WOLF'S HEAD BAY ©

JOURNEY OF THE COURAGEOUS ELEVEN

BOOK II: The Race For Home

A
THRILLER
By

Jeffery Allen Boyd

ISBN: 978-1-54392-024-6 (print)

ISBN: 978-1-54392-025-3 (ebook)

Cover photo of Bell 222 helicopter by Pedro Aragão

CHAPTER TWENTY-SIX

The Colonel had heard the entire radio exchange between his sto-len helicopter and the black Scorpion. Anger was seething from every pore. Standing before the wall of monitors in room number '13', the Auction/Control Center of the underground facility, the Colonel stared at the large main screen displaying a live feed from the Scorpion. He was so enraged he could barely mutter the words to himself through his clinched teeth. "First, the dossier. And now my *painting*!"

Seated behind him at the large control console, Shazuko looked up from her closed-circuit monitors and interrupted him. "Sir?"

Without looking away from the screen, he curtly addressed his new tech. "How much damage did it cause?"

"It was a computer Hantavirus--they are the worst, most virulent. Your system has been compromised. How badly will take several--"

"Were any specific files infiltrated or destroyed?" growled the Colonel, more annoyed than worried, confident his computer security protocols were more than adequate.

"I will need time to determine that," Shazuko replied evenly. She then turned and briefly gazed up at the Colonel, enjoying his agitated state. "You do wish an accurate assessment?"

"Yes, yes--what about his communications--were they terminated?"

"Yes," Shazuko replied tersely. With her baseball cap removed, her long black hair now fell voluptuously about her back. "As you can see we lost the image from the stolen bird after he shut down the avionics, but he did manage to land it safely in the river and you should be able to fly it back here with no problem. His radio communications and transponder signal were successfully blocked."

"Well, *Someone* heard him--helicopter Zulu November Eight Five Four."

"I have already done a computer search," she replied sharply, handing the Colonel a handwritten notation. "Anyone you know?"

Snatching the paper from her hand, his eyes seemed to glow red from reading the name.

"This Richard Skyland, is he a problem we need to be concerned with?"

"No," the Colonel lied. "What about the tracking transponders?"

Shazuko played along, aware he was avoiding the truth by quickly changing the subject. "If your young runaways should manage to evade your enforcer, there's nowhere they can go that we cannot locate them. According to the log, Ryan had them installed immediately following their arrival, and as you can see, they're all functioning properly."

The Colonel finally turned and directly addressed his tech, whom he was quite certain he didn't like. "I have every confidence Mr. Spear will capture them. Raise him on the radio; I wish to speak to him directly."

"My advice would be that he not kill any of them."

"As if I asked you for it," he rebuked her sharply.

"Yes sir," Shazuko replied, respectfully bowing her head to his authority, then turning her attention back to the bank of small monitors before her. "It appears your confidence may be well placed." She then motioned with a wave of her slender hand toward the larger monitor. "Capture may be imminent."

The Colonel turned his attention back to the main screen. "Punch up the Scorpion's four feeds. I want see everything."

Shazuko silently complied. The Scorpion, equipped with two interior, and two exterior cameras, provided a bird's-eye view of all the action, now displayed in a split-screen on the large main monitor. The nose camera's image in the upper left quadrant of the screen had a beat on the stranded Longranger in the middle of the river with someone standing off to the side and up to their knees in the surging water.

Donning a headset, Shazuko keyed the mike. "Base to Scorpion, come in."

Jeremy lunged for Ian, snatching him down from the Longranger and into his arms. The two of them looked up into the face of the flying beast. Dropping Ian to his feet and grabbing his hand, the two scrambled for shore through the deep water.

"JEREMY!" Leslie cried out from behind a huge boulder alongside the others.

Making it only half way, the beating rotor blades on top of them, Jeremy abruptly spun around. The moment he spotted Spear strapped in the rear cabin, rifle in hand, Jeremy grabbed Ian and doggedly dragged him back to the Longranger. The Scorpion screamed right over their heads, flying up and over the top of the falls, then spun around and stopped on a dime in a hover over the water. Spear took aim at Jeremy and squeezed the trigger. Hunching beneath the tail boom Jeremy shoved Ian, weighted with his backpack, to the side as the bullet streaked through the churning water near their scrambling feet. Grabbing Ian by his pack, he nearly picked the boy up, pushing him as the enforcer cocked the rifle and fired again. The steel pointed shell pierced the soft aluminum skin of the Longranger, snaking through the fuselage embedding in an upholstered seat. Ian grimaced and screamed, stumbling to his knees, splashing through the streaming water, his hands flailed for something to grab onto. Jeremy gripped Ian's pack, breaking the boy's fall, his hand sensing something familiar through the fabric, something he saw earlier. Sloshing and staggering around to the nose of the helicopter, out of the line of fire, Jeremy hauled Ian back, sliding around in front of him.

"Stay, stay!" he sputtered reaching behind, clutching Ian's shirt, keeping the boy close to his body.

"JEREMY!" Leslie screamed, the kids pressed in close behind her, their eyes anxiously darting from the trapped pair to the hovering Scorpion at the top of the falls.

"STAY DOWN!" he shouted to them.

Another shot rang out shattering one of the Plexiglas windows.

"STOP--MAKE 'EM STOP!" Ian burst hysterically. The boy suddenly bolting for the safety of the rocks where the others were crouching until Jeremy snagged his backpack, hauling him back. Spear had already cocked the rifle and took the shot.

Matthew saw what was about to happen and leaped to his feet atop the boulders screaming at the top of his lungs, "NOOOO!"

"--MATTHEW!" Leslie shrieked, clutching at his shirt and yanking him back down.

A trail of blood stained the water as Jeremy pulled Ian back. He staggered with the boy in tow through the pain in his upper left thigh. It felt like someone had shoved a red-hot poker through the skin to the muscle. Soaked and gasping in terror, Ian clamored to get away, but Jeremy held him tightly from behind, the backpack pressing into his chest. He felt it again, something hard inside the backpack. Forcing the boy down they both crouched on their knees beside the tail boom of the Longranger. Panting and out of breath, it was all Jeremy could do to ignore the pain, aided by the adrenalin surging through his body.

It was unnerving to see his blood in the water. He glanced down again at the torn fabric of his cargo shorts stained red. Stealing a quick glance inside the Longranger he saw the Glock in the side pocket, yet he was too scared to try and get it.

He turned back to Ian and his backpack. Glancing up through layers of Plexiglas; the windshield and one of the side windows, Jeremy could see a distorted Scorpion still hovering menacingly above the falls.

"Ian, turn around, buddy."

When their eyes met, Jeremy ached at the fear in his small face. "I'm not going to let anything happen to you, Ian. All right?"

Quivering from fear and the cold river, the boy nodded solemnly as water droplets beaded down the sides of his cherub face.

"Let's have a look," Jeremy said, turning Ian slightly, unzipping the top of the pack and reaching his hand down inside to something familiar from his own boyhood. Grasping the object, he pulled it out and grinned widely. Jeremy read aloud the stamped lettering along the side of the solid steel frame slingshot. "The Bone Collector. Ian, you may have just saved all our lives."

Jeremy quickly signaled the others on shore to lay low out of sight, and then turned to Ian. "Listen to me, take hold of my belt and stay behind me out of sight, okay?"

Ian quickly did as instructed, maneuvering around Jeremy through the water and grabbed onto his belt. Never so frightened in all his life, Ian trusted his friend. Suddenly his frightened eyes strayed overhead…the whine of the Scorpion's turbine and the whoop of the rotor blades seemed to be coming closer.

Jeremy looked down and saw several large stones resting in the swirling sand near his feet. He kicked one of them with the toe of his tennis shoe and reached down picking up three of them. Judging the heaviest of the three to be the perfect size and figuring he'd have only one chance to pull it off, he let the other two slip through his fingers back into the river. He gripped the stone tightly in his hand along with the slingshot and looked up just as the Scorpion began its descent. A giant deadly beast, the black Longranger slowly hovered over the edge of the falls dropping down alongside the cascading water and began moving toward its prey. Jeremy watched in horror as the beast moved in their direction. Hidden on the opposite side, he nudged Ian and slowly the two of them retreated down along the side toward the tail. Still shaking, Ian matched Jeremy's every step with precision. Leslie and the kids, hunkering down behind the boulders near shore, watched helplessly at the frightening sight of the huge helicopter, its powerful rotor downwash kicking up their hair and the water around them, glided gracefully over the river above them. The roar of the turbine bombarded their ears.

"We've gotta try and bring 'em around to this side--away from the others," Jeremy said over his shoulder at Ian, the boy's face buried in his back.

Spear's vile anger had reached a fever pitch. Soaked from his jump into the cold river water to retrieve the fishing tube, he sat riveted in the rear seat, his hands tightly gripping a M40 bolt-action sniper rifle. Probing the helicopter below through the magnified scope, his finger poised on the trigger, the pressure was mounting from the moment he spotted the teenager.

On the opposite seat lay the fishing tube.

"The Colonel, he's been calling," Lee Kwon snapped. "There may be another aircraft in the area."

Spear ignored him, concentrating on his quarry below.

"Did you hear me? He also wants them alive," Lee Kwon then warned him.

"They will be, with one exception," Spear replied coldly. "Swing around to the other side, I'm gonna cap this kid!"

"But the Colonel--"

"DO IT!" snapped the enforcer, angrily cutting him off.

The pilot looked about the helicopter with an uneasy sense, as his safety envelope shrunk and the winds began to pick up, evidenced by the strafing whitecaps out across the open river. Cautiously maneuvering the black Scorpion toward the stranded helicopter, he kept the huge boulders below and to his right, in his peripheral vision. With the rushing river just a few feet below his foot pedals, gusts were now spilling over the falls dousing the Scorpion in buffeting jolts felt through his controls. Executing a one-eighty, he brought the Scorpion around, facing the misting falls. With both passenger side doors open, Spear fluidly shifted his position and his aim to the opposite side. Despite Lee Kwon's skillful attempts at repositioning the Scorpion, the rocking continued.

"Hold her steady!" the enforcer barked.

Jeremy had watched the Scorpion spin around and saw his opportunity. Maneuvering himself and Ian back along the tail boom he turned to the boy and sputtered, "Stay close to me!"

The front left side of the stricken Longranger faced the approaching Scorpion. As Jeremy and Ian hugged the opposite side of it, out of Spears's line of sight, Ian stood in Jeremy's shadow, shaking. With the stone and the slingshot in his hand, Jeremy had only seconds. As the Scorpion backed around the nose of the stricken bird Jeremy ducked under the tail boom pulling Ian along, making sure the boy stayed behind him. Carefully remaining out of Spear's line of sight Jeremy had only his other senses to rely on, gauging the Scorpion's movement and location from its deafening turbine engine and the roiling surface of the river.

"Hold it here!" Spear barked to Lee Kwon over his headset.

Hovering out front, Spear's eyes scanned the side of the dead bird.

Jeremy hesitated, then peered back under the tail boom. His heart raced and his breathing grew shallower the moment he saw the Scorpion's tail rotor hanging above the river.

Spear cursed then ordered, "Keep going!"

On the move again, the Scorpion continued hovering backward, coming around the stricken bird, tail first. Jeremy spun around shoving Ian to his knees in the water hoping to avoid being spotted through the dead bird's Plexiglas windows. Slingshot in hand Jeremy ducked down, then cautiously maneuvered along the side of the helicopter toward the nose, trying to keep the Scorpion in view without being spotted. Sloshing through knee-deep water he stopped, hunching beside the chin bubble window.

Keep low, Jeremy mouthed back to Ian, signaling with his hand for him not to move.

Jeremy rose up just enough and peered through the Plexiglas, desperately spying the Scorpion. That's when he spotted Spear doggedly searching for them through his rifle's sight.

Jeremy had only moments.

The river was in chaos, the surface whipped into frenzy from the Scorpion's rotor downwash. Jeremy crawled back to Ian, whispering in his ear, "Stay put and don't move!"

Leslie and the kids watched from behind the cover of boulders in helpless anguish, unaware of what Jeremy was planning.

Jeremy went for the belly, crouching near the base of the tail boom. The moment he knelt in the cold water a wave of excruciating pain coursed through his thigh. He glanced down, grimacing at his blood-soaked cargo shorts. Jeremy took a deep breath and firmly gripped the handle of the steel frame slingshot, seating the wrist brace support snuggly against his forearm. As droplets of sweat and river water beaded down his face, he placed the stone in the slingshot's pouch. The moment Jeremy saw the Scorpion's tail rotor come around into full view he raised the slingshot, pulling back on the thick rubber band, and took aim at the whirling blades.

An instant before releasing the band, he muttered through gritting teeth, "Have a nice day!"

The aluminum-skinned carbon fiber composite blades were no match against the diamond-hard granite stone, shattering the delicately balanced blades to the point where one of them instantly disintegrated, exploding apart. The Scorpion suddenly bolted around, violently veering away from the Longranger, launching into an out-of-control spin. Lee Kwon's experience as a pilot in no way prepared him for the catastrophic failure that now engulfed him. He began to panic as he struggled with the controls while Spear lost his grip on the rifle, grasping at anything to hold onto. The fishing tube was flung from the seat.

"...He's gonna hit the falls," Jeremy mumbled, struggling to his feet and then shouting to the others behind the rocks. "GET DOWN!"

Leslie and the kids dove back behind the boulders as Jeremy scooped Ian into his arms, scrambling and ducking back down for cover behind the safety of the stricken Longranger.

The Scorpion spun wildly like a top, disorientating Lee Kwon. Fearing he was about to die, the innate urge to survive compelled him emotionally to continue struggling with the collective and cyclic stick to regain control of the aircraft, while his intellect told him it was useless. Grimacing from the terror that gripped his body, his vision narrowed, focusing on the erratic instrument readings while desperately ignoring the dizzying view outside. He was about to take his last breath. The enforcer merely held onto anything, watching the world whizzing by at a break-neck blur. The last thing Spear saw as his muscled body was slammed against his seat from the centrifugal force, was the waterfall coming at him.

The eighteen-and-a-half-foot rotor blades, spinning at three hundred and ninety-five RPM smashed into the cascading waterfall and sandstone rock face with the roaring speed of a freight train. The turbine engine, its deep-throated whine, violently choked off at the moment of impact, was ripped from its mounds, shredding metal into shrapnel and rupturing the fuel tank. There was an explosion of aluminum shards and chunks of rock splashing into the river and showering down over Leslie and the kids as they covered their heads. The impact sent the crumpled Scorpion crashing to the base of the falls where tons of amber colored river water doused the explosive jet fuel, engulfing the Longranger and smashing through the Plexiglas windows, instantly filling the entire cabin.

Jeremy was the first to rise up and struggle to stand, his leg bloodied, his clothes soaked and his senses dismayed at the destructive scene. The fallen Scorpion lay on its side at the bottom of the falls barely visible through the pounding onslaught of the river crashing over it. A single rotor blade, shattered and bent at a violent angle, pierced the flowing sheet and bobbed lazily from the falling water. While steam and smoke slowly rose above the surreal scene, a transparent sheen of jet fuel flowed out over the surface. The once rumbling onslaught of the Scorpion had been replaced by the quiet calm of the falls and gently gurgling river. After handing the boy his slingshot, Jeremy took Ian's hand and the two made their way through the water and over to the others, meeting them as they scrambled out from behind the boulders. Elmo and Lynn ran up hugging Ian, then helped him to shore. Elmo began to kid him because he looked like a drowned rat, soaked to the gills and appearing to barely tip the scale at fifty pounds, despite being weighed down with his ever-present, bulky backpack. Although he didn't mind the ribbing, Ian remained strangely silent. Jeremy melted into Leslie's embrace with Matthew and Travis surrounding them, their own arms locked about the both of them. Eric hung back quietly saying nothing.

Jeremy took a brief moment looking back over his shoulder at the smoldering wreckage, and wondered fearfully. What and who was coming for them next?

CHAPTER TWENTY-SEVEN

The General's open briefcase set atop his desk came equipped with a communications console complete with two small plasma monitors. In constant contact with the Scorpion, the last image they televised, before abruptly going to snow, displayed both interior and exterior vantage points. From inside he watched as his pilot struggled to control the helicopter, while the exterior's view was that of the surrounding woods and the rapidly approaching falls, whizzing across his screen until seconds later the Scorpion collided into the falls. Wu stood back gaping in dismay at the loss of the Scorpion, his pilot, and Spear, all at the hands of a teenage boy. He could actually feel the veins in his neck pulsating along with his rising blood pressure.

The Colonel's posture stiffened and he briefly clinched his fists at his side as he continued to stare at the large split-screen monitor, all four feeds gone to snow.

"Humph," he relaxed and grunted to himself, then seemingly in awe, said, "A shameful loss."

"Yes...I--I quite agree," Shazuko muttered in shocked dismay as she bowed her head. "A most regrettable loss. The pilot was a good man."

"Oh?" the Colonel said distantly. "I was referring to the helicopter. A fine aircraft."

Shazuko loathed the Colonel's arrogant nature. It took everything she had to contain her rage after his comment. She finally looked up at the empty screen again for a moment, then relinquished it for the Colonel. Shazuko glared contemptuously at him, watching as he stepped down along the control console to the end where a lone red phone sat. That's when her eyes returned to the static on the screen and she muttered reverently to herself, "...The pilot...Lee Kwon...my younger brother."

The Colonel lifted the red receiver, pressing it to his ear, and began pounding out a familiar number on the Touchtone dial pad. He waited several moments while a prerecorded female voice instructed him to leave a message.

"...My only brother," Shazuko mourned, still staring blankly at the monitor screen in front of her, her mind holding onto the last image of Lee Kwon in the doomed Scorpion.

"I have a situation," the Colonel began, "requiring a containment team. Several escaped specimens, ten in all, are loose on the preserve and need to be captured quickly. One of them has in his possession a painting, and this is critical, a flash drive containing sensitive information. It is paramount these two items be recovered at all costs. Should any one of them make it off the preserve, it would be potentially catastrophic to the Network..." The Colonel snapped his wrist, checking his watch. "The time is eight forty-five, a.m., Eastern Daylight Time." He then terminated the call, setting the receiver back in its cradle while a pensive look crossed his face.

Shazuko's obedient demeanor was typical of the subordinates the Network employed. And though she appeared to be completely uninterested in the Colonel's actions, nothing could be farther from the truth, where this steely-eyed, ruthless woman was concerned.

Finally returning to his technician at the opposite end of the console, the Colonel spoke calmly despite the calamity unfolding around him.

"When the containment team arrives, I'd like you to coordinate the entire affair. Are you up to the task, Ms.--?"

"Shazuko," the tech smiled venomously.

"Do I call you, *Ms.* Shazuko?" he asked her with equal sarcasm.

"Just Shazuko will do. And yes, I am--up to the task."

"Good. And the whereabouts of the kids?"

"I know exactly where they are. See those blips?" she continued, pointing to one of three smaller plasma screens displaying a map of the entire preserve. "The transponders easily reveal their constant location."

"Don't lose them. Our recent addition to the team, Mr. Whitehead, can assist you along with Mr. Ryan, once you locate *his* whereabouts."

Hearing movement behind him the Colonel turned. "Well, speak of the devil."

The Colonel walked up to Peter who was still in his biker gear and addressed him directly. "I want these kids rounded up and returned here, *yesterday*. Then you and Mr. Spear will immediately dispatch them, without further incident. Do you understand me?"

"Spear? But I thought he was--"

"Dead? Not likely--oh he may be banged up a bit, but hardy dead. The only way Mr. Spear is going to die," the Colonel continued prophetically, "is from a bullet!"

Whitehead nodded, silently agreeing that, after having spent the last several months in Spears' company, the Colonel's assessment of his psycho enforcer's demise would no doubt happen as he described it. Little could Peter Whitehead know that within hours his hand, and Jeremy's, would be the instruments in fulfilling that prophesy.

"Take your bike and render whatever assistance you can to him. The falls area where the Scorpion went down is near the service road, see it there?" He pointed toward the plasma screen map. "The other helicopter sitting in the river is still intact, so the both of you can use it to round up the little bastards!"

Whitehead again nodded, saying nothing.

"I'll be in my office, Shazuko," said the Colonel, turning to leave. "Let me know the minute the containment team arrives."

"Those kids aren't your only problem," Shazuko spun in her chair and announced.

The Colonel paused and turned, barking, "What do you mean?"

Shazuko nodded her head toward the small television monitor at her console. "I've got the Weather Channel on. There's something coming this way--you'd better take a look."

The Colonel stepped closer as Shazuko punched a button switching the live broadcast to the large, main plasma screen. Two seated anchors spoke conversationally while behind them a satellite image of the continental United States displayed a cyclone-like disturbance; the 'eye' situated roughly over the northern boundaries of Minnesota and Ontario, Canada. The animated image repeated every few seconds; its whirling arms embedded with bands of heavy thunderstorms extended as far out as the eastern seaboard and as far south as Georgia. The Colonel's brow furrowed and his eyes narrowed when he said, "Turn up the volume."

Shazuko complied.

"--That's right, Lisa. If this were over the ocean, it would be a Category 3 hurricane. And what makes this so unusual is that normal conditions favorable for the development of an extratropical cyclone to form over the United States is typically in the spring and fall when temperature differences are at their greatest. This is a huge storm developing very quickly just in the last seventy-two hours that began sweeping across the Midwest and much of central and western Canada, bringing strong winds, rain, hail and widespread tornados. The National Weather Service reported fifty-two tornados, while heavy snow fell in the far north.

"Meteorologists are buzzing about this one, Jim; a phenomenon called a weather-bomb because they form very quickly, often setting records for the lowest pressure measured over land. Yesterday, at seven forty-five p.m., central daylight time, the weather station in Bigfork, Minnesota recorded nine hundred fifty-five point two millibars--"

"--And since pressure is one indicator of a storm's strength," his co-anchor continued, taking up the report, "this one's measurement corresponds to the pressure indicative of a Category 3 hurricane. Right now we have our own Mike Seidel on the shores of Lake Superior at Thunder Bay, Ontario...Mike, what can you tell us?"

"Kill it," the Colonel grunted. Shazuko muted the volume, leaving the room shrouded in silence. Keenly aware that time was of the essence, the Colonel turned to Whitehead. "This could work in our favor, but it has to be done quickly. This just might make it easier to get rid of them all without any trace."

"I thought you were selling them off?"

"They've already cost me too much--in aggravation. I'll elaborate as we walk. Just get rid of them, before this monster hits!"

"Yes, sir," Whitehead grinned maliciously.

Shazuko waited a moment, watching the Colonel and Whitehead walk from the room before picking up the receiver beside her hand. "...General, he just left...yes…I understand."

Shazuko set the receiver back. A fleeting smile crossed her face, then vanished, replaced with a look of pure hate. It too then vanished, melting into an expression of sadness when she thought of her dead brother.

"Jeremy, look!" Leslie gasped at the Scorpion's battered fuselage as it lay on its side, smothering beneath tons of falling water.

Standing in ankle-deep water beside the boulders, the kids closed in behind Leslie and Jeremy where they all watched in stunned, muted silence someone's hand reaching up through the sliding panel in the window of the passenger compartment. Somehow the door had slammed shut. The assassin's hand reached out through the small opening up to his elbow, clawing through the bombarding water crashing over the wreckage, searching in vain for the door's latch. While the interior mechanism had been damaged the exterior latch was out of his desperate reach. No one said a word as the assassin's hand went limp and sunk lifeless back down through the sliding panel and into the belly of the flooded, dead Scorpion.

"God forgive me for what I'm thinking," Leslie muttered.

"Yeah, well, he deserved it," Jeremy retorted remorselessly. "Leslie, get everyone up on shore--keep 'em all together."

"Where are you going?" she asked him as he turned limping back toward the helicopter.

"We've got a long trek ahead of us. I'm gonna see if there's anything back in the helicopter we can use."

"Jeremy, your leg."

"I'll check for a first aid kit. I'll be right back."

Clearly distressed she found it difficult to look away as he hobbled through the water, the left side of his cargo shorts red with blood. "...C'mon kids, let go."

"This is stupid," Eric sneered at Jeremy, his shoes riveted in the sandy bottom of the river, refusing to move. "We're lost and you don't have a clue to where the hell we are, do you? Do you? HEY, I'm talkin' to you!"

Jeremy spun around and froze, glaring at Eric.

"C'mon, Eric," Leslie sternly prodded him, she too having enough of his attitude.

Jeremy released his angry stare and headed back out to the middle of the river and the downed helicopter.

"Eric, c'mon," Lynn softly pleaded with her brother.

The boy smirked, kicking at the water, then sloshed his way to the dry shoreline, pushing past the others and plopping down on the warm sandy beach. The kids gathered behind Leslie, anxiously watching and waiting for Jeremy. Dylan, unable to stop thinking about Charlee and where she might be, turned away from the river and walked, unintentionally, head on into Eric's penetrating stare, where he froze.

16

"What are you lookin' at?" Dylan gruffed.

"Not much," Eric replied coldly.

Jeremy recovered what he could from the Longranger, closed the pilot's door after shoving the Glock and a couple of unused rags into his pockets, and stepped back. Looking skyward, then at the pilot's seat and controls, he spoke softly as though he were bidding farewell to an old friend. "Thank you."

Travis had caught his upward gaze.

Jeremy limped back on shore with a small armload, catching his breath, and said, "I've got good news and bad news."

"Oh gee, let's start with the bad news so we can really get depressed," Eric quipped from where he sat in the sand.

Ignoring Eric and just to irritate him, Jeremy began with the good news. "We have a blanket, first aid kit--"

"Oh goodie," Eric commented contemptuously.

"...And the Glock. And, I believe this is yours," he concluded handing Dylan the smartphone.

"Hallelujah," he gasped, taking it like it was the winning lottery ticket. "Must've fell outta my pocket," he said as he turned it on briefly, examining it, and then quickly shut it back off. "It still works," he muttered thankfully.

"So it works," Jeremy griped. "What good is it? Are you sure there's no way we can call out on that thing?"

"It's encrypted--they all are. Without the proper ID the phone doesn't recognize me."

"Doesn't recognize you?" Lynn echoed sourly. "For a smartphone it sure is stupid!"

"Only the user who it was issued to at the Lodge knows its code to unlock it," Dylan corrected her. "Sorry—whaddya want me to do?"

"Fix it!" Eric growled.

Dylan merely glared back at Eric with dagger eyes.

"Don't worry about it," Jeremy said to him with a grin. "The main thing is you got us all outta that place--"

"Yeah, after he kidnapped my sister!" Eric snapped. "I'd still like to know why?"

An air of silence hung over the group, pierced only by the sounds of birds and the river beyond them.

Dylan could see everyone watching him, waiting for an explanation. He wanted to try to explain it all, but it was so complicated, more so than he thought they would understand.

"Don't have an answer? Eric began to bait him. "Can't figure that out or the phone thing, what good are you? Aren't you supposed to be our resident computer geek genius?"

The strain was clearly showing on Dylan's face, and he stared directly at Eric and sputtered, "Fuck you!"

Eric snatched a stone from the sand and bolted to his feet. "Try it gay boy and I'll shove this up your ass."

"Stop it, both of you!" Jeremy barked, hobbling in between them and interceding, his eyes focused on Eric. "We're all tired and scared, Eric, and if you haven't anything constructive to say, keep your mouth shut!"

The tense pall of hushed silence mushroomed over the group as everyone's eyes now shifted to Eric. With a relenting smirk, he let the stone fall from his grasp back to the sand and walked away.

"And now for the bad news," Jeremy resumed slowly while rubbing his forehead and temples with his bloodied hand. Still holding the first aid kit he then gingerly dug into his shorts pocket and produced the radio. Twisting the on/off switch a couple of times, the five proximity lights remained dark. "I think it got fried in the river."

"I thought it didn't have to be on for the little lights to work?" Elmo asked.

"It doesn't," Jeremy explained. "Just press this side button and the lights first flash, indicating the battery charge, then they light up, relative to the distance to the companion radio."

"Here, give that to me," Leslie said taking the first aid kit from his other hand. Noticing again the charred parts of the back of his shirt, including the redness of his skin, she gently helped him to a half-buried rock in the sand where he gingerly sat down.

"It was in my pocket and got wet, which means we've lost communication with Dane. So I'm afraid we're cut off and on our own--*WOWOUCH!*"

"Sorry," Leslie winced, apologetically, kneeling beside him trying to be gentle as she lifted the hem of his shorts examining the ripped and bloodied skin. The kids gathered around, watching.

"Is it bad?" Matthew asked cautiously.

Leslie looked up at the boy, then at Jeremy. "This is really deep and you've lost some blood."

"What's in the kit?" he asked her conversationally, shoving the radio back into his pocket while fighting back against the intense pain, doing his best to quell his brothers' fearful looks.

"Well, let's see..."

While she dug around in the small plastic case, Jeremy looked up into the anxious, grimy faces crowding before him. Their clothing wet, worn and dirty, they looked like a rag-tag group of refugee camp survivors. Off to the side, he curiously watched Ian slip off his backpack, for the first time, and proceed to sit in the sand beside it. "How you doin', Ian?" he asked the boy.

Ian looked up at Jeremy for a moment with a lost, distant expression, and then lowered his head again.

"You go quiet on us again? ...Well, that's okay. Sometimes I don't feel much like talking either. But you just hang in there, okay? I'm countin' on ya."

"And what's his problem?" Eric then sniped, taking a crack at Ian. "No Bob jokes for the occasion, kid?"

"Leave *him* alone," Jeremy growled at Eric through clenched jaws.

Eric frowned, then turned away, his seeming indifference guarded behind a hard and hateful expression.

Ian worried Jeremy. He hadn't seen the boy this withdrawn since last winter during their search for Matthew in the dead of night on South Manitou Island.

Travis could see the concern in his brother's face, yet, overwhelmed with his own concerns, asked him, "Are we a long ways from home, Jeremy?"

As Leslie began to examine his wound, Jeremy looked away, nodding. "Yep, we are. But I'll get us all home, I promise, if it's the last thing I...I mean, I'll get us back."

"How!" Eric bellowed from behind everyone with his angry frown. "We're lost, remember!"

"Shouldn't we be close to a road or highway?" Lynn offered, wanting to be helpful, while also trying to shut Eric up.

"I bet we are," Elmo blurted with excitement. "I think I saw one from the air."

Matthew burst out, "You actually took the time to sightsee during our terror flight?"

"Well, kinda."

"Good goin', Elmo--SONOFAH--" Jeremy suddenly shrieked, tensing his whole body and yanking his leg away. "Jeeeze!"

"I'm sorry, but hold still," Leslie urged him without looking up, focusing on his injury. "Jeremy, this is really deep. It's pierced the skin down to the--"

Using a small pair of metal scissors from the kit, Leslie had cut a straight line through the cargo shorts, going up his thigh about four inches and carefully peeled back the blood-soaked fabric.

The kids groaned at the gross sight.

"Yuck," Lynn winced, cringing her shoulders.

There was a deep fissure in his flesh, stretching across his mid-thigh, and it was still oozing blood. Jeremy sucked air through his teeth as he painfully straightened his other leg and pulled out the clean rags. "See if you can--oh, man, that smarts...here...see if you can use these to patch me up."

Leslie nodded, taking the rags. That's when she handed him a wooden tongue depressor. "Here, bite down on this."

"Thanks." Jeremy took it and started using it like a pointer, tapping Elmo's arm. "Any other helpful ideas?"

"Maybe," Elmo continued, digging into and pulling from his pocket, "How 'bout this? A compass. Will this help?"

"How's that tiny thing gonna help?" Eric snipped. "Where'd you find it, a Cracker Jack box?"

"Ian," replied Elmo, nodding down at the boy. "It was *Diver Dave's*. And it works. That's how he was able to tell us what direction they were heading."

"Ian, dude, you're our hero," Jeremy congratulated him.

The boy looked up and was met by a chorus of grateful smiles, especially Lynn, and, despite his diminutive size, at this moment he felt very tall, and it made him feel very good.

"Before you all start pattin' him on the back and doin' the wave," Eric jeered at them, "what about food? We don't have any, and we haven't eaten since yesterday, and I'm starvin'."

"Jeremy," Leslie said. "I've got sterile gauze to wrap and tie off the rags, and there's some antibacterial stuff here, so…"

Jeremy swallowed, then comically stuck the wooden depressor between his teeth, nodded warily at her and said, his words somewhat garbled, "In other words--"

"This is *really* going to hurt," she finished.

She then took a deep breath, removing the cap of the small bottle of antiseptic and carefully lowered it over the wound. "Ready?"

"Do it," he garbled.

Eric rolled his eyes, muttering under his breath, "Jeeze, it's not surgery."

The pain was instantaneous. Jeremy groaned and grimaced, his hands gripping the rock he sat on as if he was trying to squeeze water from its granite structure. His eyes clamped shut against the burning antiseptic flowing through the open wound, draining out and down his calf--red--the depressor clinched between his teeth until he abruptly spit it out. "AAAAYYYYEEEE, WOW...that hurts!"

"Man up," Matthew half-joked, with a stoic grin to Travis, resting his hand affectionately on Jeremy's shoulder, knowing, though, his brother's agony was real.

Slumping back against another boulder, Jeremy turned a disapproving eye to the twins, releasing the air from his lungs. "You're next, Elmo."

"No way, man, not me," he protested, lifting his bloodstained shirt revealing a dark crimson crease across his side above the hip. "Mine's healed up pretty good, see?"

"No it hasn't--get over here, Elmo," Jeremy sputtered in a serious tone, straightening and leaning forward, examining the wound. "I'm serious, I'm not playin'."

Elmo kept shaking his head.

"C'mon," Leslie said patiently.

"Get over here, you big baby," Jeremy barked.

"But--"

"Elmo, you wanna get an infection? Now c'mon."

"Ohhh, okay," the boy relented, glumly shuffling his sandals through the sand.

"Have a seat," Jeremy said, patting the boulder beside him, grinning. "Nurse Leslie will be right with you."

"Hold still while I wrap this up," she said to Jeremy.

"Why isn't anyone listening to me?" Eric said impatiently. "I'm hungry!"

"You're not the only one!" Jeremy shot back. "I'm fed up with your constant whining and complaining, causing problems. That's all you've done on this trip!"

"Me! Whaddya pissed at me for?" Eric blasted, pointing an accusatory finger at Dylan. "How come you're not pissed at him? I didn't get us into this nightmare. HE DID! And I still wanna know why!"

"Jeremy," Leslie said softly, drawing his attention the moment he began to struggle to his feet, realizing he was about to blow up.

Eric then pleaded to his sister. "...Don't *you* wanna know?"

Lynn looked at her brother, then at Dylan. Her eyes began to well up.

Dylan evaded Eric's gaze but it was Lynn's he couldn't. Without Charlee, Dylan never felt so alone as everyone stared at him. He wanted to die now more than ever. "I'm sorry," he uttered remorsefully. "I really am. I didn't mean for any of you to get caught up in this. I really didn't. ...Maybe I can make up for it with this." He then held up the flash drive between his fingers. "With this we now have a bargaining chip."

"Bargaining chip?" Jeremy asked. "Whattya mean?"

Dylan stammered nervously. He hated revealing anything about his and Charlee's life to others he didn't know and was sure didn't care. "...Before our mother died last year, Charlee and I found out who our father was, so we ran away to try and find him."

"That's the girl with Dane?" Jeremy questioned. "Charlee? She's your sister?"

Dylan nodded.

"Ran away from where, Dylan?" asked Leslie, trading glances with Jeremy.

"The Pine Ridge Reservation."

"Where is that?" Lynn asked.

"What's a reservation?" Travis winced with confusion across his face.

"It's a plot of land in South Dakota that was graciously given to the Indian people, *my people*, by the United States government, *after* they'd taken it from us in 1889. Land they didn't want. Land that was originally settled by *my people*."

"And who are your people?" Jeremy asked him thoughtfully.

"Both Charlee and I are..." The boy hesitated. For the first time it hit him. Yet, Dylan could not bring himself to admit to them, even

to himself, that he had white blood flowing through his veins. "…
we're full-blooded Oglala Lakota."

"Sounds foreign to me," Eric quipped. "Illegal alien stuff. Is that
what you guys are? A couple of illegal aliens on the run?"

"We're Americans, just like you," Dylan replied proudly. "Native
American. Oconee is my last name, or would you prefer something
more white sounding, like Smith?"

"Hey, my last name's McCaulee," Elmo volunteered, shifting his
gaze to Eric hoping to remind him of his once animosity toward him.
Now they were best friends. "And I'm just as *Indian* as you are. My
heritage is a mix of Chippewa and Ottawa of Northern Michigan;
All-American, too." he grinned to Jeremy.

Jeremy grinned and winked back at him. Probing further,
Jeremy asked Dylan, "What happened after you ran?"

"We made it as far as Detroit. That's where we met Peter, at a
bus station. He said he could help us." His gaze and voice began to
trail off. "Instead they made us prisoners."

"Dylan," Jeremy interrupted bringing him back, realizing how
difficult it must have for him to talk about it. "So, how is the flash
drive a bargaining chip?"

"I think because of what's on it. The General called it the
Caradori file."

Jeremy hesitated then half laughed with a stunned expression.
He struggled to his feet, amazed. "What! *The* Caradori file? Are you
sure?"

"Yeah. And from the way Wu was talking to the Colonel, he
threatened him with it if he didn't back down from doing something."

"Doing what?"

"I dunno. It sounded like running for office or something."

"And it's on that drive?"

"Ah huh. And let me tell you, gettin' it wasn't easy. I lifted it
from the General last night." Displaying the flash drive between his
fingers he quickly flashed it back and forth like a magician from

hand to hand. He abruptly stopped, holding out a now empty pair of palms.

"Hey, how'd you do that?" Matthew grinned. "That was cool."

Dylan stepped toward the boy, reached behind Matthew's ear and produced the small drive, displaying it between his two fingers again.

Matthew's face lit up again and he laughed. "Wow, look at that."

"This little flash drive may just insure our survival."

"Well, it won't do us any good unless we can get it to the authorities," Jeremy said.

"And someone we can trust," Dylan added.

"What's on it?" Leslie asked.

"I'm not exactly sure, but from the way the General was talking I think it's *their* little black book. You know, names, dates, that kinda of stuff. Everything about 'em. And they're not gonna stop looking until they find us and get it back."

"I don't believe this," Eric interceded loudly. "He's gotta freakin' bulls-eye on his back, and now so do we! Well, I say we get as far away from *him* as we can so when he goes down he doesn't take us with him!"

"We can't abandon him," Leslie said with exasperation.

"Why not?" Eric barked.

"KNOCK IT OFF, ERIC!" Jeremy snapped, losing his temper.

"NO!" Eric shrieked defiantly. "We're in this mess 'cause of him, Jeremy! He oughta take a leap off the nearest cliff for what he's done to us!"

Total silence engulfed the group. While some eyes fell on Dylan, they appeared to him to be accusatory and he looked away in despair. He didn't want anyone to see the hopelessness welling up in his eyes. A chill ran up his spine, his thoughts overwhelmed with Charlee and the guilt that was consuming him. He let the smartphone and flash drive fall from his grasp to the sand the moment he turned and walked from the group.

"Dylan!" Jeremy called after him. "Where are you going? STAY HERE!"

"Let 'em go," Eric sputtered angrily through clinched teeth.

"I'll go after him," Leslie said, standing.

Staring with seething anger at Eric, Jeremy said to her, "Get 'em back here. We gotta get moving. It isn't safe to stick around here much longer."

"All right."

"What about us, Jeremy?" Travis asked.

"Well, what about you?"

"We wanna help."

"Okay. You and Matt can be in charge of supplies. Gather up all our stuff."

Travis beamed as Elmo and Lynn stepped forward chiming, "What can we do?"

Jeremy thought for a moment. "Elmo, I want you to--"

"JEREMY!" Leslie shrieked in the distance through the deep woods.

Startled, Jeremy's head spun.

"JEREMY--COME QUICKLY!"

Grimacing through the pain in his thigh he hobbled off as fast as he could in the direction of Leslie's cries--the kids trailing on his heels.

CHAPTER TWENTY-EIGHT

Racing through the woods, his dirt bike suddenly began to sputter. Dane kept gunning the hand throttle but the bike continued to cough. Then, it abruptly died. When he came to a stop, he and Charlee hopped off. Dane quickly removed the gas cap and peered into the tank with a squinting eye.

"I don't believe it," he groaned in exasperation. "We're outta freakin' gas!"

"Whatta we do now?" Charlee asked leaning over his broad shoulders trying to get a look as well.

Dane straightened, unaware the girl was so close to him, and started looking around. "How do you feel about long walks?"

"Anything, as long as it gets us away from this place," she replied, pulling the radio from the leg pocket of her biker pants.

"Did they call back yet?"

Charlee handed him the radio, saying, "No, nothing. You think they're all right?"

"I hope so," Dane grumbled taking the radio from her, his frustration mounting. "Jeremy? Jeremy, it's Dane, can you hear me? Jeremy, come back...Jeremy--dang it!"

"Well?" Charlee muttered to him while her eyes scanned the surrounding vicinity. "Do you think they're okay?"

"How do I know?" he abruptly barked at her, shoving the radio into a pocket.

When she looked at him for a moment, Dane sighed heavily and said, "I'm sorry, Charlee. I'm worried too."

Charlee's attention suddenly shifted, searching the thick woods, listening. "We've not only lost my brother and your friends, but Baddog as well."

"JEREMY!" Leslie screamed again.

The terrain was rough and rocky as Jeremy, hobbling on his one good leg fended off tree branches threading his way through the dense woods, the sound of rushing water growing louder with each step. "LESLIE!" he shouted.

"OVER HERE!"

"There she is!" Elmo bellowed from the rear shooting up ahead of the others and pointing.

Jeremy spotted her leaning down over a wall of rock and immediately pressed on through the dense underbrush, rushing up beside her.

"Leslie, what--?"

The sight of Dylan, standing out on a small peninsula of rock below them at the precipice of a second set of falls, didn't register at first in Jeremy's mind what he was doing. Then he noticed the toes of his flip-flops inching closer to the edge of the stone ledge. Struggling to find some way to stop the fifteen-year-old, Jeremy knew the river, flowing swiftly around Dylan and the tiny precipice he was standing on, would make it impossible for him to get to him in time, should he decide, in the next few moments, to really jump. If what was happening before them wasn't so terrifying, the view of the thick expanse of the northern forest below might otherwise be a spectacular sight.

Jeremy nervously laughed, "Dylan, what are you doing? Are you crazy? That's at least a good sixty--that's a long drop, get back here."

The kids pressed in behind Jeremy and Leslie.

"Oh, noo," Lynn whispered looking at Leslie severely and shaking her head as if what was happening was her fault.

Leslie took her arm and held her close. The two watched as Dylan; his back to everyone, kept inching his feet closer to the edge.

"Dylan, listen to me," Jeremy pleaded. "Listen to me. You don't want to do this. No one's blaming you for what happened."

"Yeah, c'mon man," Elmo shouted, anxiously rubbing shoulders with Jeremy. "Listen to 'em."

"Don't do it, Dylan!" Travis begged him.

"Yeah, c'mon back in," urged Matthew.

"Dylan, please," pleaded Lynn. "I don't blame you. It's not your fault. If it weren't for you, we'd all still be back in that awful place."

"She's right, listen to her," Jeremy continued, the severity in his voice heightening. "Dylan, think about what you're doing. Think about Charlee. We're gonna find her and Dane, we will. I promise-- here, look!"

Jeremy then abruptly turned around reaching out and snatching Eric's shirt. "Get over here--"

"Let go of me, man," Eric barked sharply breaking away.

"Tell 'em," Jeremy snapped. "Tell 'em you didn't mean what you said, TELL'EM OR SO HELP ME!"

"Eric, please," Lynn cried, pleading with her brother.

Eric's face grew distorted in a pained expression, the anguish so deep it exploded to the surface. "What about what they did to me!"

There was a moment of confused looks until Jeremy abruptly began to swing his good leg up and over the rock wall, his bandaged thigh teasing the pain receptors with excruciating torment.

"Get back, GET BACK!" Dylan yelled, glancing over his shoulder.

"Okay, Okay," Jeremy said easing himself back down with Leslie's help. "Dylan, *please, please listen to me...*"

The boy could no longer hear him. Dylan repeatedly squeezed his eyes, fighting back the tears, but they kept flooding through, along with the inescapable images of his mother, more than a year ago as she laid in her hospital bed, dying, and there was nothing he could do to stop it. He and Charlee had been so terrified, alone and on the run. Then they were kidnapped and held captive by the Network, all the while moved around from city to city. Dylan looked out over the vast forest, the tips of the tall pines at nearly eye level and thought of Charlee. He prayed she was safe. He looked down at his toes and the river flowing around the tiny spit of rock where he stood. It was mesmerizing, almost hypnotic, the glinting sunlight, his heart racing, his breathing becoming more shallow, the water cascading over the edge in front of him in slow motion and crashing below with a deafening roar into a cauldron of boiling, churning white water. Dylan wiped the moisture from his cheeks with his hand, took a deep breath and stepped off the ledge, plummeting out of sight.

"NOOOOO!" Jeremy shrieked. "JESUS!"

"DYLAN!" someone yelled.

Jeremy abruptly tried scrambling up and over the waist-high boulders that blocked him but his wound and the accompanying pain were too much. Leslie gripped his arm, stopping him. Frozen in disbelief at what they were witnessing, Jeremy clutched at the branches of a tree, straining to see the river below beyond the falls. Everyone held their breaths looking for him, and then gasped as Dylan's lifeless body emerged from the foam and froth, floating face down in the swiftly moving current. Lynn turned away in horrified aguish, clutching at Leslie's arm.

"We've got to get to him!" Leslie blurted, leaping up and over the jagged rock wall, hurtling herself down the steep terrain just off the falls. The kids were hot on her heels scrambling up and over the rock wall, slipping and sliding along behind her, over loose dirt and gravel down to the river's edge.

Jeremy followed them, moving as quickly as his throbbing wound would allow. Once he reached level ground he immediately righted himself, running in a painful limp along the bank, shouting, "GRAB HIM--GRAB HIS ARM!"

Trying desperately to catch up to him, Leslie nearly tripped over the protruding roots of a tree the moment she reached the edge of the river. Tearing down into the cold, sixty-five-degree water, and sloshing through the gentle river current up to her knees, Leslie came to within a few feet of the boy, then lunged out toward his hand, snagging Dylan's wrist. Pulling him to her Leslie quickly rolled him over. The moment his limp body rolled over like a rag doll, his arms and legs dangling in the water as his head bobbed backward with closed eyes, Lynn and the others had caught up, panting like marathon runners. The young girl grimaced and looked away.

Jeremy shuffled up and stood at the river's edge beside the kids, asking, "…Is he all right?"

"He's not breathing--here, help me," Leslie urged. "Quickly, now."

The kids dropped down into the water spreading out around her, pitching in with waiting hands, lifting Dylan and bringing him out of the river.

"Set him down," Leslie directed them.

Shoulders bumping, the kids set Dylan on the sandy bank where Leslie quickly dropped to her knees beside his head. Placing her wrist over his forehead, she pressed downward, forcing his mouth wide open. She then clamped off the boy's nose with that hand's fingers, swept aside her long hair and put her lips over Dylan's, pumping several breaths into his lungs. With each forceful exhale of air from her lungs into his, Leslie watched the boy's chest rise. Satisfied there was no water in his lungs, she then slid her fingers along the side of his neck feeling for a pulse.

"Is he--?" Jeremy asked, afraid to say the word.

"No," she replied, then quickly directed the kids. "Get his legs, let's get him over there."

With the exception of Eric, who remained some distance away, watching, the rest of the kids scrambled to pick Dylan up and move him to drier ground.

"Set 'em down here in the sun," she said urgently, kneeling beside the boy. She again pressed her fingers against the side of his neck, while bending down closer, with her ear to Dylan's mouth. She again pumped several breaths into Dylan's lungs. With each forced breath, the only other sound was Lynn whimpering as she stood back with the other kids. Leslie paused, glancing up at Jeremy, an expression of alarm sprawled across her face.

"Whatta we do?" Jeremy asked her.

"We gotta work fast!" she sputtered, going to work on him. "Get his wet clothes off, everything, right now, strip 'em to his underwear!"

Unable to bend down to help, Jeremy directed the twins. "Boys, give her hand."

While Leslie worked, urgently removing Dylan's pullover shirt over his limp arms, Matthew unclipped his pants button, lowered the zipper, and then scrambled to his bare feet helping Travis pull the pants off. One glance up at the kids as she passed his soaked shirt to Jeremy, along with his pants, and Leslie knew she had to enlist their help. It was unnerving to see so many frightened faces looming above her.

"Listen to me, we have to warm him up, otherwise he could go into shock--Travis, go back up the hill and get that blanket, fast! Matthew?"

The boy spun around and sped along the river's edge and back up the steep embankment, his sandals spewing out rocks and dirt like spinning tires.

"Matthew, take his clothes and lay 'em out on those rocks over there in the sun so they'll dry."

Matthew gathered the wet clothing from Jeremy's hands and headed out toward the sun-drenched rocks by the river.

Leslie delivered several more breaths. Under the chilly water for only a minute or so, to Leslie's great relief, the blue tint in Dylan's lips began to fade. Finally breathing on his own he began coughing. With Leslie's help Dylan rose up to a sitting position, trying to clear his throat and his head. "--What--what happened--?"

"You took a leap off of that," Leslie said, pointing.

Dazed, Dylan lifted his head and looked out across the expanse of forest and river, thick sheets of mist rising up before a mountainous waterfall, a portion of the cascading brown water separated by a protruding ledge. He said nothing, teetering for a moment until Leslie helped him lay back down. He breathed deeply then closed his eyes.

"I got it!" Travis bellowed as he slid down the steep slope, then leaped to his feet, the blanket bundled under his arms.

Leslie quickly stood shaking out the blanket. "Here, boys, gimme a hand."

The three watched her for a moment as she maneuvered herself to Dylan's side, spreading out the blanket. The three boys, realizing what she was doing, pitched in, folding the blanket in two.

"We don't wanna bake 'em so let's move him over there underneath those trees, then cover him. C'mon everyone."

"Then what?" asked Travis. "I mean, what are we gonna do then?"

Leslie could see past his dirty and disheveled appearance, past the smear of dirt on his cheek, just below the frightened eyes, that he needed an answer. They all did. She deferred to Jeremy with a glance.

"One thing at a time, okay?" Jeremy said.

Travis frowned, saying nothing more. He bent down, joining the others and carefully lifted Dylan's limp, half-naked body onto the makeshift stretcher. Bunching the edges in their hands, the group carried him over to a grove of oaks, setting him down in the shade. Leslie went about tucking the blanket around him, after which she crawled around to his head and felt his forehead, then his cheeks, and then the side of his neck again.

"What do you think?" Jeremy asked her guardedly.

"Well, his color's a lot better, so is his pulse," she replied, matching his concern. "I think he's okay…he should rest now though."

"Thing is, we gotta get out here soon."

"Then we'll carry him if we have to."

Jeremy silently nodded his agreement. Then, as his eyes wandered over to where Eric stood alone, he said, "...All right. But first things first, though."

Everyone could see the anger in Jeremy's face as he brushed past them and hobbled right up to Eric, getting into his face.

"What the hell's the matter with you?" Jeremy growled at him.

The boy angrily recoiled, then frowned. "Get away from me!"

Leslie took a few steps past the kids.

"Look at him!" snapped Jeremy pointing to where Dylan lay.

Just as Eric turned away, Jeremy grabbed his shirtsleeve with a vise-like grip. "I said, look at him--"

"Don't touch me!"

"That's your fault."

"I didn't push 'em."

"No, but your words did."

"LET GO OF ME!" Eric shrieked, jerking away from Jeremy's grasp. "DON'T FREAKIN' TOUCH ME!"

"Don't touch you?" Jeremy barked through gritted teeth, closing the gap between them again. "Don't touch you, huh?"

"Jeremy," Leslie said raising her voice as the kids gathering behind her.

"I'll touch you anytime I freakin' feel like it," Jeremy replied nastily. "And right now I feel like sluggin' you."

"I didn't do anything!" Eric shot back.

"DAMN IT, LOOK AT HIM!" Jeremy yelled, shoving his index finger hard into Eric's shoulder pushing him back. "What's the matter with you? I really wanna know! From the moment we left, you've done nothing but gripe, complain, ridicule, and cause nothin' trouble--"

"Jeremy!" Leslie shouted.

"I have had it with you," he glared with bugged-out eyes, his hand slicing at the air beside his neck. "Up to here!"

Eric was beginning to break down as he fought back, throwing up his arms in a feeble effort to block Jeremy's continued thrusts of his hand against his chest and shoulders.

"Why can't I touch you? Huh? Why? What's the big deal? Huh?"

"Stop it!" Eric gushed in anguish. "Stop touching me!"

Jeremy was unrelenting, "Can I touch you here? What about here? Can I touch you here on your shoulder? C'mon, Eric. How 'bout here on your arm? Maybe here--"

"NOOO," Eric shrilled, violently exploding, sending Jeremy stumbling backward. He then lashed out in a fighter's stance, both his fists clinched and raised at Jeremy's face. Eric kept squeezing his eyes fighting back the raw emotion, his young face wretched in torment as he began to scream, "Don't hurt me--please, I just wanna go home…I just wanna go home…no…don't do that, please don't, don't do it, please, don't do that to me--oh God…"

Jeremy was stunned as he stood there. It suddenly dawned on him that Eric was having some sort of a flashback. "…Eric, I'm not gonna hurt you."

Then, the unthinkable flashed through Jeremy's mind. "--Oh my...God," he muttered, his brow furrowed and his eyes darted about as his mind scrambled to make sense of Eric's behavior the past few days. Jeremy held up his open hands, taking a cautious step toward the boy. "It's all right, Eric, it's okay."

Eric, frozen statue-like, his clinched fist shaking, was breathing rapidly.

Jeremy took another small step toward him, carefully choosing his next words. "Eric? What happened? Did someone do something to you?"

"I can't tell you," the boy whispered back, rubbing the wetness from his eyes with his fists.

"Yes you can. Did someone hurt you? Who was it?"

The boy spoke in a wretched whisper. "It doesn't matter."

"I think it does. It's tearing you apart...and away from all of us."

Eric shook his head defiantly.

"You can't keep this to yourself anymore. We're your friends and we just wanna help you, Eric."

With moisture welled up in all their eyes the kids closed their ranks around Leslie, listening intently.

Jeremy took a final step closer, standing just a few feet in front of him. "Eric? …Were you…did someone…did someone rape you?"

Streaming tears and agony twisted Eric's face. For a moment, his quivering fists clenched tighter. Then, becoming too much for him to endure any longer, Eric dropped them to his side and began to crumble, his whole body slumping. Stumbling toward Jeremy, crying hysterically, Jeremy grabbed and held him.

"What's he talkin' about?" Travis innocently asked Matthew as he wiped his eyes.

Matthew hunched his shoulder, raising his arm and wiped his own eyes with his tee shirt, saying nothing. Though he understood the meaning of the word, he just never knew it could happen to a boy. Ian came up and stood beside Elmo while Leslie moved toward Lynn taking her hand. Standing silently shoulder to shoulder, the kids listened to Eric's every word, swiping the streaming tears tugging at their cheeks. Although unaware of what he was reliving, all they really understood was that Eric had been hurt in a way they didn't fully comprehend.

Jeremy eased Eric back to arms-length and said, "…Eric…Eric, look at me."

The boy lifted his gaze, his red, bloodshot eyes staring into Jeremy's.

"Who was it?"

"I can't tell you," the boy uttered.

"Yes, you can," Jeremy said to him, his tone calming.

Grimacing painfully, Eric wiped his nose then bowed and shook his head. "I just can't."

Jeremy nodded in quiet understanding. He then half turned, looking at the concerned faces around him and said, "Leslie let's see about--"

"Jeremy?" Eric said lifting his head.

"Yeah."

"...I'm sorry."

Jeremy reached out cupping his neck and said, "I know you are," he said, nodding. "We'll get through this--all of us."

Jeremy focused on Elmo and said, "C'mere. I want you to stay with him."

"Okay."

"Lemme see your compass."

Elmo dug into his pocket and handed it to him. "Here."

"Thanks."

Jeremy motioned to Leslie and the two stepped away from the others. Glancing at his watch he said, "We've been here close to forty-five minutes now."

"And if we ever want to see our families again we'd better get moving," she concluded with a worried expression.

"Exactly. You think we can move Dylan?"

"We'll have to--" The moment she glanced across the beach, spotting him beginning to stir underneath his blanket she slipped past Jeremy and ran over.

"Whoa, hold on," she urged him, kneeling down next to him. "Are you all right? How do you feel?"

With Leslie's help Dylan struggled to sit up, propping himself with an arm behind him. With his other hand, he coughed deeply, clearing his throat. He leaned forward holding his head in his hands then raked his fingers through his short black hair. He gazed back at her, then up at Jeremy as he stepped carefully, favoring his good leg, and stood before them both. "What happened?--I don't--"

"You nearly drowned back there," Jeremy informed him.

"After you jumped," Leslie added.

"She brought you outta the water...then brought you back."

Dylan found it difficult to look at the both of them, avoiding their gaze, overwhelmed with guilt for drawing them into his and

Charlee's nightmare. "You two should hate me," he managed through hoarse vocal cords. "I wouldn't blame you if you did."

"We're not blaming you for what happened," Jeremy replied. "You helped us get away. Can you--do you think you can walk? We've gotta get outta here."

Dylan frantically felt where his pants' pockets should be; startled to see he had only his boxers on. "Where's the--?"

"It's right here," Jeremy reassured him holding out the smartphone. "You dropped it and the flash drive, back there, before you..."

Dylan took them and began looking around. "And my pants?"

Jeremy grinned. "You were on the verge of buying the farm--or so it appeared. We stripped you out of your wet clothes so we could warm you up. Your things are drying over there on those rocks."

"Oh," Dylan muttered.

"Rest here for a minute."

Jeremy hobbled back over to Eric and said, "I'm sorry I had to do that, but I had to find out what was going on with you, and that seemed the only way to get you to open up."

The boy nodded to him, his young face devoid of animosity.

"C'mon everyone, over here," motioned Jeremy with his hand.

"You saved my life," Dylan said in a soft hushed voice to Leslie.

When she turned Leslie met a pair of wet, vulnerable eyes and said to Dylan, "This isn't over until we get your sister back too." She then took his hand and held it, squeezing it firmly.

"I've never know white people--I've never known people like you before."

"Well, you do now."

Coming together as a group Jeremy held out Diver Dave's compass in the palm of his hand and gazed at the kids. They looked anxious and scared. "That's the way home," he pointed, roughly in the direction of Wolf's Head Bay. "And if we ever want to see our families, our homes, and our own warm beds again...then we have to start working together. No more arguing or fighting, including me. Those people chasing us? Because of what we've all seen and heard, they're not gonna give up until they find us. And if they do find us...we're all dead. Do you understand?"

Elmo took the lead stepping forward shoving aside a lock of his long hair and said, "What do you want us to do, Jeremy?"

Jeremy straightened and looked at each of them. "We're gonna buddy up. So that means you're gonna be responsible for staying with your bud--no unauthorized wandering. Elmo, you're with Eric. Leslie, you're with Lynn, and Matt, you're with Travis."

"Okay," the boys chimed together, Travis then asked, "What about you?"

"I'll team up with Dylan," he responded glancing over his shoulder at him, adding, "I may need to lean on you."

Dylan nodded with an easy smile from where he sat.

Jeremy then faced and gingerly approached Ian with a warm smile, placing a hand on his shoulder. "And you, you're also gonna be my bud."

Ian smiled up at him. It was the first one Jeremy had seen in more than a day.

"Oh my gosh," Travis gushed pointing to the bank of the river, and then bolted toward it. "Look!"

The group watched as Travis bent down at the edge, reaching for something, then gleefully held aloft the fishing tube.

"All right," Matthew grinned excitedly. "Good job, eagle eye."

"Well, I'll be," quipped Jeremy, shaking his head at the odds of finding it, then called to him, "C'mon Trav, let's go."

Travis beamed at his own cleverness for spotting the tube and started up the bank with it. Suddenly, a dark figure bolted out from behind a boulder and grabbed him.

"--AHHHHH!"

Jeremy and Leslie spun around and she gasped, "He's alive!"

"The pilot," Jeremy whispered, his heart jumping into his throat.

Everyone froze, watching helplessly as Travis, held in a brutalizing headlock, dropped the fishing tube and cried out again struggling to free himself.

Matthew started past Jeremy until Leslie snatched him by the shoulder. "Don't move," she muttered to him.

Soaking wet and wild-eyed, Lee Kwon held Travis like a sack of potatoes dragging him up from the river; the boy's thrashing feet leaving a sporadic trail snaking through the sand. Welding a gun in his free hand, the pilot took perverse pleasure aiming it at different ones in the group.

"Jeremy," Leslie whispered without flinching. "Look at his shirt."

"I see it."

"Stop squirming! STOP IT!" Lee Kwon snapped viciously at Travis, baring his teeth, aiming his weapon directly at Jeremy's head as he staggered up to him.

Travis grimaced in terror, his hands gripping the arm of Kwon as it wrapped tightly around his small neck like a boa constrictor. The boy's chest moved rapidly in and out as he gasped for air, his frightened eyes looking up at Jeremy.

Jeremy met his terrified gaze. He then looked into the dark glassy eyes of the disoriented pilot as he staggered up to him and stopped. The dazed, disheveled man raised the gun up to Jeremy's temple and winced painfully, "End of the road for you, kid!"

CHAPTER TWENTY-NINE

The Colonel had returned to the Auction/Control Center at Shazuko's request standing behind her, both of their eyes focused on the fuzzy white image on the large plasma-viewing screen until the phone rang at the far end of the electronic console.

"What's the point of having a spy satellite at your disposal if it can't break through the damn--just keep trying," he said complainingly as he reached for the receiver pressing it to his ear. "Yes?"

"Colonel!" Shazuko barked as she worked the controls, clarifying the screen's image. "We've got a break in the cloud cover."

"...I understand," the Colonel replied into the phone after receiving instructions. Looking up he nearly missed the phone's cradle as his eyes zeroed in on the plasma screen; the high-resolution image, transmitting from a hundred and fifty miles overhead by an Andromeda reconnaissance satellite, was amazingly sharp. In the upper right-hand corner of the screen were two people, one of them holding a gun to the head of the other. "Well, well. It seems Mr. Spear does indeed have nine lives...no, wait a minute..."

"It's the pilot," Shazuko said with a rare displaying of emotion.

"So it is. And it appears everyone is present and accounted for...except...now, where's our young computer genius?"

"There, that might be him, beside that tree?" Shazuko replied, her eyes probing the area along with the Colonel's.

"It looks as though young Dylan has taken ill," the Colonel quipped. He then became serious. "Mr. Spear and Whitehead should be reporting in within the hour. I want those kids rounded up by nightfall, before that weather moves in. The containment team should be landing on the helipad by noon. In the meantime, transfer all surveillance control up to my office."

The Colonel turned and rushed from the room concluding, "I have a speech to deliver tomorrow and I want no more screw-ups!"

"Yes, sir," Shazuko replied, the Colonel's final remark provoking a sly grin.

No one moved a muscle as Lee Kwon, his arm wrapped so tightly around Travis's neck that the boy's frightened eyes began to water. Travis struggled and thrashed trying to free himself, his hands clutching at Kwon's forearm until Kwon yanked on him again, spouting something in Japanese. His angry, Asiatic eyes bore into Jeremy's from behind his Glock; the barrel aimed squarely at Jeremy's face. Aghast, Jeremy remained steadfast, though, peripherally, he could see Travis's terrified expression, and Kwon's blood soaked shirt, just above the waist; the stain growing larger and trailing down his belt and pant leg.

He began again to babble something in Japanese; his contorted face a testament to his excruciating pain. Jeremy had never seen death before, and he thought he was actually witnessing the life energy ebbing from Kwon. As Kwon's face grew more flushed, he began to shudder, then the Glock became too much for him to hold onto and it dropped from his grasp to the sand. Travis suddenly bolted free and Jeremy grabbed him, thrusting the boy behind him, blocking Kwon. The disoriented man made a final gasp for air, then swayed and suddenly keeled over face first, crashing to the sand. Jeremy hesitated, and then cautiously approached Kwon as he lay crumpled on his stomach. He knelt down and touched the side of his neck.

"Is he dead?" Leslie asked breathlessly.

Jeremy suddenly stood back, nodding. He then grabbed Travis, hugging the boy. "You okay?"

Travis nodded back through a pair of wet eyes.

"It's all right, you're okay now." Jeremy took a breath, then sputtered to Leslie, "Let's get the hell outta here!"

Matthew had gone down to the shoreline, grabbed the fishing tube and ran back handing it to Jeremy. He uncapped it and pulled out the canvas partway, examining it.

"Still dry," Jeremy said looking up into a darkening sky. "The wind's picking up. Looks like there's a storm coming..."

Jeremy looked down at Kwon's weapon lying in the sand beside his body. Guns repulsed him. Despite his reluctance at using it he had to concede he felt safer having one. Was it a false sense of security he wondered? He painfully leaned down, taking Kwon's gun and hurled it as hard as he could into the river where it disappeared in a splash. Feeling the weight of Whitehead's Glock in the pocket of his shorts he withdrew it, checking the weapon's safety, making sure it was on; then shoved it into the back of his cargo shorts and the small of his back.

"I hope you don't have to use that," Leslie said to him.

"That makes two of us."

"C'mon everyone, let's go," Leslie urged them, stepping over to Dylan, now dressed and back in his clothes. "Buddy up...Dylan, you okay, can you make it?"

"Yeah," he nodded solemnly, wishing his clothes had fully dried. "I can make it," he finished, avoiding her eyes, wondered how she and the others could look at him for what he'd done to them.

Jeremy took Ian's hand and turned to Dylan, saying, "You sure? Lean on me if you have to." Dylan mumbled he was fine, avoiding Jeremy too, until Ian took his hand. The young Indian looked down at the curly-headed boy and smiled back as best he could.

Lynn stepped along with the other kids, hesitating beside Travis, her eyes scanning the woods ahead. "Are there snakes around here?"

"Sure there are," Elmo replied.

"What kind?" she asked him nervously.

"Blind ones I hope," Travis answered.

Jeremy herded the group up a gentle slope away from the river, where they quickly disappeared in the dense surrounding woods.

Whitehead spotted Kwon's body from the road and abruptly came to a stop, laying the dirt bike aside. He sped off down the slope toward the pilot. Without bending down to feel for a pulse, he could tell Kwon was dead. Mostly by the pool of blood soaked into the sand beside him and an open, glassy eye as his head lay on its side. He smiled impishly looking toward the woods and whispered to himself, "Where are you Jeremy? ...I'm gonna find you."

He spun around and abruptly found himself staring down the barrel of gun.

"Give me your radio," Spear said to him.

"Sure," Whitehead responded calmly, amazed the enforcer was truly alive.

He looked like he'd been through the rinse cycle of a washing machine; his white hair matted and disheveled, his clothes soaked, he clutched the radio as he spoke, determination etched across his rugged face. "Spear to the Colonel, are you there? ...Come in Colonel."

"Mr. Spear," the radio crackled back in the Colonel's voice. "Are you all right?"

"I am sir, thank you. I'm sorry to report we lost the Scorpion."

"I saw most of what happened. Time is of the essence. You and Mr. Whitehead get back here right away. Use the helicopter sitting in the river. It appears to be intact. We know where the kids are. When the containment team arrives, I want you to go out with them to round them up. There's also some severe weather moving in, plus, there's been a development here which I urgently need to speak to you about first."

"Understood, Colonel."

Spear handed the radio back to Whitehead and said, "I hope you're equally as good at following orders as the others."

"If you're referring to my lack of military training, you needn't be concerned. Whatever you want done sir, I'm your man."

"Good," the enforcer replied, thinking, *perhaps I won't have to kill this guy.* "Follow me."

As Whitehead hiked up the slope behind Spear, he paused for a moment when he heard a distant rumble. "Was that thunder?"

"Yep," Dane replied. "And it sounds like it's comin' our way."

"Well that's just great!" snapped Charlee. "We're lost *and* about to get dumped on. And how do you know which direction to--"

"Shhh--be quiet," Dane spun around and said.

"What for?" Charlee replied more annoyed than alarmed.

"Did you hear that?"

"I can't hear much of anything over all this wind."

The surrounding woods were alive as tree branches danced and swayed. And still Dane noticed there was something nearby in the underbrush moving about, rustling the leaves on the ground. Charlee suddenly bolted behind Dane.

"You make a great shield," she said glancing up at him nervously. "Who is it?"

"Search me," Dane muttered. He then pulled out the Glock, aiming it toward the underbrush. "WHO'S THERE, COME OUT?"

Nosing out from underneath a thicket of low hanging vines and branches, Baddog popped out his head and barked.

"--Oh, man," Dane gushed lowering the weapon to his side, then shoving it back into the pocket of his biker pants.

Charlee grinned, brushing aside her hair as it wafted about her shoulders. "There you are."

Dane and Charlee dropped to their knees, affectionately greeting Baddog as he pranced up to them, filling their waiting hands with his nose and back. They eagerly rubbed the dog's coat, eliciting a barrage of tail wagging and face licks. "Ohh, good boy, good boy, where have you been? We thought you ran away...now, you just stay with us, okay? Yeah, oh yeah, you're lovin' this aren't you boy."

Charlee saw Dane's obvious distraction and asked, "What is it now?"

"Over there...it looks like a--c'mon."

"C'mon boy!" Charlee chirped, following Dane through the thick underbrush.

Coming to a clearing, she found Dane standing before a twelve-foot fence. The height of it was daunting to Charlee and she sputtered, "I can't climb that thing."

"Won't have to...see down there?"

Looking in the direction he was pointing, she saw, some distance away, a shoreline. The fence extended several feet out into the water ending at a rusted post.

"We'll wade out and go around."

"That I can handle," she said petting the shepherd.

"Let's go," he said eagerly glancing back at them and slapping his thigh. "C'mon, Baddog."

The German shepherd bolted and leaped at Dane's feet, pawing at the ground as if he wanted to play rather than flee. Then it dawned on Dane. "Wait a minute, this is no good."

"What's no good?"

"We gotta come up with another name for this dog. Baddog? I don't think so."

The two looked down at the shepherd and thought for a moment.

"Any ideas?" he asked her.

"A foster family we once stayed with had a Great Dane named Sprinkles."

Dane frowned disapprovingly. "I was thinking something a little more masculine."

"Well, a killer dog he ain't," she quipped in a tone of finality.

"Maybe he's still in training."

"I think he failed all his courses," she said woefully. "I've seen Peter hit him."

"A real stand-up guy isn't he."

Dane knelt down in front of Baddog, affectionately massaging his neck, which the dog returned, nuzzling his arm. Baddog barked, and then stood still, watching Dane, cocking his head.

"Yep, he definitely looks to me like...like an Arnold."

"Arnold! You mean as in *Schwarzenegger?*"

"Well, of course."

Charlee shook her head at his choice, relenting with a grin.

Dane rose to his feet, doing the *Arnold* pose, bringing down his arms and flexing them, mimicking the voice of the world-famous bodybuilder; "*I'm an Arnold dog*--C'mon, boy!"

Dane took off running down toward the water, Arnold chasing after him, and Charlee following close behind.

"Shouldn't we go that way?" she called out, coming up behind them at the edge of the shoreline, pointing in an entirely different direction. "I mean--"

"Huh? Charlee, this huge fence probably goes around the entire property--"

"Yeah, but--"

"And that way you're pointing takes us back into the interior. You do wanna get outta here, right?"

"Whaddya think?"

"Well then, that's not the way. This is," Dane said to her as he began removing his boots, her sudden reluctance to leave oddly peculiar. "You'd better take off your boots, too."

Charlee nodded sheepishly, watching Dane as he rolled up his biker pant legs as far as he could, grabbed his boots and step gingerly into the cool brown water. "Charlee? C'mon."

Her blank expression vanished, replaced by a quick smile and a nod. Bending over, she began undoing the clips of her own boots. She hadn't seen Dane return to her side until she heard him asking, "What's wrong?"

Startled, she looked into his face and began to stammer. "Well, it's…it's just that…"

"Don't worry," he tried to reassure her. "I'm sure your brother is okay. He's with my friends."

Charlee's expression softened and she continued removing her boots. Rolling up her biker pants, she held her boots and quickly followed Dane back down to the water. The moment she stepped into it her toes and her face cringed in protest, mostly though from the mucky bottom. Making her way along the fence, she used her free hand, gripping it here and there for support. Arnold led the way, rounding the fence ahead of Dane. Racing up on shore the shepherd then bolted around in a circle wildly shaking the excess water from his black and tan coat. Dane, nearly there, half turned, taking Charlee's hand, helping her. Stepping from the water, Dane released her hand and looked around. The tops of the trees were beginning to bend under the strain of the wind now at a stiff gale. A distant flash of light caught his eye, the faint clap of thunder moments later arousing his complete attention.

"C'mon, let's get our boots back on. We're gonna have to find shelter, and quick."

There was another flash of light followed by an intense thunderclap.

Charlee cringed, hunching her shoulders fearfully and replied, "All right. But are you sure this is the right way?"

"Well, I'm not exactly sure," Jeremy bellowed over the wind strafing past his ears and whipping everyone's hair. Huddling the group together like ball players on the field planning their next strategy play, Jeremy spoke above the roar. "But if we keep going in that direction I think we'll run into a road, I think. Look, we gotta be close. I was sure I'd seen one from the air just before we landed."

"I'm getting cold," Lynn cried, clutching at her bare shoulders, her thin blouse wholly inadequate.

Leslie wrapped her own arms about the girl, then rubbed her shoulders briskly looking at Jeremy. "That way?"

The moment he nodded back to her, the black sky overhead lit up, followed by a thunderous roar. Everyone hit the ground, spooked by the blast.

"Let's go," Jeremy yelled. "C'mon, get up, get up, let's go!"

Jeremy got them moving, shoving them on, snatching Ian up in his arms and grabbing Dylan's arm, helping him, all the while limping from the mounting pain in his leg.

"Hey look! I see something up ahead," Dylan belted out, moving ahead of the group just as a pelting rain began to fall. "C'mon!"

The Colonel was seated at his massive desk when Mr. Spear came in. Showered and changed into fresh, dry clothes, his white hair slicked back, the enforcer approached and stood before him at muted attention. The Colonel put down his pen, closing a manila folder set before him and looked up. "Just making some adjustments to my presentation."

"You're still going through with it, even after the General threatened you?"

"Once you recover the flash drive *and my canvas,* I plan on delivering my own message to the General. It seems he has bigger plans for his girl, Shazuko, which *I* plan on squashing. Your surveillance system has been indispensable in this matter."

Spear nodded without batting an eye. With all the problems he was dealing with, he felt it unwise, at this point, to tell the Colonel the fate of his painting; lost in the river, or so he believed. All he said was, "I apologize for the loss of the helicopter, and the pilot."

The Colonel waved him off. "Shazuko thought you were Lee Kwon. Quite a blow to have lost your brother twice in one day. I know you have your hands full, but I'm afraid Shazuko will also have to be dealt with very soon now, as well. As for the rest, this has been my fault. I never should have put young Dylan in a position with that much responsibility, and freedom, despite his superior computer skills. You two made a good pair."

"He's much too undisciplined for me."

"I quite agree. And what of Mr. Howland? Have you located him?"

It galled Spear to admit defeat, but he was left with no choice. "Since Ryan hasn't returned, Colonel, I'm afraid it's safe to assume the girl's companion somehow overpowered him."

"One of your highly trained men, by another teenage boy?" the Colonel snapped, shaking his head. He then stared at Spear in a contemplative gaze musing, "Still, I was most impressed with your assessment when they first arrived. Your quick planning with the girl. Most impressive. Yet, however, despite your planning for every contingency, they seemed to have thwarted you at several turns."

The comparison angered Spear, but he kept his emotions in check. "Perhaps, but it'll all be over soon for them."

"These two are smart, Mr. Spear."

"They're still teenagers."

"That's the spirit. At least we've been able to accurately track them and their whereabouts--all eleven of them."

"We'll have them by nightfall," Spear reassured him, turning to leave.

The phone buzzed and the Colonel picked up the receiver saying, "Hold on a moment--yes?"

Spear paused at the doorway.

The Colonel's brow furrowed as he replaced the receiver.

"Containment team arrive?" asked Spear.

The Colonel shook his head. "No. They've been held up by the storm. They may not arrive until morning. So, the ball's back in your court. I want you and Whitehead to round them up. Shazuko has their location. You'll have to move quickly, though. That storm system is moving in and two of them, probably Charlee and her companion, just crossed the property line, section four, the west side corner fence at the lake."

"They won't go far. Charlee will see to it."

"So far she's failing."

Realizing he should have kept his mouth shut Spear hesitated then changed the subject. "You mentioned over the radio something of an urgent nature."

"Yes," the Colonel replied, a disturbed look clouding his face. "Henry Bartholomew has completely disappeared. Even his apartment is empty. It appears we were wrong about Lauren."

Spear only nodded his understanding, fully aware of the added complication--Bartholomew's intimate knowledge of the Network, the Colonel, and his position within the organization. He turned to leave when the Colonel called him back.

"Sir?"

The Colonel hesitated for a moment, realizing his other mistake. "My painting. I'm fully aware you had already prepared it, after I decided to keep it, rather than turn it over to that pompous fool, Wu." Resting his large hands in his lap the Colonel fully engaged his enforcer with a penetrating severe gaze. "So you realize, Mr. Spear, what's at stake here?"

"I do, sir."

"With the embedded microchip that canvas has the potential to expose and destroy the entire global Network. And Wu's flash drive has the potential to destroy me!"

Spear nodded solemnly.

The Colonel had never spoken to his enforcer in a threatening tone…until now. "These kids *must* be caught, and the canvas and drive recovered. You understand me, Mr. Spear?"

Spear again nodded obediently.

"Keep me informed the moment you apprehend them and secure my property."

"Yes, sir," Spear replied.

The moment he left the Colonel's office and walked down the hall back to his, a single thought plagued his calculating mind. *Before I do that though, there's something I need to do first…I want to know what happened to Ryan!*

CHAPTER THIRTY

Jeremy cautiously pushed on the cabin door, slowly opening it a crack, just enough for him to peer inside. Despite the time of day, roughly a little past noon, the churning black sky overhead had turned day into nearly night. A lightening flash revealed a ghostly glimpse of a room with furniture shrouded in white sheets. Water beading down the sides of his face, his blond hair matted flat against his head, Jeremy held the Glock out in front of him, shoving the door open with the barrel and herded everyone inside. He closed the door, then quickly looked around for a moment, saying to Leslie, "Stay here."

The kids were too wet and cold to do otherwise, as they clustered together in a shivering group. Like the others, Leslie shook too, soaked to her sandals. She watched Jeremy hobble cautiously into another room, vanishing in the shadows. In his absence, while the group curiously surveyed their darkened surroundings, the eerie calm of the cabin was pierced by jolting thunderclaps and the pelting rain against the roof. The kids jumped again, this time from an overhead ceiling light suddenly coming on. The kids echoed a sigh of relief, as did Leslie, the moment they saw Jeremy come back into the entryway with an armload of towels.

"Look what I found," he beamed, passing them out to anxious hands. "C'mon everyone, this way. I'll put our stuff in the dryer, otherwise someone's gonna get sick."

"It works?" Leslie asked, following behind the kids as they buffed their wet hair, following Jeremy into the kitchen.

"Yep. We got power."

"I wanna check your leg again, Jeremy."

"Okay."

"Can we turn on more lights?" Travis asked, noting the only light emanated from the tiny dome lamp over the stove.

"Sorry, this will have to do," he turned and said. "We don't wanna advertise we're here. Get all your stuff off so I can throw everything in the dryer. ...Dylan, you okay?"

Still weak and exhausted, the boy nodded back to him as he pulled off his soaked shirt.

Jeremy couldn't bend down, but did his best taking Ian's backpack so the boy could remove his own soaked tee shirt. Jeremy set the heavy pack aside, approaching Elmo and Eric.

"I got 'em," the boy replied in a low voice, nodding in Eric's direction.

"Okay," Jeremy acknowledged then turned to the twins. Matthew's hands juggled his towel and the fishing tube, which Jeremy grabbed and set aside just as it slipped from his grasp.

"Thanks, big dude."

"Your welcome, little dude," Jeremy grinned at him.

Leslie stood behind him, and when he faced her, she appeared to him more vulnerable than he'd ever seen her.

"I am so cold and tired," she moaned from behind a drawn face and a beleaguered set of eyes.

Jeremy reached out, embracing Leslie in his arms. The warmth of his strong body and the scent of his moist skin against hers caused her fatigued riddled mind to collapse inside, and she closed her eyes, leaning her head against his shoulder for what seemed like several moments.

"Okay, Jeremy," Matthew said, throwing the last of their wet clothes into a small pile. Jeremy and Leslie gathered them up and she followed him into the laundry room just off the kitchen tossing them into a large dryer.

"Well, well, what have we here..." he muttered snatching a plush bathrobe from a folded pile in the open cupboard where he'd gotten the towels. "I didn't see this--looks like your size too."

Leslie smiled in grateful relief, taking it.

"How do you like that?" he quipped, pointing to the logo on the lapel. "We're at the Ritz Carlton."

"Let's call room service."

"What would you like?"

"A massage."

"I'll see what I can do," he grinned. "In the meantime, turn around while I, ahh…"

"Oh, sure," she grinned back at him.

As Leslie slipped on the terry robe, she heard Jeremy suck air through his teeth as he gingerly pulled his shorts down over his bandaged wound allowing them to drop to the floor.

"I'm gonna turn around--"

"No, you're not!"

She did anyway, instantly reacting with concern. The blood-soaked bandage on his thigh below his boxers was alarming.

"What ya think?" he uttered while his face tensed up from the throbbing pain.

"At least your mother sent you on this trip with clean underwear."

"I mean my leg."

"It--it doesn't look infected. Why don't you go back out with the others? I'll throw my stuff in and be right out."

"Okay," he said, noticing for the first time the bruise on the side of her cheek. It appeared more prominent now. He gently touched it and asked, "Peter?"

Nodding, she could see the hurt and rage in his eyes.

"I'm so sorry," Jeremy said soothingly.

"I know you are."

Jeremy leaned in, kissing her on the opposite cheek, which she accepted with closed eyes. For a few fleeting, quiet moments, they held each other again. Her hand found the towel set on the counter beside them and she leaned back handing it to him, saying, "I'll be out in a minute."

Wrapping himself snugly, Jeremy pulled down his damp boxers through painful gritting teeth again and tossed them into the dryer. After taking a relieved breath he said, "When you come out I think we'll have a conversation with Dylan."

"Okay," she replied, too tired to ask about what. Jeremy limped back into the sparse kitchen, pausing for a moment looking around and wondering if their luck had held out. He stepped up to one of the cupboards and opened it. He made his way down the counter, opening up several more including the refrigerator. It was shut off and empty. He released a strained breath and headed back out with the others. Clad and bundled in white towels, the boys and Lynn stood waiting, looking at Jeremy.

"So where's the *sou-w-na*?" he quipped.

"Huh?" uttered one of the kids.

"Sauna?--never mind," Jeremy chuckled through his own exhaustion. He hobbled like a peg-legged pirate past them into another room with a mammoth fireplace. From a large plate glass window, flashes of brilliant light revealed a large spacious den, the furniture here also shrouded in sheets.

"How's your leg, Jeremy?" Travis asked him between thunderclaps, the concern in his voice evident.

"No downhill skiing for a while," he replied as casually as he could before leaning over, yanking on one of the sheets revealing a large couch. "Grab those," he directed Elmo and Eric.

As the boys pulled off the rest of the sheets, exposing two large leather-bound recliners, Ian came into the room dragging his weighted backpack like a stuffed animal.

"Well..." Jeremy began looking at them. "We can relax here for a while, in comfort. I checked the kitchen. It's as bare as Mother Hubbard's cupboard."

Feeling a tug at his side, he looked down at Ian beside him, holding out his backpack. "What's up? Want me to take it?"

Ian's reluctance to speak concerned Jeremy greatly, but he nonetheless treated the boy normally, hefting the weighted pack and setting it on the arm of the couch. As he unzipped the top and dug around inside, Ian settled into the opposite corner, resting his head back against the soft leather. "...Let's see what we got here, ah...the Spiderman briefs, pocket knife, looks likes some candles..." Jeremy took the small box and read the label. "Emergency candles--you really thought of just about everything, didn't you, Ian."

The boy watched with a detached expression, his eyelids hanging heavy with exhaustion.

"What else we got...the slingshot that saved our lives...every imaginable firework known to man--no wonder this thing is so dang heavy." Jeremy then stopped when he found the mother lode and grinned from ear to ear. "Once again, Ian saves our butts...lunch is served. Snickers, anyone?"

Jeremy started tossing the bars out to eager hands. Immediately the kids tore into the wrappers while settling back into the surrounding couch and chairs, quietly devouring the soft nougat covered in caramel and peanuts. It sounded like a herd of cows pulling their hoofs from the mud as they slowly savored the milk chocolate-coated bars. Their delight was enough to convince anyone they were eating a full course meal.

"Ian? Where'd you get all these?"

"I think it's his Halloween stash," said Elmo.

"There's even enough here for seconds," he said walking over and handing one to Ian. He stroked the boy's nearly dry hair and smiled warmly. "Here, you earned this."

Leslie came up behind Jeremy, touching his shoulder. "Look what I found, another first aid kit."

"Dinner is served," he smiled handing her a bar.

"Right now that looks about as good as a T-bone, medium rare."

Exchanging one for the other with her, Jeremy took the kit and limped over to another chair where he gently eased himself down and tore into his own Snickers bar. As Leslie hastily bit into hers, she dragged over a nearby desk chair, planting herself in front of Jeremy and began to carefully examine his bandage. "This might hurt a little."

"I'm a big boy," he mocked stoically between bites. "I'll try not to scream."

She grinned. Noticing a floor lamp beside them, Leslie nodded at it saying, "Jeremy, I gotta turn this on so I can see what I'm doing."

Jeremy silently agreed.

The lamp bathed them in a soft incandescent glow just bright enough to allow Leslie to go about gingerly removing the cloth bandage she had wrapped around his thigh earlier. Noticing Dylan, as he sat alone in a corner eating his Snickers, she nodded in his direction when Jeremy looked at her. "He shouldn't be alone," she said.

"Hey, Dylan, c'mon over and join us."

The boy hesitated at first. Then, clutching the smartphone and the candy bar in one hand, he stood, adjusted his towel and walked over to them.

"You all right?" Jeremy asked him.

Dylan shrugged his shoulders.

"Do you feel up to talking?"

"What about?"

Well, for starters--ahh--dang it all!"

"Sorry," Leslie winced apologetically, pausing before she continued dabbing the open wound with antiseptic.

"Oy vay, that hurts!"

"Buck up, I'm almost finished."

"Easy for you to say. Ahh, as I was saying...before I was so painfully interrupted, thanks for gettin' us outta that place."

Dylan nodded but said nothing.

"Do you know where we are now?"

"No, not really. We've never been outside the compound more than a few steps. They watched us like hawks."

"What about this guy, Spear? Who is he?"

"The Colonel's right-hand man. Does anything he wants, and I mean *anything*, if you know what I mean."

"Yeah. Well, from my conversation with the Colonel, I have a pretty fair idea of what they're doing and we're all witnesses, but... how does that..." he then leaned closer to Dylan, shielding the kids on the couch from hearing him when he whispered, "how does that warrant killing us?"

"Are you kidding? You saw what they were doing back there," the boy whispered in a desperate tone. "They sell children, around the globe, to the highest bidder. They can't let us live. They'll use every means to locate us. And they're not gonna stop lookin' until they do. And when they do find us, they *will* kill all of us because of who and what we've all seen. We all know who the Colonel is. But mostly because of this."

Dylan then held up the flash drive.

"And you've got the proof on that thing?"

"I think so. I mean it was powerful enough to make the Colonel back down when the General threatened him. And I've never seen that happen before."

Dylan hesitated, and then said, "I don't think we should stay here for very long. It could be hazardous to our health"

"Could be just as hazardous out there," Jeremy said, pointing at the picture window, rain pelting hard against the glass. "When it clears, we'll take off. For the moment, can we see what's on it?"

There was worried skepticism in Dylan's face when he said, "Okay."

"You sure we can't call for help on that?" Jeremy asked him.

They both watched as Dylan entered 9-1-1 on the key pad. An instant later the small screen displayed,

PLEASE ENTER
YOUR
SECURITY
CODE

Jeremy and Leslie closed ranks jockeying for a better view as Dylan connected the flash drive to a short adapter cable, then connected that to the USB port on the smartphone saying, "The ah, battery is still good--"

"Perfectly good goddamn phone and we can't even call out on it!" Jeremy mumbled acidly, his face a mixed reflection of helpless frustration and anger. Jeremy drew in a breath and asked, "You know what's on it?"

"Not exactly," he muttered as his fingers began to dance over the touch screen keying in commands. Several file icons appeared against a black background. Dylan scooted his chair closer to them, holding out the phone just as Leslie leaned in for a closer look.

"Can you read those?" Jeremy asked squinting his eyes.

"Yeah," Dylan murmured. "Here, let's open that one."

"I can't--what does it say?" asked Leslie rubbing her shoulder with Jeremy.

"It says clientele listing," Dylan drawled slowly. Pressing one of the keys, the file opened. He then scrolled down the list of names. As they whizzed by in a blur, he glanced at Jeremy.

"Yeah, okay," muttered Jeremy. "Try another one."

Dylan closed it, taking the screen back to the main menu.

"What are those others there?" Leslie asked, her eyes straining with the others to read the tiny print.

Jeremy squinted again and said, "It, ah, it says, photos, transactions..."

"Credit Card Numbers of Clients," Dylan finished.

"What's that one?" Leslie asked. "It says *Conspiracy of Silence.*"

"Wait a minute," Jeremy interrupted. "There it is--that's it, the one to the left, Caradori."

"Who's that?" Leslie whispered.

"He was the lead investigator assigned by the Nebraska State Legislature Special Committee."

"Want me to open it?"

"Yeah."

"What happened to him?" she asked.

"He and his 6-year-old son were killed back in 1990 while flying back to Nebraska with the evidence that was supposed to blow the lid off this thing," Jeremy explained, looking at the both of them, then back to the screen. "His plane exploded."

Leslie's mouth dropped open.

"Anything?" Jeremy asked Dylan.

She recovered, asking him, "They ever find out who did it?"

Jeremy shook his head at her. "No one knows to this day who did it or who ordered the hit."

"Maybe we do," Dylan said looking up from the small screen. He then held up the cell phone for both of them to see. "Take a look at this."

Leslie squeezed close to Jeremy as he took the phone. With two sets of squinting eyes, Jeremy described what looked like an email and scrolled down the screen reading the body of the message.

"Lead investigator has acquired open-sourced documentation--including photint--flying this evening back to Lincoln, Nebraska for meeting with Senator Loran Schmit. Imperative you take executive action to secure Caradori and dossier."

"When was it sent and from whom?" Leslie asked, trying to read it herself.

Jeremy's sharp eyes scanned the top of the message. "It's dated, July 11, 1990, and, ahh, it's from…" Jeremy cocked his head curiously. "It's from, get this, Top Dog."

"Who's that?"

Jeremy shrugged.

"Jeremy," Leslie gasped, nearly laughing, "look at the header, it was sent to UNCLE. Is it a joke?"

Jeremy shook his head. "It's no joke…too many people involved…and a lot of 'em are dead."

It was a frightening revelation and it made Jeremy begin to feel sick inside. "Here's another one…from someone named, Chairman Inzu…"

"To all board members, following message was intercepted at 3:26 p.m., EDT, United States, regarding lead investigator. Further intervention has been rendered moot as POTUS--"

"Oh, shit," Jeremy interrupted himself.

"Who's potus?" Dylan asked.

Jeremy looked at him with a shocked expression and said, "President of the United States!"

Before he continued reading, the three of them traded silent, frightened looks.

"POTUS has issued final approval. Dossier in no way threatens Network--no further action on our part is required."

"Here's one more. Look at this one…sent later that day…from Manndrake to Top Dog…"

"Concealment has been delivered."

Jeremy lowered the cell phone to his lap, reflecting distantly. He then looked at each of them. "…Whattya make of those?"

Leslie was the first to speculate. "Short and sweet, that last one. But what does *concealment* mean? Something hidden on the plane?"

"Yeah…like a bomb!" came Jeremy's chilling conclusion. "And his plane blew up in midair--and planes don't normally do that!"

Leslie thought for a moment, then whispered, "How would they know he was coming back, let alone when?"

"They must've tapped into his phone and email--and we all know how our own government loves to spy on us."

Leslie looked incredulous. "You really think they had him killed?"

Jeremy nodded, gazing sharply at both Dylan and Leslie. The fear in his face ratcheted up. "I think it was an order to assassinate him…and we may be next on the government's *hit* parade. They've done it before."

"Whaddya mean?" Dylan frowned.

"They're called GSA's--Government Sanctioned Assassinations."

There was a mixed look of doubt and skepticism in Leslie's face.

"Don't believe me? Listen to this. Back in the early 60's the CIA had plans to assassinate Fidel Castro. But they failed when it was discovered that the Cuban assassin turned out to be a double agent--"

"A what?" winced Dylan.

"An agent *provocateur*. In other words, he was, in reality, working for Castro, with the intent to get the CIA to reveal their operation. It worked too. The CIA emissary inadvertently gave the Castro operative evidence of the assassination plot, including the involvement of some of the highest ranking American government officials. It was a real blow to the intelligence community. Then, there was Ruby Ridge, Waco, Wounded Knee…take your pick."

"I know about Wounded Knee," Dylan said solemnly.

"I remember Waco," Leslie added.

"Ruby Ridge?" Jeremy queried.

They both shook they heads.

"A guy named Randy Weaver, who had no criminal record, was supposedly framed by the government after he refused to be an informant for their investigation into the Aryan Nations, an organization he had some connection with, but had little interest in. This poor guy was systematically screwed by all the various agencies involved, from the legal system, to the FBI, to the Department of Justice. A stand-off ensued in August of 1992 on his property in northern Idaho, where it escalated out of control, until in the end, three people were dead. A U.S. Marshall, Weaver's fourteen-year-old son--shot in the back by one of the Marshalls--and his wife, Vicky. She was shot in the head by an FBI sniper while holding her baby in her arms. The same FBI sniper shot Weaver in the back as well, but he survived."

"That's crazy," Dylan said.

"No, that's scary," Jeremy corrected him, glancing at Leslie.

"And Wounded Knee?" she asked him.

"That started as an occupation--"

"It started," Dylan interrupted him, looking angrily at the both of them, "as a massacre...on the Lakota Pine Ridge Reservation in South Dakota...where Charlee and I grew up."

Leslie and Jeremy listened silently.

Dylan softened his demeanor, briefly dropping his gaze as he spoke. "From the very beginning, the U.S. government did everything it could to take my people's land. They had reneged on treaty agreements to protect and feed the Lakota people after the bison herds were decimated by white settlers...with the ultimate goal of exterminating the Lakota people."

Leslie asked, "When did it happen?"

The soft light of the lamp began to glint in Dylan's growing wet eyes. "Late December, 1890. I remember our mother telling us about it, many times...so we'd never forget. A military detachment under the command of Major Samuel Whiteside intercepted Chief Spotted Elk of the Miniconjou Lakota nation, along with some 350 of our people, near a place called Porcupine Butte. The soldiers escorted them to Wounded Knee Creek where they made camp. Soon after, more soldiers arrived, under the command of Colonel James Forsyth. The soldiers were then ordered to surround the Indian camp and to set up four, rapid-fire Hotchkiss guns--they looked like small cannons on those big wheels. By nightfall there were 500 soldiers keeping watch over 350 Lakotas. And of those 350…230 of them were women and children. The following morning Colonel Forsyth ordered the immediate surrender of all weapons and the Indians to be removed from the area and taken away. Black Coyote, an old Indian, refused to give up his rifle. There was a scuffle between him and two soldiers and his gun went off. That's all it took.

"A few of the Lakota men with concealed weapons drew them and started firing. After that, the firing on both sides became indiscriminate. Most of the Lakota men, who were unarmed, were shot at close range by the soldiers. That's when the soldiers started shooting *everyone* with the Hotchkiss guns, including women and children. They never had a chance. Anyone who escaped across the prairie was hunted down and killed. In less than an hour 25 soldiers were dead. And the Lakotas? Of the original 350…there were only 51 survivors!"

Jeremy was mesmerized by the horror of his words. Finally, he said, "How do you know so much about it, Dylan?"

"Our great, grandfather was Chief American Horse. He was an Oglala Lakota chief. He witnessed the massacre."

Too upset at first to say anything, Leslie shook her head, wiping the tears from her eyes, taking Jeremy's hand, holding it tight in hers. Then she uttered, "I had no idea."

"Most people don't--or don't care. They were just Indians. Had they been your loved ones…your family…cut down where they stood…"

Dylan looked at them both, deeply anguished; the strain etched across his young face was a part of his personality that he allowed no outsiders to see. He cleared his throat and said, "The Wounded Knee massacre was considered the last of the Indian Wars, which spanned centuries, between early colonial America, the United States government and native Americans. *This* was America's holocaust.

And it wasn't the last at Wounded Knee. You were right--there was an occupation."

Dylan's moist eyes swept the room of slumbering kids as he related the events of the past he'd heard his mother, Rayna, speak of on many occasions. Events she herself had witnessed as a frightened ten-year-old Lakota. Moisture ebbed and crawled down the sides of his cheeks while he spoke of the unprovoked attacks against his people. Though his voice quivered, there was a calmness in his tone.

"Some eighty-three years later, in February, 1973, there was an occupation, which lasted for seventy-one days. In a nutshell, about two-hundred Oglala Lakota of the Pine Ridge Indian Reservation, followers of the American Indian Movement, took over the town of Wounded Knee after their efforts to impeach tribal president, Richard Wilson, who they accused of widespread corruption, failed. There was also the growing hostility toward Indians in many of the border towns, along with the failure of the justice system to prosecute the many white attacks against Lakota people. The protestors also accused the U.S. government of its continued failure to fulfill its treaty agreements with the Indian people, demanding they reopen treaty negotiations.

"The original intent of the protestors wasn't to occupy the town, but to have an open meeting to discuss the deteriorating conditions on the reservation. Almost immediately the police had set up roadblocks and were arresting people. In what amounted to a full-scale military operation, which included the United Stated Marshalls Service, FBI, state troopers and local cops, they cordoned off the entire area, for miles around using automatic weapons, snipers, helicopters, armored personnel carriers equipped with machine guns, and over a hundred and thirty thousand rounds of ammunition."

"Are you kidding," Jeremy said incredulously. "I don't recall my history books at school mentioning that."

"'Course not," Dylan replied matter-of-factly. "Seeing no other recourse, the protestors prepared to defend themselves against, what they saw as, yet again, outright aggression from the government.

About thirty days into it, the government cut off food, water, electricity and medical supplies. And it was still winter in South Dakota. They even kept the media out. Both sides were well armed and shooting was frequent. An FBI agent was killed, a civil rights activist vanished and was believed to have been murdered, and two other protestors were killed. A Cherokee, while he slept, and a local Lakota, were shot by government snipers. At that point, the tribal elders called an end to the occupation.

"In the years that followed, the violence against Wilson's opponents escalated on the reservation, precipitated by Wilson's own private militia, earning the reservation--over Detroit--the dubious title, murder capital of the U.S."

"My God!" Leslie leaned back, exhausted and overwhelmed.

"...And when it all ended, nothing had changed--except the body count!"

After a moment, the silence was interrupted by a lone crack of thunder. Dylan wiped his eyes dry with the palms of both hands and quickly changed the subject, asking, "Do you wanna see more?"

It took Jeremy a moment. What he was learning was sickening. He glanced down at the phone in his hand, took a deep labored breath, and handed it back to Dylan.

"Yeah...okay," he muttered in an undecided tone.

Dylan lowered the phone to his lap while Jeremy and Leslie leaned forward again, watching as he began scanning through several files.

"Hold it--there, that one," Jeremy blurted, coming to life again, fighting the constant fatigue. "Waaait ah minute...yeah, open that one."

"Which one?"

"Back up...that one, slave auction."

"Slave auction?" Leslie repeated with an incredulous tone. She then noticed the icon, adding, "Jeremy, this is a video."

"You're right," he said, and then pointed. "It's dated last February. Let's take a look at it."

Dylan looked at him with a disturbed expression on his face after recognizing the date.

"What is it?" Jeremy asked him.

Dylan opened his mouth but nothing came out. He looked away, focusing back on the phone.

"Are you all right?" Jeremy asked him.

"Yeah, sure," he replied distantly, opening the file.

Dylan felt like his heart had just skipped a beat. He nodded apprehensively and clicked on the file. A still image appeared, a wide-angle shot of a sprawling deck. At the far right side, steam wafted from an Olympic-sized pool while in the distant background, a decorative concrete railing encompassing the deck could be seen shrouded in snow. Opposite the steaming swimming pool, to the left, was a three-sided canvas tent housing a small stage toward the rear. Inside was a gathering of about thirty people.

"Dylan, start it," Jeremy said impatiently.

Pressing the center select key the video began to play.

The video was surprisingly clear, obviously shot in HD. As it played, it switched to several different vantage points, all from stationary cameras, possibly hidden.

From the tiny speaker, they could hear the sounds of activity and voices. It appeared to be a cocktail party. There was laughter and the soft strings of a quartet playing nearby, Mozart perhaps. The partygoers were mostly men, dressed in suits. Several of them, he noticed, appeared to be Middle Eastern, wearing the traditional long white tunic, colorful print robes, sash and a white headpiece or turban. Threading their way through the crowd were four or five waiters in tuxedos carrying trays, distributing tall-stemmed glasses of what appeared to be champagne.

Despite the cold temperature, none were wearing coats or jackets except for the handful of women present. Draped across their bare shoulders, accenting their fine evening wear, were exquisite wraps. They appeared more like decorations as they silently clung to the various men, but enjoying themselves nonetheless. The lack of winter wear became obvious. Scattered about the deck amid the gathering were about a dozen floor-standing patio heaters, all lit. With their copper finish, they looked as elegant as the people milling around them. There were also two great glowing fire pits flanking the assembly, piled high with wood, flames clawing at the air.

Leslie shrugged then commented, "Looks a little weird but so far no human sacrifices or famous people running around naked."

"Keep watching," Dylan muttered to them under his breath… as if he knew, Jeremy thought.

Leslie exchanged a curious glance with Jeremy.

After about a minute, the music stopped and the voices became hushed. It was then that they heard an announcement over a loud-speaker. The disembodied voice was soft and feminine. "Ladies and gentlemen, if you'll take your seats we'll get started momentarily."

The crowd stirred, eagerly taking their seats. In the back-ground, someone was being led from a nearby doorway to the stage. by a hulking figure of a man in a dark gray suit.

"It's Spear," Jeremy gasped. Escorting what appeared to be a boy, dressed in a white robe, his black hair neatly combed back, Jeremy thought it peculiar the way the boy walked with his head bowed, not so much out of any kind of respect, but it seemed more like out of fear. It was strangely eerie, almost like a master handling a prized pet at a show. It was impossible to see the boy's face. "What the hell is this?" he drawled slowly.

The image switched to the boy on stage.

Jeremy and Leslie's eyes widened at what was unfolding on the pool deck. Jeremy abruptly grabbed the cell phone from Dylan and pressed the pause button freezing the image. His jaw gaped open as he looked at Dylan. "I don't believe it!"

"It's you!" Leslie looked aghast at him too.

"Dylan, what is this?" Jeremy asked him pointedly.

"It's a slave auction."

Jeremy was at a loss for words.

"Keep going," the boy uttered unapologetically, feeling a sense of relief washing over him as the truth unfolded on the tiny screen.

Resuming the video their eyes focused on a woman in a black evening gown that walked up and stood behind the podium beside the platform.

"If you will all take your seats," she said into the microphone. "We'll get started. My name is Lauren. I'd like to thank you all for coming. I hope you all forgive the venue, but the Colonel felt that it was such a beautiful day he thought holding today's auction outside would be more fitting to this winter wonderland that surrounds us. Before I introduce your host, I'd like to share with you a taste of this afternoons offering."

Both Jeremy and Leslie felt the cold fingers of terror crawling up their spines.

"Head up, please," Lauren warmly coaxed Dylan. "There we are…although we have confined today's auction to males, our forth-coming auction this spring in Las Vegas will feature a more varied selection of sexes and nationalities. For today, this young man is typical of our candidates. He is both drug and disease free, fully inoculated and is of course a virgin. Untouched, as the pure white snow that surrounds us," Lauren joked coldly. "He is fifteen years old, and, as you can see, of Native American heritage. As always, the majority our selections today will include those of pure Aryan heritage. I trust that will satisfy the requests of some of our Middle Eastern buyers this afternoon."

Lauren then nodded to Spear who had been standing off to the side. He then obediently led Dylan off the platform and back inside.

"You all have your catalogue of today's stock in front of you, which you were given upon arrival. You are all aware of the rules and conditions governing the auction. All sales are final and, as always, the bidding will begin at fifty-thousand for each of our selections today."

"It's goddamn nightmare!" Jeremy declared.

Suddenly the entire group rose to their feet and began to clap. An unusually tall man with broad shoulders strolled out before the gathering. The tall man waved, then gestured for his guests to sit.

"Ladies and gentleman," Lauren announced graciously, "our host, the Colonel."

Dressed in leather loafers, tan corduroy pants and a white ski sweater, the Colonel towered above Lauren in her Christian Louboutin stilettos as he strode past her to the podium. He bent over slightly to adjust the microphone, then addressed the chic gathering. "Sit and be comfortable, my friends," he stated warmly. "I'm pleased you could all make this special weekend. My home is yours. If there is anything you require that you don't see, do not hesitate to request it. The champagne will flow as long as you all can stand it…"

Jeremy again paused the video, freezing the image of the man behind the podium. He stared at it for a long moment, then asserted, "Look who it is…I just don't believe it!"

"Odd how he doesn't seem concerned at being recognized," Leslie commented.

"Why should he?" Dylan explained. "He rewards his friends and destroys his enemies. You remember Senator Hatcher?"

Jeremy's mind raced to the recent past. "That was about two years ago…"

"I remember," Leslie too recalled," didn't he die on a boat or something?"

"That's right," Jeremy continued, "Hatcher disappeared while out on his yacht cruising to the Bahamas--"

"The authorities ruled it a suicide," Leslie concluded, recalling the bits of information of the subsequent investigation reported by the media.

"That's right," Dylan confirmed, then corrected her. "*After they* found all that nasty stuff on his computer, including his off-shore bank account. All of it Spear's handiwork. He's real good at framing people…and killin 'em, too!"

"But why?" Leslie queried.

"With all the surveillance throughout the facility I was able to spy on the Colonel and Spear myself. I heard 'em talking about it once. Hatcher had been wary about the Colonel for a long time--supposedly had something on the Colonel--what I don't know. But it was enough to get him killed!"

Before Jeremy pressed play again he and Leslie exchanged an alarmed expression.

"...following the auction," the Colonel continued, "dinner will be served in our dining salon overlooking our lovely lake. So, until then everyone...enjoy yourselves."

The Colonel strolled off the stage and disappeared inside through the nearby door. Jeremy's hand, holding the phone, dropped to his lap as he slumped back. Mounting fear was rising up in his throat like putrid bile as he realized what they'd just watched.

Indistinguishable voices continued emanating from the phone until Dylan pleaded with tears in his eyes, "Please shut it off."

The three then were speechless.

Finally, Jeremy asked, "What happened--with you and Charlee?"

The room suddenly lit up with lightening flashing across their muted faces followed moments later by a distant deep rumbling that rattled the plate-glass window. Leslie looked over at the kids passed out in the couch and chairs, and then looked compassionately at Dylan.

It took Dylan a moment. "They sold me...to some sheik. Charlee was next. I had to do something. I was able to convince the Colonel I could help him with his computer issues at the lodge, but only if he kept us both there. He went for it. That was last winter."

"And you and Charlee have been there ever since?" asked Leslie.

"Yes," he replied as he unclipped the cable and flash drive from the phone, and then shut it down, adding, "We should get this to the cops, or someone? Right?"

"What about the government?" asked Leslie.

"Can we trust the government?" Jeremy countered with a dubious arched brow.

Dylan was pensive for a moment then said, "Sure, we can trust the government. Just ask an Indian!"

Jeremy leaned forward, leveling a hard gaze at both Dylan and Leslie as they too straightened, sequestering their conversation from the kids, just in case one of them might be awake and listening. "Cops, the government?" Jeremy answered them both in a hushed voice bordering on a whisper. "Who did you have in mind? Who can we possibly trust when this thing involves powerful people in Washington and around the world, going all the way to the top, right up to the doorstep of a U.S. President, for God's sakes? The Colonel admitted to me they've had others killed, including Caradori. And the dossier of evidence? That supposedly vanished years ago."

"And now we have it," Leslie said grimly.

"Yep. And now *we* have it. And anyone who's ever gotten close to exposing this has wound up murdered! I wouldn't know who to take this to."

Leslie thought for a moment between lightning flashes and said, "We've got to get it to someone in the media."

"Okay...who?" asked Dylan.

Jeremy looking wearily at the both of them and replied, "That's the million dollar question now, isn't it?"

Somewhere in the dense woods, while the rain continued to fall in buckets, Charlee huddled close to Dane, snugly ensconced beneath the overhang of a huge rock, while Arnold curled up beside him under his arm. Remaining fairly dry, the thunder was fading to a distant rumble, while occasional lightning flashes lit up the black sky and surrounding forest. Dane could hardly keep his eyes open any longer and the still steady, pounding rain was putting him to asleep. The moment he began to drift off, Charlee anxiously saw her chance and began to ease herself, as quietly as she could, from the ledge.

The rain began pelting her the moment her feet touched the ground. Though her instructions were to stay with him and find out all she could, she was also instructed to somehow prevent Dane from leaving the property. Her mind was awash in confusion as to what she should do next. She feared for Dylan and knew she was placing Dane in great danger. She couldn't handle any more. When a rogue thunderclap overhead startled Dane awake, Charlee panicked and bolted, stumbling awkwardly through the downpour. She could hear Arnold barking. Running over the rough and muddy terrain, she slipped and fell. She screamed the instant someone grabbed her from behind hoisting her back to her feet.

Dane spun her around. "What are you doing? Where are you going?"

"I--I--"

A brilliant flash momentarily revealed to him a frightened face behind the muddy water droplets cascading down the sides of her cheeks. "Look, I know you're worried about your brother, I know that," he said, trying to sooth her. "I'm sure he's all right."

She nodded back, too frightened to say anything.

He thought it peculiar that she would try to get away on her own. He was her best option for reuniting with her brother. Dane dismissed it and simply smiled back at her encouragingly. "C'mon, let's get back, before Arnold thinks we've left him."

Bands of squally weather were moving through the area, raking the forest with high winds and heavy rains. By the time Spear and Whitehead reached the abandoned, dilapidated cabin on their bikes, there was a break and the rain had stopped. Removing his helmet, Spear dismounted the bike, withdrew his Glock and cautiously approached the opened door. Whitehead remained on his bike as Spear instructed him. Confident no one would be there, he nonetheless pushed the door open with the gun barrel and walked inside.

The interior was a shambles, but clearly evident from the shoe marks in the dirt on the floor that someone had recently been there. Spear was about to turn and leave when something on the floor in the next room caught his eye through the partially closed door. He opened it, peering inside. As he entered he recognized Ryan's boots, then the rest of him. Spear was no stranger to death. Ryan's open, empty eyes were enough.

He knelt down beside the body and felt the side of his neck. He surmised Ryan had been dead for some time now, as the flesh was cold and stiff to the touch. Spear's brow furrowed in astonishment as he performed a cursory examination. While Ryan's radio was still clipped to his belt, his Glock was missing. With no apparent signs of a struggle or a gunshot wound, the thought of his lieutenant, a trained professional, killed at the hands of a boy, was slowly boiling to the surface. How was it possible? Although his friendship with Ryan never entered his calculating mind, he fully expected to vent his rage on whomever it was that cut Ryan down.

Waiting out front, Whitehead pulled off his helmet and examined the dried blood inside. He then felt the gash on his head, his fingers revealing the blood there too had dried. The pain though was fresh, and he resolved to make sure Jeremy paid for it--if necessary--with his life.

Spear said nothing as he walked back outside, slipped his helmet on, then mounted his bike. "Can you hear me?"

Whitehead nodded as the enforcer's voice came through on his own helmet's intercom communication headset then said, "Shazuko just radioed their location."

"Spear to base, come in."

"This is base," Shazuko's voice crackled over the radio. "Go ahead."

"Ryan is dead. Get me the Colonel."

"The Colonel is indisposed at the moment," replied Shazuko. "Your instructions are as follows: The target's location is constant. They haven't moved in 20 minutes. You are to apprehend them, recover the flash drive and the canvas. Then you're to kill them--all of them!"

"Roger, stand by," Spear said, then turned to Whitehead. "You are to follow my instructions to the letter when we get there, do you understand me?"

Whitehead nodded and the two of them started up their bikes and roared off down the muddy two-track in the direction Shazuko was now instructing them to follow.

CHAPTER THIRTY-ONE

Jeremy sat silently staring at nothing in particular as Leslie fin-ished wrapping a length of first aid tape snugly around his upper thigh, over a fresh hand cloth she had found in the kitchen.

"Jeremy...I said how does that feel?"

"Oh--yeah, it feels okay, thanks."

"I've wrapped it as tight as I can--there didn't appear to be any infection, but you're probably going to need stitches--when we get home."

That last part got his attention. When his eyes met hers she said, "We are going to make it home, right?"

"I'll make sure of it," he said softly with an intent look. Jeremy then gingerly rose to his feet with Leslie. "I'm gonna look around. I saw a garage just off the laundry room. Maybe there's a car or something in there we can use."

"I'll go with you."

"Okay," he said.

Passing through the laundry room, Jeremy noticed the dryer had shut off. When he opened it, he found a packed dryer of warm, dry cloths. Pawing through the bundle, he found his boxers, cargo shorts and tee shirt. He then motioned with a twirl of his finger and Leslie turned her back to him. He shucked his towel and gently slipped his underwear and shorts back on, along with his tee shirt. The warmth of his clothing against his skin felt exhilarating. Opening a nearby cupboard, he took out the Glock where he'd stashed it for safekeeping. After checking the safety he shoved it safely between the small of his back and his cargo shorts. Running his hands through his tangled hair, he stepped over to the door opposite the kitchen and opened it, nodding at Leslie. "Coming?"

"I'll be right there," she said and began searching for her own clothes.

Jeremy's eyes quickly adjusted to the faint light coming in through a large window over a workbench for him to see there was no car. He flipped a wall switch to his left and a series of florescence lamps overhead ignited. Though there was no car, what he saw raised his curiosity and his hopes nonetheless. Several large--he counted four--objects covered in blue tarps. He approached them, lifted one of the corners and threw it up and over.

Jeremy's heart sank. "Damn."

Leslie came up behind him, adding to his bleak assessment with, "Snowmobiles. It had to be snowmobiles!"

Jeremy nodded grimly. Glancing over his shoulder he decided to scrutinize the workbench for anything useful, while Leslie headed over to a huge map hanging on the wall to her left. She walked up to it and immediately began trying to identify landmarks, hoping to figure out exactly where they were, specifically; the river where they had landed and the Scorpion had crashed. As her eyes pored over the landscape, she gradually began to recognize certain features. To the north was the Lake Superior shoreline...taking a step closer, she was able to identify the state roads surrounding the property, marked in green highlighter: only one of them led into the property, she noticed. From inside the preserve her eyes backtracked, following the highlighted road as it snaked through the countryside outward to where it passed through the perimeter fence to the east at a gate, becoming Justamere Road. That's when she noted the boundaries of the fence. Some distance south from Lake Superior was the northern boundary. The fence formed three sides of a 'box'; the east and west sides of it extending southward encompassing several thousand acres and dead-ending at the shoreline of a large lake. Leslie's mouth gaped open absent-mindedly as she studied the map, spotting the lodge in the northern section of the massive property, marked in red highlighter. The green highlighted road passed by it. She followed as it continued to the south, eventually skirting past a wide river with boulders and falls. It wound through the deep woods past two small cabins, and then on to a third, this one also marked in red. The road went on and finally ended at the lake which she estimated to be less than a mile away, directly south of the third and last cabin.

Her eyes narrowed on a hand-written notation beside the third cabin.

you are here

Those three words sent shivers crawling up her spine the moment she suddenly realized where they were, "Jeremy!"

"What is it?" Jeremy blurted, rushing over to her side.

"Look!" Leslie cried, pointing at the notation. "No wonder we haven't seen any park rangers—we're not in the state park—the park's way over there. Jeremy, we're still inside the nature reserve!"

Wild-eyed, Jeremy turned and exclaimed calmly, "Get the kids dressed, fast!"

"Right," Leslie replied breathlessly, dashing from the garage then abruptly turning back. "What about you?"

"I got an idea--hurry!"

Jeremy sped back over to the workbench where he frantically looked out the window. He then spun around, glancing at the half-exposed snowmobile, his mind racing. There was only one option, he thought. Spotting a magic marker among the tools on the bench, he grabbed it and immediately went to work.

Spear's voice came through loud and clear over the communication headset inside of Whitehead's helmet despite the dirt bike's sputtering gas engine. "I don't want to spook them, so we'll stop a quarter mile from the cabin..."

The two bikers roared down the muddy dirt road, dodging potholes and puddles, with Whitehead doggedly maintaining a distance of only a few yards behind Spear.

"...We'll approach the rest of the way on foot. When we get there, I'll take care of them. You handle anyone who tries to get away. No one is to be left alive, understood?"

Though Whitehead knew he was no match against this naked brute of the enforcer, he had his own plans for Jeremy and merely replied, "Understood."

Leslie scrambled into the laundry room tearing open the dryer and gathered all the clothes into her arms. Racing into the next room where the kids were still sacked out on the chairs and couch she began waking them, starting with Dylan.

"Dylan!"

"Huh?"

"We're in trouble. We gotta get dressed and get outta here, now!"

Half-asleep, Dylan suddenly bolted awake from the floor, fumbling with and then clutching the phone and flash drive in one hand while his other dove into the pile of clothes.

"Matt, Trav, Ian," Leslie whispered with quiet urgency. "C'mon, get up; we gotta get goin."

"Huh? Now?" one of them muttered followed by a chorus of groggy confusion.

"What is it?

"What's going on?"

"Leslie, whatta we doing?"

"C'mon kids, get your stuff on," she repeated, hastily throwing out to each kid what they had been wearing. "There isn't time to explain…"

"…Lynn?" Leslie said rousing her awake, trying not to startle her. "C'mon, let's get dressed."

The girl sleepily rose up from the couch beside the twins, brushing aside her long, tangled blond hair and then looked instantly worried. "Something's wrong, isn't it?"

"We have to go," Leslie repeated as she helped the boys collect their shoes.

Hopping like a rabbit in an effort to slip into his jeans, Dylan snapped at Jeremy the moment he raced into the room. "They're coming, aren't they?"

Jeremy didn't reply for fear of frightening the others. Helping Ian, he grabbed the boy's backpack not realizing it was left open. The contents shifted, spilling out onto the floor. He knelt painfully, shoving everything back into the pack until an idea struck him and he paused for a second. Despite their near disaster in the river with the Scorpion, the fireworks inside of Ian's backpack had remained dry. Jeremy quickly threw everything back inside the pack except for the fireworks, a roll of masking tape and a lighter. He zipped it closed, handed it to Ian and turned to Leslie. "Take all the kids out into the garage and wait for me there."

"What are you going to do?"

He snatched the fishing tube from the floor, handing it to Matthew. "Take this and don't lose it; I'll be right out."

"Jeremy?"

"It'll be all right. Please, do as I say."

She nodded anxiously, taking Lynn by the hand and led everyone through the laundry room and into the garage. When she saw what Jeremy had done with the magic marker, she traded a wide-eyed glance with Dylan.

"Is he crazy?" Dylan exclaimed.

Jeremy's heart was racing as he scrambled back to the small pile of fireworks on the floor and quickly gathered them up setting them in the fireplace. There were three or four packs of firecrackers, but the mother lode was the five Roman candles. There was also another long strand of fuse cord left, about five feet, which he quickly went about twisting the fuse from each of the Roman candles to the longer fuse cord at various lengths. He then ripped off several strips of the masking tape and wrapped each connection tightly. Jeremy bolted to his feet then froze when he heard something from the foyer down the hall. He scrambled to the archway of the den and hugged the wall.

The room was silent, pierced only by the sound of a metal doorknob slowly twisting back and forth. Jeremy nervously peered around the corner and saw in the fading light of the hallway the front doorknob moving. His breathing was deep and loud, and he seemed to shake all over. Holding the lighter, he raced over to the fireplace where the end of the fuse lay on the floor and lit it. It glowed red, sizzling and smoking, snaking toward the first Roman candle. He went to reach for the Glock in the back of his shorts, grimacing the moment he realized it wasn't there--he'd placed it in the storage compartment of one of the snowmobiles. Spotting a fireplace tool set, he picked up a heavy brass poker and gripped it tightly in both hands. Taking deep breaths, trying to quiet himself, Jeremy reeled back into the shadows when the door exploded open on its hinges, banging against the wall.

Spear stealthily stepped inside, his cold, steely eyes aiming down the Glock as he swept it from side to side, moving down the wide hallway. Ahead of him at the end of the hall was a large archway.

He moved toward it, stepping lightly up to the edge of the archway.

He then abruptly swept around the corner, his index finger poised on the sensitive trigger.

Spear's brow furrowed and he gritted his teeth in confusion at the sight of a room filled with sheet-shrouded furniture.

Jeremy froze the instant Whitehead abruptly appeared from around the archway and stood there aiming the Glock in his face.

"Spear must be cursing up a storm by now," he quipped with a grin. "I ah, told him you all were at the first cabin, I'm bad. But I so wanted to spend more quality time with you, Jeremy. So, ah, where are the others?"

Spotting the burning fuse in the fireplace Whitehead carefully stepped over to it, keeping his eyes and his weapon trained on Jeremy, bent down, and yanked the string of fireworks from the hearth.

Jeremy stepped toward him, trying to divert his attention, stopping the instant Whitehead snapped the Glock up at his head, taking aim. "How's your head feeling?" Jeremy quipped sarcastically, noticing the dried blood wiped from his shaved scalp.

Whitehead smiled venomously. "You can't beat me. But you can go ahead and drop that..."

Jeremy reluctantly complied, letting the brass poker clank to the floor.

Whitehead then pointed with the Glock, "...Now, let's go find the others, shall we?"

Jeremy moved slowly across the room while his eyes searched for another weapon. That's when he caught sight of the still burning fuse, still burning down to the first Roman candle. He had to stall.

"Spear's orders are to kill all of you," Whitehead explained conversationally. "But I wanted that privilege for myself."

Jeremy stopped and spun around facing him. "You've got me. Let the others go. The kids haven't done anything to you, or Leslie. Let 'em go, please!"

"I love it when you beg," growled Whitehead. "I'm gonna make you pay."

"For what?" Jeremy snapped in anger. "Your own warped paranoia?"

Suddenly, from behind, there was a whoosh followed by an explosion of light and color as pyrotechnic fireballs began shooting out across the floor from the first candle as it lay on its side. Seconds later the other candles, two of them upright, ignited shooting multicolored flares in all directions. Jeremy ducked, shielding his face from the onslaught as they ricocheted off the walls and ceiling like a meteor shower. One of the bright, burning fireballs struck Jeremy in the shoulder singeing his skin while another slammed into Whitehead's chest. He violently waved it off as if shooing a fly away. The instant his hand holding the Glock went up trying to protect his face, Jeremy lunged for it, grabbing Whitehead's wrist. The two teetered off balance in a furious spasm, spinning around in a death dance, struggling for control; Jeremy grunting as he violently shoved Whitehead's hand downward squeezing as hard as he could, forcing him to release the weapon. Whitehead's red-hot anger erupted in a loud guttural rage swinging his muscled arm and the Glock upward, squeezing the trigger. The weapon discharged; the first bullet smashing through the wooden ceiling, raining splinters followed by a second blast, the 9mm bullet ricocheting off one of the granite rocks of the fireplace and piercing the wall across the room.

Jeremy cried out, straining with everything he had, terrified he was about to die and released the hold of one of his hands and began yelling like a wild man, punching Whitehead directly on his sternum repeatedly as hard as he could. Whitehead gasped in a pained convulsion, dropping the Glock and stumbled for a moment. Jeremy grabbed him by the shoulders and shoved him backward toward the picture window and right on through it in a shattering explosion of glass. Jagged shards fell everywhere: one of them slicing Jeremy's hand. He stumbled, gasping for air, nearly tripping, until Leslie caught him. Startled, he cried out as he spun around.

"IT'S ME, IT'S ME," she shouted, struggling to hold him as he swayed and fought to breathe.

"--Let's go!" he sputtered in a drunken-like confusion, his heart pumping like a jackhammer on speed, his body dumping adrenalin throughout his system.

Jeremy could feel his legs beginning to buckle beneath him but somehow he kept moving. Jeremy leaned on Leslie as the two staggered into the garage where the kids were all nervously milling around three of the uncovered snowmobiles. He gathered his strength, hustling around in front of the machines and the group, wiping the blood from his hand on his shirt, all the while still trying to catch his breath.

"Your hand!" cried Travis.

"It's okay--listen to me--I checked 'em. They're full of gas and ready to go. I used a magic marker and scribbled your names on the--on the seats. The weight has to be as balanced as possible for where we're going."

"Where exactly are we going?" Leslie asked reluctant to move.

"Just get on and do exactly what I tell ya to!"

"Are you kidding--on these?" Matthew gushed in a confused, frightened tone. "There's no snow out there."

"Would you rather make a run for it on foot? They'll run fine over the ground."

"Not for long," Elmo sputtered as he quickly began examining one of the sleds. "We'll burn out the hyfax."

"I know all about that," Jeremy interrupted him as he turned and hoisted the garage door open, leaving a smear of his blood on the handle. "Trust me. Now get on and follow me!"

"How far can we get on these things?" gushed Eric.

"I don't know but let's not debate it now--just get on!"

Leslie anxiously mounted hers with Travis, and Lynn climbing on behind her. Elmo grinned eagerly and hopped on his followed by Matthew and Dylan. This was something he'd always wanted to try but never thought he would.

"C'mon, get on," Jeremy sputtered as he snatched a towel from a workbench and wrapped his hand in it. "Ian, you're behind me. Eric, you'll be behind him."

The boys nodded, nervously climbing on behind Jeremy. Eric quickly helped Ian squeeze in, showing him where to hold onto Jeremy. Eric wrapped his own arms about Ian's waist with the boy's near empty backpack sandwiched tightly between them. With Ian's head burrowed deep against Jeremy's back and his eyes squeezed closed, they could both feel him shaking.

"Now all of you hang on tight!" Jeremy shouted to the group. "And stay close to me, you hear me, HOLD ON!" He then half-turned gently repeating himself to Ian and Eric--he knew they were scared. "--Hold tight you two."

Jeremy, Leslie, and then Elmo each started up their snowmobiles, squeezed the throttle and tore out of the garage in a deafening roar of blue exhaust. The trio of snowmobiles had barely made it to the end of the drive, spinning out onto the main dirt road, tearing off down toward the lake, when seconds later, out of nowhere, a dirt bike screamed up the road behind them followed by a second.

Spear barked at Whitehead through his microphone, "Where the hell did you go?"

"I called you but you didn't--"

"Don't argue with me!" he snapped cutting him off.

"I'M NOT!" Whitehead shot back.

Without the cushion of snow beneath the Carbide runners and spinning track, it was a bone-jarring ride; all of it painfully taunting Jeremy's wounded thigh. He was in the lead followed by Leslie, with Elmo in the rear. Racing down the hard gravel road, the trio repeatedly dodged from side to side, avoiding the minefield of potholes and puddles, now carpeted with broken tree limbs from the violent storm. The instant Jeremy gunned the turbocharged engine, the powerful four-stroke accelerated the sled to breakneck speed, the blast of cool summer air tugging at their hair. He could feel Ian's grip tightening at his side. He glanced back, making sure Leslie and Elmo were close behind. All three snowmobiles quickly picked up speed, a sizable gap beginning to build between them and Spear.

"They're pulling ahead," Whitehead yelled.

"I'll run this first one off the road," Spear replied quickly, accelerating his bike, swerving and just missing a downed broken limb. "You go after the next one."

"What about the lead ski?"

"He won't abandon the others--do as I say!"

Jeremy snapped his head around catching Spear closing in on Elmo's snowmobile. He squeezed the throttle to the limit accelerating the sled even faster hoping the others would follow his cue and keep up. He kept looking back; Spear was still closing in, his bike swinging erratically from side to side, dodging ruts and scattered limbs. Jeremy swerved his sled just in time missing a huge pool of standing water. Elmo saw the pool ahead and grinned. Leslie saw it too, swerving to the right, flying by and barely missing it. Hearing the approach of a sputtering engine, Elmo glanced to one side catching Spear rapidly closing in on his left side. Dylan and Matthew saw him as well. Like three peas in a pod, the two boys clung even tighter to Elmo's back.

"HOLD TIGHT!" the boy bellowed over the wind strafing their ears. Elmo let up on the throttle. Spear's ego saw an opportunity not realizing he was being set up for a fall and accelerated. He came to within a few feet when Elmo then gunned the throttle, swerving back out in front striking the pool of water head on. Spear veered too late sliding into an airborne wall of muddy water, losing control and careening off into the woods.

Elmo momentarily looked back, grinning from ear to ear at his own cleverness. "HA! ONE DOWN, ONE TO GO!" he shouted to his clinging passengers.

"LOOK!" Lynn shouted to Leslie over Travis's shoulder. Travis briefly craned his neck around Lynn trying to see it as well. While his one hand held a death grip around Leslie's waist, his thigh resting tightly over the fishing tube, Travis shouted back the instant he saw what lay up ahead, "LAKE--YOU GOTTA GO AROUND IT!"

Leslie gripped the handlebar so tightly her hands were getting sore. She worked the throttle trying to catch up to Jeremy and glanced back over her shoulder looking for Elmo. The late afternoon sun hanging low to the west broke through the distant storm clouds, casting long shadows through the woods and flickering across Dylan's face. That's when she noticed that Jeremy seemed to be pulling far ahead of her. Jeremy spotted the lake as well and throttled up again in its direction.

Spear quickly recovered, ignoring the pain and mud he was coated in, but not his escalating rage. Adjusting his helmet, he picked the bike up, grabbed the handlebars, forcefully climbed back on, started it up and flew back out onto the road screaming up behind Whitehead.

"We've got 'em," Spear grunted coldly. "The road dead-ends at the lake. Up ahead it splits off then circles back around at the shoreline. We'll both cut 'em off there. Here it comes, you go right, and I'll go left. We'll meet up and corner 'em--GO!"

Jeremy glanced over his shoulder and saw the two speeding dirt bikes split off in different directions. With the shoreline just ahead of them he pulled to an abrupt stop revving the sled's throttle.

"We lose 'em?" Eric cried the instant he came to a stop alongside Jeremy.

"Not exactly," Jeremy said just as Leslie pulled up on the opposite side and stopped.

"Which way Jeremy?" Leslie asked in a breathless, panicked tone. "Right or left?"

"LOOK!" Elmo shouted pointing down the shoreline on his right.

Suddenly a fast approaching buzzing sound snapped Jeremy's head left and he gaped at the sight of the other bike tearing up the opposite side of the beach toward them.

"They've got us cut off on both sides!" Leslie shrilled.

"Head straight for the lake," Jeremy shrilled back flatly. "We're going across!"

"What?" she gasped. "On these things?"

"Are you nuts?" Eric bellowed. "We'll sink."

"No we won't!" Elmo blurted excitedly shaking his head. "It's called watercross--I've seen it done--keep the throttle full open and we'll shoot across like a bat outta hell! We can do this!"

Spear and Whitehead were nearly there.

"When you hit the water," Jeremy barked, looking directly at Elmo then focusing his eyes on Leslie, "open'er up all the way--gun it! GO!"

The terrified group of drivers squeezed the throttles and all three snowmobiles spun out in a hail of dirt, leaves and stones leaving Spear and Whitehead converging in a near collision right behind them.

Spear jumped off his bike throwing down his helmet and watched in mounting dismay with a *Where do they think they're going* expression as all three snowmobiles roared down the sandy beach, one after the other, and splash into the water like an amphibious armada.

"...I'll be damned!" the enforcer muttered as he watched the three snowmobiles shoot out over the rippled lake...all of them remaining afloat!

He withdrew his Glock and took aim.

They had made it free of the compound. And now the stakes just went up. Despite the continued deteriorating weather, he was surprised and angered when spotting a group of teenagers nearby on waverunners wakeboarding. Thinking it best not to fire he lowered the weapon and stood there grinding his teeth.

It was a wild sensation Jeremy thought as he glanced down at his feet on the sled's runners. The water parted like a speedboat as they rocketed over the open water at sixty-five mph knowing that if he stopped or slowed, even the slightest, they would abruptly sink like a rock. And without lifejackets out here in the middle of the lake, far from shore, he knew he'd be risking disaster. The others couldn't stop and help, not without risking a similar fate and maybe even drowning. He didn't get them this far to fail out in the middle of some lake, not like this. No doubt the kids on the waverunners would rescue them. But then he would be risking their lives as well. Jeremy just wanted to get to the safety of the other side of the lake. He glanced off to his side exchanging looks with Leslie and Elmo. The three snowmobiles shot past the kids on the waverunners and wakeboards eliciting wild and excited catcalls with pumping fists in the air. Whizzing past them, Jeremy felt like James Bond as he simply smiled and nodded his head in their direction.

Whitehead stood behind Spear with a sneering smile. "...Now what, big guy?"

Spear turned ignoring him, picked up his helmet and replaced it, speaking decisively. "Spear to base, we were unable to apprehend targets. They've escaped across the property line, too many mushrooms (*innocent bystanders/witnesses popping up unexpectedly*) present for us to take further action. We are returning immediately to implement 'Operation Shoebox.'"

"Affirmative," Shazuko replied curtly.

"What the hell is that?" Whitehead gruffed with a snickering laugh.

First Spear, then Whitehead picked up his bike and climbed back on. As Spear started his, he replied smartly, "I know exactly where they're heading, and by morning we'll have them."

"Just like that?"

Spear smiled with a smirk, "Oh, we'll have a little help of course...from Charlee."

The two bikes tore up the sand as they spun out heading back to the lodge.

CHAPTER THIRTY-TWO

The sight of three snowmobiles jetting across the surface of the lake in August was jaw dropping, if not surreal, for the few inhabitants of this remote area. Though it was unclear to Jeremy who might be watching, other than the kids on the waverunners they'd left behind, there was no one else in sight, at least on the water. There were also no shoreline homes or cottages of any kind. He figured this was state land and what few people were around left quickly when it appeared the storm wasn't through with them. The sun's brief appearance was over as Jeremy witnessed the next band of thunderstorms closing fast, evidenced by the gradually building whitecaps marching across the surface of the water in their direction. A mammoth cloudbank that filled the entire western horizon was slowly bearing down on them, an angry steel-gray billowing mass crawling across the summer sky like a slow-motion explosion.

Jeremy hastily signaled the others and pointed toward a spot up ahead on shore that was open, and to head in its direction. With Jeremy still in the lead, all three snowmobiles, their wakes fanning out behind them and spreading out across the surface in crisscrossing patterns, roared toward the shoreline on the opposite side of the lake.

They were less than a quarter mile from land when the wind and waves churning in their direction slammed into the trio. Jeremy snapped his head around and caught Leslie bouncing over a series of whitecaps, plummeting hard against the surface of each, the resulting spray dousing her, Travis and Lynn. Jeremy quickly realized they were all now in danger of capsizing. If any of them lost control, it was all over.

Elmo, on the other hand, was fearless and loving every minute of it. With his tongue curled in the corner of his cheek, Matthew and Dylan had pressed themselves as close as possible to his back, and to each other, connected by unrelenting death grips. Elmo deftly worked the throttle and steering, maneuvering his snowmobile over the assaulting waves like a skilled professional. Leslie was close behind and off to his left. With her hand clamped down on the throttle, she grimaced against the cold soaking spray, shaking her head free of the water droplets cascading across her face and clouding her eyes. Leslie prayed they would make it to shore without sinking. She was exhausted, drenched and cold and just wanted off.

The shoreline was now fast approaching when Jeremy looked down at his right hand on the throttle and saw the trail of dried blood from the cut he received from the flying glass had snaked up his arm. It was quickly washed away by the torrential spray of water. In a fleeting moment of anxiety, he wondered how much more they would have to endure before they reached home. About to make landfall on unfamiliar terrain, Jeremy abruptly but cautiously eased up on the throttle the moment the Carbide runners swooshed up on shore and the caterpillar-like rotating Kevlar belt track bit into the muddy ground spewing out clumps of dirt and muck as it howled up a gentle slope. Elmo, followed by Leslie's sled swooped up on shore with a final splash and the two tore up the slope right behind Jeremy.

Up ahead of them the open expanse quickly converged with a dirt two-track where the trio was swallowed up by the surrounding woods. The quiet calm of tall-timbered yellow birch, beech and two-hundred foot white pines streaking past them was pierced not only by the roar of the three machines but now also by the gale force winds coursing through them. Abruptly one of the machines sputtered and smoked to a dead halt in the center of the trail. Jeremy fearfully looked back as he had several times and saw Leslie waving her arms. When he stopped, Elmo slid up beside him and bellowed, "What's wrong?"

"It's Leslie," he barked to the three of them, pointing. "She's in trouble, stay here!"

Elmo, Matthew and Dylan anxiously craned their necks watching as Jeremy ran back toward the stricken trio meeting up with Leslie the moment she crawled off the sled. "It quit and I can't get it to start," she bellowed at him. "Your hand!"

"It's all right."

Clutching the fishing tube, Travis, then Lynn stiffly climbed off while Jeremy hastily fiddled with the lanyard, depressing the starter button. Nothing. Seeing how cold and drenched the three of them were he sputtered, "Leave it, let's go."

Jeremy quickly herded them back to the other two waiting sleds nearly bumping into Elmo the moment the young boy bounded from his sled, pumping his clenched fist high in the air shouting, "That was kick-ass cool! Did you see us shoot across that lake--sweeet!"

Jeremy was amused but knew they were short on time as he sped around, opening the forward storage compartment of his sled, withdrawing three large white bath towels, handing them to the damp and shivering trio.

"You are a Godsend," Leslie gushed, taking one of them.

"These three were the last ones on the shelf," he said. "I thought they might come in handy."

He passed the other two to Lynn and Travis's shivering hands. "You three squeeze on--"

"Jeremy, it won't work, "Leslie spewed. "We can't fit on these two, there just isn't room."

Jeremy's mind spun, searching for a solution. He finally said, "Elmo, shut it down."

The frightened group of kids huddled close to Jeremy while above them the fierce winds howled through the deep woods. The carpet of leaves on the forest floor whipped to a frenzy all around them and the towering pines swayed and groaned under its unrelenting force. Suddenly one of them bent too far and the trunk split open with a thunderous crack. The kids abruptly dropped to their knees covering their heads just as the upper half of the tree came crashing to the ground not fifty yards from them in a swirling hail of pine needles, bark and splinters.

Jeremy bobbed his head above the others shouting, "HOLY!--THAT WAS TOO CLOSE--WE'RE SITTING DUCKS OUT HERE! WE GOTTA KEEP MOVING."

"WHICH WAY?" Leslie shouted back.

Jeremy's eyes scanned up the two-track to where the seemingly abandoned road snaked deeper into the forest and disappeared. A distant rumble echoed over their heads. "WE GOTTA FIND SHELTER, FAST. LET'S FOLLOW IT."

Clutching the towel as it fluttered wildly about her shoulders, Leslie nodded, acknowledged Jeremy's open hand and took it. The two of them quickly began herding the kids up the road.

"Oh, wait a minute," Jeremy muttered to her, darting back to his sled. They all watched, especially Travis, as he opened the storage compartment, withdrew the Glock, checked it and then shoved it into his pocket. Gazing skyward for a moment, then over at the two snowmobiles including Leslie's back down the path, Jeremy uttered softly to himself, "Thank you."

Spear and Whitehead roared down the road on their bikes toward the covered bridge. In the distance, they both witnessed the arrival of another Longranger out on the distant helipad on the hill landing alongside the two-toned, blue and white one. They flew into the cavernous garage, coming to a screeching stop, then killed their engines. Spear removed his helmet, setting it on the bike's seat, and spoke decisively as Whitehead followed suit with his. "I want you to wait here for me. I have a meeting with the Colonel. This shouldn't take long."

"Does it have anything to do with who just landed?"

"Depending on the severity of the storm, we may have to suspend operation 'Shoebox' until morning."

"Some of your NSA friends?"

"In any event I want you ready to go. If you like, get something to eat--it's going to be a long next twenty-four hours."

"Are we having two different conversations?" spat Whitehead.

Spear engaged him directly. "You'll know what you need to know at the proper time. For the moment, your job is to simply follow my orders, period, without question or hesitation. Can you do that? Otherwise you're no good to me, if you get my drift."

Whitehead glared back at the enforcer, unafraid and said, "I do."

"Good. Now, I want you to go to the Auction room and monitor the weather."

After he watched Spear calmly walk from the garage and down the hall, disappearing around the corner, he headed for the Auction room, muttering to himself, "Whatta freakin' psycho."

With Arnold at his side Dane tramped through the thick woods, threading his way through the gale force winds strafing his body, hampering his every step. He paused at the base of a pine, it's towering upper half swaying gently and clutched at the shepherd, patting him behind his ears. He then called back to Charlee. "C'MON, YOU OKAY?"

When she reached his side, clutching his arm, she leaned into him saying, "We should've stayed where we were. I don't like being out here in a storm."

"You afraid?"

"Yes."

"Bull."

"What?"

"I said, bull! You're not afraid of anything, Charlee."

"Whattya mean by that?" she repeated, shoving aside her fluttering hair.

"Look, I know you're worried about Dylan, but you've been dragging your feet ever since--"

"I have to tell you something," she blurted unexpectedly, rubbing her right ear again.

"You gotta earache or somethin'?"

"No," she abruptly snapped, dropping her hand.

"What's going on with you?"

"I-I--," she stammered, avoiding his eyes. A distant thunderclap did little to shake her thoughts. He was right. What she was doing was a betrayal. And now she was having her doubts. Was it too late, she wondered as she looked at him, clutching his arm?

"Charlee. What is it? What's wrong?"

"...It's nothing, forget it," she muttered, looking away. "I think we should head in that direction."

"Why?"

Charlee nervously looked at Dane. "I think there may be a road in that direction."

"How could you know that? You've never been out here, you said, remember?"

Arnold barked as if he were growing impatient.

"If you don't wanna go that way--"

"Sure, why not. Whaddya say, boy?" he said patting the dog's neck and back. He then looked skyward, saying, "I think we're gonna get hit again...we'd better get goin.'"

Charlee nodded, refusing to release his arm. She gripped his hand tightly for the first time as he led her through the howling woods. She was beginning to allow herself to trust and feel safe with Dane. But was it the right thing to do, she questioned?

Spear stepped from the elevator into the warmly lit hall and walked casually toward the Colonel's office. Despite his disheveled appearance from his wipeout on the dirt bike, he took only a moment to remove his soiled jacket. Though he didn't show it, he was eagerly anticipating what was about to transpire. The Colonel and General Wu were about to face off. He grinned to himself at the prospect. He knocked briefly and then entered the Colonel's office, quickly appraising the situation. The Colonel sat characteristically behind his massive desk while the General stood nearby, accompanied by Shazuko at his side.

"Come in, Mr. Spear," General Wu purred, ignoring for the moment the dried splatters of mud on his pants and boots. "We were just about to start."

As the enforcer strolled in, his damp boots caressing the thick pile carpet, the empty space above the mantel where the Colonel's prized painting had hung elicited a stolen glance. He stopped and stood opposite the General, ignoring the Colonel.

"Allow me to begin," Wu announced in his usual arrogant manner.

"Brevity, if you please," the Colonel sneered casually.

Wu nodded elegantly in his direction. "Mr. Spear has informed me that you intend to pursue your current political agenda. And I believe, Colonel, I have already spoken to you as to the...provocative nature of such a course of action..."

From behind a set of steely eyes and a poker face, the Colonel watched Wu move about the room, all the while putting the final mental touches on the General's impending death.

"Our global Network is a surreptitious organization operating in complete and total secrecy. And your current political ambitions are now jeopardizing that. At the time of your appointment when King retired, we were well aware of your political aspirations...and we were justifiably concerned. However, your Washington connections over the years have proven quite beneficial, especially where potential troublemakers were concerned, as with the Caradori affair and those connected to that entire investigation. Add to that the increased profit margin you brought to the Network. Nonetheless, Colonel, despite these attributes, it has been unanimously decided by the board that--"

A prolonged buzzing sound emanating from the Colonel's phone pierced the tension-filled room. Lifting the receiver and pressing it to his ear, the Colonel listened for a moment, then replied, "He's right here."

Visibly angered by the abrupt intrusion interrupting his hold over a captive audience, General Wu caught the Colonel's dark penetrating gaze the moment Spear crossed in front of him, taking the receiver.

"Yes?" Spear said listening. Several moments passed, then, "I understand. I want you to make sure both helicopters are properly secured. Then show our guests to the conference room. I'll join you shortly to brief them."

Spear returned the receiver without making any eye contact with the Colonel and obediently stepped back opposite the General and said, "Mr. Whitehead informs me that the additional security team you requested has arrived. Also, the weather is rapidly deteriorating."

"Well, well," The Colonel smirked. "Betrayed by my own enforcer."

"Do not blame Mr. Spear," Wu said, facing the Colonel, his tone sarcastic. "He may be your enforcer but I own him, as I do so many strategically important individuals within the organization. What's that saying, Colonel? Keep your friends close, but your enemies even closer?"

The Colonel glared at Wu. "If you think for even a moment, General, that I'm going to stand idly by while you move in and take from me the Network I have built--having made vast improvements that King couldn't even have imagined in the beginning--I'd think again if I were you. I've taken the entire organization to new levels, and with no help from your people."

"You've no choice, Colonel," Wu stated flatly. "As I was saying, regardless of what you've done for the Network, no one can be allowed to threaten it, not even you! Therefore, it is the board's unanimous decision that your retirement go into effect immediately."

"And who's to be my replacement?" the Colonel fumed.

"That does not concern you. And you will of course refrain from further political endeavors. The board also strongly suggests that you not consider running for another term, but rather retire from public office altogether. That is, of course, if you wish to remain as a consultant, Colonel. That is the board's decision, and there is no court of appeals."

The Colonel remained silent, glaring up at the General, then at Spear.

Turning his back on him, who the Colonel perceived as a final symbolic gesture, Wu said to Spear, "What is the latest update on our escapees? From your appearance, Mr. Spear, I gather you were less than successful in apprehending them."

"The oldest one has proven to be quite resourceful."

"The blond teenage boy?" Wu snickered at him. "Their current location?"

Shazuko stepped over to the Colonel's desk where she picked up the television remote and depressed a button activating one of the flat screens. A map of the preserve including several square miles of the surrounding area appeared. She zoomed in on a portion of it where six glowing dots appeared. "The transponders are still functioning. As you can see they all appear to be stationary now, no doubt taking refuge from the storm."

"Hopefully *not* in the company of others," the General muttered in a disgusted tone.

"Unlikely," Shazuko remarked. "This is a very remote area."

Wu looked at her. "I hope you are correct. And Charlee?"

"There she is," Shazuko said pointing to a single stray blip a short distance from the others. "So far, she's been most cooperative. Correct?"

"Oh yes," said Spear. "I've kept her on track. She won't gamble with her brother's life."

"And my flash drive?" Wu asked.

"Dylan's with them," Spear assured him. "We'll have no problem recovering it by morning."

"See to it!" the General snapped.

A heavy stray branch carried by the howling winds slammed onto the deck just outside the French doors catching everyone's attention, most notably the General's. The sight of the massive trees in the yard gently swaying, their leaves rustling violently, elicited an uneasy, distant response. "...Reminds me of the monsoons of my... what about this weather?"

"Flights have been grounded throughout most of the state," Shazuko replied. "There have been reports of downed power lines, outages, that sort of thing. However, conditions are expected to improve by morning."

General Wu grinned with a satisfied sneer. "At that time you will take our security hit team and dispatch each and every one of them without further delay. Have I made myself clear on this--to both of you?"

"Absolutely," Spear replied while Shazuko bowed obediently.

"Excellent," replied Wu. He then turned to Spear. "I'll be returning home tomorrow and I want you to fly me out to the airstrip to meet my plane the moment this weather clears."

"Of course, General," Spear replied.

"Now then," Wu concluded facing the empty space above the mantel, his hands coming to rest on his hips. "When may I take possession of my painting?"

Travis, standing behind Jeremy, the fishing tube tucked tightly in his grasp while he clutched the towel about his shoulder, peered out from behind him. The others closed ranks scrutinizing what was left of a dilapidated farm house kitchen. Floorboards were missing here and there while a good portion of the ceiling was gone; the sink hopelessly rusted beyond any use and not a single window left intact.

The wind howled and swirled all about them.

"Here we go again," Travis muttered.

"At least the other place had a roof," Matthew added.

"And comfortable chairs," Elmo remarked.

"It doesn't look like anyone's live here in years," Leslie said.

"Yeah," Jeremy muttered back. "I saw a barn out back. Let's check it out."

Turning to leave, they followed Jeremy down the rickety porch steps and around the side of the weather-beaten house. Travis paused when he saw a flash of lightning in the distant black sky, followed by thunderous crash. "--HEY! Wait for me!"

Trampling through waves of knee-high grass, the group was greeted by an obscuring veil of thick green vines hanging down over the barn entrance. Jeremy paused cautiously, then said to Leslie and the others, "I'll take a look. Everyone wait here."

Still so very cold and tired, still clutching the towel about her shoulders, Leslie nodded wearily, watching him duck inside. Thirty seconds later, he reappeared and announced, "C'mon everyone, it's okay."

Jeremy held back the vines hustling all the kids inside. "How you holding up?" he said to Leslie as she came up to him, bringing up the rear.

"I'm working on my third wind. You?"

"I'm hangin' in there," he said to her with a smile.

He pushed aside the vines and led her through.

When she straightened and her eyes began to focus in the waning light she said, "Now this is more like it."

"More like what?" Travis quipped. "My room's cleaner than this."

"So is our garage," Matthew added.

"Correction. *My half* of our room."

"You gonna start that again?"

Travis relented with a frown to his twin as Jeremy darted past them over to a narrow set of stairs along a far wall and went up about half way. "You were expecting the Grand Hotel? C'mon everyone, it's a little tidier up here."

Leslie led the way as the weary and exhausted group of kids shuffled toward the stairs and staggered up the steps to a second story loft. They all grinned in approval when they reached the top step.

"Our luck is holding out," said Leslie as the kids slowly filed past her.

"Let's hope it continues," Jeremy uttered disparagingly to her under his breath. "We're still a long ways from home."

CHAPTER THIRTY-THREE

General Wu stepped into Spear's office after the enforcer requested a private meeting with him following their conference with the Colonel. Spear rose from his control console and faced the General.

"I've always been impressed with your talents, Mr. Spear," Wu purred. "I'm glad to see you're going to be joining *our* team."

"You didn't leave me much choice now, did you, sir?"

"Perhaps not," the Asian snarled with a contemptuous grin. "But a most wise choice nonetheless on your part. The board is purging those undesirables that have proven to be a detriment to us. And the Colonel is one of those. He's dangerous."

"Is he to be killed?" Spear asked him bluntly.

"An accident. They happen so...unexpectedly."

"And who is to be my new boss?"

"Shazuko is to be his replacement, taking full control of the North American Network. This facility will of course be shut down and dismantled."

"I see."

"Do you approve, Mr. Spear? Can you take orders from a woman?"

Spear nodded. "Yes sir--to both questions."

"Good," muttered the General as he looked about the control room and its battery of monitors along the wall. "Why am I here, Mr. Spear?"

"Dylan, our young computer genius, has in his possession one of our smartphones."

"The fool!" the General snapped with a frown, referring to what he felt was the Colonel's blatant stupidity at placing a runaway youth, despite his superior computer skills, in charge of the lodge's vital computer system. "Why the Colonel allowed him to--he can't use it, can he?"

"He's disabled the secondary protocol I.D. code," Spear lied, knowing it was impossible for Dylan to break the complex code. "If he should disable the primary protocol, then he'll be able to make a call. This kid's very smart."

"Damn!" Wu growled through clenched teeth. "Whose does he have?"

"Ryan Howland's."

"I won't ask how he got it. Just shut it down."

Spear was betting on the General's ignorance when it came to cell phone technology when he explained, "It will require that I shut down all of the phones within our local network. It could affect *your* phone as well."

"Only until tomorrow when you recover Ryan's. Correct?"

"Yes. But it'll mean you'll be out of touch with the Board, and your pilot."

The General's face glowed red from his rapidly elevating blood pressure. "I will not allow this organization to be brought to its knees by a band of insignificant teenagers and an incompetent idiot. Do it. Shut them all down!"

Spear gambled and won. "Yes sir. I'll take care of it immediately."

The General took a calming breath, then said as he turned to leave. "I'm going to the lounge for a nightcap. I leave it in your capable hands, Mr. Spear."

"Thank you, sir."

Wu paused as he opened the door. "And my painting?"

Spear smiled. "You'll have it with you when you leave tomorrow. I'm having it carefully packed for your trip home."

"Excellent. I look forward to a long and trusting relationship with you, Mr. Spear."

"As do I, General Wu," the enforcer replied from behind a false veneer of respect. "As do I."

A pile of towels marked the top of the steps of the loft of the old abandoned barn. Surprisingly clean and sparse though dusty cobwebs dangled everywhere, there was a bonus. Two bales of hay. How they got there and why was a mystery. They were thankful nonetheless. While the kids spread out the hay with their feet and hands, the overhead beams creaked and groaned in protest against the heavy winds outside, eliciting looks of concern from Lynn. Leslie joined in to help her, trying to take the young girl's mind off her fears, clearly etched across her face. It didn't help when minutes later the black sky overhead opened up with a thunderous crash, releasing a deafening downpour that pounded against the old shingled roof. She clung to Leslie for a moment, her eyes gazing up at the rafters along with the other kids every time there was a flash of white light.

"I wish it would stop," Lynn sputtered.

The kids froze, ducking their heads in anticipation of the roar of thunder that followed, shaking the rafters above. Abruptly deciding the hay was spread well enough the group quickly sat down in a circle nervously waiting, as if the roof was about to blow off. Jeremy stood apart from the group, staring out the only window in the loft. Through the dirty glass, he watched in awe, as distant trees danced and swayed in the torrential rain, the nightmarish scene splashed with flashes of blinding light. The Glock, weighing heavy in his shorts pocket, Jeremy pulled it out and set it on the ledge below the window. He then felt another tug on his shorts and looked down to see Ian staring up at him. The boy held out a candy bar for him. He glanced over at the group on the hay as they tore into their evening's repast. Jeremy bent down grimacing slightly, meeting Ian's gaze. Jeremy took the bar asking, "Where's yours?"

Ian shook his head.

Jeremy grinned at him. "You go ahead, I'm all right. I'm still full from lunch."

Ian continued to hold out the bar for Jeremy to take.

"No, I want you to eat it, okay?" Jeremy repeated gently.

The boy looked down until Jeremy lifted his chin, raising his gaze back to his own wet eyes. "You ever gonna talk to me, Ian? Or, wrinkle your nose at me again?"

Jeremy took the bar and gently placed it in Ian's hand. He then brought the boy close and hugged him whispering, "Whatever it takes, I'll get you home. Do you believe me?"

He released Ian and the boy nodded, a smile easing across his dirty face.

"You look awfully serious," Leslie said coming up to them, her voice barely heard over the din above them.

Jeremy winked at Ian and nodded toward the other kids. "Take this now and go hang out with the others. We'll join you in a few."

Ian reached out with his small hand and caressed Jeremy's cheek, wiping away the moisture. Jeremy stared back intently at the boy, took a breath, and finally rose to his feet, watching as Ian returned to the others.

"You okay?" Leslie asked him.

Jeremy wiped his nose and eyes, looking away uneasily for a moment, until a flash of light streaked across both their faces. Leslie flinched and suddenly found herself burying her face against his chest. She jumped at the clap of thunder. A moment later, she stood back, echoing Lynn's own anxiety. "I wish it would stop too. I wish this whole nightmare would end!"

Jeremy took her hand and held it. She looked down, returning the touch and warmth in his with a gentle squeeze. "Does it hurt-- your leg?"

"I hurt…all over," he replied with a tired grin. "A few stitches from Doc Gibbs and I'll be as good as new."

Leslie's smile melted into a grave expression and she muttered, "I'm scared, Jeremy. I'm really scared."

"I know," he uttered looking over at the kids on the bed of hay, talking somberly and listening to the storm. "…so am--"

A furious gust of wind suddenly rattled the roof above their heads grabbing an upward glance from all of them. Jeremy and Leslie held their breath, exchanging concerned looks as the heavy, aged wooden beams groaned and creaked against the onslaught. They each took a nervous breath and then returned to the others. Jeremy, noticing Eric had separated himself from the others, sitting off to one side by himself, left Leslie's side. He stepped over to him, gingerly settling down on the hay beside the boy. "How 'ya doin'?"

Eric, at first, shrugged his reply, then added, "I'm okay."

"At some point you've got to tell us who--who it was that hurt you."

Eric sat in silence for several moments, looking away, before he said, "I just wanna forget about it,"

Jeremy thought for a moment, then said, "Eric, you can't. You have to face this, for your sake. Listen to me…this is not gonna go away unless you talk about--let it out. Okay? You've already taken the first step in healing yourself by opening up about it. And we'll help you through this. But you've got to remember one thing… you've done nothing wrong. You've nothing to be ashamed of, do you understand me? You remember that. You did the only thing you could…you survived. …Okay?"

The boy finally met Jeremy's steady gaze but could only nod his reply. Jeremy then placed a hand on his shoulder for support and stood. "You think about that."

"Here, Jeremy," Matthew said holding out a candy bar for his brother. "There's one left for you."

"Did everyone eat?" he replied, taking it.

"Yep," Travis quipped from behind his twin, then winced, "Dinner was scrumptious, but I'm still starving."

Settling down beside Leslie, Jeremy tore into the wrapper and began stuffing a good portion of the bar into his mouth. Savoring each mouthful of caramel chocolate, it tasted as grand as a thick, juicy steak.

The rain continued its sporadic dance across the roof while bursts of light pierced the gaps in the weathered siding eerily casting shadows all about them. While the kids cringed with every jarring thunderclap that rocked the old barn, an uncomfortable silence fell over the group. It was then that Leslie noticed Jeremy's eyes and attention beginning to stray again. Aside from their predicament something else was on was on his mind. Drawn and exhausted herself, she could see the toll in his face and it worried her. She looked around at the kids then announced wistfully, trying to take their minds off the storm, "You know something?"

At first, no one so much as budged or batted an eye.

"…I do believe this is absolutely the best candy bar that I've ever had in my entire life. Really. The *best ever!*"

Matthew grinned impishly in her direction adding, "I've had better."

"I dunno. You can't beat a Baby Ruth."

"I could eat ten more of these," Travis added grimacing while rubbing his stomach.

Elmo leaned forward massaging his knee just above his prosthetic leg and said, "This is the first I've eaten since…man, since… breakfast Sunday morning--and that was--what day is this anyway?"

"Monday, I think," Leslie replied soberly, savoring the last bite of her bar then adding, "And you're right. That was the last meal any of us had, except for these, thanks to Ian."

"I know it was for me," said Elmo.

"What are you doing?" Lynn asked watching as he began removing his prosthesis.

Elmo laughed, "Sometimes it itches below my knee where I put it on."

"Man, that was a million years ago too," Matthew said crumpling his candy wrapper, practicing his aim as he prepared to toss it in Dylan's direction like an NBA player in a free throw.

Travis grinned and laughed, "It wasn't *that* long ago.

"Tell that to my stomach."

"You're just missing mom's cookin."

"You can say that again."

Dylan's timing, despite the smartphone in his hand commanding his attention was right on the mark as he glanced up and batted the wadded candy wrapper with his hand like a ball player, then returned to the phone. Frustration clouded his face as his mind ran through every conceivable code, even some phrase, he could come up with that would unlock it; yet nothing worked. For a moment, he just stared at the device, cursing it and his lack of ability to crack it. He then immediately went back to work; his fingers dancing over the mini keypad.

Squeezing close to Leslie's other side, Lynn asserted, "It's getting awfully dark in here."

"What's so interesting, Dylan?" Travis asked.

"Just checkin' it," he muttered without looking up.

"I was just thinking the same thing," Leslie replied looking overhead. "And I don't see any lights up there either."

"What'll we do?"

"Hey--wait a minute!" Elmo said eagerly after popping his prosthesis back on. "Lean forward Ian," he quipped to the boy. "...Are you ever gonna take this thing off?"

Munching the last of his own bar, Ian shook his head as he leaned forward. Elmo unzipped the top and bent over peering inside. He then dug down inside, his hand rummaging through what was left.

"Careful. He might have a lion or somethin' in there," Matthew joked.

"I never knew you to be so resourceful…you and your Spiderman underwear."

Elmo then hoisted the colorful briefs aloft for everyone to see.

The kids laughed as Ian frowned swiping the briefs from Elmo's hand.

"What else we got in here? …Hold it, hold it," Elmo grinned. "What have we here?"

Stretching up to see from where they sat on the hay, the group watched with eager anticipation as Elmo brought out the box of emergency candles. "This kid thinks of everything--Jeremy, you still got the lighter?"

"Oh yeah," he said, gingerly digging into his shorts pocket. "Hopefully it survived the dryer. Finally withdrawing it, he flicked it producing a tiny flame, then tossed it to Elmo.

"I'll give you a hand," Leslie volunteered.

The two of them placed each of the four, five-inch candles strategically around the loft, away from the hay and lit them. The effect was warm and soft and in an odd way, it made them feel safe. The moment Elmo lit the last candle, the rain started to ease up, and the rumbles of thunder finally tapered off, although the wind continued rattling the walls of the barn occasionally. Jeremy left the group and stepped over to the small window where he watched the storm's wrath across the forested landscape.

"You know what I miss?" Lynn said softly, nuzzling close to Leslie. The other kids moved in close together, finally beginning to relax.

"What?" Leslie asked her.

"I know what I miss," Travis jumped in and said. "A big bowl of vanilla ice cream."

"Oh, yeah," Elmo grinned. "Smothered in caramel and chocolate."

"Mmmmm," Travis purred.

"Pizza," Lynn said with a smile. "That's what I miss. Whisker's Tavern has the best pizza in town, too, you know?"

"Boy, you said it," Matthew agreed, elaborating, "With pepperoni, onion, ham, green pepper and pineapple."

"Pineapple, yuck!" said Elmo.

Lynn looked over at her brother and said, "What about you, Eric?"

The boy looked back at her but only shrugged his shoulders.

Leslie knew it upset her, the private torment her brother was in the moment she caught the subtly pained expression in her face.

"Hey Ian," Elmo leaned over, coaxing the boy. "What about you, whatta you miss?"

Cross-legged on the hay, the boy inched closer to the group, up to Leslie's side.

"C'mon Ian, tell us," Elmo repeated.

Ian reached out, taking Leslie's hand and turned it over. With his index finger, he began to 'draw' on her palm.

As he did Elmo read aloud what he 'wrote'. "M--y--my, m--o--m...d--a--"

"My mom," Lynn said gently.

"--And dad," Elmo finished.

There were several moments where no one spoke a word as a brief smile came to Ian's dirty face, then faded. To their great disappointment the boy remained steadfast in his self-imposed silence as he laid back on the hay.

"...Whatta you miss, Leslie?" Elmo asked, breaking the spell.

"A warm bubble bath."

"Jeremy...hey Jeremy," Travis called to him at the window. "Whatta 'bout you?"

"I'm with her," Jeremy finally turned and said.

The boys giggled.

"But in my case, a hot shower...*alone*, you bunch of *maroons*," he sternly corrected them, easing into a warm smile.

Travis had been curiously watching Dylan when he absent-mindedly blurted before catching himself. "Hey, Dylan...whatta about you?"

They were surprised when he responded with, "An outlet and a charger cable."

Matthew then asked, "Aren't you even worried about your sister?"

"Of course I am," Dylan responded, his eyes and fingers totally absorbed with the smartphone. "But I'm more worried about us."

"Any luck with that so far?" Jeremy asked him.

"Nope, I just can't figure out Ryan's password--it could be anything. A perfectly good phone in my hand and we can't even use it to call for help. Problem is all I'm doing is draining the batteries."

"Forget the phone," Jeremy said. "We've got the flash drive. There's enough evidence on that thing to blow the top off the entire slavery Network, exposing a lot of prominent people. And that's all we need."

"Maybe, but *this phone* is our backup," Dylan corrected him. "If anything happens to that flash drive we've got this. This phone, like all the ones they use, has a 32 gigabyte, high capacity security memory card. Before we left the Lodge, you remember, I downloaded the entire dossier. So, all we need is one of these to prove what's going on and who's involved. And whichever one that turns out to be, makes *it, the* Holy Grail. Then there's the other problem. We still don't know who to give it to."

"We need to get it to a television station." Leslie said. "Saw that in a movie once."

"Know anyone at a TV station?" Dylan quipped back, his eye catching the phone's screen going dark. "Someone we can..." Dylan suddenly stiffened, his fingers abruptly freezing over the tiny keypad, as though he'd done something wrong, but hadn't. "...Ah-oh... oh, shit...damit!"

Jeremy stepped away from the window asking, "What? What happened?"

"Well folks, we just lost our phone."

"Whattya mean?" Jeremy continued, drawing near him, looking at the darkened smartphone in his hand. "The batteries?"

Dylan slumped and muttered dejectedly, shaking his head. "It's dead, but I don't think it's the batteries--they're still fully charged."

"It's been working fine so far," Jeremy mused, snatching it from his hand and looking at it himself. He then began fussing with it, pressing several keys yet nothing happened. "What else would it--"

"I was afraid of this. He shut down."

"Shut it down? Who?"

Dylan looked back at Jeremy and said, "Spear."

"They can do that?" Jeremy pressed, panic edging his tone while his brow furrowed.

"Yep."

Dylan then pulled the flash drive from his pocket, reassuring himself, secure in the knowledge that it was still safely in his possession.

"And the memory card in the phone?" asked Jeremy.

"That they can't touch."

Once Spear completed his task of shutting down all of their smartphones, he picked up the phone receiver from the control console in front of him and punched in an extension. It rang only once before being answered. "It's done, sir," he said flatly. "All of our phones have been neutralized to minimize the potential threat, as we discussed… yes sir, I understand," he calmly replied, ending the call.

With the region fully engulfed by the 'weather bomb' storm system, there was little Spear could do until morning, but lay in wait. At daybreak, weather permitting, he and his supreme commander would make their move, setting in motion, uncontrollable, and unintentional forces that would rock the worldwide slave Network.

A somber mood settled over the loft, pierced only by gusts of wind howling above them, while thunder continued rumbling in the distance.

Jeremy's eyes wandered about the loft focusing, though, on nothing in particular, until they caught sight of the fishing tube resting casually beside Travis's leg. He thought for a long moment, then pointed and asked Dylan, "Whatta 'bout that?"

"What about it? It was your idea to bring it along."

"I know that," Jeremy replied snidely. "The Colonel sure valued it. Is it worth anything?"

"I dunno,"

"Let's have a look at it again."

Dylan rose to his feet and Jeremy followed him over to where the twins were sitting. Dylan bent down picking up the tube and popped the cap off.

As he gingerly began to withdraw the canvas, Jeremy left his side for a moment. He'd been watching Ian who had become the first one to succumb to sleep deprivation. Teetering back and forth, as the boy sat on the hay, his eyes had become slits, fighting to stay awake and listen. Jeremy went over, knelt painfully beside him and gently eased his backpack off. The boy languidly complied as Jeremy then laid him back down. The moment his head touched the bed of hay his body went limp and he closed his eyes. Jeremy felt the side of his face, his thumb gently stroking his cheek and whispered, "Sweet dreams, little guy."

When he finally stood, grimacing against the continued pain in his leg, he approached where Dylan had gently rolled the five-by-four-foot canvas out onto the hay. Anxious to get a closer look at the painting herself, Leslie stood up and moved in behind them both. The kids, too, gathered closer and watched as well. Leslie picked up one of the burning candles and moved in closer beside Jeremy.

"Careful," he said nodding his head at the dry hay.

Leslie nodded back and cautiously held the candle aloft so everyone could see the painting. "Who painted it?"

Dylan shrugged. "Search me."

Leslie reached down and with the tip of her index finger felt the edge where the paint merged with the canvas. "This is incredible—it's beautiful. And it's an original. Look at the cracks and the brush strokes…looks very old…I don't see a signature in the corner though."

Jeremy studied it for several seconds, and then asked Dylan, "Where did the Colonel get it?"

"I dunno. But I do know they're stolen. There were six paintings in all he had me work on."

"*Work on*?" Leslie repeated.

A small hand squeezed in between Jeremy and Leslie and was about to touch the canvas when Jeremy slapped it away.

"Hey!" Matthew yelped.

"Don't touch."

"I was only--"

"What exactly were you *doing* to these paintings?" Jeremy asked incredulously.

"Not the painting…the back of it--turn it over and I'll show you."

Jeremy gently turned the canvas over. The aged canvas back was dirty and spotted in places, yet nothing otherwise appeared unusual--to the naked eye that is.

"There," Dylan said pointing. "See it, up there in the right hand corner?"

"Looks like a staple," Jeremy muttered as he leaned closer, squinting.

"That's what it's supposed to look like. It's actually a computer chip--acts as a GPS too."

"Did you make it?" asked Leslie.

"Oh no, not me. I just programmed it. Spear then attached and sealed one of these to each of the canvases."

Jeremy straightened and looked at Dylan. "What does it do? And why six?"

"Spear wasn't much for conversation. He told me nothing. But the lodge is heavily secured with surveillance. It was easy to eavesdrop on him and the Colonel. The deal was each painting was to be given away as gifts. One to the head of each Network. The North American, Eastern and Western Europe, Africa, South America and the Middle East. This one was supposed to go to General Wu; he's in charge of the Southeast Asia slave Network."

"Then what?" Leslie asked, unable to take her eyes from the obviously magnificent work of art.

"Well, the Colonel wants to control the entire worldwide slavery Network, yet he knows he can't. So then, what better way to spy on each of the Network heads than via his own 'Trojan Horse'."

"Huh?" Elmo grunted, squeezing shoulder to shoulder with the other kids.

"Because each of the paintings is stolen, they can't be displayed out in the open. Therefore, of course, the Colonel suggested they each hang them in their private offices where they can enjoy them. And all of 'em did."

Jeremy thought a moment, then asked, "So they were all sent out. And the 'Trojan Horse' thing?"

"As long as each painting, or chip, is within range of that particular Network's computer, and they all were, it gave the Colonel complete and undetectable access. That tiny chip emits a signal allowing him to tap into the Network's data base."

Leslie then asked, "How does that help us?"

"Each chip has a five-digit code. I know 'em all. But I also gave 'em a second code, my own."

"A backdoor?" Leslie asked with a knowing grin.

"Ah-huh."

"Whaddya mean by a backdoor?" Travis asked.

"A way to sneak in," Jeremy beamed, matching Leslie.

"Oh," Travis added, then frowned. "I still don't get it."

"What's the code?" Jeremy asked him.

"They all have the same one--Double Oh Seven."

Jeremy chuckled. "Are you kiddin' me?"

"I like James Bond," Dylan replied in earnest. "He's cool. And he never loses--well, almost never."

Jeremy stepped away from everyone and began to pace the floorboards of the loft, thinking aloud. "What are the chances they've changed or blocked access of the codes?"

"A hundred percent," Dylan said soberly. "I'm sure they have--I would. But they don't know about the backdoor. I can still gain access--to the entire mainframe system of the Network."

"Through that tiny chip?" Leslie asked in astonishment.

"Yep. All I need is a computer."

"Oh my God," Leslie suddenly gasped, staring at Jeremy. "Do you realize what this--Dylan--"

"Ho-lee," Jeremy gushed in growing understanding. "Do you know what this means?"

"What?"

Leslie traded stares with Jeremy, reading his knowing expression and said, "You said the chip is also a GPS?"

"Yeah."

"That means you can locate each of the six paintings, right?"

"Well, sure--oh, man."

"And if they're stolen and famous..." Jeremy drawled with a slow nod and arched brow.

"What do you mean, Jeremy?" asked Matt, just as confused as the other kids.

"Then the powder keg we're sittin' on?" Dylan rasped, "...just got a whole lot bigger!"

Jeremy traded alarmed stares with Dylan and Leslie, then declared, "Not only can we gain access to the entire slave Network, but we can also locate each of the stolen paintings--"

"Including," Leslie added stoically, lowering the candle, "the identity of all six executives running each of the slave organizations."

CHAPTER THIRTY-FOUR

For Jeremy, Leslie and Dylan, the frightening reality of what they had in their possession: a micro chipped, original oil painting, possibly famous, definitely stolen, was just beginning to sink in. And for each of them it was different. Dylan was terrified of being recaptured, along with Charlee, and ultimately disappearing, never to know their father and a normal life. Leslie feared for all of them, especially Eric and the smallest one, Ian. The physical pain that Jeremy was in concerned her even more.

While Jeremy stared back at the muted face before him, trying to sort out in his head what to do next, he abruptly turned away, trying to conceal the alarming expression that gripped every muscle in his tense face, and stepped over to the loft window.

While his mind raced to come up with a plan, he tuned out the howling wind, the assaulting rain on the roof, and the accompanying cracks of thunder, until finally, he couldn't stand it anymore.

"I don't believe this!" he uttered incredulously, nearly laughing at the absurdity. "Of *all* the major events to rock this country in the last half century, maybe with the exception of the Kennedy assassination, *this one* is the biggest, *and* the least known, mostly because of the orchestrated cover-up. And *we*…are squarely…in the middle of it!"

"Who covered it up, Jeremy?" asked Dylan.

It took Jeremy several moments to collect his wits...and his thoughts. "The ahh, the first Bush administration...back in the late 80's. Almost no one has heard of it because they clamped down on much of the news coverage. Then it all just quietly went away."

Dylan was still curious and asked him, "How do you know so much about it?"

"One of my political science professors at college was into this stuff. We spent a couple of weeks last spring semester covering various scandals in American politics, some of it, like this, sounding like good ol' conspiracy theory stuff. Never in my life would I have imagined, or even believed something like this was possible. But after what I saw back there and what's on that flash drive, yeah, I'm a believer. And for that touch of irony, I also did a research paper on this stuff."

"Jeremy, how'd it start?" Leslie asked.

"With the Franklin Credit Union scandal of Omaha, Nebraska. There were hundreds, supposedly, thousands of victims--all of them children. Our professor even said that during the 80's when all those kids had disappeared, the ones who were profiled on posters and milk cartons, had been kidnapped and sold, *sold,* into the global sex trade. That's what these people are operating...a human trafficking Network...modern day, twenty-first century slavery."

"Slavery?" Matthew blurted.

"Is that why they're after us?" Elmo asked.

Jeremy nodded tiredly. "And from what we've all seen, it's apparently true."

"I don't understand, Jeremy?" Matthew winced. "Slavery ended with Lincoln."

"Yeah, that's right," Travis rasped innocently. "It was called the Emancipation Proclamation. Everyone knows that."

"The Emancipation Proclamation, you're right, little brother. That was in 18...?"

"'63," Travis finished.

Jeremy grinned and nodded. "Yeah, 1863. At least that's what the history books tell us. What they don't say, is that within the last thirty, forty years, the slave trade has reemerged and evolved into an organized, global Network, involving many nations, corporations and government leaders. And that includes the United States of America."

"I don't believe you," Elmo shot back angrily. "Not us, not this country. You're wrong!"

"Am I?" Jeremy responded. "What about you Dylan…am I wrong?"

"Dylan stared off blankly with distant, pensive eyes. "No… you're not," he spoke softly. "It would make you sick to hear the things that Charlee and I've seen…what they did…" his voice abruptly trailed off.

Jeremy approached the boy and gently gripped his arm. "Better put that away for safe keeping," he said, nodding down at the canvas on the hay. When Dylan looked up into Jeremy's eyes, the boy knew he understood and nodded back.

Overwhelming fatigue was beginning to claim a hold on Jeremy but he continued to fight it off as he looked about at the drawn, muted faces around him. He then sat down on an empty crate, and, for a moment, buried his face in both his hands, rubbing his forehead and temples. He took a breath, then released it with a deep sigh and said, "People and institutions you'd never dream of in a million years are a party to the most horrific crimes against children. How do you fight this kind of corruption? It's everywhere. Ever hear of a company by the name of DynCorp International?"

"No," Leslie replied somberly.

"How about Halliburton or the UN?"

"I've heard of Halliburton," she said.

"*The,* United Nations?" Elmo clarified.

Jeremy released another deep breath. "In 2002, a pedophilia scandal was uncovered by UPI, operating within the U.N. It involved sexual abuse against West African refugee children in Sierra Leone,

Liberia and Guinea. They reported that Senior U.N. officials actually *knew* of the widespread pedophilia activity, and did nothing to stop it. They took no action against the perpetrators and even went so far as to cover it up. The following year AP reported that UN officials had chartered a ship for 'peacekeepers', and were using it to traffic young girls from Thailand.

"When the civil war began in Darfur in 2004 thousands of innocent people were being murdered. Did the United States or any other nation rush in to help them--as we do the oil rich countries? Nope, we sure didn't. Bush stood on the sidelines, looking away, along with the rest of the world. Whole villages of people were being slaughtered. After the peacekeepers finally arrived, under the control of the United Nations, reports of abuse began to surface in the media.

"Several major news outlets, including the BBC, reported on a systematic scale of child sex slavery. It's been alleged that hundreds of children were subjected to rape and prostitution, not only in Darfur, but also in Sudan and Haiti. And all of it involving United Nations peacekeepers, military police and civilian staff. It just goes on and on, with no end in sight."

"Jeremy?" Matthew said softly.

"Huh?"

"What is, pedo--pedo--"

"Pedophilia. It's adults, hurting children--in the worst way imaginable."

"Why?"

Jeremy shook his head. "I don't know, little brother."

Leslie said, "What about Halliburton--how are they involved?"

"DynCorp, which is a subsidiary of Halliburton, is a U.S. based private military company headquartered in Falls Church, Virginia. They provide primarily law enforcement training and security services, mostly overseas in places like, ah, Bolivia, Bosnia, Somalia, Haiti, and, ah, Colombia, lemme see, where else…Kosovo, Kuwait… and ah, oh yeah, Afghanistan. Any of these places sound familiar?"

"How are they connected to what's happening to us?" Leslie probed.

"This ought to blow your socks off," Jeremy continued, recalling his research. "When I read this stuff while writing my paper I couldn't believe it. This has been going on since the 90's, and little has been done to stop it. Certainly not by our own government. DynCorp was commissioned by the U.S. government to provide training for the Afghani police. Many of its employees doing the training at the time were ex-Green Berets, including veterans of some other badass elite units. Now, who pays for all of that training? The United States tax-payers funded more than 95 percent of DynCorp's $2 billion annual revenue. Now, some of that two billion actually went for the training. However, investigative news reports discovered that a larger chunk of it went to Afghanistan drug dealers and pimps--pimps of children. Girls and boys--some as young as..." Jeremy stopped himself the moment his eyes fell on Ian, sound asleep.

"...This is a billion-dollar government contractor, and not the only one, engaging in, according to two company whistle blowers, fraud, corruption and wide-scale child prostitution. Eight to fifteen-year-old boys and girls bought and sold by DynCorp employees and supervisors--for sex. It's all fully documented in numerous articles. And if you think that's frightening, listen to this--these bastards have even been investigated. The few who were caught were forced to resign. That's it. Not one single person was held accountable or ever prosecuted. How scary is that?

"Later, in 2005, during hearings on the DynCorp scandal, Donald Rumsfeld told Representative Cynthia McKinney, that it was not the policy of the Bush administration to reward companies that engage in human trafficking with government contracts. Rumsfeld even tried to shift the blame *away* from the DynCorp hierarchy to one or two employees. *One or two employees? Is he kidding?* Hello-- it's widespread, for God's sake!

The president even called for the punishment of those involved in the sex trade. In the end, nothing was ever done, and DynCorp continued to receive government contracts.

"But here's the real stunner--listen to this. That same year the US Defense Department drafted a proposal prohibiting *any* defense contractor from engaging in human trafficking and sex slavery. Can you imagine? Anyway, what ended up happening was that several defense contractors, among them Halliburton *and* Dyncorp, sent their lobbyists into high gear, *assisted by the Pentagon*, in an all-out effort to kill the legislation that was supposed to ban human trafficking by U.S. contractors. The fact is that human trafficking and sex slavery is a practice condoned by companies like DynCorp and Halliburton. And because to this day the Pentagon refuses to ban it, it still goes on. Children, *children for God's sakes*, are being sold into a life of slavery, while transnational corporate giants, elected leaders, including *our own president*, either participate in, or simply look the other way."

Jeremy stood, clearly agitated. "Look at the drug cartels in Mexico; they've murdered thousands of people--*thousands*. They run that country and they're in ours. What's being done about it? Well, we're building that really long wall.

"How 'bout the Catholic Church--who knowingly moved, hid and protected their own pedophilic priests for decades. Children brutally victimized and church officials, including the Vatican, ignored them; that is, until the public outcry finally drowned out the church's *very loud* silence. Well, if you ask me, if *that* doesn't define evil, I don't know what does!"

No one said a word as Jeremy turned back to the loft window and stared past the rain slashing against the glass. "How in God's name do you fight this shit?" he growled. "What chance do *we have*, against that much evil?"

Eric stirred from his corner and offered, "Maybe there's no God. If there is, how can He ignore what's going on in our world?"

"Maybe He's just given up on us," Elmo muttered.

At first, Jeremy hadn't heard his brother's voice over the roar. Travis stood, cleared his throat and took a step closer to him. "I said, you're all wrong--God will protect us."

"He will, will He?" Jeremy turned and replied soberly. "Is that what you think?"

"Don't you?" Travis replied looking at Jeremy searchingly. "You always said that He does. Remember Alligator Light?"

"Yeah, I remember."

"What's Alligator Light?" Leslie asked.

Matthew chimed in with, "That was a blast."

"Hasn't he so far?" Trav continued. "He got us across that lake on those snowmobiles--who'd a thought."

"No, *I* got us across that lake on those snowmobiles."

"Well, what if we had gone to a different cabin, one that didn't have any snowmobiles--they would have caught us."

"And what if there had been a car at one of those other cabins, Trav?"

"But no gas."

"Or bicycles," Leslie interrupted them. "C'mon now, what's Alligator Light?"

"We were lucky, Travis."

"I'd call it a miracle."

"A miracle?" Jeremy snapped with a frown, his mood abruptly becoming more angry. "I hate that word!"

Travis dropped his gaze just as Jeremy gingerly limped over and stood before him. "Travis," Jeremy said softly, "look at me."

The boy did so reluctantly.

"I know it bothers you that I don't believe--about what happened to you--"

"But why, Jeremy? Why don't you believe me? Mom and Dad did."

From the look of disappointment on the boy's face, Jeremy suddenly regretted what he had said.

"Well, I don't care," Travis stated softly, then pointed at Leslie. "She saw 'em too--just as I did, and just as you did--in the lighthouse. You said so yourself."

"I was mistaken."

"No, you weren't."

"Travis, listen to me."

"No, I won't listen," he sputtered angrily, turning his back to Jeremy.

Jeremy reached out grasping his brother's shoulder and gently spun him around. "I'm sorry. I just don't--"

"You don't what? Believe that I've been to the other side?"

"You're still on that kick?"

"It's not a kick!" the boy frowned at him. "It happened, I was really there!"

"Okay, so you think you were there."

"I don't *think I was there!*" Travis shouted angrily, "I *was there*, period! What's the matter with you?"

"What's the matter with me? Look around you!" Jeremy snapped and then shouted back. "WHATTYA THINK'S THE MATTER WITH ME!"

Startled by Jeremy's sudden outburst, Travis's own anger turned to dismay. The others stirred uneasily. Ian, who could have slept through an air raid attack, stirred too and lazily sat up.

The pressure Jeremy felt came boiling out from his lips. "And don't give me that miracle crap! When was the last time you saw or heard of a real, honest-to-God miracle? Humm, Trav? Name me one!"

Travis' eyes were beginning to well up when he replied sheepishly, "They're in the Bible."

"Yep, that's right, they're in the Bible. How about the parting of the Red Sea? Remember that one? If I remember my Sunday school lecture correctly, so the Israelites could escape the evil Pharaoh, God parts the Red Sea so all of His people could cross over from Egypt into the Promised Land--and we're talkin' a lot of water here, millions of tons of it being pushed apart, for what had to be the better part of a day. And no natural phenomenon gonna do that, so I'll give you that one. Yep, in my book, that would definitely qualify as a truly certifiable, honest-to-God, bona fide, *miracle*. Now, heard of any more recent ones?"

Travis choked on the words he wanted to say, but they wouldn't come out. Instead, tears began to stream along both sides of his face.

"Cat got your tongue? Lemme help you out. Remember that plane crash in Denver last year?--made all the headlines. And remember the woman talking to reporters afterwards? She said it was a *miracle* that she survived. Remember that? I do. Not a scratch on her. But the little kid seated right next to her, an inch from her elbow--now he wasn't quite so fortunate. He didn't make it, along with his entire family, including the other fifty-two passengers! God, in his infinite wisdom said, "I'll grant this one woman a miracle and let her live, but screw all the others!" I dunno, maybe God was pissed off that day. Call me funny, call me peculiar, but that was no miracle. She was just *damn lucky!*"

Jeremy limped to the far side of the loft, his face shrouded in shadows. "I've read the Bible too. Back then, God seemed to talk to, or at least communicate with a lot of folks--prophets. Like Moses, Abraham, Elijah, Jeremiah--does He do that today? Nope. And apparently *not since* Biblical times. So, it's been a while. And if He did, if someone said they actually spoke to God, had a conversation with Him, they'd be thrown in a straightjacket and tossed into the loony bin. And if anyone were to admit to having a chat with the Almighty, my money'd be on the pope. And unless you know somethin' I don't, I haven't heard *him* admit to any one-on-ones."

Jeremy spoke to the window, his eyes staring past the raging cauldron outside. "We've got this cousin…she's always sending our mother these religious emails--you know the ones--the kind you have to forward to ten friends in order to receive God's blessing or prove your faith. She sent us this one, from some woman who had snapped a picture of these clouds. They look like two hands clasped together, as if in prayer. They really did too. It came with the caption: proof of God's loving existence. You've heard of others like that-- right? Like the ones people proclaim are the images of Jesus…in ice crystals, on some guy's car windshield, or the restaurant owner who swears the image of Jesus is burnt on the inside of his oven, or the woman who saw Jesus' face on a cake, or how 'bout the image of the Virgin Mary…*on an oak tree.* C'mon…gimme a break! If God really wants to reach out to humanity I can think of a lot better ways for 'em to do it than through ice crystals, burnt ovens, cake frosting or some tree stump out in the middle of the woods!"

Jeremy emerged from the shadows, his face wretched in raw emotion and tears, changing the subject. "Evil is like Visa, it's every- where. And so is global slavery. It's on the rise and it's illegal every- where. Yet government corruption around the world allows it to thrive and go unpunished, including the United States. What else we got? --Wars, suicide bombers, WMD's, dictators killing their own people to keep 'em in line…"

Leslie rose to her feet in tears and simply spoke his name, "Jeremy."

Throwing up a hand in protest, Jeremy closed his eyes and rasped from memory, "Judges, 3:20. Ehud killed the king of Moah, Eglon; it was God's punishment because of his eighteen years of repression against the people of Israel. 'And Ehud came to him, as he was sitting alone in his cool roof chamber. And Ehud said, "I have a message from God for you." And he rose from his seat. And Ehud reached with his left hand, took the sword from his right thigh, and thrust it into his belly.'"

Jeremy took a breath, wiping his eyes, then gritted his teeth angrily as he continued. "They say people have turned their back on God. I think it's the other way around. I think God has turned his back on us. Look at our world! Repression and genocide in the Middle East. Although we got Saddam Hussein and Bin Laden, I don't see God going after the rest of those monsters over there, 'cause they ain't the only ones. There's more of 'em. How 'bout North Korea's,

Kim Jong--remember that psychopathic freak--a short Hitler with a bouffant? The North Korean people don't dare fart without state permission. Oh, yeah, and his prisons camps? The atrocities? They're teaming with over 200,000 *political* prisoners. In other words, average folk like you and me--and growing. How about Hitler? There had been several attempts on his life, and every one of 'em failed. Was *evil*, protecting him? If God is so almighty powerful--why didn't the *first one* take? The lives that could have been saved, atrocities prevented. Even Mother Teresa, at the end of her life, after all the misery she'd seen, expressed doubts in the existence of God. So, if there was ever a time for God to put in an appearance in our world, and exact some of that justice that he was so fond of dishing out back in the old days, *now would be good!*"

"He can't!" Trav blurted through tears.

"Whattya mean He *can't*. Why the hell not? You talk about miracles? Here's one He should consider. Why doesn't God simply stop their hearts? Just stop 'em all beating in their evil tracks, including these bastards who are after us. Well, I'm not gonna be holdin' my breath. So don't talk to me, little brother, about God and miracles…"

Jeremy then pounded his fists together. "I said I'd get everyone home, safe and sound, and goddamn it, that's just what I'm gonna do!"

"--Oh, Jeremy," Travis cried in anguish, looking at him.

Jeremy broke down too, the instant Travis ran to him. Jeremy enveloped his brother with his arms and the two of them wept.

While the side of Travis's head pressed against Jeremy's stomach, he muttered, "And Jesus said, "I am the way, and the truth, and the life; no one comes to the Father, but by me.""

"Travis, what father turns his back on his children, while they're being slaughtered?" Jeremy muttered back, his voice hoarse with emotion. "I'm trying to get us all home."

The boy pushed back, looking up into his older brother's tired and wet eyes and said, "You have to have faith, Jeremy, we have to trust in God--"

"We've been lucky so far--"

"He's showing us the way."

"Showing us the--?" Jeremy was at a loss for words as he stared back into Travis's eyes, wet but bright with hope and belief. There was calmness in the boy's expression as he spoke. The others remained silent, watching the two of them, their own wet eyes glinting in the soft candlelight. Finally, Jeremy cried, "What makes you so sure?"

"I died out there on the river last year, remember? I saw him."

"Who?" Jeremy replied with a confused expression. "Our grandfather or God?"

Travis hesitated to answer him.

Jeremy relented with a lopsided look and a disbelieving shake of his head. "Leslie, help me out here."

"He's got you," she replied, wiping her eyes. "And what he said earlier, I mean about what I saw? He's right. I did see 'em, there in the hallway at your house."

"God?"

Leslie smiled. "Well, no, I don't think so. He looked exactly like the old man in that portrait above your fireplace."

Jeremy's eyes burned into Travis'. "I don't know what I saw."

"You did see 'em," Travis urged him.

"Was it our grandfather?"

"He's our guardian angel."

"Angel or not," Leslie interrupted, sniffling back her tears. "I still wanna know about this, Alligator Light?"

"Well…" Jeremy began, his eyes locked on Trav's. He then relinquished them and look at the others. "A few years ago we took a family trip to Islamorada, in the Florida Keys."

"That was sooo much fun," Matthew beamed, wiping his own eyes with his palms.

Jeremy nodded. "We went out on…the ahh…"

"The Happy Cat," the twins chimed in together.

"Yeah, that's right," Jeremy grinned in recollection. "The Happy Cat snorkel boat, out of Robbie's Marina, right there in Islamorada."

"Hey, remember Bubbles, the dog?" Travis beamed with a widening grin.

"Oh, yeah," Matthew recalled matching his twin's gazing smile.

"Who's Bubbles?" Lynn queried with a chuckle.

"She was a cool little dog at the Kayak Shack," said Travis.

"Yeah, she'd sit in a kayak on the deck and bark at other dogs," Matthew related.

"Until her owner yelled at her to stop," Travis laughed.

Jeremy laughed too. "Yeah, that was funny. And if you'd say to her, 'Gimme five, Bubbles', she'd high-five your hand with her paw."

"Ahhh," Lynn cooed.

"...Anyway," Jeremy continued, his demeanor becoming more serious. "We went out to this huge lighthouse at the edge of the reef--'bout five miles off shore."

"The water was swimming-pool blue, wasn't it, Jeremy?" added Matthew.

"With an awesome white sandy bottom. It *was* pretty gorgeous out there. And it's called Alligator Light. We snorkeled beneath it--"

"And there were tons of tropical fish hanging out under this thing," Matthew beamed again, a grin stretching from ear to ear, both his hands stretched out sideways. "Barracudas too, this big."

"The lighthouse doesn't look like a regular one," Jeremy went on. "It's has an iron skeleton framework with a housing platform, stretching to about 130 feet above the water. Below the housing platform was a smaller, plank one, roughly fifteen by fifteen--about ten or twelve feet off the surface of the water. Well, people were climbing up and jumping off it into the water. Looked like fun, so these two daredevils dragged me up there and we started jumping off it too. It was pretty cool."

"Tell 'em what happened next, Jeremy," said Travis.

"We were clowning around, pushing and shoving each other, and I started to step back...and that's when I heard a voice. Not an audible voice, like your hearing me now, but it was in my head. And I knew it was in my head."

"What did it say?" Leslie asked.

"It said, three times, very calmly; 'Look behind you, look behind you, look behind you.'. So I did. *One more step* and I would have fallen through a huge, gaping hole in the planking, which I hadn't even noticed before. I more than likely would have been seriously injured or even killed as I went down striking all that iron-webbing framework below. Not kiddin' you, one more step and our vacation could've come to a tragic end. It was kinda weird."

"Wow," Elmo whispered.

"Was that my guardian angel?" Jeremy turned and asked Travis. The boy nodded.

"Okay. So maybe God can't save us."

"His angels can, if we're listening. Then it's up to us to choose."

Jeremy just shook his head. "But they don't warn everybody, do they? I can think of a few thousand people, especially their families that probably wished they'd have been warned before they boarded some planes and walked into two New York City towers. You know that missing person poster on the tack board in Dad's office at the shop?"

"Yes," Travis answered solemnly. "Jacob Wetterling."

"Travis, Jacob was abducted in the fall of 1989, when he was just eleven years old. He was just a year older than you and Matthew. What's happening to us may be what happened to him. And he's never been found. Now, you ask me to believe in a God that in Biblical times, performed miracles, almost routinely, but cannot seem to be bothered to work a few today. Save an innocent boy from who knows what awful fate awaited him, let alone save us? What you're telling me Trav doesn't make any sense. Who am I, that I was warned about those missing planks?"

"When God made people, Jeremy, he gave us the freedom to choose," the boy replied earnestly. "We can do right, or we can do wrong. And if we're not free to choose evil, then we're not free to choose good either. So He can't interfere. If he does, he takes away our freedom, and our humanity."

"But Trav," Jeremy replied calmly, "if you really believe in the Bible, then you already know that in Biblical times He intervened many times, breaking *His own rule.*"

Travis was at an impasse unable to find the words to refute his brother. Finally, he said, "He will see us through this."

"You really believe that?"

"Yes."

"And what if He doesn't? What if we all don't make it home?"

"It'll be all right, Jeremy."

Jeremy straightened, the timber in his voice strengthening. "Bullpucky! Look Trav, I love you but I don't care what you or anybody says. If Klaatu can come all that way to talk to us *and* neutralize power all over the planet, in an effort to get our attention--and he was an *alien*--then so can *God*!"

Travis frowned, cocking his head and winced, "Klaa--?...Who?"

Jeremy just shook his head, tiredly grinning down at his brother, and leaned in, kissing him on the head.

Jeremy's hand shot up in protest, anticipating Leslie's next question. "It was an old 50's sci-fi movie."

Leslie grinned.

Jeremy could feel the weight of Travis's stare and knew he couldn't shake it. Finally, he blurted with a direct look, "What?"

"I saw what you did back there," Travis said accusingly. "I know you believe."

"Whattya talkin' about?"

"Back there," the young boy began to elaborate motioning with a tilt of his head. "In the river, after that creepy guy in the other helicopter tried to kill you. When you went back afterwards to get stuff out of our helicopter, I watched you...you looked up into the sky for a moment and said something...and just now, back in the woods, after we made it across the lake and Leslie's snowmobile broke down...and you went back to get the gun. You again looked up into the sky and said something…what were you doing? …Were you thanking God?"

Jeremy was at an impasse. He wasn't sure what he believed anymore.

"I'll bet you were," Travis said to Jeremy.

"I dunno what you're talkin' about," Jeremy responded impassively.

Travis let it go, glaring briefly at his brother.

While the tension in the loft seemed to soften, along with the rain patting the roof above their heads, Jeremy limped over to Leslie and carefully eased himself down beside her. He felt Ian's radio in his pocket pressing against his leg and tried to move it. Briefly withdrawing it without looking at it, he was about to shove it back down inside his pocket when he hesitated. He wasn't sure why he was holding onto it since it no longer functioned, or so he believed. Jeremy decided instead, since it was causing him so much discomfort, to reach over and drop it down inside Ian's open backpack.

Matt wasn't entirely sure why, but when he searched the gloomy faces around him, something funny popped into his head. "Whaddya call a guy with no arms and no legs who washed up on the beach?"

The kids perked up a bit and began displaying mounting grins.

"Okay, I'll bite," Leslie said. "What *do you* call a guy with no arms and no legs who washed up on the beach?"

"Sandy," quipped Matt.

The kids broke into smiles, then laughter.

"Whaddya call a guy," he continued, "with no arms and no legs but who's only pretending to have no arms and no legs?"

Matt hesitated with a big smile plastered across his dirty face and said, "…Josh."

The loft would remain their safe haven for only a few more hours. After the worn-out group of refugee-looking kids closed ranks snuggling close together on the bed of hay, Lynn took up the cause.

"…Whaddya call a girl with no arms and no legs who keeps turning up? …Penny."

Dane and Charlee found themselves huddled together in their tiny shelter like two peas in a pod as the storm raged around them.

"I know we're lucky," she said rather loudly over the roar of wind and pelting rain against the waterproof fabric, "but what is this thing?"

"A hunter's blind," Dane answered back. "What a stroke of luck that someone left it out here and you spotted it, camouflaged and all."

"Wasn't too hard--the bright colors don't exactly match the surrounding foliage--what are you doing? Oh, don't call him again--"

"Perfect though for the fall colors, I guess--ARNOLD!" Dane shouted through a small mesh window. "C'MON BOY...ARNOLD! HERE BOY!"

"Dane, stop," Charlee crowed, covering her ears as he whistled for the dog, his repeated, earsplitting shrills piercing the onslaught outside and shredding her nerves. "You're not going let him in here, are you? We're actually staying dry in this thing. We'll be drenched if he comes in here."

Dane ignored her, straining to see through the downpour. "Nothin'," he muttered back. "Why'd he run? Hope he's all right."

"I hope my brother is all right."

Dane turned and looked at her blankly.

"...And your friends," she added consolingly.

Dane relented with a smile, noticing a card or something in her hand. After closing the small flap, he surveyed their cramped interior again, observing the bellowing canvas and said, "It's a little tight, probably built for one."

"I'm grateful. Right now, the last place I wanna be is the other side of that thin canvas. So what happens now?"

Dane thought for a moment, then dug into the pocket of his biker pants and pulled out the Glock and the small radio. He set the weapon aside in the corner of the blind beside him, then took up the radio. When he pressed the side button activating the battery check, the lights flashed again, this time all five vicinity lights glowed green. He pressed the call button on the side, but there was still no response. He then turned it back off, conserving the battery.

"Why don't they answer?" she asked him gravely.

"I don't know," Dane replied distantly. "Maybe they can't."

"But they're close by, right?"

"According to this, within a mile. And they haven't moved. So they must be holed up somewhere, like us. I wonder what happened?"

"What do you mean?"

"They didn't get very far. They should've easily made it to a highway or an airport. Something went wrong. And we could be walking into a…"

"Into a, what?"

Dane looked at her. "I don't know."

"So, whatta we do?"

"We wait…until morning," he said thoughtfully.

"And then?"

"And then, we go find my friends, and your brother." He then nodded at her closed hand. "What's that?"

"Just an old photograph of my father."

"Can I see it?"

Charlee handed it to him and Dane studied it for a moment. "He looks like Roy Rogers."

Charlee grinned at the comparison. She lay back, curling herself into a ball on her side, closing her eyes and did the only thing she could. She began to pray silently.

Jeremy blew out the next to the last candle, at the edge of the bed of hay beside Matthew and stared down at his sleeping brother. Travis had curled with him and the two boys lay face to face. He gently stroked each of their blond heads, unable to look away. Finally, he whispered, "I won't let anything happen to either one of you…"

In the waning light of the single candle, Jeremy looked around the loft at the faces of the other sleeping kids. "…And that goes for the rest of you guys, too."

It was the first time Ian appeared so peaceful. Eric, even asleep seemed restless as he intermittently tossed and turned on the hay. Elmo felt protective of his friend and had fallen asleep next to him. Noticing that Dylan still lay awake, Jeremy spoke softly and asked him, "You think we'll be safe here tonight?"

"Well," Dylan replied looking briefly at everyone, then at Jeremy, smiling, "For our sakes, we'd better not linger over breakfast in the morning."

Jeremy nodded and grinned back at him. "We'd better get outta here before sunrise. You better try and get some sleep, too."

"Okay," he yawned and stretched his arms, finally lying down.

Leaning into Jeremy's side, feeling the warmth of his body, Leslie took his hand and squeezed it lightly. "How's your leg feeling?"

"I'll make it," Jeremy replied tiredly, gazing back into her own languid eyes. He reached up and stroked her cheek. "I'm scared, Leslie," he admitted to her.

"I know," she whispered back, her eyes searching his. "Me too."

"I won't give up--not until we're all home."

Jeremy reached out with his hand and snuffed out the flame of the last candle with his thumb and index fingers. The moment it fizzled out there was a flash of light through the cracks of the loft's weathered slats. A distant crack of thunder signaled the storm was moving off. The two fell back onto the hay exhausted. Jeremy rolled onto his side with Leslie curled up close to his back. Just before she lost consciousness, she reached around him. The moment he felt her warm hand come into his he held it close to his chest and she heard him whisper, "Please God…help me get us all safely back home tomorrow."

Jeremy couldn't hang on any longer. His mind was awash in a myriad of vague thoughts and disconnected images as he began to descend into darkness. Although the rain had subsided, the flashes lingered. He thought he heard something and rose up his head for a moment, looking about the loft. It was just the wind; a tree branch had fallen on the roof overhead. In those fleeting moments during which there had been several strobe-like flashes, something caught his eye. Just a few feet away from him lay one of Lynn's sneakers, which she had taken off. There was something shiny on the side of it, something poking out from the heel. He tried to focus on it, but he simply couldn't think clearly. It was too late. The moment before he closed his eyes for the last time, in a final flash of brilliant white light, Jeremy's drained mind surmised it was probably a piece of the reflective fabric of her sneaker coming loose.

It was not.

PART 4

DISASTER ON THE MIGHTY MAC

CHAPTER THIRTY-FIVE

The Last Day...

Monday, August 25, 2014

Special Liaison to the President of the United States
Washington D.C.

Manndrake is his name. And that was all anybody within the Capital Beltway knew about him. Few had ever met him, knew what his full name was or even what he looked like. Professionally, he is literally a shadowy figure within the United States Government.

Manndrake had one job within the nation's capital. It required stealth and unlimited access to whatever resources and funds he might need. It also required of him on occasion to operate outside the law. So be it. He had no office, so to speak, only an encrypted cell phone number. He is the second individual to fill the position since his predecessor retired in the late 1980's. Special Liaison to the President, which does not exist anywhere on paper, was created and funded in secret by Congress following the Nixon impeachment. It was decided then that the office of the presidency, the very institution itself, is too vital to our national interest to be threatened. It was Manndrake who originally advised then President Clinton to admit to his indiscretion with Monica Lewinsky. And yet against that advice Clinton lied under oath. The resulting impeachment proceedings, though they had never come to fruition, nearly cost him his presidency. And that is something those within the government vowed must never be allowed to happen to a U.S. president.

Ever!

It wasn't until Congressman Theodore Denis began making inquiries into the Caradori plane crash that the red warning flags were raised again throughout Washington. Although any connection between the presidency and Caradori's investigation, including his subsequent death, had been cloaked in secrecy, even to this day, what is known is that what began with the Franklin Credit Union scandal abruptly ended when President H. W. Bush ordered a crackdown on the media coverage. When the news began to circulate among the power elite of the nation's capital of the Congressman's renewed efforts to reopen the investigation into Caradori's suspicious death few, if any, actually believed it would get off the ground. At first the investigation once again floundered, leaving it in limbo.

That is until the August night when Denis's Lear jet went down in Lake Erie.

Then a year later, Dr. Wringwater's email, sent by Henry three days prior, and intercepted by the DNI, was immediately forwarded to a point man within the current White House administration.

Privately assigned to monitor the situation the point man considered this a new and growing threat, and deemed it necessary to alert Manndrake. When he received the call from his contact and was briefed, Manndrake knew immediately who to contact.

D.N.I. – Director of National Intelligence

McLean, Virginia

Deputy Director, Vincent McNeil hadn't gotten much sleep during the previous night. Hourly updates allowed him only to catnap until he awoke abruptly just before the alarm clock on his desk, set to chime at 4:30 A.M., had a chance to go off. Although it wasn't his custom to sleep in his office, the long couch in the corner had proven to be fairly comfortable on those rare occasions. And the General's out-of-the-blue call to him yesterday had turned this into one of those occasions. As project manager of operation *Marco Polo*, the call left him no choice. He remained so he could personally oversee the situation room, and their operative in the field. When McNeil finally sat up, swinging his stocky legs around and planting his stockinged feet on the thick carpet, he thought for a moment, yawned, and then shook his head in disbelief at the strewn intel papers laid out on the coffee table in front of him. The General's file was comprehensive.

He was still mildly shocked at hearing directly from General Tusamo Wu. When he surfaced on the phone yesterday, McNeil knew it was a desperate measure on his part. It had to be. The General was playing with fire, he reasoned. To risk exposing any aspect of the global human trafficking network, the most secretive and clandestine operation in existence today, was a dangerous prospect. He wasn't surprised at the General's own intel, concerning *Marco Polo*, since secrets don't stay secret for very long in the spy game. What did intrigue him, though, was why the call at all. McNeil was also irritated, since the General's call had not only thrown the entire operation's timetable out the window, it had also set into motion the events of the next 24 hours. Lives and reputations around the world were on the line. Glancing at the digital clock on his desk, he determined he had about thirty minutes until his next update from his staff, and then another twenty before the General's scheduled call.

Stepping into a small bathroom to freshen up, he emerged several minutes later freshly shaven and wearing a clean linen shirt. With a small hand towel resting on his forearm, the palm of one hand containing his favorite aftershave, he rubbed his hands together, then lightly patted his face and neck. Taking the towel, he stood before the thick glass window of his sixth-floor office drying his hands. Though sunrise was still a good thirty minutes away, he couldn't help admiring the predawn view. Facing east, despite over-looking a portion of the parking structure and parking lot below, a wooded area, including the Virginia countryside beyond, reminded him of his childhood home. During late fall the colors were stunning. The smile which had absent-mindedly spread across his face suddenly ran away when his phone's private line rang. Glancing over at it, he instantly noted the security light flashing.

McNeil tossed the towel into the bathroom where it slid off the counter and right into a small wastepaper basket. The way this operation was going he hoped that wasn't a bad omen. He walked over to his cluttered desk, sat down and read the caller ID.

REPAIRMANN

It wasn't the General.

When he picked up the receiver the security light blinked, then remained solid, indicating the call was indeed secure. McNeil recognized the unmistakable twang in the voice at the other end and listened for several moments before speaking. "If you're involve then the president, or whichever one of 'em has misbehaved, is in trouble…and it doesn't get more serious that that!"

"You know why I've called?"

Seated at a large mahogany desk in the near darkened shadows of his private study, the receiver pressed to his ear, the only light that softly doused the aged features of his face was from that of a small lamp at the corner of the desk surrounded by family photos. Clad in a bathrobe, he hesitated momentarily, gazing out through a large plate-glass window, listening to the churning surf. Still smothered in darkness, Chesapeake Bay could only be heard--crashing against the gigantic boulders surrounding the shoreline estate.

"I have a pretty good idea," McNeil reply soberly over the phone. "Still, I'll need confirmation that this is indeed who I think it is."

"The reason, Mr. McNeil, that very few of our corrupt politicians and presidents ever see the inside of a prison cell is because that's my job. To see to it that they never do. And it is a full-time job!"

McNeil smiled benignly, then shook his head at the absurdity of it all. "…My team and I were alerted by the mission supervisor that you were involved and we were to provide you with any and all necessary intel. So, Manndrake, what can I do for you?"

"I'd like the latest update, Mr. McNeil?"

"Nothing's changed, not yet. I'm expecting the General's call within the hour."

"Do you believe him?"

"You mean, do I trust him--to turn over the Caradori dossier?"

"That's exactly what I mean," Manndrake replied evenly, recalling his recent briefing by the head of the agency and his Secret Service liaison.

"Yes, I do. And in light of the Colonel's recent activity, which I believe now constitutes a threat to national security, I thought it imperative that we alert our asset inside the Colonel's foundation."

"Speaking of your asset, that was a stupid and careless thing for him to do--sending that email to a former FBI agent."

McNeil was too tired to argue and took the criticism in stride, offering little in the way of rebuttal other than, "Perhaps. We've been monitoring the foundation's communications for some time now…and it seemed the only way to force their hand."

Sensing his remark had fallen on deaf ears, Manndrake change the subject. "You know what has to be done, Mr. McNeil," he said intently, his arthritic index finger tapping the desk. "They have a cell phone, it's to be recovered. And the Dossier…that also is to be recovered--then destroyed, once and for all. Do you understand me?"

"I'm assuming you're aware of the latest problem."

Manndrake bristled, as he spoke, shifting in his leather chair. "I am. I've been informed there are now a group of kids somehow involved. And one of them, a young Indian boy by the name of Dylan Oconee--"

"Excuse me sir, Skyland."

"What?"

"Sky--"

"Yes, yes, I know all about that, thanks to your asset!" Manndrake responded testily. He took a moment to calm himself. "How in the hell did this Oconee kid--Skyland, or whatever you want to call him, get his hands on the dossier?"

"I've no idea, sir. But considering these events, our time to move will have to be this morning--within the hour. Our asset learned only a few hours ago the exact location of the group. He had one helluva of time getting to the location due to the storm, but he's there now, on site and into position. He's prepared to eliminate any hostiles and recover the cell phone and dossier. We'll do what we can to keep the kids out of harm's way. Will that be satisfactory to the president?"

There was a long pause, then, "Mr. McNeil, listen to me carefully, because I'm going to say this only once. And I just want to make sure we're both on the same page concerning this. We've been tapped into the organization's cell phones for quite some time now, and I've been informed by my sources that these kids have somehow accessed the dossier through one of them, within the last few hours in fact, including the videos. So now we have, not just one, but several eyewitnesses."

McNeil listened, knowing where the conversation was headed.

"Do you understand--what has to happen here?"

"I think I do, sir."

"Good. Because I want them to go away, Mr. McNeil, all of them. No witnesses."

McNeil was a hard-minded professional, never one to hesitate because of his own emotions. He had a job to do, plain and simple.

Or so it seemed to him, until this very moment in time. There was an edge to his tone as he spoke. "Just so we're understanding each other...are you asking me to initiate a standing kill order on nine Americans--kids--children?"

Manndrake bristled, then said, "I will not allow the presidency to be tarnished, threatened, let alone destroyed because of a..." his voice suddenly broke off. After a moment he recovered and continued. "As I recall, with your agency's assistance the Clintons made Whitewater disappear. Make this disappear, Mr. McNeil. Make it all just go away, permanently. Accidents happen all the time. Remember, we're a team, Mr. McNeil. I'll do my job and you'll do yours. Your career depends on it!"

Manndrake then abruptly ended the call, setting the receiver on the phone cradle within the bottom drawer of his desk.

McNeil gazed briefly at the receiver before setting it back in the cradle. He rose from behind his desk, entered his small bathroom and retrieved the hand towel from the wastepaper basket. Distractedly, while his mind mulled over his instructions, he wadded the soft terry towel into a tight ball. Then, with the same explosive zeal of a pitcher on the mound, he heaved the towel with a grunt as hard as he could at the thick glass window of his office where it harmlessly bounced off and fell to the floor.

Clutching the phone again in his hand, Manndrake's bony index finger pressed the '6' key on the speed-dial pad. It was only a few moments before an intense, feminine voice answered.

C.I.A.–Central Intelligence Agency

George Bush Center for Intelligence
Langley, Virginia

Ops Division Director, Carol Langford, adjusted, first the Prada glasses resting across the bridge of her nose, then the phone headset she wore, as she stood before a 200-inch Ultra-definition LCD flat screen. Surrounded by four other technicians at various monitoring stations in the relatively small operation center, one of several at the notoriously clandestine facility, the woman with long brunette hair and dark pantsuit spoke decisively.

"Interesting call. I know McNeil. He'll get the job done."

"Frankly, Carol, I don't trust him."

"The storm has cleared that part of the state, and the satellite retask by McNeil's team, which we've tapped into, is sending exceptionally crisp images. We have a clear view of their operative and the structure. What is it you want me to do?"

"My impression of our conversation was that Mr. McNeil doesn't quite share my enthusiasm. I want that flash drive and their cell phone recovered, then destroyed. I needn't remind you that if this information should reach the press or the internet, it would have repercussions for your agency as well. And this is equally imperative--no witnesses--there must be nothing to connect these kids to any of this, or to the president. Is that understood?"

"I know my job, Manndrake."

"Of course you do. And as always, Carol, we never had this conversation."

Manndrake set the receiver back within the bottom drawer and slid it closed. Like an old friend, the pounding surf once again drew his attention. When he looked out over the compound estate, his eyes caught the first glimmer of golden light peeking just above the distant horizon. He loved this view of the ocean from his private den. As he slowly rose to his feet and tightened the terry belt of his robe, he muttered confidently to himself, "Yes, I do believe it's going to be another beautiful day in paradise."

Lodge helipad

The windsock at the northwest corner of the helipad, lit from below by a single flood lamp, was fully inflated like a horizontal balloon, buffeting in the 25-knot gale that streaked across the hilltop above the Lodge. Still shrouded in darkness, the only other visible light on the helipad was that of the Scorpion II's interior cabin LED lamps. The pilot, dressed in blue overalls with a baseball cap pulled tightly about his head, completed the preflight check, removing the tie-down lines from the tail and main rotors last. Opening the baggage compartment in the belly of the helicopter, he tossed them in alongside a garment bag and what appeared to be a lifejacket. He was about to close it when the radio in his pocket chimed. He removed it and answered the call.

"Yes?" he said loudly over the wind.

"The General will be down in a few minutes," Spear's deep voice crackled over the speaker. "Have everything ready when we arrive."

"It will be," the pilot answered.

Shoving the radio back into his pocket, the pilot then walked down the wind-swept hill from the pad to a black Hummer. Opening a rear door, he reached in and removed a large four-by-five-foot sheathed canvas. Struggling briefly with it against the gusts that seemed to taunt him, he kicked the Hummer's door closed, gripped the frame more tightly in a streamline manner with both hands and walked back up the hill to the Scorpion. After placing the sheathed canvas in the rear passenger cabin, securing the door, he then removed the lifejacket from the baggage compartment, picking it up with considerable effort. It was a uniquely designed 'jacket' filled with fifty pounds of lead pellets, which he set on the concrete, out of sight, on the opposite side of the Scorpion. The wind seemed like it wanted to push him over as he leaned back and relaxed against the Plexiglas nose of the Scorpion. The pilot then reached inside the breast pocket of his uniform and removed a Robustos. Rather than try to light it, he merely planted it between his lips, savoring not only the tobacco flavor on his tongue, but the highly anticipated moment of Spear and General Wu's arrival.

CHAPTER THIRTY-SIX

The man lying prone on his stomach gently maneuvered his body
against the cool ground, adjusting the high-powered Barrett M82
sniper rifle in his hands to a more comfortable position. So completely camouflaged in his ghillie suit, from head to toe, even a
trained expert would have difficulty spotting him amid the rustling
trees and foliage. The buffeting wind posed no real problem for him.
With the type of caliber he was using, coupled with a corresponding
maximum range of 1,800 meters, and estimating his distance from
his intended targets of roughly 100 meters, a relatively short flight
path of less than the length of a football field, accuracy would not be
an issue for him. An expert marksman, he was considered the best.
An elite government assassin, he killed only those who were themselves killers.

Setting the rifle aside for a moment to remove a stick of gum
from a pack he'd set nearby, he unwrapped and popped it into his
mouth. As he began chewing, savoring the flavor, the sniper mulled
over in his mind how he came to be on the hilltop overlooking a
long abandoned and weather-beaten old barn. His instructions, as
yet, were incomplete. He still waited for his final orders. Despite the
fact that he had killed before, performing each hit with precision,
it had been nearly ten years. But then again, he thought to himself,
one never loses the talent. And he was actually looking forward to it.
He had grown tired of what he felt was a much too long deep cover

assignment as an undercover operative inside the global slave network's U.S. operation.

At forty-eight he was tired of the game. Having amassed a small fortune, he felt it was time to enjoy life. Before he even realized it, he'd made his decision. After today he would retire from the business, leave it all behind him and live a contemplative life--on his recently purchased island, hidden in the South China Sea.

Checking his watch, and then scanning the distant horizon from his high vantage point, he could see the first hint of sunlight peeking above the tree line. He then peered through the rifle's telescopic sight making mental notes of the area; specifically, which locations afforded the cleanest kill, including the vine-shrouded entrance to the barn. He lowered the rifle and for the moment, allowed himself to relax. After he dug out the disposable cell phone buried in a special side pocket, he set it beside the rifle and lay in wait for his quarry to arrive; thinking to himself…timing is everything.

Hearing the approach of a vehicle, the pilot came around the nose of the Scorpion, shoving the unlit Robustos back into his breast pocket, and watched as another black Hummer cruised up the dirt road. Passing the burned-out hulk of the RV, it pulled up to the base of the helipad and parked beside the other black Hummer. Spear slid out from the driver's seat and stepped to the rear, opening the door. Grasping a small bag and an aluminum briefcase from the seat, he moved aside and waited like a servant as General Wu grunted across the leather seat, planting his custom made loafers on the ground. The moment he stood in the stiff breeze, he straightened his jacket, then raked his fingers through his silver hair, and proceeded toward the walkway leading up to the Scorpion. The pilot, watching all of this, smiled as he stepped back around the nose of the helicopter and out of sight. As Wu huffed and puffed his way up the steps, Spear passed him the instant he reached the concrete helipad. Wu stopped just short of the huge Longranger's passenger door and waited as Spear set the bag and briefcase down and opened the door. The General's face beamed when he saw the sheathed canvas. As he took a step toward it, eagerly anticipating his prize, Spear reached into his coat pocket and carefully slipped onto his middle finger a special fluid-filled ring.

General Wu briefly glanced about the helicopter while clandestinely slipping a hand into his slacks pocket, gripping the small revolver, expecting to see the Colonel. Though he was aware that Shazuko had confined him to his own suite, he ordered that the Colonel be present at the helipad for his departure. His goal was to murder the Colonel. And if necessary, he had every intention of murdering Spear as well. Paramount in his mind this morning was getting his hands on the Colonel's flash drive. He put it on the back burner of his thought for the moment, and like an excited child, said to Spear, in his typical demanding manner, motioning toward the sheathed canvas, "Show it to me."

Spear dutifully reached in, and with his free hand, pulled apart the Velcro top portion of the canvas. Aware of the General's excitement, Spear then respectfully stepped aside and motioned for him to remove the remainder of the protective cover himself. The General, still gripping the revolver in his pants pocket, took an anxious breath, reached over with his free hand and grasped the cover, pulling it down, exposing a portrait.

It was to be the last thing the General would ever do.

Wu had barely reacted with a confused furrowed brow to the Elvis image on black velvet when he felt the prick of a capillary needle at the base of his neck. The paralyzing effect of the curare compound was instantaneous. As his body went numb and he slumped forward inside the cabin, the gun slipped from his grasp, sliding down inside his pocket while his head came to rest on the carpet. His first thought was this cannot be happening to him. His second was, how could he have been so blind, allowing himself to be taken by such a deadly surprise? The General's anger quickly turned to fear. Despite the complete paralysis of his body, he was still breathing, though now more rapidly, and Wu could hear everything going on around him. He just couldn't move. The only other physical thing he could sense was his heart--beating ever faster--in anticipation of his own death.

Spear roughly manhandled the robust Asian from behind, hoisting him from the cabin. Setting him directly down onto the open weighted jacket where the pilot had just laid it on the cool concrete, Wu's hand flopped out from his pocket, falling to his side. Splayed out on the helipad like a car crash victim, the powerful general was at Spear's mercy. The moment the enforcer moved out of the General's line of vision to open the passenger cabin the pilot came into his view, bending over him.

"Good morning, General," the Colonel said, removing the baseball cap and tossing it aside. "And how are we feeling today?"

Wu's shock couldn't register on his face, but it did in his brown, terrified, blinking eyes.

The Colonel nodded up at his enforcer saying, "It's going to be a lovely day, just look at that sunrise. What do you say, Mr. Spear, how about a morning flight?" He then glared down at Wu, the corners of his mouth curled in a sadistic grin. "I've heard the lake is a spectacular sight this time of day--from five hundred feet!"

"I couldn't agree with you more, sir." Wu heard Spear say. He then watched helplessly as Spear and the Colonel knelt down on either side of him, rocking him roughly, one way, then the other, shoving his arms into the jacket. Spear zipped it up around his rotund chest and the two of them hefted Wu into the passenger cabin, pushing his legs inside. The Colonel then climbed in and Spear secured the door behind him.

Spear climbed into the pilot seat, securing his door and immediately went about powering up the Longranger, flipping switches while his trained eyes scanned the various instruments.

"Let's get this done," the Colonel barked. "We have a schedule to keep. You have a flash drive, phone and a painting to recover, along with some brats to round up, and I have a speech to deliver later today. And I don't intend to be late!"

As the turbine howled and the rotors began to spool up, the Colonel jostled Wu around like a rag doll. He gripped the General by the collar of the weighted jacket, yanking him up to a sitting position, then pushed his limp body back against the cabin seat. Wu's hands clumsily came to rest along his thighs. The Colonel could see the mix of hatred and terror in his narrow eyes and smiled vengefully at him.

"So you thought you'd hand me my hat--you arrogant fool!" glared the Colonel. "Say goodbye to this world and hello to the next. Shortly you'll be enjoying hell. You should have never tried to blackmail me, General. I don't take kindly to threats against me, or my empire."

Wu's eyes glanced over to Spear in the pilot's seat which the Colonel caught. "You'll have to forgive Mr. Spear. But loyalty runs deep with him. He was mine first--let's go!" he barked over the high-pitched whine of the turbine and whirling rotor blades overhead.

Spear, always the professional, remained on task, ignoring the Colonel while he monitored the instruments. The Longranger hummed and vibrated beneath the spinning blur of the rotor blades. Satisfied, he donned his headphones, motioning for the Colonel to do the same. With gusts blowing across the helipad at a right angle to the Scorpion, Spear, using fluid-like control, brought the power in, lifting the Longranger off the pad, turning the nose into the wind, and climbed into a cloudless blue sky. The Colonel watched as the helipad dropped away and the tips of the oak and maple trees quickly slid beneath the Longranger. The view ahead in all directions was the wide expanse of the forest canopy. The Colonel looked down, turning his attention back to General Wu.

"Did you really think I'd go quietly into the night?"

The General was a proud man. He resigned himself to show no further fear in the presence of the Colonel. He would face death like the soldier that he was. The Colonel sensed this, and became irritated, swearing that, despite the paralyzing effects of the drug, Wu now carried a smug expression.

"I have plans," the Colonel continued, determined to wipe it from his arrogant, fat face. "I'm taking over, General. And you and the board are not going to get in my way. But should they have any concerns, I've already taken the liberty of contacting each member and relating to them that, if any of them should attempt further efforts to thwart me, I shall expose each of them to the world. And I have the means to do it. And just so Shazuko doesn't become concerned this morning, I took the liberty of contacting your waiting jet at the airstrip informing them that you decided to stay on a bit longer and so should return to the airport without you to await further instructions."

The Colonel glanced over Spears's shoulder, then glared back at Wu. "I trust the jacket isn't too tight? Rather stylish, don't you think? I'm sure you're familiar with one of these."

The Colonel could see the mounting rage in Wu's eyes and enjoyed it.

"Quite a handy little item. Looks just like a real lifejacket, doesn't it? Though instead of foam, the lead pellets of the—death jacket—produce a far different affect. Never dreamed you'd find yourself in one of these, did you? Now, do try to relax, it won't be much longer. Oh, and, do try to enjoy the ride. It's going to be your last!"

The Colonel craned his neck looking over Spear's shoulder again and barked into his mike. "How much longer?"

The sun had cleared the eastern horizon, bathing the great forest that lay before them in a bright golden aura. The enforcer pointed out front over the instrument panel. Beyond the boundary of the forest to the north, the Colonel could see the deep blue waters of Lake Superior, dotted with whitecaps. Within minutes the Scorpion, cruising at five hundred feet, glided out over the shoreline.

"Can you handle him?" Spear asked over the intercom.

"Did you want to come back here and give me a hand?" The Colonel replied in a rare humorous moment. "I think I can handle this," he then answered with a gleeful expression before removing the headphones.

Moving to the opposite cabin door--that slid open sideways rather than opening outward, the Colonel pushed down on the handle and forcefully shoved it open. The door latch caught, locking it into position. The blast of air flooding the cabin suddenly sent anything not secured flying, included Elvis.

"Careful, Colonel," Spear warned as he banked the Scorpion around into the wind, easing back on the controls and bringing the Longranger to a smooth hover. "Let me position her first."

While the Colonel steadied himself, The King's portrait suddenly ricocheted against the rear seat and abruptly out the opened door. The Colonel crawled over Wu's legs and looked over the edge, his hair and collar snapping in the gale, watching in amusement as it sailed toward the rough water below, slamming into it with a great splash. He leaned back inside and glared down at Wu in mocked shock.

"Well, General, there goes your painting. You better go and get it!"

And with that, the Colonel grabbed General Tusamo Wu, one of the most powerful and dangerous men in the world-wide slave network, and with all his strength, shoved him head first, tumbling out the open door.

The landing skid, the blast of air against his ruddy face, the roar of the turbine and thumping rotors--then only the air whistling past his ears--blue sky--the black Scorpion racing away from him--were the last things General Wu saw and felt before closing his eyes as he free-fell through the sky like a sack of potatoes.

The Colonel watched with detached fascination as seconds later the two hundred pound Asian careened into the churning lake with a monumental splatter, disappearing beneath the foaming surface. The weighted death jacket continued the General's descent to his watery grave, never to be seen again, leaving behind a crimson-stained, rippled surface, which quickly vanished among the whitecaps.

Not one to linger on sentiment, the Colonel replaced the head-phones and barked, "Let's get back!"

Twelve minutes later, the black Scorpion was approaching the helipad. The moment the skids touched down, Spear locked the flight controls and shut down the turbine. While the spinning blades gradually slowed, Spear hung up his headphones beside the Colonel's. After engaging the rotor brake the two of them exited the Scorpion. The Colonel stepped down from the cabin and from the rear baggage compartment in the belly of the helicopter removed a garment bag, setting it on the edge of the cabin. "You understand what you're to do?" said the Colonel after unzipping it. He began stripping off the overalls, revealing a white, cotton fitted shirt and tan slacks. "I don't mind telling you, Anthony, I'm a little concerned about this…I've backed myself into a corner."

"I won't let you down sir," said Spear, standing behind him.

"I'll return to my suite until you leave. Once you're gone I'll have one of our pilots fly me up to the resort. I plan to arrive by 10:00 A.M. We'll rendezvous then. Just make sure Shazuko goes with you to round up our band of troublemakers."

"She will. From monitoring her communications, I understand the board has insisted on it."

"The board," the Colonel sneered contemptuously as he pulled from the garment bag a Gucci tweed jacket with matching leather loafers. "A bunch of fossilized relics overseen by that dinosaur, Inzu!" Regaining his train of thought after slipping into the loafers, the Colonel faced Mr. Spear. "I've already instructed our hit team as to what is to transpire this morning, understood?"

Spear nodded obediently, checked his watch, then hesitated, an expression of grave concern on his pale, taut face.

"Something else, Mr. Spear?"

"Yes sir. Your flash drive."

"What about it?"

"Are you sure it's a good idea to take it with you? Wouldn't it be safer simply to lock it up in your safe at the lodge?"

"Oh no," the Colonel replied adamantly, briefly patting his neckline. "I feel better knowing *exactly* where it is at all times. Besides, you've been so busy you're not aware of the latest development. Shazuko informed me that Dylan's little virus he unleashed on our system virtually destroyed the original dossier. She has since neutralized it, but the damage is done--it's gone!" He again placed his hand consolingly at the neckline of his collared shirt. "It's still quite safe, though."

Spear nodded.

Glancing at his Rolex the Colonel placed a hand on Spears' broad shoulder. "Get those kids, the cell phone, my canvas and Wu's flash drive!"

"Yes sir, I will. Without fail."

"Oh, and if you wouldn't mind," the Colonel added with a smirk, nodding his head at the General's bag and briefcase left on the pad, "Get rid of those."

Snatching up Wu's belongings, Spear followed the Colonel back down to the Black Hummer.

Spear hurried through the facility and briskly entered the Colonel's office where he found the General's beautiful, but deadly second-in-command seated behind the massive desk waiting for him.

Annoyed, he kept his usual cool as he spoke. "Mr. Whitehead said you wanted to speak with me--it's already past sunrise and we need to move quickly."

"I'm well aware that time is of the essence..." Shazuko replied calmly. She gazed upon the hulking enforcer with contempt as she rose from the Colonel's chair. As he wasn't Asian, he was, therefore, not to be trusted. And it was no secret where the man's loyalty lay. However, the General trusted him. So for now, Shazuko reasoned, she would too, utilizing him and his skills until he could be replaced. She came around the desk and faced the enforcer directly. Despite that he towered over her by a good four inches, she was neither afraid nor intimated by him as she spoke.

"I want to outline the plan one final time," she growled. "Do not fail again. You're to take the four members of the hit team along with Mr. Whitehead, the two RV's and collect the runaways, splitting them into two groups. You're to separate the two oldest ones from the rest of the group--the younger ones will no doubt look to them for strength. This must be removed. I am also going along with you to supervise this operation--and to personally recover the flash drive and the smartphone. We'll then cross the Mackinaw Bridge, head to the farm where they will all be disposed of."

Although he despised this woman who stood before him, he never let it show.

"One final thought. I also want it clearly understood that I am now in charge of this facility and the entire American Network. Will that present any problems for you, Mr. Spear?"

"None at all," was Spear's veiled response.

"Excellent."

"Will there be anything else?"

"Charlee and her companion, what is their status?"

"She'll meet us at the rendezvous point. If she doesn't, she knows I will kill her brother. And she won't risk anything happening to him. Anything else?"

Shazuko smiled a satisfied, but smug grin. "And the Colonel?"

"Confined to his suite, behind a locked and guarded door-- where you put him."

"The Board and I will deal with him on my return," she spewed. "Wait for me downstairs, I will join you directly."

As the enforcer turned to leave, Shazuko pulled on his leash one last time.

"Oh, Mr. Spear? Did the General make his plane on time?"

Pivoting in the archway of the door, Spear replied coolly with a poker face, "We dropped him off."

CHAPTER THIRTY–SEVEN

Grand Traverse World Resort and Spa
Traverse City, Michigan

Miles Montgomery was everything an on-air television reporter should be, and more. He was young, single, good-looking, a natural talent when it came to investigative reporting, and articulate in front of the camera. With his slightly graying black hair groomed back, put him in a tux, and he was the spitting image of Cary Grant, straight out of the opening scene in *An Affair to Remember*, right down to his cleft chin. Miles was well-liked, respected by his peers and co-workers of the local NBC-affiliated television station. There were no daggers thrust into his back when it was turned. And to top it off, there wasn't an arrogant bone in his trim, tanned body. After several years of hard earned work, he was ceremoniously given the 6 P.M., thirty-minute news anchor slot, *the* coveted lead-in to the nightly national network news broadcast, and there wasn't a hint of jealousy from anyone. Ratings soared. He had arrived, someone had told him. He did have it all, and he was grateful for it. Only thing was, after seven years, the itch was setting in. Even his close associates could see it. Miles was terribly bored.

From beneath a gradually lightening sky where a glowing orange ball had begun its ascent, Miles strolled in the moment the twin glass doors parted, carried on a gust that briefly ruffled the line of potted flowers along the floor of both sides of the hotel atrium.

"Let's go, boys and girls…gather 'round," he announced to his entourage that trailed in behind him. Spotting a collection of empty plush couches arranged in front of a stone fireplace, Miles steered the group toward them. Weighted down with gear, shoulder packs of supplies, some of them lugging equipment on wheels, they willingly followed him, assembling in a loose circle. Miles, no stranger to getting down and dirty with the crew, heaved a heavy box from his arms down onto one of the couches. Loosening his tie, he picked up his tweed jacket from where it lay across the heavy box and distractedly scanned the grandly appointed lobby done in warm earthy tones, leather and wood. "Okay everyone, listen up--anyone seen Stewie?"

"Thar he blows," came a weary announcement in the back from his twenty-something makeup assistant, Clarissa, annoyed at the early morning call.

"Where have you been?" his young, fastidiously dressed, Alex P. Keaton-look-alike assistant sputtered, handing him a clipboard.

"Traffic, Stewie." Miles replied, taking it, briefly scanning through several sheets.

"I *hate it* when you call me that."

"I know, but it fits you to a tee, Stewart,"

"That's more like it--here," Stewart quipped, taking back the clipboard.

"It's crazy out there, worse than Cherry Festival. You'd think the president was coming." Miles leaned in and muttered gleefully, "He isn't, is he?"

"Nope, just the senator."

"Rats. So why all the hubbub?"

"The scuttlebutt is he's gonna announce--"

"Hey, Miles--" groaned an out of breath burly man, loping up to the group.

"Not now, Brian, my team and I--"

"Yes, now, Miles. You're wanted."

"Carl?"

"The one and only. You'd better high-tail it over to the Governors' Hall. They've got everything set up in there. That construction up in the Trillium room has thrown our schedule off and everyone's in a lather--especially--"

"Say no more...wait a minute--you mean the as yet unfinished restaurant that was supposed to be done for this major event, but due to red tape, unions and expired building permits is still a mess up there?"

"Yes, yes, that one," Brian sputtered, nodding and throwing up his hands in protest. "The boss man wants you on set, go!"

"Ah, my producer. Probably wants to speak to me about my upcoming assignment to the Middle East--wants to embed me in a roving convoy--"

"The only thing you're gonna find yourself embedded with is the toe of his loafer up your ass if you don't get to the set. He wanted you there ten minutes ago."

"I'm on my way," Miles sputtered back cheerfully, then half-turned, pausing, "--Hey, you and Sandy, get my anniversary gift I sent?"

"Came last night--thanks, Miles."

Grinning back, Miles flashed him a double thumbs-up and a wink as he tore off.

Standing shoulder to shoulder, Brian and Stewart both shook their heads, watching as Miles tore off down a wide, carpeted hallway. Finally, Stewart sputtered, "He's so annoyingly lovable."

"And in this business," Stewie concluded with a sigh, "That's just not right."

The Grand Traverse World Resort and Spa was considered *the* premier resort in all of Northern Michigan. Its 26-story, 250-room, bronzed-glass high rise was a gleaming jewel. Below the tower was the hotel complex consisting of an additional 200 rooms, including the central plaza with its gallery of shops sprinkled throughout, including a diverse selection of restaurants and lounges. There was the 7,000-square-foot spa, and an impressive, 100,000-square foot health club with a partially glass-enclosed Olympic-sized, indoor/outdoor swimming pool. The only thing missing was Esther Williams poised on a rope swing over the water.

The crown jewel atop this golden tiara of the north was the elegantly appointed Trillium Room, the main dining salon on the 24th floor. Its 16, floor-to-ceiling, plate-glass windows, encompassing the entire northwestern side of the dining room, afforded some of the most stunning panoramic views of the countryside. The brilliant tower was a landmark beacon surrounded by 900 acres of manicured lawns laced with sand traps and ponds, making up some of the best championship golfing this side of Lake Michigan. In the distance were rolling hills dotted with lush green northern woods and pines that migrated out to the emerald waters of East Grand Traverse Bay. Over the main dining room, the high ceiling supported a breath-taking, 35-foot-diameter, smoked glass skylight. Just beyond the skylight was the rooftop helipad. On the opposite side, set back toward the rear half of the tower allowing for unobstructed views through the skylight were the machine rooms for the four elevators, including maintenance and storage, making up the 25th floor. There was also one other architectural structure located here. Partially sunken through the roof, extending down through a portion of the maintenance floor was a 240,000 gallon, 31-foot diameter, steel water tank, painted in an attractive Caribbean blue.

It would have been the perfect venue for the day's event were it not for the 24th floor's complete disarray, along with an accompanying reminder in the way of a small sign posted at the lobby elevators:

> Please pardon our mess,
> Trillium Room closed
> due to remodeling.

Carl Thibodaux, senior producer, chewed on his cigar as he and another man, dressed in overalls, huddled together at the far end of the Governors' Hall ballroom, poring over a schematic diagram spread out over a large lighting control panel. At the opposite end of the great ballroom, beneath elegant chandeliers, technicians were completing work on the stage platform, while busboys in red smocks buzzed around the four dozen tables, putting the final touches on each of the place settings. Miles hurriedly threaded his way through the throng, nearly colliding with a young hotel staffer as she placed the last vase of fresh roses at the center of a table.

"Oh good, you're here," Carl said the moment he looked up from the panel as Miles strolled up. Dismissing himself from the man in overalls, Carl came around the lighting console and other equipment, stepping over the miles of cables that snaked across the floor and placed a fatherly hand on Miles's shoulder.

Miles sputtered, "Please tell me we got coffee brewing somewhere around here."

"Gallons of it over there--now look boy, you gotta be on your toes today."

"Whoa, look at this place. Fit for a king--or a president."

"Would you settle for Senator Toddhunter, due to arrive by helicopter at one o'clock?"

"The helipad is finished, right?"

Carl nodded with a sarcastic grin. "That's the only thing upstairs *that is* functional."

Miles turned and faced Carl. "Any word from the brass?"

"Miles, we may not be as big as the networks, so *I am* the brass, and the answer--"

"C'mon Carl--"

"Now Miles, listen to me. We've been through this. Enough."

"Just one little assignment, a few days in Afghanistan, Carl, I can do it--"

"Which I have no doubt you could, but Miles, *your job is here.* And this is where I need you. Now listen to me--"

"Carl--"

"Miles! Now listen to me, one devilishly handsome Richard Engel from the network, in the field, is enough. I need you to focus. Stay with me, now."

Miles finally relented with an exasperated sigh, then said, "Okay, okay. Gimme the poop. But you're gonna regret this someday."

"Until such time, work with me, please, will you? Now, Senator Toddhunter, as I said, will arrive at approximately 11:30 A.M. He has his own security people. I've met his head of security, slash campaign manager--big bruiser of a guy--probably moonlights as a hitman. He's due to arrive at 10 o'clock. The actual luncheon begins at 12:30. Now Miles, after you introduce the Senator and he makes his speech and announcement, you'll have about five minutes with him afterwards. We're coordinating with the network in New York. This could be a nice piece provided you don't blow it."

Miles shot Carl an *are you kidding, me--blow it?* arched eyebrow expression.

"Good boy. Did Stewart give you a list of questions?"

"You mean these?" Miles replied, dully holding out a sheet. "I'll grill 'em like the professional I am."

"Yeah, well don't grill too hard. Go easy, save the gritty stuff for another time. Short and sweet."

"Okay, but why the kid gloves?"

"According to his campaign manager he's going to make a major announcement."

Miles nodded, distracted by all the activity, and his disappointment.

"Well don't get too excited, as emcee this could be another feather in your cap."

Miles kept looking about, nodding at the throng that was slowly gathering. "...A cap you keeping stepping on. ...Look at this place, Carl, it's going to be a madhouse."

"A madhouse. And you wanna go to Afghanistan?"

Miles gave him a blank stare.

"…I hate it when you give me that look," Carl replied with a roguish expression. "Now, buck up and listen to me. They're also setting up for some huge outdoor function at the pavilion for later on, a wedding or something. I've got some script notes here for you…"

Carl was about to elaborate when he spotted and recognized two people nearby, a tall, stocky man standing beside his wife, an attractive woman with shoulder-length, topaz hair. Carl caught the woman's attention and flagged them both over with a wave of his hand.

"Oh, Miles, these are two good friends of mine, and a couple of our hardworking volunteers…"

"How do you do," Miles said warmly, extending his hand to them as they walked up.

"Miles, this is Caroline and Robert Hodak."

Robert gripped his hand and pumped it. "A pleasure."

"Hello," Caroline said meeting his enthusiastic smile with her own.

"Hey, we're part of this crew," came a warm voice standing before a small group.

"Oh, absolutely," Caroline beamed apologetically. "Carl, Mr. Montgomery--"

"Please, call me Miles."

"Miles, these are my parents, Emmy and Leland Lerue."

"How do you do," said Miles, making the rounds shaking hands.

"And…this is Tom and Lorrie Thigpen, Lisa McCaulee, and this is Jeff Sumner."

"A pleasure to make all your acquaintances." Miles then focused on Caroline. "Now I remember you. I met you and your husband last spring at the special volunteer committee meeting. And if recall you were quite pregnant. What did you end up having?"

Caroline smiled proudly and said, "After three wonderful boys, a beautiful baby girl. We named her Elise."

Miles smiled back and nodded approvingly. "That is beautiful. I'd love to see her. Did you bring her along?"

"We left her home today. Jeff's wife, Shelly, is taking care of her."

"I see. Well, I'm truly sorry I missed her."

"Don't forget me," a stately voice announced from behind.

"Never," Caroline replied, still beaming and motioning with a hand for the last one in their group to come forward.

"…This is a dear friend of ours, and a valued helper here this morning, Dr. Everett Gibbs."

Despite favoring his cane to support a bad knee, the spry doctor strolled forward energetically through the parted gathering, extended a hand toward the newsman and said, "Very pleased to meet you, young man."

"The pleasure is mine, Doctor."

Jeremy awoke to the cries of an infant. When he rose up and stood, he found himself standing in the middle of a waist-high, wheat field. Everywhere he looked, the pristine golden grass swayed and rippled on a gentle breeze like a great ocean. He quietly listened. At first the cries were so very faint, nearly imperceptible. But they were there. He felt a sudden surge of fear.

It was Elise.

The cries were becoming louder and he became more frightened. He could now hear her clearly. Jeremy spun around trying to--at first he couldn't tell from what direction they were coming. He listened; looking in all directions…her cries seemed to be all around him. Jeremy gasped fearfully and spun around again, but he just couldn't--wait a minute--now her cries were coming from just ahead of him. But all he saw was the endless sea of billowing golden wheat.

Elise was in danger.

He began walking toward the cries, his eyes darting back and forth, sweeping the entire field laid out in front of him. Her cries were getting louder, yet she was nowhere in sight.

Panic began to set in.

He bolted through the wheat, cutting a swath, frantically spreading the grass with his hands as he ran. Then he abruptly froze in his tracks. The crying had stopped. Panting breathlessly, sweat beading down his face, he looked everywhere, listening. Jeremy spun again as the cries intensified, from behind him this time. He sprinted back the way he came, running as fast as he could. Suddenly his feet went out from under him and he fell to the ground. Scrambling to his feet, he gasped when his eyes caught sight of her, resting in the arms of Peter Whitehead. As he held Elise, rocking her gently, he glared back at Jeremy, smiling with a malevolence that could only come from the devil himself. Jeremy's eyes widened and he cried out, lunging for Whitehead. He missed him, going down into the wheat with an--*umph!*

Jeremy snapped awake.

He sat up, in a momentary fog, clearing his head. Breathing rapidly, he reached up and felt his chest; beneath his soaked tee shirt, his heart was pounding like a jack-hammer. He held up his hand over his slit eyes, trying to focus. Everyone around was still sound asleep, including Leslie, curled in a ball beside him. Then he saw from where the bright intrusion was coming from. The small window. Though the storm appeared to be over, it was still quite windy, evidenced by the shadows dancing against the floor of the loft. Scattered sunlight was filtering in, spilling at his feet, bathing one of the kid's shoes in a warm glow. That's when he noticed something glinting.

He swallowed and sighed quietly, calming himself as he reached for it. Realizing it was one of Lynn's sneakers, he began to examine it closely. Curiously, something small was protruding out from the edge of the sole where it was normally glued to the fabric. It had come apart and something--metallic--was…his eyes abruptly strayed when he heard a faint creaking from below, like the sound a boat makes as it shifts against the pier. Still breathing nervously, Jeremy cautiously struggled to stand, favoring his good leg. His jaw dropped open and his eyes widened in terror the moment they met the barrel of a gleaming gun aimed directly at him. His dumbstruck gaze then locked on the dark, menacing orbs of Peter Whitehead, grinning from ear to ear, as he stood on the steps leading up to the loft. Frozen like a park statue, Jeremy glanced at the others standing behind him. A small Asian woman flanked by four men, all dressed in black uniforms, and all brandishing hand guns.

Jeremy expected to see Spear, yet the brutish man was nowhere in sight.

"Good morning," sneered Whitehead at his stunned enemy. "Ah, I see you found the transponder hidden inside Sweet Thing's shoe. But where are my manners? Did you have a good night's sleep? It was your last."

CHAPTER THIRTY-EIGHT

Dane found it nearly impossible to remain asleep during the raging storm which lasted on and off throughout the night. He'd drift off only to be abruptly awakened by either a clap of thunder or the constant rustling of the hunter's canvas blind around them, as if they were encamped on the summit of Mount Everest. Charlee on the other hand had no difficulty whatsoever, he had noticed. She slept on her side like the proverbial baby, rolling over only occasionally. As exhausted and worried as he was about his friends, he finally succumbed and fell deeply asleep around four A.M. by the last glance of his watch. When he awoke on his back, it wasn't from the chattering fabric of the hunter's blind or even from the sunlight flickering through the leaves flapping wildly on the trees overhead, but from the faint sound of someone's voice. He abruptly sat up and listened. The disembodied male voice sounded…faint…but nearby. When he rose up on his elbows, a puzzling expression clouding his rugged features, Charlee began to stir, rolling over on her other side away from him. More distinct now the voice repeated *her* name.

"Charlee…Charlee, answer me, now. Do you hear me, Charlee? If you don't answer me…"

Dane searched the cramped blind, following the faint voice with his eyes. It was definitely coming from somewhere inside.

"Charlee, I know you're close by. I know you can hear me. Come out!" Spear's tone and inflections were growing more threatening, as were his words. "I have your brother, and if you want to see him again, come out, now! Charlee, if you don't answer me, I'm going to execute him, along with the others. Do you hear me? Charlee? CHARLEE!"

Dane eye's looked down and settled on Charlee's flowing hair as it splayed out on the ground behind her. The agitated voice continued. He pushed aside her thick hair and the moment he found the source the voice stopped. A small earphone device of some kind lay on the ground. Dane frowned as he picked it up and began examining the earpiece. Confusion clouded his features as he pressed it to his ear listening. Then abruptly the voice shouted--"CHARLEE!"

Dane snapped the earpiece away, holding it at arm's length. Clutching it angrily in his fist he yanked Charlee by the arm.

"AHHHHH--" she shrieked in a high-pitched terror.

"WHAT IS THIS--?"

"What are you doing--?"

"WHAT THE HELL IS THIS?" he continued to yell, dragging her from the blind.

"Dane--stop--STOP IT!" Charlee shrieked, kicking and fighting against him as he pulled her outside into the morning sun and churning winds. "--LEMME GO!"

He released her and she fell awkwardly to the ground, her hair swirling wildly about her face, shock etched across her frightened features.

His clothes still damp, his mind fatigued, Dane was at the breaking point as he stood over her, his eyes narrowing in a fiery explosive rage, waving the earpiece at her while shouting, "WHAT IS THIS--WHAT ARE YOU DOING--WHO THE HELL IS THIS?"

"Stop yelling at me!"

"WELL?"

"It's not what you think!" she cried.

Dane tried to calm himself. "Isn't it? I've been trying to get us outta here and you've been--"

"They're gonna kill my brother--!"

"Along with my friends! What's the matter with you? We're so close to them now."

"Please, Dane--listen to me--"

"I thought something was funny the way you kept trying to lead us back the way we came. I should've known after your conversation with Ryan!"

"Whatta you mean?"

"C'mon Charlee, remember what you said?--'I did what you asked'--remember? You're working with them! WHY?"

"It isn't what you think," she whimpered through tears, dropping her head in defeat, the howling gale swirling her hair.

"Oh yeah?"

"HOLD IT, right there!" ordered a disembodied, harsh voice from behind.

Dane froze as instructed.

Charlee twitched and her head snapped up, looking first at Dane's wild-eyed expression, then at the man standing behind them, his arms outstretched, a gun gripped in both hands aimed directly at Dane's back. Dane caught the young girl's eyes widened, not in terror but seemingly more out of mounting recognition.

"Both of you--don't move!" the commanding voice again ordered. "You! Muscle boy..."

Muscle boy? Dane mouthed with a frown.

"Step away from her and put your hands on your head... NOW!"

Mother Nature was an unrelenting tormentor, evidenced by the constant groaning of the loft's thick wooden beams overhead. Jeremy's personal tormentor was equally unrelenting as he slowly ascended the creaking old staircase, closing the gap. Jeremy couldn't believe his eyes as he watched and listened in dumfounded shock to Whitehead.

"You don't look so good, Jeremy…did you honestly think you were gonna get away?" he glared, his lips curled in a smirking, satisfying grin. "From the look on your face I guess you did."

From behind Jeremy everyone in the loft stirred to wakefulness at the sound of Whitehead's deep rasping voice. Afraid to be without it, like a security blanket, Ian quickly slipped on his backpack.

Whitehead stopped at the top landing just in front of Jeremy. Shoving his Glock into an inside pocket of his biker jacket, he took the shoe from Jeremy's hand and held it out under his nose, displaying the side of it where a tiny electronic gadget protruded through a small split in the sole, like a ruptured hernia. "We've been tracking you since your escape. That's why we collect all the shoes--we do that with everyone. It prevents escape--all that rough terrain--hard on your bare feet. Then of course there's this--a transponder--in all of the kids shoes. If someone *should* get away, we can find 'em like that!" he concluded with a snap of his fingers.

Leslie rose up and stood behind Jeremy, her face drained of expression and white as a sheet. The kids closed in behind her, Lynn and Ian finding their way under her protective arms. Eric stood up too, behind the group, his back intentionally blocking the window and the ledge…where Jeremy had left his Glock.

"Just like we found you," Shazuko said, slyly slithering up the steps behind Whitehead like a viper.

"Here's your shoe back, Sweet Thing," Whitehead said in his usual warm, schizophrenic manner. "You're gonna need 'em this morning, for a little while at least."

Like a mother bear protecting her cubs, Leslie took it instead. Whitehead grinned at the both of them, then again at Jeremy. "You never had a chance. But that snowmobile thing across the lake--that was ingenious…and pretty cool."

"I'd call it inspired," Jeremy quipped defiantly.

"Whatever. But it's over now."

Still stunned Jeremy tried desperately to gain back his composure. He ignored Whitehead, knowing it would piss him off, focusing instead on the beautiful Asian woman behind him. "Who are you?"

Shazuko came around Whitehead, saying nothing and began examining the loft. She spotted the fishing tube and called out to one of her black uniformed henchmen below. "Where's Mr. Spear?"

"Outside."

"Get him."

She picked up the tube and removed the cap. "And what have we here?"

Briefly examining the canvas after pulling it out part way, she said, "I understood this left with the General this morning. How is it all of you have it?"

Met with silent stares, Shazuko gently pushed the canvas back inside and recapped it. She then surveyed the frightened group of dirty and disheveled youngsters. Eric moved slightly, hoping to continue blocking her view of the window. She unwittingly obliged him.

She then looked at Jeremy. "I asked you a question."

Like her henchmen, the petite Asian woman wore a one-piece black outfit, although hers was form-fitting. And for a moment she seemed to Jeremy like an evil femme fatale from a James Bond movie, and probably just as deadly. Jeremy had to remind himself this was no movie. And the large weapon holstered to her shoulder was no prop filled with blanks.

Shazuko walked up to him, engaging Jeremy's eyes and said, "Are you the young man who killed my brother?"

Inches away he could smell the delicate scent of her perfume and feel the warmth of her skin on his face; yet it was her eyes that drew him in. They were a cold set of orbs, calculating and cruel. For a moment he hesitated, confused, then replied, "--What?"

"The black Scorpion helicopter?" she said tersely, her dark eyes boring into his. "The pilot--Lee Kwon. He was my brother--and you murdered him!"

"Yeah, well, sorry 'bout that," Jeremy snarled, his teeth clenched. "But he was trying to *kill us*!"

"Perhaps *I'll* have better luck," she sneered back at him. "And this canvas?"

"It was left in one of the elevators, so I grabbed it."

"Really." Shazuko replied curtly. That didn't make sense to her but for the moment she dismissed it. She then held out her hand. "I'll take the cell phone and the flash drive, if you please."

At that instant one of her henchmen arrive at the landing and announced, "I don't know where Mr. Spear is, ma'am."

"We don't have them," Jeremy responded boldly before thinking it probably wasn't a good idea to provoke her.

"Really?" she said coolly, before calling out to her henchmen below. "Find Mr. Spear, now. We're leaving!"

"Yes, ma'am."

Shazuko then turned her eyes to the black-suited man at her side, cocked her head in the direction of Leslie and said, "Take her."

"ALL RIGHT!" Jeremy cried trying to block the hulking henchman as he snatched Leslie's arm. In a flash he struck Jeremy across the head knocking him to the floor, the pain in his thigh exacerbated the moment he hit the floor. The kids cried out at the sudden savage attack. An instant later, like lightening, Elmo leaped onto the henchman's back. Matthew and Travis scrambled to their brother's side while Lynn held onto Leslie, the both of them recoiling backward from the henchmen. Leslie, trying to fend him off, thrust herself in front of Lynn to protect her. The henchman, tiring of Elmo's interference easily shook the boy off, sending him to the floor with a thud! In a swift judo move, Shazuko violently spun Leslie around like a top, dropping the fishing tube, and restrained her in a choking hold to her throat. Whitehead watched with a smirk on his face as Leslie's eyes bulged in terror. It abruptly vanished when something shiny in the corner of his eye caught his attention. A young, angry voice then captured everyone else's.

"Stop--STOP IT! ...Let her *go*, you BITCH!"

Everyone stopped, their eyes falling on Eric and the Glock pistol gripped in his quivering hand, aimed at Shazuko. The sinister Asian released her hold and Leslie staggered a few steps, coughing, gasping for air. Shazuko moved away from the group, subtly shaking her head at her henchman signaling him to reholster his gun. She then smiled gamefully at Eric, drawing the frightened boy's attention to her. Jeremy struggled to stand with the twins' help and they staggered to Leslie's side. Jeremy stared in horror at Eric, his mind retracing where he'd left the weapon the night before…on the damn windowsill!

"Oh my God," Leslie whispered.

The disposable cell phone lying on the ground beside the sniper in the camouflaged Ghillie suit trilled. After witnessing two large RVs approach along a dirt road and park some distance away, he carefully monitored the movements and positions of the seven occupants through the telescopic sight of the high-powered Barrett M82 sniper rifle in his hands. He watched them as they exited, handguns drawn, stealthily head in the direction of the deserted barn. He made meticulous mental notes as four males, dressed in black followed a fifth, a bald, husky individual outfitted in a black and silver motorcycle ensemble. Behind them in tow, also in black, was a small, slender woman with jet black hair, kicked up by the unrelenting gale. They seemed to know right where to go, cautiously ducking beneath the vine-shrouded entrance and into the barn. All of them with the exception of the seventh male with spiked white hair; a bandage along the right side of his hairline from a recent injury. Dressed in tan slacks with a white-collar dress shirt, plain tie and light jacket, he moved off in the opposite direction and disappeared into the woods. The sniper lowered the rifle, reached for the cell, opened it and said, "Marco."

"Polo," came the sharp response, the voice electronically altered to sound male. "Your orders are to kill everyone. No witnesses, no survivors. Then you're to collect their cell phone and the flash drive. Understood?"

"...Understood."

The sniper closed the phone, laid it back by his side and picked up the rifle, focusing his eyes and his aim at the barn entrance before scanning the vicinity. Until now, the sniper never hesitated on an order. He couldn't put his finger on it, but something about the voice, the inflections, regardless of the electronic scrambling, didn't sound right. And his original orders were explicit. He was to follow directives from Vincent McNeil *only*. And his intuition was telling him that that wasn't McNeil!

Despite the surrounding foliage and trees whipped to frenzy by the furious winds, his trained eye caught someone moving slowly along the west side of the barn. Whoever it was appeared to keep low, maneuvering beneath the thick cover of bushes. He followed him through the scope, trying in vain to identify who it was, his finger poised gently on the delicate trigger.

Director of National Intelligence, Deputy Director, Vincent McNeil stared unblinking in mild confusion for a moment at the image before him. Far advanced beyond anything on the public market, the state-of-the-art, ultra QHD, nano-plasma flat-panel display covered an entire wall. Finally, he sputtered, "What the--what just happened, people? Who was our operative just talking to--'cause it wasn't us?"

The situation room's six technicians, seated at various stations before the massive screen in the conference-size room monitoring their own individual computer screens, snapped into action calling up additional data, searching for an answer.

"Someone talk to me!" McNeil barked. "Simpson? What's going on?"

Paul Simpson, a young twenty-four-year-old technician in the agency, specializing in high-tech communications, feverously scanned the information on his small screen pinpointing the problem and stated, "I think our operative just got hijacked."

"What!"

Simpson took only a second to double check his findings. "According to this, our cell tower signal is being blocked. And the call he just received won't track."

"That's impossible."

"See for yourself, sir."

McNeil didn't have to. Simpson knew his stuff. This kind of sophisticated manipulation of cell phone signals could only be done by another spy agency--someone else, McNeil concluded, was in the game!

He frowned at the thought. "How much you wanna bet our *cousins* are behind this!"

In the world of spy game lingo, the kinsman remark was a direct reference to their counterpart; the CIA. McNeil's eyes then hardened as he stared at the lofty image of their camouflaged operative on the hill, whom they were now apparently unable to communicate with. Despite his blending concealment, his body was clearly outlined in a red hue by the inferred lens of the geostationary satellite camera some two hundred miles overhead. McNeil glanced at another young technician and said, "Mr. Thompson, initiate a level five protocol diagnostic. I want to know who's tapping into our satellite!"

"Yes, sir."

McNeil continued to stare at their red-hued operative, and then announced loudly through pursed lips and clenched teeth, "I want to know what the hell is going on, people!"

Dane did as he was ordered. Still facing Charlee, bewildered by her expression, he raised his hands behind his head, lacing his fingers together, and slowly began to inch away from her. The look of startled recognition on her face could only mean one thing. They'd been found. For a brief moment his mind raced--the Glock wasn't in his pocket--where was it? ...That's right, he'd set aside in the blind. Not at all adept or skilled in the use of any weapon, he wasn't sure if it was a blessing or a curse. He feared he was about to find out.

"Okay, okay--I'm moving," muttered Dane.

"Turn around!" the tense voice ordered.

Dane stopped. In that instant he became acutely aware of his thumping heart and how deeply he'd been drawing his breath. He warily turned. A man with dark chestnut hair, dressed in a grey Hilfiger button collar shirt beneath a leather gun holster strapped to his shoulder, stone-washed denim jeans and worn cowboy boots, stood before them.

"All right you, hold it right there."

Charlee was still staring at the stranger. It was as if an old, faded photograph had come to life.

"Roy Rogers, I presume?" quipped Dane.

"Roy Rogers?" Charlee gasped. "...Dad--? Daddy?" Cha--Charlee--?"

Richard's eyes and the gun in his hand guardedly danced back and forth from the overwrought muscled young man to his left to that of the dirty, disheveled young girl to his right on the ground and he sputtered again, "Charlee--is--is that--?"

"Oh, Daddy!" she cried leaping to her feet. In a torrent of raw emotion and tears streaming down her face Charlee ran into her father's arms and clutched him in a bear hug. As she broke down, sobbing uncontrollably, Richard did his best to hold his own emotions in check, keeping his eyes and his gun trained on the young man.

"Charlee--oh my God, Charlee--is it--is it really you?"

Dane started to lower his hands until Richard advised him otherwise with a stiffened arm, thrusting the gun in his direction.

"It's alright--his name is Dane--he's a friend," she wailed with her face buried in his shirt.

"Some friend," he shot back, glaring at Dane.

Charlee pulled away from Richard, wiping her face and eyes, looking up into his, "They have Dylan, and his friends."

"Who has Dylan?--Hold it, I said!"

"Look, if you're gonna shoot me," Dane growled in final protest, dropping his hands to his side, confident he wasn't going to get shot--he hoped, "then get it over with 'cause I'm too dang tired to hold 'em up any longer!"

"How did you find us?" Charlee asked Richard.

"It's a long story," he replied, before shifting his steady gaze back to Dane. "Just who are you?"

"My name is Dane Bergman. I was camping with my friends when we ran into *her* brother. He kidnapped one of my friends--a young girl--and a small boy!"

"That's not true--exactly," Charlee gushed through redden eyes and streaming tears, defending her brother. "He didn't mean to. They made him do it!"

Dane wasn't sure what to think anymore and it showed in his dark sullen eyes and the grim features of his rough, unshaven face.

"They?" Richard said in an urgent tone, finally lowering the gun, shoving it into the shoulder holster. He looked first at Charlee, then at Dane. "The Monarch Foundation?"

Releasing a thankful sigh, Dane's expression suddenly intensified and his eyes narrowed. "Yes, but, how did you know?"

"Charlee's email led me to 'em. Do you know where they are now?"

"Email?" Charlee winced questioningly.

"The one sent from Dr. Wringwater."

"Dr. Wringwater? I don't understand, you just got that? She sent that last summer"

Robert shook his head. "Apparently she didn't. I just received it…three days ago."

"Three days ago," Charlee echoed. "Who sent it to you?"

"Doesn't matter. Do you know where Dylan and the others are right now?"

"Not far from here, I think," Dane said. "But that still doesn't explain--*this*!"

He opened his hand holding out the earpiece.

Richard walked over, keeping Charlee close to him and took it.

Dane's eyes stared into Charlee's. "She's been in contact with 'em since we all escaped--what's up with that?"

"Spear said I was to find out who you were," she began to explain, looking first at Dane, then to Richard. "They've held us prisoner since last year. He told me if I didn't do what he wanted he would kill Dylan and the others. And he's killed before. I was hoping to buy some time, figure out some way to--I didn't know what to do. It's the truth!"

"It's okay, it's all right," Richard said gently, still holding onto her.

"What are we gonna do?" she cried softly, looking up at him. "We've got to find them before it's too late."

"We will," Richard replied emphatically. He turned his attention to Dane and said, "How do you know they're close by?"

Dane dug the radio from his pocket, turned it on and held it up. Then he pressed the side button. The proximity lights first flashed, then steadily lit up. "The green lights are a kind of cheap GPS. They first indicated the battery charge--and they're getting low, then they indicate how far away or how close we are to the companion radio, which my friends have. They're all lit, so they should be within a mile of us."

"Can you talk to them?"

"Nope. And I don't know why, but they don't answer."

Richard left Charlee's side and took a few steps, facing the deep woods. He focused his intense, wary eyes on them and wondered what lay beyond. He looked down at the earpiece in his hand, then clinched it tightly in his fist and angrily threw it away. He knew now from his experience at the Foundation what to expect and in his mind, a plan was formulating.

Finally, he turned to Dane and Charlee, the wind snatching at the young girl's jet-black hair and said decisively, "Let's go and get 'em!"

CHAPTER THIRTY-NINE

Eric held the Glock anxiously in his outstretched hand, the muzzle pointed directly at Shazuko. His face was a mixed collection of fear and rage. When she began to slowly move away from Whitehead's side his aim followed her every step. Eric's lungs gushed air in shallow yet rapid bursts and he was beginning to feel lightheaded as if he were going to pass out. Watching her as she slithered off to the side, her dark Asian eyes bore back into his with a playful malevolence he'd never seen before, in anyone. That terrified him even more. His senses were so overwhelmed by this point that he wasn't sure what was worse, her evil stare, the hunger pangs stabbing at his gut or the fear of holding a real, loaded gun in his hand. It was fairly light, the metal cool against his hand. Afraid it might actually go off, he kept his finger wrapped around the trigger guard rather than the trigger itself. Sweeping the weapon from side to side, from Shazuko, then over to Whitehead at the loft landing then back again, Eric shook all over, down to his quivering knees, unsure as to what he was going to do next.

"Eric," Lynn whimpered to him, shaking her head. "...Don't."

"Eric, listen to me," Jeremy implored softly. "Put the gun down- *-put the gun--*"

"Nooo," he growled through taut lips and anguished eyes.

"Well, well, well. So the little boy really has a set of balls after all," Whitehead glared at him.

"We haven't time for this," Shazuko snapped. "Take his gun!"

"NOO!" Eric shouted again, nervously panning the weapon back and forth. First at Shazuko, then at Whitehead.

Shazuko.

Whitehead.

His breathing intensified, almost snorting like an angry bull, his teeth bearing down when he muttered at Whitehead, "You! You always get a thrill out of hurting others?"

"Yeah, actually I do. *It is* kind of a thrill for me."

"I remember how you watched what he was doin' to me."

"Well, we all have our little vices."

Eric's hand gripped the gun tighter as he winced tearfully, "He was hurting me and you enjoyed it!"

Curious, Shazuko remained silent, allowing the drama, for the moment, to continue.

Jeremy caught what he said and stepped closer. "Eric? Is he the one?"

"No...but he watched." Eric's face then twisted in agony. HE WATCHED AND DID NOTHING!"

"C'mon, he was just havin' a little fun with ya."

Eric wiped his livid eyes with his free hand, then spat angry words that were a mix of hatred and spit. "FUN? IS THAT WHAT YOU CALL IT? FUN?"

"Who was it?" Jeremy said looking at Whitehead. "Who?"

Whitehead only smiled back at him.

Lynn took a step toward her brother, barely noticing Leslie clutching her shoulders drawing her back. The scared kids closed in behind them, listening and watching in their own innocent dismay at what was unfolding.

From across the loft Jeremy's mind raced through their conversation over breakfast at the cabin the other morning, his eyes mindful of the gun in his hand. "...The boy at McDonalds...you called him the 'n' word."

"Why, Eric," Whitehead uttered in mocking shock. "I'm surprised at you."

"You're no racist…no more than me or the rest of the kids… which leaves only one person at home--doesn't it?" he concluded, looking again at Whitehead. "Ron Hardy."

"He's not black," Travis said softly.

"Bing-go," Whitehead uttered with a gleeful smile. "Good ol' Ronnie, my mulato friend."

"Huh?"

"Multiracial," Jeremy clarified to his brother. "His mother is white and his father is African American."

"And not that you could really tell so much," Whitehead explained casually. "He just has that really nice tan all year 'round-- Ronnie, I mean. And he does have that nappy head of hair when he'd let it grow out, which he rarely did."

"Eric told everyone the kids at camp had beat up on him," Jeremy said to Whitehead, limping slowly in between the two of them, favoring his good leg. "But he left out the part about being raped. It never happened at camp. It happened at home, last summer. Didn't it?"

"Move outta the way, Jeremy!" Eric grimaced.

Jeremy raised his open palm while still facing Whitehead. "You threatened him? His family--the other kids—didn't you?"

Whitehead shrugged innocently and said, "I may have--I really don't recall."

"I do!" Eric winced hatefully, recalling the attack in vivid flashbacks.

Jeremy continued. "*Hardy* attacked him, and *you* enabled him. Later, when it finally came out what had happened, in order to protect himself and the kids, he made up the camp story. Is that about right?"

Whitehead chuckled, grinning coldly and said, "Well, I'm not sure what you mean by *enabled*…but what can I tell ya. Ronnie likes boys. Especially the chubby ones."

There was fiery rage in Jeremy's face. Whitehead wasted no time and came right at him--the two face to face. Whitehead never stopped grinning as he spat, "Whaddya gonna do now, Jeremy, huh?"

"Enough!" Shazuko intervened with a bark. "A most touching scene for which I'm afraid we have no more time."

She walked up to Eric, yet he held his ground, terror etched in his face. He shook and moaned, "I'll shoot you--I will, I swear I will--"

"Not likely," Whitehead sputtered as he left Jeremy and came up beside Shazuko. The instant he snatched the weapon from Eric's hand the boy jumped back at his bold act, gasping for air.

"It helps kid if you take the safety off," Whitehead muttered as he fussed with the weapon for a moment, then thrust it back into Eric's hand, forcing the boy to hold it point-blank against his chest. Whitehead's dark malevolent gaze drilled into Eric's terrified eyes as he spoke. "Now it's ready. Wanna shoot me?"

"Leave 'em alone," Jeremy barked.

"Back off--go ahead, kid."

"Stop it, Peter!"

"Back off, Jeremy! C'mon Eric, let's see what kinda man you really are."

"Goddamn it--*leave 'em alone!*"

"And I said *back the fuck off!*" Whitehead glared at him with a brief twist of his head. "Here's your chance, Eric, your chance to really kill me. Go ahead, boy, do it."

"ERIC!" Lynn cried out.

Though Shazuko felt pressed for time, she nonetheless found perverse pleasure in their exchange.

The boy cowered, breaking down as waves of anguish washed over him. He couldn't hold onto the gun any longer and he nearly dropped it until Whitehead grabbed it from him, stepped back and thrust the muzzle against Jeremy's temple, violently shoving him stumbling backward. Eric's own festering rage began gushing from his lips the instant he suddenly lunged for Whitehead. Instantly fending the boy off, Whitehead shoved him violently into Jeremy. The two went down, followed by a weapon's blast from behind, sending the startled kids to their knees, screaming and ducking for cover with their hands.

"What the hell is this?" Spear fumed at Shazuko as he came up the stairs, his Glock aimed at the rafters overhead. "This your idea of control?"

She glared back at him with contempt and said, "Where's the girl?"

Jeremy exchanged a worried glance with Dylan.

Spear's anger was so intense he wanted to kill Charlee the moment he saw her. In his sociopathic mind she was nothing but a tool, a means to an end. His equally ordered mind also considered her a dangerous loose end that had to be eliminated. They all were. Regardless of Shazuko's instructions, he had his orders from the Colonel and that's all that mattered. *His* were the only ones he would follow. He held his emotions in check the moment he entered the barn, passing behind one of the black-suited operatives, and came up the stairs, firing his weapon overhead.

"I asked you--"

"I heard you the first time," Spear replied brusquely. "I don't know where she is. She refuses to answer."

"No matter. We will attend to her later."

Shazuko stepped over to where the fishing tube lay containing the canvas and picked it up, handing it over to Spear. "Perhaps at some point you can explain this."

Spear took it, returning her contemptuous glance with his own glib expression, with little intention of doing so. Shazuko turned back to Jeremy. "I won't ask again."

Jeremy dug into his pocket and withdrew the flash drive, handing it to Shazuko. He then motioned to Dylan. Dylan couldn't swim to save his life, he never learned how. And now it was as if he was being threatened, while floating in deep water, to remove his only lifeline--his lifejacket that had kept him from drowning. Reluctantly

Dylan stepped forward and handed her the smartphone...their last lifeline.

The woman took them both, the smartphone and flash drive and deposited them down inside the hip pocket of her suit. Satisfied, she smiled before turning to Spear and saying, "Take everyone outside--now."

"Let's go!" Spear growled, pointing with his Glock rather than the fishing tube. "Downstairs!"

Jeremy didn't know what to do at this point, except as they were ordered. Taking Leslie's hand, he nervously limped down the stairs, leading the way, his heart leaping into his throat, his eyes desperately searching for a way out. He paused at the bottom landing looking at each of them, trying to keep the kids close to him. One by one they filed past him. Matt, Dylan, Elmo, Trav, Lynn, then Eric. Frightened as they were, each was bolstered by Jeremy's determined, defiant expression. Following closely behind, Leslie held tightly to Ian's hand.

"You'll never get away with this," announced Jeremy to the kidnappers. "Our families are by now already looking for us--please, just let us go...we can't hurt you. You got want you wanted. Let them go and keep me--"

"I said, outside," Spear calmly repeated, cutting Jeremy off and pointed with the fishing tube. "Or I'll shoot each of you here and now."

Jeremy's face froze in terror as he stared into the gray empty eyes of the enforcer, knowing he wasn't kidding. At first no one heard him come in. Emerging from the shadows after crawling in through a missing wooden panel in the corner of the old barn, Arnold entered the arena.

"Well, I'll be--here's that miserable dog of yours," Spear said to Whitehead. The kids watched as the curious German shepherd paused for a moment, sniffing and looking about the barn.

"And here I thought you'd run away, dog. C'mere Baddog, before I beat ya again."

Arnold heard his master's voice and looked up toward the top of the loft landing where Whitehead was standing. When he saw the bald, hulking figure at the top of the stairs, the long, thick hairs around his neck rose up and he began to growl. He remembered the beatings, being kicked and forced into the tiny wire cage for so long. He remembered being hungry, too.

"C'mere, you miserable mutt!"

Spear then spouted, "I told you and Ryan this one wasn't trainable--shoot 'em."

"No!" Eric cried out. Arnold heard the fear in his voice and went right up to him, nuzzling his leg. Eric bent down protectively petting the soft fur along his neck, then cupped one of his ears, rubbing it gently, all in an effort to hold onto him.

"Why you good-for-nothing--!" Whitehead spat.

Arnold turned toward him the instant he started down the stairs and unleashed a torrent of furious barking. The German shepherd took an attack stance, all four legs poised to propel him directly at Whitehead.

"NOOO!" Eric cried out again as he watched Whitehead, the gun still in his hand, raise it and casually take aim. Jeremy lunged for Eric, trying to hold him and the other kids back. They screamed Arnold's name just as the animal leaped for Whitehead but it was too late. Cut down by the blast of Whitehead's Glock, like being hit by a truck, the bullet tore into his brisket, tearing flesh, exiting out the other side of his chest in an explosion of scarlet and fur. The next instant, when the others looked, the dog was lying on the dirt floor, unable to move, whimpering, trying to draw air into its lungs.

"FOR CRISE SAKES!" Jeremy lashed out. "YOU DIDN'T HAVE TO SHOOT HIM!"

Jeremy went for the injured animal, only to be grabbed roughly by Spear and shoved into the wailing, panic-stricken kids.

"Get them outside!" Shazuko demanded. "This is getting out of control--and separate them!"

Spear waved his weapon in the direction of the vine-en-shrouded opening and shouted, "GO! GO!"

Shazuko leaned into Spear, nodding in Whitehead's direction and murmured, "When we get to the farm, get rid of him as well--he's trouble!"

Whitehead leaned into Jeremy's face, pressing the Glock force-fully against his shoulder and winked.

Through spit and sweat Jeremy raged, "I am gonna fuckin' stop you--all of you!"

"Then you'll be needin' a little help," Whitehead leered back before shoving him on. "'cause no one's been able to yet,"

The last thing Jeremy and the panic-stricken kids saw as they were forced at gunpoint from the barn was Arnold panting in a spreading pool of blood, his paw twitching desperately.

Richard and Charlee moved quickly through the dense woods lead-ing the way, emerging out to open pasture. Loping behind, Dane caught up to them, then abruptly stopped dead in his tracks. Sensing the absence of Dane's footfalls through the knee-high grass, Richard tugged on his daughter's hand and turned.

"C'mon--what's wrong?"

Dane stood there for a moment, staring past them. He finally said in a dreaded tone, "What is that? *Airwolf?*"

"Hey, that's pretty good--it's the same model all right," Richard replied. "A Bell two-twenty-two to be exact. C'mon."

"You ah, you came in that--not by car?"

"Nope, just that."

"Ahh, jeeze," he winced softly. "And I suppose I gotta get in it?"

"That's the idea--unless you wanna remain out here."

"C'mon, ya big baby," Charlee sputtered. "My brother and your friends are in trouble. Suck it up and let's go!"

"But those things on top that spin around…"

"The rotor blades? What about 'em?"

"Ahh, what if…well, you know, what if, one of 'em were to--you know, come off?"

"Well then," Richard mused thoughtfully, "It'd be a really short trip."

"Yeah…that's what I thought."

"You're not worried, are you?"

"No, not exact--well, now that you mention it…"

"Trust me, Dane. Those things are bolted on--P.D.T."

"P.D.T.?"

"Pretty darn tight."

Dane's brow arched up his forehead and he said, "Did you bolt 'em on yourself?"

"Nope. My underpaid mechanic did. Now, come along, unless you wanna be left behind."

With a dreadful look of alarm, Dane watched Richard and Charlee sprint on ahead in the direction of the sleek helicopter, then muttered to himself, "Oh shit!"

Spear led the way with Shazuko in tow, both of them walking briskly up the road toward two large RV's while Whitehead and the four henchmen brought up the rear. Jeremy clutched Leslie's hand tightly, keeping the kids clustered about them as they moved nervously along the dirt road. "What are we going to do?" she whispered to him.

"I don't know. I wish I knew where Dane--"

"Ah-ah," gruffed Whitehead as he ran up alongside to escort them. "No talking in the ranks."

Spear stopped at the Baddog RV, handing off the fishing tube to Shazuko as she went on ahead to one parked in front of it. He popped the door open and began barking directions to the four henchmen. "You two remain here with Mr. Whitehead. You're taking the younger kids. You other two, you're with us. We'll be in the lead RV with these two older ones."

The two operatives nodded obediently while the two remaining immediately began waving their weapons in Jeremy and Leslie's face, prodding them on.

"Wait a minute!" Jeremy demanded.

"Let's move it," one of them barked.

"Jeremy!" Matthew cried.

"Where are you taking us?" he demanded of the henchman. "Where are you taking us?"

"A little farm on the other side--"

"Shut up!" Spear snapped at him. "Go on. Keep moving."

"Don't make me use this, kid," one of them snarled, hoisting his gun aloft.

"It'll be all right," Jeremy called to the group of frightened faces as the henchmen began to forcefully segregate them, herding the younger kids into one of the RVs while Spear directed Jeremy and Leslie toward the RV up ahead. One of the henchmen started to move in on Leslie, grabbing her arm.

There was panic in Jeremy's voice when he suddenly erupted. "Don't touch her--don't you hurt her--!"

An instant later Leslie screamed in horror as the henchman abruptly reeled backward, his chest erupting in a bloody explosion. As his entire body convulsed she recoiled from his twitching grasp as blood splattered across her line of vision, strafing her face. She screamed again as he crumpled to the ground, making a pained gurgling sound. Spear spun around just as the second henchman next to him convulsed backward against the RV, his face imploding and the back of his head blowing out in a hail of bloody hair, flesh and bone fragments. As his body slid down the white side of the RV to the ground he left a splattered and smeared trail of red. Screams erupted from the kids just as Jeremy grabbed Ian and the others, shoving them all to the ground next to the RV. Leslie awkwardly pulled Ian close to herself, covering him with her body.

Spear launched into action, bellowing at Whitehead and the two remaining henchmen. "GO! TAKE THEM!"

Whitehead snatched Elmo first. Terrified, the boy lurched toward the open RV door, yelping and covering his head. In succession Whitehead grabbed each kid yelling and shoving them toward the open door. Elmo grabbed an arm bringing Lynn with him.

In his frenzied rush, paranoid of being without a weapon, Whitehead scooped up one of the dead henchman's Glock from the ground stuffing it down inside the pocket of his biker pants.

Jeremy tried to stop Whitehead until Spear struck him along the side of his head. He reeled backward, his bare arm sliding along the smeared blood on the RV, stumbling over the dead henchman and falling to the ground. Spear pressed his Glock against Jeremy's neck, yanking him as hard as he could back to his feet and shoving him forward to the other RV. "Get up in there!"

As they were being split up, Leslie took her eyes from the kids for only a second, scrambling to help Jeremy, gasping and screaming for Spear to stop. The instant he grabbed her arm, tighter than a vise, she felt it was about to break and thrust her foot against his calf as hard as she could. It was like kicking the trunk of a solid tree, having little affect. Spear swung her around, then instead of going for the Glock in his shoulder holster, he snatched the both of them with the help of the fourth henchman, shoving them ahead to the other RV's open door.

The third henchman snatched the last kid and hustled Dylan through the door of the other RV. Tripping over the step Dylan twisted, landing on his butt. He had barely looked up through the chaos when the black-suited henchmen, scrambling through the door in front of him suddenly froze, his body jerked and arched backward unnaturally. His face contorted in a pained, horrifying grimace as he realized his body had just been pierced by the hot poker effect of a bullet slamming through it. Dylan reeled back, gasping, watching as the man's shocked expression drained from his face. In a desperate, futile attempt to hang on, grabbing the door frame and handle, the henchman lost his balance falling backward outside and crashed to the ground in a dead heap, leaving the RV door banging open against the side.

"What the hell is going on!" Shazuko screamed at Spear.

"I don't know," he hurled back at her, suspecting the board was behind the attack.

She then shrieked at him, "Get us outta here--DRIVE!"

The fourth henchman scrambled behind Leslie and Jeremy, away from the open door, fending Jeremy off as he continued to fight to get back outside, explosively shoving the both of them to the back of the RV.

"I'll handle them--get to the other RV," Spear ordered his remaining henchman.

"Sit down!" Whitehead yelled at the cowering kids, nearly out of breath from the surprise, brutal ambush. The remaining henchman dodged inside right behind him, slamming the door. Promptly tossing his Glock to the empty passenger seat, Whitehead scrambled into the driver's chair and started the engine. He cursed the unmoving RV in front of him. "C'mon, c'mon, LET'S GO!"

"Get back there and sit!" Shazuko ordered, calmly recovering but clearly stressed, as she moved past Spear, taking his weapon and pointing it at Jeremy as he held on to Leslie. Spear plopped down into the driver's seat, turned the ignition and engaged the gear shift.

"Humph," The sniper grunted, watching through his scope as the two large RV's tore down the wet country road, splashing through potholes and mud. "I missed one!"

In the event of a hasty departure, which Richard had planned on, he skimmed briefly through the checklist since he'd already performed a thorough inspection just after landing. He feverously went about hitting switches and activating systems. The helicopter immediately came to life, vibrating and humming, the huge main and tail rotors gradually spooling up. As the powerful twin Lycoming/Honeywell turbo shaft engines whined and the *whop-whop-whop* of the main rotors spinning overhead built to a fever pitch, Richard nudged Dane in the co-pilot's seat, to open his eyes. He motioned to both him and Charlee, in the rear passenger cabin, to don their headphones. After scanning the vicinity, Richard pulled on the collective stick at his side and the light blue *Airwolf* Bell 222 lifted gently from the field, flattening the grass beneath it. Retracting the forward wheel into the nose and the side landing gear into the stub wings, Richard continued ascending into the sky.

An instant later their headphones crackled with his voice. "They should be just over the next ridge. We'll be there in a couple of minutes."

CHAPTER FORTY

C.I.A .– Central Intelligence Agency
Langley, Virginia

It was days like these--when things went horribly wrong on a mis-sion--that Carol Langford loathed her position as Ops Division Director at the CIA. And so, once again, in those rare quiet moments she seriously contemplated retirement. And again, she dismissed the thought, refocusing her mind on the task at hand, thinking, could things get any worse.

They just did.

"Ma'am?" the technician repeated.

Staring up at the 200-inch ultra-definition LCD flat screen, Langford finally reacted with dismay, tossing down her Prada glasses onto the control console. She tiredly rubbed the bridge of her nose and sighed.

"Ma'am…he missed the targets."

"He certainly did," she snapped wearily. She took a moment, shaking the strain from her mind, allowing the anger she felt to reenergize her. Finally, she straightened, forcing herself to look away from the screen and the glowing, camouflaged operative lying prone on the ground, focusing on her technician.

"Your orders?" he asked her.

Langford smiled malignantly at the tech and said, "Contact our intercept team…tell them the word is…*go.*"

"Yes, ma'am."

"Director?" another technician called out from a nearby console. "Better have a look at this."

"What is it?"

"There, upper right-hand side of the screen…just coming into view…"

D.N.I. – Director of National Intelligence

McLean, Virginia

"…I see it," McNeil groused. "…Now who the hell do you suppose that is?"

"Light helicopter, sir. It's not ours," Thompson replied.

A subtle grin crossed Vincent McNeil's youthful, unshaven face. "And they thought they could highjack our own operative," he muttered softly to himself.

"*They* may still be trying."

"That they may," he replied with a nod, studying the image as the helicopter moved across the screen in the direction of the abandoned barn. "Mr. Thompson, enhance the tail section. Let's get a look at its call letters."

"Excuse me, sir?"

"Yes, Mr. Simpson?"

"Do you want me to get Manndrake on the line?"

"No, that won't be necessary," he replied candidly. "I'll not assassinate nine kids just so he can hide the indiscretions of… National security my ass. I'll inform him myself…and if they want my resignation…they can damn well have it!"

"Yes sir," the savvy tech replied as if he were in a trance, totally absorbed in his own monitor like a child with a favorite toy, working diligently to contact their operative.

"While some of us are still young, Mr. Thompson…"

As Thompson's fingers danced over the keyboard, the clear overhead image froze. The super imaging computer zoomed in on the aircraft, enlarging the fuselage even farther, and then turning the image on its side. He continued to manipulate the picture until a few seconds later the call letters appeared, completely legible, as though it had been photographed from only a few feet, instead of from the actual 212 miles overhead.

"Zulu November Eight Five four," Simpson announced.

Thompson said, "A Bell two-twenty-two, and definitely not ours."

McNeil said, "You're sure about that?"

"No Bells of that designation in our fleet, nor is it transmitting our transponder code."

"All right then, Mr. Thompson, let's find out who it is."

"Yes sir."

"And Mr. Simpson, continue to reestablish communication with our operative."

Dane had been clutching the radio so tightly in his hand he'd been unaware for several moments the helicopter had just bounced to a soft landing. The first thing he saw after he unclenched his eyelids was the radio in his lap. "Hey, all the little lights are--we've landed!"

"You gonna make it?" Richard asked him, surveying the dilapidated farm house off to his right side, then the weathered barn just beyond. Richard quickly set the controls, locking the collective and reducing the rotor rpm. He paused, glancing at Dane.

"I don't know whether I need a beer or a barf bag."

"Go with the beer--your color's still pretty good."

Dane shook his head, releasing a deep sigh of relief. Removing the headphones, he began unclipping his safety harness, asking, "This the spot?"

Richard nodded at the radio in Dane's hand and said, "The little lights would so indicate. They're all still green and there are no other structures around. So yeah, I think this is it."

Charlee threw off her headphones, leaning into the cockpit for a moment, spouting loudly over the whine of the turbine, "C'mon--c'mon!"

"Hold it!" Richard sputtered back, unclipping his own harness. "You two stay here."

"Are you kidding?" Charlee barked at him.

"Listen to me--*listen to me…*" he said urgently, sensing the tenseness in the young girl's voice and the fear in her facial expression. He cautiously spied the deserted-looking house, then turned back to both of them, patting Charlee's cheek. "Let me check it out first, the two of you remain here. I mean it, okay?"

The two nodded and Richard exited the aircraft. They watched him intently as he withdrew the pistol from his shoulder holster and slowly approached the weather-beaten structure. Approaching the nearby dirt road, located at a right angle to the house and barn, he stopped and appeared to stare down the length of it. The tall overgrown grass swirled around him in the gale as tree branches danced and swayed in the background. Richard's heart sank when he had spotted what looked like three adult bodies on the ground on his approach. He nervously prayed he wouldn't find Dylan or the other kids like that--*Please God, no*, he thought. As he walked in their direction, pivoting instinctively, scanning the vicinity for anyone who might be hiding, he stopped halfway when he could see they were indeed adult males in one piece, black suits. Despite his professional training and experience in the field, the splattering of blood and body parts caused him to grimace. He'd seen it before. A violent ending, perhaps deserved, to three suspected contract operatives trained to kill. This time *they* were the hunted.

There was also no doubt in Richard's mind, considering the type of weapon used, that it was a professional hit. And that gravely worried him. That's when he noticed the two sets of heavy tire tracks in the muddy road. Richard spun around and quickly headed toward the barn. Pausing briefly at the vine enshrouded entrance before he ducked inside, he turned, motioning with his hand for the two to remain inside the helicopter.

The seconds passed like an eternity. Dane looked down at the radio in his hand with its five glowing lights.

A moment later one of them blinked out.

"Ah-oh," Dane uttered gravely. "Something's wrong!"

"What--what's wrong?" Charlee blurted at him.

He flung open the co-pilot's door and bounded from his seat, along with Charlee hot on his heels. As they raced across the field toward the barn they collided head on with the reality of their situation, both of them spotting the three bloody bodies in black up the road.

"Oh my God!" Charlee cried.

Dane was equally shocked at the grizzly sight. He snatched Charlee's hand, pulling her along after him. They were met just as Richard abruptly emerged from the vine sheathed entrance to the barn, clearly distressed.

"What is it?" Charlee blurted, on the verge of tears, "What's wrong? Are they--?"

"No, no, they're not there, but--"

"But, what!" Dane blurted without waiting, tearing past them, ducking beneath the vines. Richard grabbed Charlee's hand, following immediately after him. Dane instantly spotted Arnold and dropped to his knees beside the still laboring-to-breathe German shepherd "--Oh, no!"

"Arnold!" Charlee gasped, kneeling beside Dane, briefly looking about. "Where are they?"

"I dunno, but someone's been here--you know this dog?"

"Yes," she cried.

Dane quickly removed his jacket then tore off his tank top shirt, gently pressing it against the dog's red soaked fur. He was horrified at the pool of blood on the wooden floor surrounding the dog's head. Arnold's eyes blinked at Dane in seeming recognition. "Hold on, boy, hold on."

"I'll get the first aid kit in the ship."

Richard slipped from the barn, dashing back to the helicopter. He grabbed the kit and a large towel from a compartment, then paused abruptly when he noticed the radio.

"He'll be okay," Charlee said to Dane.

Dane was moved close to tears as he moaned, "Oh God--he's lost so much blood."

"Here," Richard bellowed the instant he raced back into the barn. Kneeling beside the two of them, dropping the towel, they watched as he opened and removed several items from the plastic medical kit. Richard spoke succinctly as he leaned closer, examining the shepherd's bloody chest. Removing a small pair of scissors, he began to carefully cut away the dog's blood-soaked fur from around the wound. "He's been shot, Dane."

"What?"

"Listen to me--hold this--we must have just missed 'em--the radio's lights are nearly out."

"Dammit I forgot, that's what I meant to tell you," snapped Dane, taking a bottle of antiseptic from Richard and unscrewing the cap, handing it back along with some gauze. "Hand me some of those--yeah, here--I'll patch 'em up, but we gotta get outta here or we're gonna lose 'em."

Both Dane and Charlee watched as Richard tore into a sealed syringe and immediately plunged the inverted needle into a small bottle of clear liquid. "Hold him."

The two laid their hands gently on the shepherd as Richard, short on time, doused a small area on the dog's thigh with antiseptic, then inserted the syringe and squeezed the plunger. Arnold whined and struggled for a moment.

"What is that?" Charlee asked her father.

"Are you a vet?" asked Dane.

"No, but a close friend of mine is--Charlee, hand me some of that gauze. This will lessen the pain and keep him calm."

Richard looked over at Dane when the bodybuilder asked through wet eyes, "Who would shoot him--why?"

"I don't know, but no doubt the same people who have Dylan and your friends."

"Is he gonna make it?"

"I've patched the wound, but we gotta get goin', right now. Gimme that towel."

Richard spread out the large beach towel next to Arnold, folding it in half. "C'mon, help me…gently now."

The three slid their hands beneath Arnold's head, shoulder and hindquarters lifting him with great care onto the towel. The shepherd tensed his weakened body, whimpered, then seemed to relax.

As Dane quickly slipped his jacket back on, Richard said, "Bunch the corners together. We'll carry 'em and put him in the back with Charlee."

Gathering their ends of the towel like a hammock the two men prepared to lift Arnold.

"Ready? On three. One, two, three."

Hustling him back out to the whirling helicopter, Charlee raced ahead, opened the rear passenger door and climbed in, helping to ease the seriously wounded animal inside. Dane hopped in and the two gently hefted the dog onto the seat. He then scrambled back outside leaving Charlee seated beside Arnold's head, buckling her harness. Richard secured the door behind her, then slid into the cockpit. As Dane got in he picked up the radio from the co-pilot seat, then slammed his door tight, gasping, "The lights--all of 'em--they're out!"

After donning their headsets, Richard barked, "Buckle in and hold on!"

Dane braced himself, watching Richard bring the throttle in with a twist. The turbine whined with power as the rotors built up speed, casting shadows from the rising sun, fluttering across the cabin through the spinning blades. A few moments later Richard pulled the collective, angling the cyclic into the gale and lifted the helicopter smoothly from the ground. The wheels retracted and he maneuvered the sleek blue and white helicopter smoothly into the sky. Watching the treetops racing beneath his feet through the chin window, Dane's vision shifted uneasily to his hands. Like Richard's they were coated with Arnold's blood.

Shazuko leaned out the open door of the motor coach, grabbed the handle and slammed it closed just as Spear turned onto a main two-lane highway.

"Your Colonel is a dead man!" she barked.

"Excuse me!" Spear fumed back, looking at her through the oversized mirror above his head. "You think he ordered that? He's under house arrest, remember? That was no doubt *your board* in action!"

"Ridiculous!" she snapped with a dismissive glare.

Jeremy sat beside Leslie on a plush couch below a large window. Reaching around his head, he grimaced as he gently rubbed above his ear.

"You all right?" whispered Leslie.

"Head hurts from these jerks whacking me--"

"Quiet," Shazuko barked at them.

Taking the seat opposite them she sat erect with her gun and her cold steely eyes trained on the both of them. While Jeremy's hand became tightly entwined with Leslie's, she leaned into his shoulder thinking of home and her mother. Jeremy's thoughts were elsewhere; primarily the safety of the others and how to retrieve the smartphone and flash drive from the hip pocket of Shazuko's suit. The fishing tube lay on the floor beside her. From the corner of his eye he kept tabs on her, noting her unusual nervousness as she checked her watch several times before finally relaxing. Perhaps she wasn't used to being shot at like a deer in a scope. Swiveling in her leather chair away from them, she momentarily ignored the two of them, watching the passing scenery out front through the panoramic windshield.

Jeremy then said aloud, "Neither one of you strike me as nature enthusiasts."

"Excuse me?" Shazuko replied with a momentary glance.

"These two huge RVs--you and Spear go camping a lot?"

"Hardly," she replied with another short glance accompanied with subtle roll of her eyes. "We use them to shuttle kids across the country."

"Would that include abductions?" Jeremy probed.

"You ask too many questions," she replied without looking at him.

"I'm just getting started. Where are you taking us?"

"To the *farm*."

"The farm?"

"A place where undesirables are taken and terminated."

"Where is it?"

She finally faced the two of them. "If you must know, on the other side, across the Mackinac Bridge."

"*Mackinaw*."

"What?"

"Mackinaw--it's pronounced *Mackinaw*."

"If it pleases you," she quipped with a blasé pout. "It won't be much longer now."

As the massive 45-foot Baddog motorcoach sped down the highway, taunted by gusts, Elmo kept everyone clustered together on a long, side couch, toward the rear. While Ian sat on his lap clinging to him like a bear cub, his head resting against his shoulder, Elmo observed just behind them at the rear of the coach, two motocross bikes, the wheels supported and locked in a track embedded in the floor. Behind them the entire back end opened downward on two thick cables like a ramp. Elmo scanned the faces of the others and he knew what they were thinking. Lynn was gripping Eric's hand so tightly it felt to him like his fingers were going numb. He gently shook it, relieving her death grip on him. Beside them, shoulder to shoulder, Travis sat with streaming tears, clutching Matthew's hand.

"He'll be all right, Trav," his twin brother whispered.

"No he won't," the boy uttered through a tortured expression. "...You saw all the blood."

Staring out the window, Dylan sat motionless on the end of the couch, ignoring the henchman standing over them with his arms folded across his chest, a gun clutched in his hand. Dylan looked up at him, then turned to Lynn beside him. Sensing he was staring at her, she turned her head and met his gaze.

"I am sorry," he said to her in a quiet voice.

"I know," she replied softly with sympathetic eyes. Without looking away, she slid her hand, resting on her lap, over to his and held it.

The blue and white Bell helicopter clipped over the forest at two hundred feet streaking southwest, closing in on the Lake Michigan shoreline. Richard's voice broke over the intercom. "Helicopter Zulu November Eight Five four to Skyland Stables, come in Skyland Stables, Christine are you there?--Dane, listen to me, the nearest--"

"Skyland Stables, this is Skyland Stables, Richard, I hear you, are you all right? Did you find the kids?"

"This is Zulu November Eight Five four, yes, Christine, I found them, but we have a medical emergency which requires your veterinary skills--a German shepherd with a bullet wound to the chest.

Grab your stuff, jump on '75' and head north. I'll keep you posted as to our location--right now we're heading southwest to the Mack. Do you copy?"

"Affirmative. I'm on my way, Skyland Stables out."

"If they're gonna fly outta here, the nearest airstrip or airport is back toward St Ignace, so they've gotta be heading there. But in these fierce winds I doubt they'll even be able to take off."

"With all of them?" Dane's voice crackled, his eyes frantically scanning the road and cars below. "They'll need somethin' bigger than a Cessna--might draw some attention."

"I agree, I think they're headed south."

"South. Across the bridge?"

"Most likely."

Dane glanced down at the radio in his hand, all the tiny lights still dark. "We don't even know what they're in?"

"There were a couple of sets of very heavy duty tire tracks back there--I'm thinkin' two large RV's--so keep a sharp eye."

"Okay."

"We'll find 'em." Richard assured him. "They gotta be on this road--Charlee, how's he doing?"

"So far so good, I think."

"Hang in there, dog," said Richard. "Help's on the way."

"Yeah, hang in there, boy," Dane muttered over his shoulder with a quick glance at the stricken shepherd. Putting aside his fear of flying, or at least trying to, Dane prayed like he'd never prayed before that Arnold would survive…and his friends were safe.

Jeremy stared out the large picture window, organizing his thoughts, when he noticed his and Leslie's reflection. For a second he didn't recognize the dirty and disheveled face of the boy in the glass. He looked scared. And it reminded him of a recurring thought. What had it been like for the people aboard the doomed airliners that slammed into the World Trade Center Towers? Is this what they felt? Not just the terror, but having no choice. No way out. No deciding in their own fate. Looking out the windows of those two airplanes, seeing how low they were to the city, did they perhaps know, they would never see their families again. Never see their children grow. Never see and do the ordinary, mundane things that they had done only days or hours ago. Death was but minutes away. Is this what evil tries to do, he thought? Take your life, your loved ones, your very soul?

Where was God in all of this, he wondered?

Jeremy felt trapped and he knew he was rapidly running out of time. But he still had a choice, he reasoned. And he wouldn't give up until his final breath, if that's what it took to save everyone. Then he had another thought. The tension and animosity between Shazuko and Spear--could he somehow use that--pitting them against each other?

Jeremy reached up and gently touched, wiping away a smudge on Leslie's cheek. They stared into each other's eyes, searchingly, until he said to her in a determined tone, "I'm not gonna be a victim here," he declared. "None of us are."

She returned his gaze with a confused, concerned expression, and then watched him rise to his feet.

"Sit down," Shazuko ordered.

"You seem to have some powerful enemies out there," Jeremy said, looking down at her.

Shazuko stood and with a deadly gaze said softly, "Sit...down."

Jeremy glared back at her through gritting teeth and said, "Make me!"

Surprised, but unamused by his defiance, she delivered a quick blow to his stomach. Jeremy stumbled backward into Leslie where she broke his fall, then crumpled to the floor, clutching his abdomen, gasping and wheezing for air. Shazuko turned her back on the two, conferring with Spear.

"What are you doing?" Leslie whispered to him in a terrified tone.

Jeremy labored to speak between breaths. "Trying to…save us."

It was several minutes before Jeremy could stand. When he finally struggled to his feet, he began pulling out drawers in the small galley.

Shazuko turned and said, "If you're looking for a weapon or something…"

Jeremy ignored the woman, but Leslie couldn't.

"…You won't find it."

He kept looking. That's when he spotted a small fire extinguisher mounted on the wall, just off the kitchenette, out of sight. He thought, it worked once before.

"Sit down," Shazuko barked, "before I hurt, *her*."

Jeremy stopped and returned to the couch beside Leslie. She clutched his hand tightly in hers, looking directly at Shazuko and said, "You can't get away with this."

Shazuko ignored her.

Jeremy baited her. "Don't waste your breath on her, this one's not too bright?"

Jeremy waited but Shazuko refused to play his game.

"I'm not going to let you hurt any of us," Jeremy finally said, his words energized with grit.

The Asian woman merely smiled at him and replied, "You don't have much choice."

Jeremy's eyes shifted outside to the passing scenery. Cruising along the highway that skirted Lake Michigan Jeremy watched with detached interest the endless expanse of shoreline battered by the onslaught of crashing whitecaps. In the hazy distance he spotted the familiar twin towers of the Mackinaw Bridge and muttered to himself, "What would Dirk Pitt do?"

"What--who?" Leslie asked him, unfamiliar with his favorite Clive Cussler character.

Elmo stared at the henchman standing over them. The moment his attention strayed he nudged Matthew's ribs. The boy looked and Elmo cocked his head toward the picture window across from them and whispered, "The Bridge."

Matthew looked, along with the others.

"Hey, you," Whitehead called back to the surviving operative. "Instruct the kiddies that their silence is requested when we get to the bridge toll booth. Remind them of what will happen to any one of them if they try anything cute--like calling out for help."

"I think they understand," the brute sneered, glaring down at the group of frightened faces. "But just in case they don't, you two the blond look-a-likes, lower those blinds!"

Matthew and Travis stood apprehensively, reached over and each pulled on a dangling cord of the opposite windows, lowering both blinds.

"We're coming up to the bridge," Spear announced loudly, then ordered, "just in case those two get any ideas of attracting someone's attention, close those blinds!"

"You heard him," Shazuko snapped at the anxious pair.

Mackinac Bridge Authority

St .Ignace, Michigan

Steven Armstrong had been director of operations with the Mackinac Bridge Authority overseeing the daily operation of the bridge for the last thirty years or so. Retirement was unthinkable. He loved his job. From the small command center located at the toll plaza in St. Ignace on the Upper Michigan peninsula side, he and his assistant could monitor bridge conditions via an array of sensors embedded in the bridge's superstructure, along with weather conditions from instruments also strategically placed on the bridge. An observation platform in the way of a console housing a bank of eight live-feed bridge cams, including one for the National Weather Service's live Doppler regional and local NEXRAD radar, provided a complete visual display of all traffic and conditions. And today's high winds definitely warranted close monitoring. If necessary, Armstrong knew he could close the bridge altogether. Rare, but not unusual for him to do so.

"How we lookin' Andy?" the slimly built man with short gray hair asked his assistant. Coming into the operation center, a mug of steaming black coffee in each hand, he paused, looking out the large window. Like looking down the length of a long runway, the twin steel support towers in the distance rose some five hundred feet above the sparsely traveled four lanes like two massive sentinels.

Seated before the bank of live monitors, the portly assistant with dark hair and mustache replied, "That was one helluva storm yesterday. It's good to be back up and running again. Traffic's low, so far. The winds are holding at twenty-eight miles per hour, gusts clocked at thirty-two. However, they've been steadily climbing for the past hour. Currently we've resumed a wind warning, not a wind escort condition, but have a look at this."

"Here…have some coffee."

"Thanks, boss," Andy replied, exchanging a sheet of paper for one of the mugs, continuing his briefing. "I've alerted all personnel to be on their toes, conditions and speeds electronically posted for all drivers to see, and *that* is the latest forecast and wind advisory from the National Weather Service. …You think we'll be able to remain open today?"

Armstrong scanned the figures carefully, then glanced at the wall clock, noting the time and spoke from his years of experience. "We're gonna try. I'd hate to be shut down two days in row."

"That'd be a first."

"Yes it would, Andy," he replied, his eyes still absorbed in the figures. "But we'll do whatever safety dictates...says here the winds are expected to go back up, possibly to severe. Let's keep a close watch on things, shall we? I'm gonna give Rick a call at the main office. I'll be at my desk. I'd like updates every five minutes."

"You got it, boss."

Spear continued maneuvering his 30-foot motorcoach along the churning Lake Michigan shoreline on US 2 until it moved inland, merging with Interstate 75 where he turned and headed south. He glanced at Whitehead's motorcoach through his side mirror, then put his sights on the Mackinaw Bridge ahead. "When we get to the toll--"

"I have it well under control, Mr. Spear, thank you," Shazuko irritably cut him off.

Spear bristled as he gripped the wheel, anxiously anticipating the moment he would kill the annoying Asian woman.

"For the duration," Shazuko glared at Leslie and Jeremy, "you two are to remain seated. Do you understand me?"

Leslie's nod and nervous stare was the most she could muster for a response while Jeremy's eyes deliberately ignored Shazuko altogether, gazing past her, out front, through the panoramic windshield. Ahead and fast approaching was the Mackinaw Bridge, its iconic white twin towers soaring high over the roadway. Jeremy's mind raced for ideas. If the high winds don't prevent them from crossing, he was going to make his move. He'd wait until they got to the bridge, past the toll booth--past the point of no return, when it would be too late for Spear to turn around. Was he being foolishly risky with all their lives? He was fast running out of options, he kept thinking. He had about a minute left, he figured.

Still gripping Leslie's hand, Jeremy squeezed it lightly. She turned and silently met his eyes. From them she knew he was going to do something. Though it terrified her, she trusted him. They both nervously watched the traffic through the panoramic windshield. It was light and cars were still apparently being allowed to cross, streaming ahead and converging at the open tolls, like people flowing through the gates at a football stadium before a game. The motorcoach slowed to a crawl. There were several cars ahead of them in line. Jeremy craned his neck, looking out the back window. They were boxed in. It was now or never, he thought. He squeezed Leslie's hand again, then let it go, bracing himself.

"Hey Spear," he bellowed. "You do know what she's gonna do, don'tcha?"

"Silence!" Shazuko snapped, trying to keep things calm.

The motorcoach lurched forward.

"Think about it…after she's killed us--"

"Shut him up!" Spear yelled.

"I told you to be quiet!"

"Then she'll kill *you*! Just how *stupid* are you anyway?"

"For the last time--"

"I can handle this!" Shazuko shrieked at him before leaping to her feet.

"Disrespects you--cuts you off--walks all over you, *like a door mat!*"

"One more word out of you," Shazuko cooed as she stood over Jeremy and Leslie waving her gun threateningly. "And I will shoot her."

For effect Shazuko looked directly at Leslie with her cold, empty eyes. Though she saw fear in the young girl's own eyes, her subtle expression was the same as Jeremy's. Quiet defiance. And that enraged her. How she wanted to kill them both right there--yet she knew to do so in such close proximity to the tolls would be risky. Perhaps once they have cleared them…yes…perhaps that would be advisable, her twisted mind thought. For the moment she needed to keep them under control!

"That might draw a lot of attention, don'tcha think?" Jeremy guessed, looking up at her.

It had become a standoff. Shazuko bristled behind an ever tightening jaw.

Spear brought the motorcoach to a jarring stop behind the last car in line before the toll booth, nearly knocking Shazuko off her feet. He slipped the gear into park and leaped from his seat. He roared at Jeremy, grabbing him, his muscled elbow knocking Leslie aside, yanking him up from the seat. "I'm gonna enjoy puttin' a bullet in your head kid!"

Shazuko intervened, grabbing his arm and spat, "We haven't time for this, get back in your seat!"

Face to face with a trained, professional assassin, Jeremy leaned into his ear and whispered, "See."

Spear couldn't believe he was actually listening to this boy. He knew what Jeremy was doing and reacted violently, shoving him backward into the galley cabinetwork where he fell backward to the floor. Leslie dropped to his side, anxiously kneeling beside him.

Spear returned to the driver's seat.

"Get behind me," Jeremy whispered to Leslie, grimacing through the pain, stealing a glance at the fire extinguisher above them on the wall.

She flashed him a quizzical expression.

"Get around behind me!" he sputtered urgently under his breath to her, positioning himself for the moment he could pounce for it.

CHAPTER FORTY-ONE

"What are those?" Charlee gushed over her headset breaking through the muffled drone of the turbine and whooping rotor blades overhead.

"It's the Mackinaw Bridge and those are her twin support towers," Richard replied.

"Haven't you ever seen a bridge before?" asked a surprised Dane, his eyes focused on the distant suspension bridge.

"Yes, I've seen a bridge before!" Charlee replied testily. "But never one *that big*. Are we going to go over it?"

Richard didn't immediately answer her. His eyes and his mind were focused on both the road below and the bridge ahead in the distance. Finally, "…Not sure, maybe,"

Dane was equally absorbed, glancing back and forth, from the massive distant structure, to the radio in his lap, hoping for a change in status, everywhere but frighteningly downward. Dane had seen the bridge a million times growing up, but never like this, and never from this height. Below it, and spread out as far as the eye could see, whitecaps speckled the endless blue expanse, crawling their way southward across the straits.

The year was 1884 when it was determined that year-round service across the Straits of Mackinac by boat was a failure. So an alternate route through Michigan had to be found. The inspiration for the five-mile-long Mackinaw Bridge was the Brooklyn Bridge, which opened the year before in 1883.

In the beginning the idea languished for years during which other proposals were considered. Two ambitious projects were concepts for a floating tunnel while the other connected Michigan's two peninsulas through a series of bridges and causeways. Starting at Cheboygan, 17 miles southeast of Mackinaw City, the route would traverse northwest out over the water to Bois Blanc Island, Round Island, then to the southern tip of Mackinac Island and then on out across the channel to St. Ignace. Neither concept ever got off the ground. In 1923 a ferry service was established. Within a few years, traffic became so heavy that then Governor Fred Green ordered the State Highway Department to once again reexamine the feasibility of a bridge directly across the Straits. Some progress was made only to be eventually scrubbed. Then in 1934 the Michigan Legislature created the Mackinac Straits Bridge Authority, empowering it to investigate the feasibility of construction and financing, through the issuance of revenue bonds, of a suspension bridge.

Over the next 20 years, setbacks along the way continued to dog the project. Most notably was the projected cost: upwards of $32 million. In 1934 and 1936 the Federal Emergency Administration of Public Works was solicited for loans and grants for its construction. Despite the endorsement of the U.S. Army Corps of Engineers including late President Franklin D. Roosevelt, who favored the bridge, both applications were denied. Additional studies were then commissioned, from traffic, geologic, to ice and water currents. Finally, with the advent of the Korean conflict all progress on the bridge came to a stop. And in 1947 the State Legislature abolished the Mackinac Straits Bridge Authority, effectively killing the project. The future of the Mackinaw Bridge looked pretty bleak.

Supporters of the bridge were not discouraged. They established a citizens' committee in an effort through legislation to restore a bridge authority. By 1950 the legislation was enacted but came with a stipulation; the new Authority would be required to consult with three of the world's foremost long span bridge engineers and traffic consultants. And still the delays continued; primarily due to the Korean War causing a shortage of materials and a lack of investors.

The winds of fortune began to shift in the spring of 1953.

A private investment banker came on board, agreeing to manage a group of investment companies and underwrite the sale of the revenue bonds. Unfortunately, there were not enough investors due to a weakening money market. In an effort to sweeten the deal and make the bonds more appealing, the Legislature passed an act covering the annual $417,000 operating and maintenance cost of the bridge through gasoline and license plate taxes. Despite this added inducement the project faltered. But then, by late 1953, with an improving market, enough investors purchased the bonds and the project was finally ready to move ahead.

On May 7th, 1954 construction of the world's longest suspension bridge began. Mobilizing the largest bridge construction fleet of its day, the project employed a total workforce of engineers, workers at the bridge site, including quarries, shops, and mills of 11,350 people. Built over the wild and turbulent waters of the Straits, it used a total length of 42,000 miles of wire in the main cables at a diameter of 24 ½ inches, weighing in at 11,840 tons. There is 931,000 tons of concrete, 88,000 tons of steel, including a concrete roadbed weighing in at 6,660 tons, making it truly an amazing feat of engineering.

During its three-year construction, five men lost their lives.

The Mackinaw Bridge opened to traffic on November 1st, 1957.

Soaring out from the natural landscape of the upper and lower peninsulas of Michigan, the Mackinaw Bridge rose to its greatest height of two hundred feet at mid-span above the churning water. Like frozen giant behemoths, the twin support towers soared five-hundred and fifty-two feet into the cloudless blue sky, their shroud-like cables sweeping downward in a graceful arc, extending to the road deck.

"Hey! I gotta light--two of 'em in fact," Dane suddenly belted out. "Make that three!"

Richard said, "That's it. They're heading for the bridge and going across."

"But in what?" Dane uttered discouragingly, his eyes trained on the line of tiny vehicles at the toll entrance. "We still don't know."

"According to the tracks in the mud back there--gotta be two RV's--has to be," Richard replied as he shoved the cyclic stick forward, pushing the airspeed to the limit.

Spear pulled up to and stopped at one of the four southbound toll booths, only three of which were open due to the combination of light traffic and current weather conditions. Jeremy and Leslie heard the side window slide open, then voices. They held their breath for what seemed like an eternity the instant Shazuko pointed her Glock in their direction and said, "Not a peep from either one of you."

Seated shoulder to shoulder, Leslie glimpsed Jeremy's hand on the seat, out of Shazuko's sight, inching toward the small extinguisher on the wall. Anxiously tightening her grip on his other hand, she glared at Shazuko in an effort to distract her. "You use that on us and I'll scream my *guts out!*"

"Not if you're *dead!*" the ruthless woman replied matter-of-factly.

Richard began to ease back on the airspeed, slowly descending toward the bridge, leaving behind the pines and the hardwood forests that dotted the landscape below. The cabin swayed and rocked against sporadic gusts buffeting the aircraft. Charlee held onto her harness with a tightening grip while she tried to comfort Arnold with her other hand as he lay beside her on the seat. The German shepherd whimpered in pain with every jarring movement. She did her best to soothe him, despite her own intense fears as she peered downward. Cruising out over Lake Michigan, she grimaced painfully at the water below crawling up the shoreline, crashing in massive waves and spray. Glancing directly ahead at the parade of tiny cars moving slowly through the distant toll plaza, Richard abruptly spat into his headset microphone, "There, look. See 'em! How much you wanna bet…"

"Yeah, I see 'em," Dane said, reaching for a pair of binoculars at his feet, his finger feverously focusing the lens, finally blurting, "And there are two of 'em all right--wait a minute--I don't believe it…"

"What?"

"The second one…it looks just like the one from the campground. I'd bet my life on it!"

Richard said, "Can you see anything?"

"Yep…they're goin' through."

"You think it's them?" Charlee's strained voice broke in.

"It has to be."

"It is, look!" Dane replied after he lowered the binoculars and held up the radio.

"They're all lit," Richard noted, exchanging a stricken look with Dane. "It's them."

At about one hundred feet above the bridge, he immediately swung the helicopter into a wide arc flying parallel to it. With the roadway now off their left side, he began a slow descent toward it.

Spear slowly accelerated the motorcoach along the four-lane south approach to twenty mph, the speed the toll agent had advised. He checked his side mirror, making sure Whitehead was following in the same right-hand lane. They were almost home free, he thought. Get across the bridge, then to the farm to eliminate all the passengers, *including Shazuko*. Spear grinned privately to himself. He had no doubt her orders from the Board included killing *him*. It was an interesting deduction by the teenager. But he had no intention of allowing her to succeed. About to turn the tables on *her*, he was aware that she more than not, suspected it. No matter, he continued thinking. He wouldn't be caught off guard by her. She didn't even know the Colonel had left the Lodge hours ago, thanks to *his* loyal crew at the lodge. He abruptly lost his bemused expression as the taunting gusts, felt through the steering wheel in his hands, became more apparent, rocking the motorcoach.

Like the previous twenty-four-hour period, during which the extratropical cyclonic event or *weather bomb*, as it's been termed, descended over most of the northern part of the country and Canada, including Michigan's Upper Peninsula, the longest suspension bridge in the western hemisphere was once again coming under its brutal assault. Designed to move so as to accommodate changes in temperature, wind and weight, the main cables supporting the 104,400-ton steel superstructure began to groan under the strain. Far below great heaving waves lashed and battered the base of the two massive support piers. As the severity of the winds continued to increase, the center span of the road deck between the two towers began to actually move, pushed ever-so-slightly in the direction of the wicked onslaught. Of the four lanes, between the two towers, two northbound, two southbound, the inside lane of each was open steel grating. Gale force winds filtering up through them were beginning to create a particularly hazardous condition. In 1989 high winds gusting up through this steel grating actually lifted a Yugo compact car up and over the 36-inch-high railing, plunging it and its lone driver to the lake far below.

Richard descended the helicopter, leveling off at two-hundred feet, cruising alongside the bridge at road level. They were behind and just close enough for them to easily see the two motorcoaches traveling among a caravan of other cars.

"Can you see anything?" Richard asked.

Dane focused the binoculars, scanning the pair. "The blinds are closed. I can't see crap--can you get closer?"

Richard shook his head in frustration, his eyes darting between the instruments and the looming bridge off to his left, support cables whizzing past them. "I'm already breaking FAA regs."

Dane lowered the glasses. "What're we gonna do? Once they exit the bridge on the other side we're gonna loose 'em. And if they split up..."

Charlee hastily unclipped her harness and leaned over the seat into the cockpit, pleading, "Stop them! Can't we stop them?"

"On the bridge?" Richard sputtered back, his eyes taking in the whole scene while his mind raced for ideas.

"It might be our only chance," Dane uttered in a desperate tone. "Between the two towers, where the main support cables dip in the center."

"You want me to land? I can alert the state police--"

"And what're they gonna do? C'mon, you saw what they did back there!"

Charlee gasped, "Listen you two--he's my brother--I won't lose him now!"

"Richard, they have your son and my friends!"

"I could cause an accident--get 'em all killed--goddamn it!" Richard snapped, the complexity of the situation straining even his skills. But this was pushing the limits and he had only seconds to determine what to do.

"They're approaching the first tower," Dane announced, focusing the binoculars.

Richard said, "Charlee, get back there and buckle in!"

"What're you gonna do?" she asked.

"Break about a dozen more FAA rules!"

Andy's casual sighting of a helicopter captured by one of the bridge cams at first didn't raise any red flags in his mind, until, that is, it appeared to be moving in *closer*. He abruptly straightened in his chair, craning his neck over the console, trying to spot it in the distance near one of the towers. Unable to see it clearly the heavy man grunted to his feet, reached for a nearby drawer and pulled out his binoculars. "What the--hey boss! …You better have a look at this!"

When Armstrong came into the room he found Andy standing at the large observation window, absorbed at something through the binoculars, muttering to himself.

"Problem--an accident?" he asked gravely.

"Nope, take a look," Andy said, handing him the glasses.

"Where--what?"

"Off to the right side of the bridge, near the first tower."

It took him a moment to focus them, then, "…Is that a heli--? What's he doing?"

Sweeping the telescopic sight of the binoculars along the steady stream of traffic flowing slowly along in both directions, he caught sight of two large motorcoaches. Armstrong lowered the glasses and looked at the wind gauge. The electronic needle had been hovering at the twenty-eight mph mark for the past fifteen minutes. Then, in the span of only moments, both men watched in stunned disbelief as the wavering needle of the gauge began to slowly creep upward. They both held their breath.

….29 mph

….30 mph

….31 mph

….33 mph

….35 mph

An abrupt buzzing alarm snapped the two men out of their trance.

"I don't believe it," Andy spat.

Armstrong dashed for the control console slapping a large red button in the center activating the emergency toll suspension, essentially alerting all toll operators to the conditions and locking down the four southbound toll gates located on the St. Ignace side of the bridge. He then immediately lifted the phone receiver and pressed a single key. "…This is Armstrong, alert the State Police, quickly, I want all northbound traffic at Mackinaw City stopped from entering the bridge. …Yes, you heard me correctly. We have an emergency, do it--now!"

Whitehead was the first to spot the blue and white helicopter off to his right through the passenger window the moment it swooped down to eye level, about a hundred feet out. It was a peculiar sight as it moved in closer, separated by the thick vertical support cables fluttering by. It was close enough for him to see someone in the passenger seat staring back at him through a pair of binoculars. He watched as it quickly moved ahead toward Spear's motorcoach. The kids in the back saw Whitehead's distraction and wondered fearfully what was happening.

Dane gasped, looking over at Richard, "I don't believe it, it's him!"
"Who?"
"The creep who kidnapped my friends."
"--You see 'em--Whitehead?" Charlee sputtered.
"Yep."
"Okay," Richard said as he double-checked his instruments, preparing his next maneuver. "Let's let 'em know we're here. Hold on."

Leslie noticed Spear's attention repeatedly shifting from the road ahead to the right-side passenger window and nudged Jeremy's side. When he looked, Spear shouted to Shazuko.
"We got trouble!"

"Stay put," she ordered the two of them.

Shazuko stepped down into the stairwell of the door and peered out at the mysterious helicopter cruising alongside the bridge.

"One of *yours*?" the enforcer spat.

"No," she replied steadily studying the helicopter. "And it's not the police...what's he doing?"

"I don't know," Spear growled, gripping the wheel tighter. "But we'd better get off this bridge, fast."

"Stay within the speed limit," Shazuko barked. "We cannot afford to be stopped with all these kids."

Spear ignored her, accelerating the motorcoach, unaware of the torrential gusts raging up through the left-hand lane's open steel grates ahead of them. He moved into the left lane, passing other vehicles, approaching the first tower, and the open steel grates.

Elmo sensed something was happening and anxiously craned his neck to see what it was. Spying the distracted henchman, he saw his chance and leaped for the dangling blind cord. He yanked it and the blind snapped up and open. Before the henchman could react, Elmo caught a glimpse of the helicopter and suddenly blurted out, "Hey... look at that!"

The rest of the kids snapped to attention and could see it too. The henchman, about to dash back to close the blind instead spun around and looked, spotting too the strange helicopter. He quickly moved up and stood in the stairwell of the door and frowned angrily. "What's going on--who the hell is that, cops?"

Whitehead grinned knowingly, saying nothing, gunning the accelerator and following Spear, steering unaware into the left-hand lane and disaster.

Armstrong watched in sickening, stunned disbelief as the wind gauge needle on the console quickly crawled around the dial to fifty-six mph and hovered there. He grabbed the binoculars again, looking toward the hapless traffic near the center of the massive bridge, including two huge motorcoaches and muttered under his breath, "Almighty God!"

Great massive air currents enveloped the bridge, ripping across the roadway, tugging and pushing at the parade of vehicles creeping their way across. The instant the heavy duty tires of Spear's motorcoach rolled over the steel grating, just after passing beneath the first tower, the undercarriage sang out a monotonous hum. A violent dance ensued from the wind bursts screaming up through the grates. The 63,000 pound motorcoach was an unwilling partner as she began to minutely rock and sway in protest. Jeremy and Leslie were still seated on the floor, their shoulders bumping with every jolt, Jeremy's arm resting on a bench seat, his hand poised near the fire extinguisher, all the while his eyes watching Shazuko. He noticed her cool, stone-faced exterior was beginning to crack. Gripping the edge of her seat, her other hand still clutching the Glock, a bead of sweat appeared on her temple. The motorcoach abruptly lurched to one side, causing the woman to awkwardly stagger on her feet and, uncharacteristically, wince in fear.

In that instant Jeremy laid his hand on the extinguisher.

Shazuko ignored her captives and turned to Spear as he worked the steering wheel, playing tug-of-war with Mother Nature.

Shazuko snapped at him, "Slow down!"

"Would you like to drive?" Spear retorted, working overtime controlling the heavy vehicle.

The woman shoved the Glock into her shoulder holster and stood fast, grasping the passenger seat for support. They both kept glancing at the helicopter still flying alongside the bridge. Again, the motorcoach rocked sideways, forcing Shazuko from her feet to the floor with a gasping chirp. Leslie cried out as she and Jeremy rolled to one side. He then suddenly grabbed the extinguisher, ripped it from the wall, pulled the safety tab and awkwardly leaped to his feet. From the overhead mirror the sudden movement caught Spear's roving eye and he yelped at Shazuko, "--HEY!"

Shazuko staggered back to her feet, instinctively grabbing the Glock from her holster, but she was too late; her face met with an explosion of dry chemicals clouding her eyes, mouth and nostrils. She cried out, waving her hands in front of her like a shield, while the gun dropped to the floor, along with her knees, in a thud. Jeremy continued unleashing the entire contents of the small canister, bathing the woman in a white powdery cloud while she coughed, gagging for air until there was none for her lungs to take in. Spear could only watch helplessly, cursing out as he literally had his hands full. Jeremy threw the canister aside just as Shazuko's writhing body fell over in a heap. As she lay there wheezing, Leslie staggered to Jeremy's side, groping his arm for support.

Spear took his angry eyes from the road, glaring up into the mirror at Jeremy, still cursing him, momentarily unaware of a car moving out front into his lane. When he saw it, he suddenly spun the wheel, swerving, trying to miss its rear fender. Leslie grabbed onto Jeremy as the two of them lost their balance, tumbling to the floor. Like a slow-motion death knell, the motorcoach struck the car's rear side with a dull crunch, sending it sliding toward oncoming traffic. Spear lost control of the massive motorcoach, desperately spinning the wheel in the opposite direction in an effort to steady it. The vehicle lurched up onto the foot-high curb railing with an explosion of sparks underneath, until one of the wheels caught something, slamming it sideways. Jeremy clawed at the couch and window ledge, holding on, catching a fleeting glimpse of the bridge railing and vertical support cables streaming past the window, and far below, the churning white water. Jerking to the left, pushed by the howling winds strafing the road deck, the motorcoach's right side wheels abruptly left the pavement. Leslie screamed as the cabin began tilting wildly. Jeremy grabbed onto her and yelled to hold on. Covering his head along with Leslie's as they went over, he did his best, shielding her with his body as they slammed against the cabinets.

Chaos ensued.

Cupboard doors swung outward and drawers slid open, raining their contents everywhere in a frenzied avalanche. Spear, not easily moved, watched in dismay as the roadway out front pitched over sideways; the pavement smashing into his left-side window. Shazuko, barely coherent, could do nothing to help herself as her body slid, then slammed against the galley cabinetry in a loud hail of loose objects.

The motorcoach careened downward against the pavement in a thunderous crunch, sliding sideways against the embedded road grate, metal screaming against metal. Shazuko felt a rumbling through her hands and gasped the moment her eyes focused, through the confusion and chemical residue, at the sliding road grate screeching just beneath her. Her body had come to rest atop the large plate glass window. As she rose up on her hands and knees, staring with gaping terror, the last thing her satin blue eyes beheld was her own disheveled ghostly reflection staring up at her. An instant later the picture window exploded in her face. Shazuko's authoritative voice was drowned out in a gurgling, sickening shriek as she was sucked down through the grate like a meat grinder; first her delicate hands with the exquisitely manicured acrylic nails, then her smooth, slender forearms, followed by the rest of her body, torn apart in blood splattering black fabric, flesh, and body parts.

Startled drivers in both the north and southbound lanes scattered in a panic, screeching to a stop in skewered angles trying to avoid others the instant the motorcoach went over onto its side, sliding and finally coming to a rest in the center of the two lanes, a crimson trail in its wake.

Dane gasped, "Did you see that!"

"Oh, no," Charlee cried over her headset, leaning in the cock-pit, watching, too, in horror at the unfolding scene below them.

As Richard maneuvered the helicopter into an ascending arc over the center of the bridge between the two massive towers, the Baddog passed beneath them. He spun her around into the raging gale and immediately came to a seventy-foot hover above the roadway.

Whitehead was intrigued by what was happening ahead of him; the thought of seeing blood aroused him. As he slowed, threading the Baddog through the myriad of stopped cars, he and the hench-man watched in silence, coming up to and easing right past the motorcoach lying on its side like a dead dinosaur.

The henchman said, "Better keep going."

Whitehead nodded his intention, saying, "Looks like our plans have changed."

The henchman shrugged and said, "It's your call. Why not just dump 'em at the farm and leave'em?"

"I got a better idea. Besides we may need some hostages. Spear is supposed to meet up with the Colonel this afternoon. I say we join 'em. Can you fly a helicopter?"

"Yeah, sure. Why?" the henchman lied.

"While the Colonel's busy we'll borrow his."

"Where is it?"

"You'll see," Whitehead toyed with the henchman, revealing nothing more.

The professionally trained assassin knew he was dealing with an amateur. For the moment he'd allow Whitehead to think whatever pleased him. At the proper time he would kill him.

The moment Whitehead looked up at the frightened faces of the kids reflected in the mirror above his head, the corners of his mouth curled in his trademark malicious grin.

The kids had leaped to their feet, their faces hugging the glass of the big window, looking back, straining to see. They winced in horror, catching a fleeting glimpse of the overturned motorcoach. One of the twins cried out Jeremy's name. It was Travis, who then bolted over to the door in a panic, struggling to open it. Dylan went for Travis to stop him. The boy fought him off until the burly assassin jumped back into the cabin where he grabbed both boys by the arm and whirled them around and back onto the couch, frightening the other kids into frozen submission. Screaming hysterically, Travis's face was wretched in agony as he spat through tears and spit, "JEREMY!--JEREMY--!"

Whitehead snapped, "Shut that kid up!"

Matthew, his own face wretched with terror and his eyes reddened with tears, swarmed around his twin, gushing over and over, "It'll be all right--it'll be all right."

Lynn was overcome. She'd never seen either of the twins cry like this before. Once when Travis fell off his bike and skinned both knees and his chin, he wailed for maybe a few moments. Then he wiped the blood away with his tee shirt, got back on his bike and took off. This was different. The fear was for Jeremy and what was happening to their older brother. She then couldn't help noticing her own brother. Eric sat silently, apart from everyone else, in a single padded lounge chair, staring at the floor. Unaware of the approaching henchman, a moment before he dropped the blind, Lynn caught sight of a helicopter hovering over the center of the bridge and slowly descending. The brief glimpse gave her a surge of hope the moment she wiped her eyes.

"My God, I don't believe it," Armstrong sputtered in jaw-dropping disbelief standing at the observation window, nearly dropping the binoculars. "An RV just flipped over…and now it looks like that helicopter out there…I think it's going to land!"

CHAPTER FORTY-TWO

"The other RV just went under us!" Charlee exclaimed over her headset, still leaning into the cockpit and pointing wildly at the Baddog motorcoach threading its way through the chaos below. "See it? There it goes."

"I see him," Richard said, glancing at it briefly, fleeing the scene. Like a jet stream tearing across the bridge deck at right angles, the winds taunted and played with the helicopter. Every ounce of his skill and attention was in full throttle and high alert as Richard's eyes danced across the instruments, flashing over to the bridge's thick support cables, a scant 30 yards from the tail rotor, and then to the chaotic scene below them, determining where to set down--if he even could at all. In full command of the Bell 222, his hands firmly gripped the controls.

"And there he goes," Dane yelped, watching it too, then snapping his head in the direction of the overturned motorcoach he gulped to Richard, "We gotta get down there, if the kids are in that one--"

"Along with their armed abductors--Dane, listen to me. I can't land her on the deck, it's too dangerous, which means I can't leave the helicopter. You'll be on your own. I'll bring her down light on the wheels but don't move until I say so. Charlee you stay put. This is gonna be damn dangerous!"

Dane nodded, sucking in a deep breath as he felt the helicopter begin to slowly descend.

Richard spotted an opening.

Keeping the nose of the helicopter into the wind he eased the Bell as close as he safely could to the overturned motorcoach. Concentrating, he could feel the aircraft through his body, while his eyes and his mind choreographed where he could set down with regard to the proximity of the myriad of cars and their occupants below, some of them clinging to the outside of their vehicles in the gale. Richard cursed the instant he spotted two men dashing beneath him, running toward the stricken motorcoach. Coming down to eye level, the underside of the motorcoach facing him, Richard released the wheels from their interior bay compartments and gently brought the helicopter to the pavement. The tires bounced, then settled lightly.

Richard said, narrowing his eyes. "Okay, I'll hold her here."

Dane nodded apprehensively as if to say, whatta I do if…

"Hold on," Richard said, reaching into the side pocket of his door and held out a stubby .45-caliber Warthog handgun. Uncertain if it was a good idea--the last thing he wanted was the boy in a gun fight--but, he quickly reasoned, he was left with little choice. "Take this, it could make the difference. That's the safety there--ever fire a gun before?"

"Recently," Dane replied pointedly shoving the weapon into the side pocket of his biker pants.

"I'm going with you," Charlee spouted at them.

"No you're not!" the two of them bellowed at her in unison.

Dane pushed opened the door as the gale force wind pushed back. He squeezed out, securing it behind him, and scrambled in the direction of the overturned motorcoach, the loose hem of his shirt flapping at his waist.

Richard suddenly felt a whoosh of air and snapped his head around just as the passenger cabin door banged closed. He yelled repeatedly after her, but she was too fast. All he could do was hold the Bell steady, watching helplessly as Charlee bolted after Dane.

Jeremy's head floated, his thoughts swirling in a disoriented state for several moments following the sliding rollover. Once the inside of the cabin had settled and stopped raining debris, he stirred, then groaned. Every part of his body ached as he rose up on his elbows, then rolled over on his side and off of Leslie. They were covered in seat cushions, supplies, kitchenware, utensils and canned goods; everything in the motorcoach that hadn't been secured away in cupboards or nailed down. He kicked at, then pushed away several heavy items including a large padded chair. Leslie joined him, taking several exhaustive breaths as she sat up next to him, brushing away the remaining debris. Looking around quickly, they had ended up near the rear of the coach, protected by the close quarters of the narrow hallway.

Taking Leslie's hand, Jeremy said, "Are you all right?"

"I think so."

He began helping her to her feet. "C'mon, let's get outta here!"

Charlee caught up to Dane, grabbing his arm.

"What're you doing?" he turned and barked at her.

"He's my only brother."

He clutched her hand. "C'mon."

The girl suddenly recoiled in revulsion and cried out, "OH GOD!"

A few feet in front of them, partially embedded in the steel grating of the roadbed, was the remains of a bloody hand torn from its arm at the wrist. Two of the slender fingers had been ripped off leaving three blood-spattered digits, Shazuko's acrylic nails still intact. Their eyes followed a bloody trail leading the fifty yards or so up to the overturned motorcoach.

Dane too winced in revulsion at the shocking sight "Unless your brother or my friends had their nails done recently--it's somebody else."

Dane gritted his teeth, grabbing Charlee's hand. They raced toward the overturned motorcoach where two men were surveying the damage, determining how best to scale the undercarriage to the door now facing skyward and a midmorning sun, when one of them turned.

Dane shouted at them, "My friends are in there, help me up."

Without hesitation the two men laced their fingers together. Dane planted his foot, gripped their shoulders and hoisted himself upward. They grunted under his weight just as he snatched the edge and pulled his muscled body effortlessly up and over. Scrambling to his knees, he heard a muffled scream.

Horrified, Leslie turned away, burying her face in Jeremy's neck. He looked over her shoulder, then down at the shattered picture window and grimaced. Resting on the trailing edge of the frame was a bloody tangled heap barely recognizable as Shazuko's willowy legs, still sheathed in her tight-fitting black suit. One of her black shoes was missing, violently shaken loose, exposing a small, delicate, lifeless foot. Wide-eyed, Jeremy then looked up toward the front. The driver's seat, now sideways, its seat belt dangling in the gale streaming in through the shattered windshield, was empty.

The two of them suddenly jerked out of their skins.

Dane banged on the door a second time, cupping his hands together. "Leslie? Jeremy? Is that you?"

"YES!" came Jeremy's muted reply from inside. "...HOLD ON!"

Jeremy snatched one of the overturned lounge chairs from a pile and quickly positioned it beneath the door over his head. He propped himself atop the seat reaching for the lock and unlatched it. Twisting the knob and shoving it upward, Dane caught the door and swung it open hard; the stainless steel handle clattered against the siding. He peered down inside, completely forgetting the .45 wedged in his waistband, then remembering it, reached behind himself poised to grab it.

"You guys okay?"

Jeremy nodded up at him briskly. "Here, help Leslie…c'mon," he said to her.

Dane's tense hand relaxed and he relinquished further thought of the .45.

Leslie flinched, her eyes avoiding the bloody scene at their feet. Climbing gingerly onto the cushionless chair which Jeremy steadied for her, she eagerly reached up for Dane's waiting hands. With Jeremy's assist, Dane took her hands, hoisting Leslie upward through the open door into the gale. She gasped at the torrential winds howling through the bridge's thick support cables, then at the tangle of cars on the road deck and the people milling around them. Hovering in the distance a few feet above the road deck, she noticed the blue and white helicopter. She leaned over Dane's shoulder, steadying herself in the buffeting winds, sweeping aside her long hair and holding it, looking, too, for Jeremy as Dane shouted down inside the empty doorway.

"C'mon Jeremy, let's go, get your ass up here, whaddya doing?"

"Wait a minute!" he shouted back.

Jeremy's eyes flashed across the destruction, searching until they spotted the gray fishing tube. Broken glass crunched beneath his tennis shoes as he awkwardly made his way over to it, the capped end poking out from under the rubble of a smashed entertainment center that had come loose. It was at that moment he remembered where the flash drive and smartphone were.

"Oh Jesus," he moaned at the thought of what he had to do next. He forced his gaze down at Shazuko's blood-soaked torso and grimaced at the outline of the small portable storage unit and smartphone in the pocket of her pantsuit.

"Jeremy, whaddya doin' down there?--takin' a coffee break--c'mon, c'mon!"

"Wait a minute I said!"

The agonizing vision in his stressed mind of the Baddog vanishing with his brothers and the other kids was tearing at his insides. He had to focus and work quickly. He inhaled deeply several times as if he were about to free dive into hell. Kneeling down beside what was left of the Asian woman, the beige carpet soaked in her blood, he reached out, grimacing through tight eyes. His index and middle finger gingerly felt the flash drive beneath the fabric along her hip. Moving up to the open slit of her pocket, it felt like he was reaching into a jar of spiders. Jeremy winced as his fingers slipped inside, probing until they hit pay dirt. He grimaced, sucking air through his gritting teeth at the warmth his fingers detected as they clamped down on the small unit before pulling it out. "…Oh God this is creepy."

Inhaling deeply, he went for the smartphone and pulled it out, then thankfully stuffed them both down into his cargo shorts pocket.

He abruptly appeared at the overhead door, shoving the tube up in Dane's face. "Here, take this." Handing it off to Leslie, Dane reached back down, glaring at his friend. "What're you waiting for, Christmas?"

Jeremy was about to reach up and take Danes waiting hands when he took a final haunting glance at the empty driver's seat.

"Now Jeremy, now would be good!"

Reaching out, Dane hauled him up into the bright sun and howling wind strafing the road deck and said, nodding at the tube in Leslie's hands, "*That's* what you were lookin' for?"

"I'll explain later--let's go!"

With the help of the two men, the three climbed down from the overturned motorcoach, bid their thanks with handshakes and dashed to the hovering Bell. Wheels still extended, Richard brought the helicopter back down to the deck. The moment Charlee, Leslie and Jeremy climbed into the passenger cabin, Dane secured the door behind them. Charlee immediately checked on Arnold while Dane settled into his seat dropping the .45 weapon into his door's side pocket. Richard's eyes quickly swept across the instrument panel, then the vicinity around the Bell and announced boldly, "All right, everyone, buckle in and hold on!"

Ramping up the power, immediately lifting the helicopter from the road deck, everyone watched breathlessly as the snarled vehicles dropped away sharply, followed smoothly by the massive steel structure of the south tower in the distance, rising above it, replaced by a pristine blue sky.

"Say again?" the 911 female operator repeated with unusual dismay after listening to the excited voice on the other end of the line. "You have an overturned RV and a what?"

Armstrong didn't miss a beat. "I repeat: we appear to have a one-vehicle accident, an overturned RV at the center of the bridge and a helicopter landing--no, wait a minute…he just took off!"

She said, "Can you see the call numbers on the aircraft?"

Andy hadn't budged from the large window where he'd been standing with the binoculars glued to his eyes, observing the frightening drama unfolding. "Ahh, yeah, I can see 'em."

Armstrong said, "Read 'em off."

"Ahh, yeah, hold on…yeah…Zulu November Eight Five four."

"Zulu November Eight Five four," Armstrong repeated for the operator. "And it looks like he's heading south!"

Spear sprinted along the narrow walkway skirting the road deck, hoping to blend in as best he could with the chaos. An emergency ambulance, with lights and siren blaring, screamed past him toward the mayhem at the center of the bridge. He managed to make it off the bridge, pausing at the entrance of a packed parking lot when two police cruisers, their sirens wailing and lights flashing red and blue, sped past him. A moment later they were followed by the rhythmic beat of rotors slapping the air. Spear looked up, shielding his eyes against the sun and watched as the Bell roared overhead, flying southward. He then turned his attention back to the lot, smirking maliciously at his pick of cars.

"He's alive!" Jeremy gasped over the drone of the turbine the moment he saw Arnold sprawled on a beach towel on the rear passenger seat.

"How's he doing?" asked Leslie in equal but thankful amazement.

Charlee squeezed in between the two of them. "The bleeding stopped…but I--I'm not sure how he's doing. I mean, he looks so weak."

Jeremy uneasily shifted his attention from the injured German shepherd to the sparsely populated ribbon of highway whizzing beneath them at 110 knots, his eyes desperately searching for the Baddog. He snatched and donned a spare headset exclaiming wildly like a madman, "We've lost 'em--they're gone! Did you hear me? The RV's nowhere in sight down there. Whoever you are, do something!"

Richard replied calmly, "I am. Dane, anything on your radio?"

"No--nothing."

Jeremy bolted across to the opposite passenger seat, kneeling and shoving his head into the cockpit. "The radio isn't working. I put it in Ian's backpack."

Dane turned and replied through a strained set of eyes. "You're sure? The GPS thing still does, the little proximity lights on mine still work. That's how we found you."

"But we couldn't raise you."

Jeremy was at a loss, then he sputtered, "Well, they were only ten bucks--plus ours got wet--maybe that's why." Jeremy then turned his attention to the pilot. "Look, I don't know who you are but you gotta find 'em. They have my brothers and friends."

"Including my son," Richard shot back.

"What--your son?"

"Charlee and Dylan are my kids. Jeremy, is it?"

"…Yes."

"Jeremy, they only have three choices, US 23, 31 or I-75. US 31 splits off of 75 up ahead--where are they heading?"

"I don't know."

Leslie donned the last headphone set and squeezed in beside Jeremy, listening.

"Well think! You must have heard something--have some idea."

"I tell 'ya I don't know."

"The farm--remember?" Leslie broke in.

"Oh yeah, that's right, someplace called the farm."

"Where?" snapped Richard.

"I dunno," Jeremy replied, his tone agitated, the frustration he felt growing. "The farm--that's all she called it. And she didn't say where it was, just somewhere on this side of the bridge where they…" Jeremy's voice abruptly trailed off.

"Where they, what?"

Jeremy hesitated the instant it dawned on him that they had in fact now crossed the bridge…and the Baddog RV was nowhere in sight.

"Goddamn it, kid, what?"

"I think they're gonna kill 'em," Jeremy answered solemnly.

"Who was driving?"

"His name is Spear."

"What happened to him?"

"I dunno that either. He disappeared from the RV after the crash."

"Who's driving the other one?"

"Creep by the name of Whitehead."

Richard went silent, his desperate eyes scanning the terrain below. They were beginning to cruise over the shimmering waters of Carp Lake, leaving both highways to split off. He could see them both in the distance, Interstate Highway 75 on his left, US 31 off to the right. Jeremy's own eyes began to well up. Then he frantically wiped the moisture away, his mind racing.

"Wait a minute, wait a minute, there was something else--when I was in the Colonel's office I saw a notation on his day planner. Today's date was circled and he had written on it, 'G T W Resort, ten a.m.'"

Richard's attention snapped back to the cockpit. "Wait--what did you say?"

"G T W Resort, ten a.m."

"No, before that, you said, the Colonel--*the* Colonel?"

"Yeah. The one and only."

Richard was dumbstruck. ". . . Are you sure?"

Jeremy said, "You know who I mean, don'tcha?"

"Yep. And I don't believe it."

"Believe it! I saw 'em with my own two eyes, and spoke with him--we all did. It was him all right!"

"I know where they're headed then," Richard replied emphatically.

Dane queried back. "G T W? Are you thinking the Grand Traverse World Resort?"

Richard nodded.

"Why head to the resort? What's there?"

Richards's headset crackled with static, then he uttered, "The end of the line."

"Hey look, I gotta light!" Dane suddenly shouted holding up the radio, a single LED light glowing.

The cabin erupted in cheers.

Richard pushed the cyclic over, changing course. "If they're in a hurry they'll more than likely be on seventy-five." With a flip of a switch on the avionics panel he activated his cell phone over his headset. They all listened as it chimed only once.

"Richard, where are you--is everyone all right?"

"Christine, we're fine. Listen, we're heading south over seventy-five, just left the bridge. Where are you?"

"I'm south of Gaylord. Where do you want to meet?"

Richard thought for a moment, his mind computing his speed in relation to Christine's, and her estimated distance from them, then answered her. "Christine, the Grand Traverse World Resort, isn't there a political function going on there today?"

"Yes, a political luncheon fund raiser--supposed to be a big deal."

"OH SHIT!" Jeremy suddenly blurted out with. "...That's right--I forgot."

"Hold on a moment Christine."

"My parents are gonna be there--all of 'em, in fact. They've all volunteered to help out at that thing today."

Richard thought, then said, "We haven't a moment to lose, Christine. We'll shoot for Indian River--we'll have to make the transfer quick."

"Roger, Indian River. How's your patient doing?"

"He's holding his own."

"Please be careful Richard--all of you."

"We will, see you soon."

Richard clicked off the connection and pushed the cyclic and the Bell's airspeed to the maximum limit.

The stage in the Governors' Hall ballroom was fully dressed with the exception of two lighting technicians climbing the scaffolding over Miles's head, adjusting several spotlights, while a handful of hotel staffers ran around like ants making last minute place setting arrangements. Miles stood at the podium holding out his hand, shielding his eyes against the intense glare. Dressed in a charcoal gray pinstripe with a blue stripe button-down shirt and red oxford tie, his collar bristled against his neck. Brought on by his makeup girl's unfinished business, the tissue paper kept chaffing his skin. Surveying the dozens of elegantly dressed tables throughout the ballroom, he cleared his throat, preparing his television voice. "Check, check, four score and seven years ago our fathers brought forth on this continent a new nation, conceived in liberty, and dedicated to the proposition that all men are created equal...how do I sound, Brian?"

The techs voice boomed over the sound system. "Okay Miles. That's perfect, take a break."

Miles resumed studying his notes on a clipboard set before him on the podium. Standing out front between two television cameras, their operators absorbed in conversation over their headsets, Carl, chewing on an unlit cigar, frowned at the floor. Absorbed in his own conversation over his wireless headset, he went silent, his eyes darting around the ballroom as he listened. A moment later he looked up at Miles with a relieved grin while shoving the cigar to the corner of his mouth. Checking his watch, he approached the young newscaster with an energized gaze. "We're actually ahead of schedule, the senator just landed. They're on the helipad upstairs, be down in just a few minutes. Odd thing, though."

"What's that?"

"The senator's security guy is late, never made it. No one knows where he is."

"Maybe he's out killin' someone."

Carl frowned playfully, shook his head, then said, "Now here's the plan. I'm waiting on word from the network if we're going to open the noon newscast with a live feed from here with Senator Toddhunter's announcement, followed by your interview with him."

"Noon?" Miles echoed glancing at his watch. "It's ten now. We gonna be ready?"

"Absolutely. Whatever the network wants to throw at us, we'll be ready."

The red warning light on the avionics panel blinked for only a second. But it was long enough to snag Richard's roving eye. He gazed at it for several moments then reached out, tapping it. Rather that light up again it remained dark. Other than the high-pitched whine from the turbine and the whoop, whoop, whoop of the rotors overhead, no one in the cabin spoke a word. Everyone's eyes were trained on the highway below. Traffic on the Interstate, mostly cars, trucks and

SUVs and the occasional RV, was light. But nowhere in sight was the behemoth Baddog motorcoach.

For a moment Leslie closed her eyes. When she opened them again she was looking down at her hands in her lap. Her dirty and broken nails reminded her of her last conversation with Lynn. The next time she was in Wolf's Head Bay to see Jeremy they were going to get together for a girl's afternoon out for lunch, then later, the works; she would treat Lynn to her first manicure and pedicure. The excited look on the young girl's face haunted her to tears.

Charlee's heart raced. She tried to calm herself, staring at the swiftly passing landscape below, but there was nowhere her thoughts could go for solace. She couldn't remember a time when she didn't worry about Dylan. Her eyes kept welling up, brought on by the thought that she might not ever see him alive again. She found herself gently stroking Arnold's side as the dog lay motionless, his eyes closed, his chest heaving gently. She gripped his paw and Arnold blinked, looking up at her.

Richard loosened his grip on the controls in an effort to stay alert. His emotions were ricocheting across the landscape of his mind. Out of the blue, he discovers a son and daughter he never knew, never saw grow up. Now, his son…still missing and being held against his will. Where was he?

Dane was so pissed off he could have chewed nails. He not only forgot his fear of flying, but he'd forgotten the radio as well for several moments. When he looked down at it in his lap, he saw the unthinkable. "Something's wrong," he blurted out over the mike system, his tense voice shattering the silence. He held it up. The one LED that had previously lit up had gone dark. Exasperation clouded his unshaven features as he looked at the others and said, "We've lost 'em again!"

Richard's eyes darted out across the landscape racing below them. "He knows we're after 'em."

"What if he's pulled off somewhere," Jeremy gushed in disbelief. "The farm! You gotta go back--do you hear me? You gotta go back!"

Richard suddenly pushed the cyclic over, changing course, departed the interstate and headed westward.

Jeremy shouted, "Go back around!"

"Where're you going--what're you doing?" Dane snapped looking at Richard.

"Trying to save those kids!" he said. His eyes ignored Dane as they scoured the other highway on the distant horizon that they were fast approaching. He clicked on the cell phone. The moment she answered he said, "Christine, change of plans."

Miles paused at the podium as instructed. "Camera one, give me a wide shot…yeah…just a bit more…hold it, yeah, right there. Good."

Bert Mather, news director, scanned the camera monitors from inside the TV mobile control room, a small van parked on a service road just outside a rear door of the Governors' ballroom. The electronics hummed as the young director, dressed in denim jeans, black Skechers and a black Def Leppard T-shirt, his short blond hair hidden beneath a baseball cap, looked over his clipboard, then adjusted his headset. He swiveled in his chair, consulting another similarly dressed technician seated beside him before he continued. "Okay camera two, tighten up on Miles ugly mug…yep, littttle more…yeah, right there, that's good, hold it. Okay, guys, that's it, stand by. …Carl? We're set here."

"An hour and forty-five minutes to show time, Miles" Carl said, coming up from behind. "And I just got the go-ahead from the top brass."

Miles spun around facing Carl, the whites of his teeth gleaming like a beacon from behind those tanned, chiseled features. "That's great news."

"And that's not all," Carl beamed. "For the icing on the cake, we'll be going national, both at noon *and* this evening with Brian Williams."

Miles's face continued to shine like a boy on Christmas morning spying the toy he'd been eagerly anticipated under the tree, just waiting to be unwrapped.

"And *you* wanted to go overseas!"

Miles deadpanned, "What *was I* thinking!"

"The senator said he's ready when we are."

Carl stopped chewing nervously on his cigar, nodded, then removed it from his mouth and used it like a pointer. "See over there in the corner? We have a second camera set up where you'll do your live interview with him on the noon broadcast following his speech."

"God, I love this job!" Miles sputtered jubilantly.

"C'mon, Sport. Take that tissue paper off and I'll introduce you to the senator."

"You were right, look!" Dane barked excitedly to Richard holding the radio aloft. The first LED light glowed red. A moment later a second one popped on, followed by a third. "We're closing in on 'em. Look around, does anyone see 'em?"

There were several anxious moments until Charlee, her face nearly pressing against the Plexiglas peering below at the rapidly passing highway, shouted, "Yes, I see 'em. There they are. Look up ahead!"

Jeremy, then Leslie, squeezed in beside her, spotting the Baddog motorcoach.

"Whatta we do now?" Leslie asked nervously.

"Talk to 'em. Let's try the radio again," Jeremy growled, leaning through the bulkhead into the cockpit. "Hand it to me."

Dane passed it to him and Jeremy began pressing down on the call button like an angry, anxious patient repeatedly calling his nurse.

The kids sat in a terrified cluster along the length of the long couch below the picture window. While Elmo kept watch on the henchman standing over them, the others averted their eyes from their menacing guard, too scared to look at him. Elmo's eyes drifted about the cabin looking for anything they might be able to use as a weapon or a means to escape. There wasn't much, nothing that he reasoned would stand up against an armed killer. Behind him he spotted, near the ceiling, a small panel with three large buttons; a green one marked, 'OPEN', a yellow one marked, 'STOP' and a red marked 'CLOSE'. He was wondering what they operated until his concentration was abruptly broken when the radio in Ian's backpack began buzzing. Elmo's eyes snapped wide open.

The henchman barked at the kids, "What's that?"

"What's what?" Elmo replied, feigning ignorance.

Whitehead heard it too, cocking his head at the henchman. "Is that a phone? Get it!"

The brute man stepped toward the kids, glaring down at the young Indian, his ears and malevolent dark eyes following the buzzing. "*Don't* make me take it from you."

Elmo swallowed while his eyes bore back into the henchman's. Reaching behind Ian, he unzipped the top of the backpack and grabbed the radio, handing it over to the henchman's large waiting hand.

"Give it here," said Whitehead.

The henchman stepped forward, passing it to Whitehead's open hand poised above his right shoulder. While watching the traffic ahead he pressed the talk key. "Hello Jeremy."

"You've nowhere to go. Stop and let the kids out and you can leave."

Whitehead's other hand clamped down tighter on the steering wheel while he scanned the vicinity in front of the motor coach, including the side mirror. He did a double take when a large helicopter in the distance flashed briefly in the mirror's field of vision. He pressed the talk button. "There you are."

Jeremy's voice crackled over the airwaves. "Let them go!"

"Or what, Jeremy? Whatta you gonna do?"

"I swear to God if you--"

"Swear to God, Jeremy? What God! You think he's gonna stop me? He can't any more than you can. So if I were you I'd *back off*, or I might just get so pissed that I'll pull over and have my friend here put a bullet in every one of their little heads. Whatta you think of that?"

Jeremy's face drained of color as he leaned back in his seat at a loss as to what he should do. His hand clutching the radio dropped to his lap as though he held a brick. He stared down at it, closing his eyes, tuning out the whine of the turbine, the rotor blades overhead biting the air and the sudden intrusion of a whistle through the headsets. His eyes opened sharply recognizing the main rotor chip detector. His head shot around peering into the cockpit scanning the avionics panel. He watched as Richard fussed with several switches, but the light remained solid.

Richard said, "Listen up everyone, we've gotta problem--I gotta set down."

"No you can't!" Jeremy shouted.

Richard said, "We have to."

"No!"

"Jeremy. I've no choice!"

Jeremy slammed his closed fist against his chest several times, crying out in anguish. "Nooo...we're gonna lose 'em--AGAIN!"

"If I don't land and check this out we could *fall* out of the sky. It'll take just a few minutes."

"They'll be gone in a few minutes! And if he shuts the radio off it's over--we'll never find 'em--never!"

Richard gripped the controls trying to stay focused, looking for a place to land. As the helicopter began to lose altitude Jeremy spun around, watching helplessly from the window the swiftly departing

Baddog below. Throwing off his headset, he turned his eyes upward at the open sky and screamed, "If you're not gonna help us then at least stop throwing us under the bus!"

"Where'd they go?" Whitehead barked at his companion. The hench-man peered out the large picture window and reported the helicop-ter appeared to be going down. The kids became alarmed while Whitehead's leering grin never seemed to leave his evil, injured face.

Slowly descending out of an ocean blue sky, Richard maneuvered the helicopter over and just south of a sprawling dealership.

CHAPTER FORTY-THREE

Jeremy caught sight of a separate lot of vehicles as they passed over the dealership from about a hundred feet. He immediately noticed they were huge and his mind began racing, looking for a solution in the event the helicopter was grounded. There were several more, parked out front skirting the highway. Motorcoaches--big ones just like the Baddog! The seconds were ticking along right with the 45-foot Baddog motorcoach, lumbering off down the highway, fading into the traffic.

The Bell 222 came down in a vacant field where its wheels bounced smoothly, the amber grass bending flat beneath the rotor wash. Richard quickly locked the controls and began shutting down systems. The cabin was tense with anxiety as everyone realized their situation was sinking fast. While the rotor blades spooled down, Dane hopped out from his seat, opened the rear door and climbed into the passenger cabin.

"Listen…" Richard said hastily to everyone in the back, tugging on the overhead rotor brake. He pulled his headset off and opened his door a crack. "This will take a few minutes but I'll work fast. I'll call Christine and let her know what's happening--how's the dog?"

Dane just shook his head and frowned at him after quickly examining Arnold's bandaged wound.

"Charlee, give me a hand," Richard barked as he climbed out. Racing to the rear, opening a storage compartment in the belly of the aircraft, he lifted out a small tool chest, opened it, taking out a wrench along with a dirty rag. He paused at the cabin door, looking at Jeremy. "I'll work as quickly as I can--we'll get 'em back, safely, all of 'em."

Jeremy barely nodded before Richard slipped from view followed by Charlee squeezing past him out the door. He could hear the clanking of metal overhead as Richard opened the engine compartment cowling. Jeremy looked back over his shoulder, focusing on the line of brand new motorcoaches out by the highway.

"What is it?" Leslie asked him, snagging Dane's attention away from Arnold.

Jeremy turned and shrugged at the both of them, then stuffed the radio down inside his other pocket. "C'mon, let's see what they're doing."

Exchanging a worried glance with Dane as she followed him out the door, Leslie knew he was distracted by something more than the missing kids.

Richard had extracted a small stepladder from the compartment and stood on it, peering inside the engine compartment, his hands moving about inside. Charlee stood beside him watching. Dane stepped outside, joining them. Jeremy stood there too, watching, clenching and unclenching his fists at his side. He looked down the highway, past the parked motorcoaches, as if he were trying to see Baddog. Every second they were getting farther away, he feared.

Every second.

He felt like he was about to explode.

Richard grunted as he removed something and held out a greasy set of fingers examining something in his hand. He sighed, then went back to work in the compartment. Jeremy turned briefly and stared in the direction of the motorcoaches, almost salivating like a hungry dog. Rather than watching Richard, Leslie watched Jeremy. She could see the wheels turning in his head.

"C'mon, what's the verdict?" Jeremy asked impatiently.

"...I'm not...sure yet..."

Jeremy gritted his teeth and spun back around, his eyes glued on the distant row of motorcoaches. Grabbing Dane's wrist, he quickly led his friend around to the opposite side of the Bell, out of earshot of the others and got in his face. "Take off your clothes."

"Never on a first date."

"I'm serious, c'mon." Jeremy begged, tugging at his biker jacket. "I'm gonna try and get us some wheels, but I can't go lookin' like this."

Dane's mouth gaped open, about to say something, but instead relented with a confused look on his face as he watched Jeremy tear off his tee shirt and cargo shorts down to his boxers holding them out to his friend.

"Let's go--c'mon," Jeremy snapped.

Dane slipped out of the jacket handing it over. While Jeremy shoved his arms through the sleeves Dane unclipped and removed the boots then immediately pulled off his biker pants down to his boxers.

"Pink?" quipped Jeremy.

"Hey, they were a gift," Dane sputtered after his head popped through Jeremy's shirt, pulling it on, the cotton material stretched tightly across his thick muscular pectorals. He glanced down shaking his head. "We gotta pack some more muscle on you."

Jeremy spoke hastily between breaths as he as if he were trying to catch a bus. "…If you get this thing going, follow us."

"Follow you?" Dane whispered, "Follow you where? Whatta you doin'?"

"I'm doin' the Indiana Jones thing," he huffed with each tug, pulling the full-length boots over his feet.

"What's that, I'm afraid to ask?"

"I'm makin' it up as I go along."

"Oh man--you want me to go with you?"

"You better stay here with the dog," he sputtered, slapping down each of the four buckles on the boots. "…Oh, and whatever you do, *don't* let that fishing tube outta your sight."

"Will do."

Jeremy bolted then abruptly spun around snatching his cargo shorts just as Dane was about to step into them. "Oh, man--almost forgot. I might need this."

"Hey, *I need those!*"

"But I need these!"

Hastily pulling out the flash drive, smartphone and the radio from the pockets of his shorts he stuffed them into small pockets along the sleeves of the biker jacket then tossed the shorts back to Dane's waiting hands and disappeared around the Bell. Richard was so absorbed in what he was doing, Charlee too, watching her father, that neither of them had noticed Jeremy snatching Leslie's hand and their sprinting off across the field in the direction of the dealership.

The moment their feet touched the pavement of the lot he squeezed her hand slowing their pace to a quick walk. His eyes scanned the lot, looking for any approaching busybody salespeople, then narrowed in on the motorcoaches. What he had in mind was straight out of the movies, he thought. It was crazy. And if he made a mistake, there would be no retake. But he was running out of options...and ideas. And this actually seemed plausible to him. He specifically looked for an RV with a ladder on the back of it. He spotted one and headed for it.

"Jeremy...?" Leslie gushed breathlessly between steps. "...What are you--?"

"How's your driving skills at high speed?"

She abruptly halted, snapping her hand from his and stood staring at him, panting, a frightened look mounting across her tanned face.

"Jeremy, what are we doing?" she pleaded with him.

He didn't have time for explanations and simply snatched her hand again. "You *don't* wanna know."

"Hey Fred, looks like you got a couple of live ones out front from that helicopter!"

Fred Williamson, father of five, happily married to the same woman for thirty-two years, overweight, balding and dressed in his daily work attire of slacks, leather loafers and sports jacket strolled from his office onto the sales floor before a small gathering of co-workers. He straightened with anticipation, displaying his trademark grin of eager salesmanship. Giving his loose tie a neat tug, checking his breath against the palm of his right hand, Williamson marched across the sales floor toward the double glass doors announcing boldly, "See you boys later. Don't wait up for me."

"Go get 'em, tiger," one of the salesmen grinned.

Leslie's worried expression hadn't escaped Jeremy. He drew her around to the rear of the motorcoach below the large window where he spun about closing the gap between them like he was about to share a deep, dark secret with her. "Listen to me, I need you too--"

"Good morning," boomed Fred's deep baritone voice across the lot, his hand out ahead of him. Despite their youth, Leslie's disheveled appearance and the helicopter out in the field, which they appeared to have come from, Fred's curiosity was most certainly heightened.

Startled, they both turned, Leslie feigning her 'happy surprise' expression. Jeremy, though less enthusiastic, immediately hid his frustration from behind a spreading grin, matching the approaching salesman's.

Leslie whispered to Jeremy, "Follow my lead, *honey*."

"Whatever you say, *dear*," Jeremy muttered agreeably.

"Good morning, good morning," Fred beamed again, moving right into their personal space, engaging their eyes. "She's a beauty isn't she? I see you've noticed the window there. We're very proud of that feature."

"A window?" Jeremy quipped.

"Oh, no young man. But this particular one opens, slides downward…" He then dramatically swept his hand across the horizon and skyward wistfully adding, "…for those, quiet, romantic evenings, as you're lying there with your significant other in your arms, watching the stars as the two of you drift off to sleep." He then leaned closer as if to share a private thought. "You can even set it with a timer to close on its own, should you two fall blissfully asleep."

Feeling like she'd just stepped out onto the veranda of Tara to greet Ashley Wilkes, Leslie launched herself into character, smiled back at him, gallantly taking Fred's open hand. "Oh yes, that does sound verrry romantic, doesn't it, honey?" she said, passing the ball.

Jeremy glanced at her first, then at Fred, meeting his hand too. "--Oh, it does indeed, honey. And it seems to be the right size for what I need."

She never stopped smiling. "And, dear, what exactly is that?"

"Wellll, honey, you know…"

"Gosh, darling," she said turning to Fred, flashing him her southern hostess party face, arching her brows. "You never really shared with me sweetie, exactly *what that was*."

Fred grinned at her widely, cocking his head saying. "Are you two newlyweds?"

Leslie draped her arm about Jeremy's shoulder and replied, "Whhhhy not."

She then maneuvered herself between Jeremy and Fred, hooking their elbows and began escorting the both of them down the length of the motorcoach, spying a quick glance at the salesman's name tag pinned to his jacket. "You know, Fred, is it?"

He grinned back at her, "Williamson, yes, but--"

"Well, Mr. Williamson--"

"But you can call me Fred," he grinned, tipping his head.

Leslie swept her hair back, matching his toothy smile. "Fred, how sweet. Well, Fred, my ah, husband and I--that's our little ol' helicopter out there…well, there we were, flying high as a kite to our honeymoon destination when we spotted your little dealership here.

I mean, we just love the great outdoors and all, open road and such, but up there, we're so high up, it's hard to see anyyything. Everything looks sooo tiny. Well, hubby here, he says, let's go down and check those out."

Fred said, with an ever-wider grin, "Y'all didn't rob a bank, did 'ya?"

Leslie laughed, glancing at Jeremy for help, waving off the suggestion, "A bank? Heavens no."

"Not likely," Jeremy responded drolly.

Fred was studying them but not coming up with much. "Well, what is it y'all do, I mean, for a livin'?"

Leslie heard Jeremy draw his breath about to speak but cut him off, flashing more teeth at the salesman. "--He, ah, inherited his daddy's yacht company."

"Really?"

"Oh, yes," she said with frowning seriousness.

Fred peered around the blonde at Jeremy.

"It's ah, a rather large operation," quipped Jeremy. "Huge in fact."

"Really? Well, isn't that interesting."

"Yes, indeed," Leslie said pouring it on thick, moving in and smoothing out the lapel of Fred's jacket. "And what we were hoping for, Fred, was a quick little demo. You know, let us take her out for a spin around the block, to see if it'll meet our needs--isn't that right, honey?"

"That's it exactly." Jeremy was then the one to lean into the salesman. "Whattya say, Fredo?"

Still smiling, Fred reached for the door handle, opened it and gestured with an invitational open hand. "Key's in the ignition. All aboard."

Leslie grinned in Fred's face as she slid past him and up the stairs. Jeremy glanced over at the Bell. Spying Richard still atop the stepladder, his hands inside the engine compartment, he politely gestured for Fred to go ahead of him. As he followed behind the salesman, Jeremy nervously swallowed, rolling his eyes skyward, wondering if he was completely out of his mind and muttered, "All aboard."

Quickly closing the door behind him, he steered Leslie to the driver's seat while Fred settled into the passenger's.

Fred asked, "First time behind the wheel of one of these?"

Totally engrossed with gripping the large steering wheel and settling into the leather seat while her eyes darted around the unfamiliar instrument panel, Leslie muttered softly, absent-mindedly forgetting her southern belle demure before stepping back into character. "There've been a lot of firsts lately...I mean, ahh, yes, indeed."

"Well, not to worry. I'll walk you through it."

"I can hardly wait."

"Excuse me."

"I mean, let's do this."

"Well then, let me point out a few things before we hit the road..."

Jeremy anxiously settled into a large leather chair directly behind them. His hands were sweating profusely as he nervously rubbed them together. Since they were about to *steal* the massive motorcoach *and* kidnap the hapless salesman, he began to wonder how he was going to look in an orange jump suit supplied free of charge by the county. Yet he couldn't risk doing anything that might alert or startle the man. Not until they were under way so he wouldn't be able to flee. He just sat there quietly and listened.

"That's your GPS navigational system there," Fred said to her, eagerly pointing everything out. "Forty-channel CB radio, tire pressure and temperature monitor system, radar--"

"--Ah," she interrupted him with a wink, "why don't we get going and then you can point all this nifty stuff out to me as we drive?"

Fred hadn't stopped smiling. "Excellent idea--keys in the ignition there." He then winked back at her after clipping his seatbelt. "Go ahead and give her a go."

Leslie did the same with her belt, then turned the key. As the massive RV smoothly rumbled to life Jeremy craned his neck, looking over his shoulder through the picture window at the Bell. He grit his teeth, grimacing in anger at the sight of Richard's hands still buried in the engine compartment.

Leslie slipped the gear shift into drive, braked, looked both ways down the highway, and when it was clear, pressed the accelerator. As the heavy vehicle slowly lumbered across the ruddy grass lawn of the dealership, Jeremy cautiously rose to his feet and stood behind her. He wanted to get far enough away before he said or did anything. He didn't want Fred jumping ship.

Dane's brow arched up his forehead, his eyes widening the instant he caught a glimpse of Leslie behind the wheel of the departing RV pulling onto the even pavement of the highway and muttered, "Oh-oh, OH-OH!"

Charlee turned, bumping shoulders with him, asking, "What's wrong?"

"Look!"

"At what?" she sputtered

"Where are they going?" he sputtered.

"Who?" Richard said, pulling his head from the engine compartment.

"The RV, see it? Leslie's behind the wheel!"

"What?" gasped Richard, as he nearly tripped stepping down from the ladder. "What're they doing?"

Watching the motorcoach roar off down the highway in a cloud of dust, Richard grabbed his cell phone from his pocket and dialed Christine. The moment she answered he spewed, "Honey, 'nother change of plans."

The elevated, panoramic windshield gave Jeremy a wide, unobstructed view of the road ahead. As Fred picked up his orientation, where he'd left off, Jeremy scanned the cars in the distance. He momentarily dropped his gaze, noting the speedometer. Gently squeezing Leslie's shoulder, he bent low and said, "A little faster, Sweetie."

"AM, FM radio with CD--sure, open'er up a little," Fred bubbled on with a curt wave of his hand. "Let yourself really feel the power behind this little gem. Just stay below the speed limit so we don't arouse the attention of any cops--I mean any state troopers that might be cruising the road. We wouldn't wanna do that."

Jeremy looked down at Leslie, meeting her wary gaze. "Yeah, we don't wanna do that, *not now*."

"…I'll ah, I'll do my best," she nervously muttered up at him.

The serene atmosphere inside the Baddog belied the undercurrent of terror. It was deathly quiet, save the gentle hum of the engine and the mild rocking motion, cruising at sixty-five. Whitehead chewed relentlessly on a fingernail as his other hand gripped the wheel, his mind obsessed with Jeremy. He knew his nemesis was not about to give up. And Whitehead was desperately counting on it. When he looked up into the mirror over his head, the kids had taken to staring out the windows on either side of the cabin, all except Elmo. The young Indian was staring back at him. Whitehead smirked, thinking some more, then, finally decided to pull off to the side of the road.

"Whatta you doing?" the henchman asked, turning slightly in his chair directly behind him. Determining the kids presented no threat he had returned his gun to his shoulder holster, yet kept his eyes trained on them as he stood.

"Preparing for our guest," he grunted as he steered onto the dirt shoulder, braking to a gentle stop.

"Guest? What guest?"

Whitehead shifted the gear into park leaving the engine idling, then rose, meeting the henchman's steady gaze. "We're going to have company soon and I wanna be ready for him."

"Company? Whatta you talking about?" the man sneered.

"Trust me," Whitehead said to him. "You don't know Jeremy Hodak like I do."

"Yeah, well, when he gets here you can deal with him," the henchman said acidly, dismissing Whitehead and turning his back to him, facing the group of frightened kids on the couch. His dark eyes then zeroed in on Elmo's. "In the meantime, I'm taking over."

Elmo became even more terrified, sensing the henchman had something especially in store for him.

Whitehead glared at him. "I don't--"

"You don't, what?" spat the henchman turning on his heels, withdrawing his gun in a swift move, holding it up to Whitehead's temple. Whitehead glared back at him, watching the henchman reach down to the passenger's chair where he'd dropped the Glock and pick it up, slipping it into the pocket of his suit. The henchman's expression was one of stone cold indifference as he continued to glare steadily back into Whitehead's eyes, his hand slipping inside Whitehead's biker jacket and removing his Glock. "I'll just hold onto this for now," he said, shoving it down inside a side pocket of his own suit. He then concluded coldly, "*Don't…interfere.*"

Whitehead, bristling, held his tongue, saying nothing.

"I have *my* orders," the henchman explained, removing a Bluetooth headset from his pocket and placing it in his ear. "And from here on out, *you,* take orders from *me!*"

"Orders?" Whitehead repeated to him with equal chill.

"If Shazuko fails--and I believe she did--*my orders* are to proceed to the resort and complete my job."

"And what job is that?"

The henchman sheathed his gun and said, "Need to know… and you don't need to know nothin'. First things first, though," he said, returning his icy gaze toward Elmo. "You seemed to be the tallest of the bunch, leader type. Bet they look up to you, don't they?"

"I'm no leader," Elmo answered with a tense shake of his head from the couch.

"Stand up, kid," snarled the henchman. He then lunged threateningly at the kids, reaching for one of them, startling the group. Recoiling back against the couch, Matthew and Dylan tried blocking the trained killer's hand, only to have him roughly rebuff the boys, shoving them aside like annoying puppies with his muscled arm. He reached down, grabbing Elmo, violently dragging the boy to his sandaled feet. Elmo briefly struggled against the brute force of the henchman until he drew the boy closer to his unshaven face. The moment Elmo shoved aside his long black hair, his eyes were met by the henchman's stark, empty orbs, his mouth parted in a vicious grin. He was so close Elmo could smell the remnants of his aftershave along with his foul breath.

Turning away and wincing, the boy murmured bravely, "Whatta you gonna do?"

Having snatched his upper arm so tightly, Elmo could feel the blood constricting in a painful tingle. Hesitating, enjoying the moment, the henchman finally drew Elmo even closer. "If you and your little friends want to see your next birthdays, you're gonna behave and sit there quietly. And to insure that you all do, I've got something special in mind...just for you."

The boy grimaced and swallowed from behind a set of panicked sea-green eyes.

Fred was beginning to freak. Stealing a sweaty glance at his wristwatch he realized they'd been gone from the dealership for close to an hour--not your typical test drive, and still heading south. He kept thinking something just wasn't right with these two. They had paid little attention to him during his orientation, seemingly distracted.

Their odd attire should've been enough, but the helicopter slash honeymoon story, at first sounded plausible to him. Now it was beginning to alarm him, appearing to be bogus. But in his zeal he fell for it. And he'd spent the last several miles kicking himself, becoming uncharacteristically quiet, until a familiar intersection appeared in the distance. Clipping along at sixty-five, it was coming up fast. Fred pointed it out saying, "Oh, ah, see that corner coming up, the gas station? You can turn in and go around and we can head back to the dealership."

"If you don't mind, Fredo," Jeremy said in a friendly tone, kneeling beside Leslie, his eyes focused on the road out front, "we're gonna keep going."

"Oh my God," moaned the salesman as his face drained of color, watching the gas station and intersection fly by. "You did rob a bank!"

Jeremy remained focused on the road ahead, his eyes scanning the vehicles for the massive Baddog. He turned and looked at the worried salesman, "Would you stop with that bank stuff? We didn't rob anything."

"Whatta you call this?" Fred spouted while he began to hyperventilate, breathing long and rapid as he fumbled with the strap on his wrist, removing his watch, then digging into his slacks pocket, withdrawing his wallet. Sweat gathered across his brow as he pulled out a wad of bills. He gathered it all together in his hands and held it out in front of Jeremy.

"We're just borrowing your RV, we'll give it back. Whatta you doing?"

"Here, you can have my watch, it's a Rolex, and I've got a couple of hundred bucks here--probably doesn't come close to your take--"

"Take?"

"Yeah, here, you can have it, just please don't hurt me."

"Now, stop that, I said, and put that away. We didn't rob a bank. We're not going to hurt you. Just sit there and watch the scenery and relax, okay?"

Fred slumped silently back into the passenger seat, his wallet, watch and bills slipping through his gathered hands to his lap. Clasping his hands together they too settled to his lap. He then uttered, "I think I'm going to be sick."

"The head's back there if you need it."

Fred grimaced. "It isn't operational."

"Hey," Leslie barked, concentrating on the road and the feel of the massive vehicle through the steering wheel. "Now that the cat's out of the bag, why am I driving? *You* should be here."

"I thought of that," Jeremy explained. "But I might be busy."

"Not another bank job I hope," Fred said.

"QUIET!" the both of them snapped at him in unison.

"...Sorry," he replied timidly, his gaze returning to the passing scenery.

"Jeremy, what are you planning to do?"

"I'd explain it, but there isn't time."

"We appear to have plenty at the moment."

"No, we don't," he said pointing. "There they are, look."

Far up ahead, leading a pack of cars was the 45-foot Baddog.

Leslie said, "I guess he doesn't believe in exceeding the speed limit. Whatta we do now?"

"Stay back here. We'll follow 'em and see where he goes."

"If he's heading for the resort, we can stop him there, right?"

"I hope so, but..."

"But what?"

Jeremy thought, and then said, "Why is he goin' there in the first place?"

"It must have something to do with that event today."

"It doesn't make any sense."

"It does to him," replied Leslie glancing at Jeremy.

Jeremy stepped away to think. He pulled forward a cushioned chair and planted it just behind Leslie then sank into it. Fred glanced over at the boy's sullen face and thought to himself, all was not what it appeared to be. Perhaps they didn't rob a bank.

Jeremy looked up, staring at the distant Baddog and said, "Don't get too close to him."

"Okay," Leslie replied softly.

"I lied," Fred said quietly.

Jeremy lifted his head and looked at him. "What?"

"I lied--about the watch, I mean. It really isn't a Rolex. Got it at K-mart."

Jeremy laughed, then smiled at him.

"He's slowing down," Leslie announced, getting Jeremy's attention and chasing his smile away.

"Match his speed."

"Okay," Leslie replied, concentrating.

The air within the motorcoach was thick with palpable tension as they could do nothing for the moment except stealthily follow behind the Baddog. Mile after agonizing mile they trailed a good distance behind them. All Jeremy could do was think about his brothers and friends and how he was going to save them. They drove through Petoskey ironically going right past Leslie's house on the bluff overlooking Little Grand Traverse Bay. The moment her eyes caught sight of the clapboard house, she traded a quick glance with Jeremy.

"You'll be with your mom by tonight," he reassured her.

Whitehead turned off onto US 131, heading south. They crawled through the small towns of Walloon Lake, Boyne Falls, Mancelona and Antrim. Approaching Kalkaska, Jeremy was on pins and needles and simply couldn't stand it anymore. He pulled out the radio from the pocket on his sleeve and looked at it.

Leslie watched him through the mirror and asked "You gonna call him?"

"I gotta do something," Jeremy said, trying to break through the frustration. "What if he doesn't go to the resort? What if he heads through town--we might lose 'em. Then what? I just can't shake it-- why is he going to the resort? Where's he gonna go from there?"

"Maybe it *is* the end of the road for him," Leslie said prophetically, locking eyes with Jeremy through the mirror.

Jeremy said, "Which can only mean he's intending to hurt someone. Maybe a lot of people, including my parents."

"Does he know they're there?"

Jeremy shook his head. "I don't see how. I never mentioned it to him."

Jeremy stood up, thinking, gripping the radio in his hand, and flicked it on. "We gotta stop him. And we gotta do it now."

Jeremy took a deep breath, then pressed the talk button. "Peter…I'll make you a deal…pull over, let the kids go and you can have me."

His heart pounded beneath his sternum while he waited.

Nothing.

Jeremy cleared his throat before pressing the talk button. "Whitehead? Do you hear me? I said you can have me if you let the kids go. Whatta you say?"

Still nothing.

Fred was having second thoughts about these two as he watched Jeremy kneeling beside Leslie, flashing her a grave look before spying the Baddog, a good half mile out in front. A road sign fluttered by and Leslie announced their position, "Kalkaska, ten miles."

Jeremy pressed the radio to his lips and growled, "Answer me you sonofabitch!"

The radio remained silent.

Jeremy could feel himself starting to lose it as he raised his voice. "Did you hear me? Whitehead? Did you? If you hurt them, if you do anything to any of those kids…Whitehead? Do you hear me? DO YOU?"

The radio crackled for a moment, and then Whitehead's voice boomed through the tiny speaker. "Hear you loud and clear."

"Don't touch those kids!"

"Are you presuming to tell me what to do?" Whitehead growled back over the airwaves. "Lemme tell you what you're gonna do…you're gonna do nothin'! And I'd better not so much as see a cop car with flashing lights on my ass, either, you got it?"

"WHATTA YOU WANT FROM ME!" Jeremy shouted into the radio.

"YOU!" Whitehead goaded him.

Jeremy lowered the radio, staring at the Baddog out across the chasm of streaking highway between them. His fear and confusion suddenly faded to the back of his mind, replaced by sheer rage. He turned and faced the rear of the motorcoach, tossing the radio to his chair. He took a step across the carpet, formulating a plan in his mind. Pivoting, he looked back at Leslie through the mirror. She could almost see it in his eyes, what he was planning.

"What's he mean, Jeremy--what does he want you to do?

"He's challenging me…to come after him."

"What are you gonna do?"

Calmly, Fred looked across at Leslie, then up at Jeremy, his eyes narrowing, when he said, "Yes, young man, what *are you* going to do?"

"Answer his challenge and rescue my brothers and friends," Jeremy growled boldly, his mind racing.

There was a sudden ringing sound, emanating from the vicinity of Fred. It startled the salesman for a moment until he realized it was his cell phone in the breast pocket of his suit coat. He cautiously withdrew it, scanning the face.

"It's, ahh, the dealership," he announced resolutely. "It's been over an hour and they're probably wondering where I am."

Leslie exchanged a stricken look with Jeremy.

"I'm gonna have to answer it. If I don't…they may call the police."

PART 5

INTO THE FIRE

CHAPTER FORTY-FOUR

Unknown to everyone attending the formal political luncheon today, the stage had been unwittingly set for a deadly, high-rise confrontation, confirmed by the arrival of Senator Toddhunter's security/campaign manager--his right-hand man. Even he had no idea what was coming. Backstage, amid the flurry of activity, Miles couldn't help watching the two men engaged in a lively discussion off in a quiet corner. He would've given a month's salary to hear what they were talking about. When he was introduced to the senator earlier by Carl, the man seemed unusually anxious. He was reputed to be a controlling, cold, no-nonsense senator. It sure seemed to fit him, thought Miles. It must have been more bad news, because now the senator appeared to be seething with anger the moment his right-hand man stepped away. Miles watched him too. Carl was right, he mused. The hulking security/campaign manager did look like a hitman.

It was 11:00 A.M. and out front the triple set of double doors at the far side of the Governors' Hall were swung open. As streams of the senator's supporters began flooding into the ballroom, conversing in hushed tones, today's event had the feel of a casual affair, yet the gathering was excited and energized, many of them socializing, while others dispersed, eagerly planting themselves at the various, elegantly dressed tables. Within minutes the Governors' Hall was filled to capacity with an electrified crowd.

"Will you hold still and stop fidgeting," Clarissa chided Miles in his barstool/makeup chair as she gently dabbed his forehead, applying a powder bronzer, giving the dashing anchor that shine-free TV appearance. "You're as bad as my five-year-old nephew every time I cut his hair."

"So you do hair as well?"

"Among my many talents," she said conversationally, nodding at the large mirror propped atop her makeup cart with a head-shot photo taped to the inner frame that Miles travels with. "A guy might have a photo of his girlfriend or wife...what's with the guy there? Why do I think you're gay--it wouldn't bother me if you were."

"Maybe because I dress better than you?"

"*Whaaat?*"

"Missy, there's a thin line between looking Vogue and looking homeless," Miles playfully chided her, "and I think you crossed it."

"Look here *GQ*, my attire is very comfortable, especially for a five-a.m. curtain call."

"Okay, okay, that explains the five-a.m. look. How do you explain the way you look the rest of the day...they actually let you come in through the front door of the station dressed like the 80's version of Cindy Lauper?"

On the job only a few weeks, fresh out of college and doing her internship at the station, Clarissa and Miles often traded gibes with each other. Yet beneath the playful sarcasm there was deep respect for one another. Clarissa stopped dabbing his forehead, stood back and just smiled back at him, steering the conversation back to her original subject. "I have an uncle...tall, blond, handsome and tanned like you. He does waverunner tours in the Florida Keys. And he's gay. I love him and wouldn't change him for the world."

"I'm glad to hear that."

"So, c'mon...who is he?--he's cute. Your brother?--though you two look nothing alike."

"That, my young, ambitious makeup--"

"*Person*," she warned him, playfully wagging a taut index finger. "Don't you dare say 'girl.'"

"I stand nearly politically corrected," Miles said with an ever-so-faint frown, accompanied with a roll of the eyes. He then became reflective, adding, "He was a top news reporter...and a good friend."

"Was?"

Miles nodded thoughtfully. "David had made it to the big leagues as an NBC News correspondent in Iraq, where he was embedded with the Third Infantry Division, reporting directly from the battlefield in what became affectionately referred to as the Bloomobile, his mobile satellite truck. He was a go-getter all right. We attended Pitzer College together in Claremont, California."

"I didn't know that," Clarissa said softly.

"David Bloom died unexpectedly in 2003 of a pulmonary embolism from something called DVT, or deep-vein thrombosis. Left a wife and three beautiful daughters. We'd catch up as often as our, or should I say, his, schedule allowed. He was a great mentor. ...I miss our conversations."

So absorbed in listening to Miles, her soft blue eyes misting over, Clarissa's hand remained frozen-like beside his cheek, pausing from applying the finishing touches to his face. Finally, Clarissa mumbled, almost absent-mindedly yet with great empathy, "I'm sorry, Miles."

The small-town newscaster smiled stalwartly and said prophetically, "Life goes on, right?"

The ballroom was buzzing with hushed but lively conversations over the soft tinkling of glass and silverware while the anxious gathering grazed over their lunch of Chicken Alouette, apple iced tea, vegetables tossed in olive butter, cranberry congealed salad, followed afterwards with coffee and chocolate boxes with raspberry mousse. The senator had insisted that no expense was too extravagant.

Carl came up behind Miles, rousting him from his barstool chair, and confirmed with him that all was on schedule. As the two men continued to review and confer over each other's notes, Clarissa came up to them, her eyes gazing past them and said, "What's with Abbott and Costello over there?"

"Huh?" Miles grunted, looking at her, then, following her gaze to the far side of the back-staging area, the three of them watched as Senator Toddhunter's hulking security/campaign manager returned to his side with a steaming Styrofoam cup of coffee. "The senator still appears to be peeved about something," Miles then noted. "They are an odd couple, aren't they."

"You said it," Clarissa muttered.

"I wonder what's got him so riled?" Carl mused.

"I wish I knew," Miles replied earnestly. "They are a pair."

"Yeah, but a pair of what?" Clarissa mused back to the both of them with an arched brow before excusing herself.

Carl then glanced at his wristwatch. "Getting close to show time. Let's get you set up. We go live at noon for your introduction of the senator and his big announcement."

Jeremy stood beside Fred, staring down at the man long and hard and said, "What are you going to say?"

Fred relaxed for the first time, raised his hand in a calming gesture, then brought the cell phone close to his lips. "Hee haw, boys, what's up?"

Jeremy suddenly blurted, "They have my--"

"Hold the line a moment, Jake."

Jeremy engaged Fred's eyes with an imploring gaze. "They have my brothers and our friends whom they intend to kill…unless we can stop them…do you hear me?"

Fred nodded with his confident salesman's face. "…What was that, Jake?"

"I said, the boss wants to know how much longer you're gonna be, and did you make the sale? You've been gone over an hour."

"They love this little gem. We're on our way back now. I'll be home soon enough--see you soon."

Fred tapped the screen ending the call, then inserted the phone back into his pants pocket. "That should buy us a little more time. All I ask is whatever you're planning, please don't scratch this thing."

Jeremy broke into a relieved expression and said, "Thank you. And we won't, I promise."

He then turned and dropped beside Leslie. Kneeling, his eyes glued on the Baddog some distance ahead, his voice was decisive. "We'll have to stop 'em. Can you come alongside and--"

"Alongside?" she spouted at him wide-eyed, gripping the wheel tighter in her sweating hands. "You want me to--"

"It's four lanes, all you have to do--"

"Jeremy--"

"Listen to me," he argued. "We've lost the element of surprise; we can't run 'em off the road--"

"Run 'em off the...Jeremy--I'm not a stunt driver!"

"You are now."

"I'm terrified driving this behemoth," she uttered sharply, the power of the massive RV felt through her hands on the steering wheel as if she were handling an eighteen-wheeler. "And you want me to cruise up alongside of him while you're...while *you're* doing *what*?"

"Oh, I didn't tell you? I'll be on the roof--"

"The roof!"

"When you get close enough I'll cross over and--"

"Oh my God, Jeremy!" she gasped, her eyes riveted on the busy highway out front. "Are you crazy--really?"

"Goddamn it, it's the only way! You gotta better idea?"

"What about the police? You can call 'em on Fred's phone."

"You heard what he said no cops, remember?"

"Even if you make it, then what--how are *you* gonna stop 'em?"

"Please, Leslie, one thing at a time."

"Pull over," Fred shouted out after listening to their exchange. "*I* can help you."

The two of them looked over at the salesman dubiously.

"Oh, I'm a pretty good judge of people," he offered. "I didn't really think you robbed a bank. And I'm also pretty good behind the wheel of these…behemoths. C'mon, pull over, I'll drive."

Leslie exchanged a wary look with Jeremy until he finally relented with a nod. She eased onto the gravel shoulder and braked to a smooth stop, slipping the gear shift into park, leaving the engine idling. Breathing a deep, grateful sigh of relief as she struggled to stand from the driver's seat, stretching her legs, Jeremy helped her to her feet. Fred moved to the rear of the motor coach, removing his jacket and tossing it to the couch. Jeremy and Leslie followed him, watching as the hefty salesman picked up a small black remote device from the night stand beside the queen-size bed and handed it to Jeremy. "You'll need this, it opens the window here."

"Okay," Jeremy said, taking it.

Fred said, "Are you sure there's no other way to do this?"

Jeremy shook his head. "I know this guy. It's the only way. But if you have any ideas…"

Fred shook his head, briefly studying the floor, then engaging the boy's eyes, replying, "All right. You'll have to go out here, carefully climb the exterior ladder to the roof, and then, when we get close enough--"

"I'll bang on the roof just before I go."

Fred nodded. "From there you'll be on your own. You look like a strapping young man. Whatever you do, don't fall off!"

Jeremy, a little wild eyed, nodded back and said placidly, "I'll do my best."

Fred got his mojo back and flashed his salesman's smile at them both. "It *is crazy*, but…let's get going. My wife is serving one of her roasts for dinner tonight and I'd really hate to miss it…that is of course, assuming, we're not all sharing a jail cell this evening!"

Fred squeezed past the two kids, their relieved smiles warming his heart and quickly slid into the driver's chair and adjusted the seat and corresponding belt. As Jeremy zipped up the biker's jacket to his neck, Leslie suddenly hugged him. He pushed back, staring into her eyes, and then leaned in, kissing her passionately. After several moments, her smooth cheek slid along his rough, unshaven skin until her lips caressed his ear. "You be careful now and come back to me, with everyone, you hear me?"

Jeremy straightened, his eyes diving into her and whispered, "You know I will."

They nearly lost their footing as Fred steered the motorcoach back onto the highway and accelerated. Jeremy turned and stepped forward.

"It'll take us a few minutes to catch up to 'em," Fred bellowed while keeping a steady eye on the crowded highway streaming past them. "That's a sturdy ladder, but it can be slippery. Grip it tight, make your way to the roof, then bang on it to let me know you're in position, okay?"

"All right," Jeremy bellowed back.

"As you said, we've lost the element of surprise, but not completely. They don't know what you're in. But I'll have to be quick. I'll slide up alongside as best I can--you'll only have seconds so you'll have to be fast and nimble, got it?"

"Got it."

Jeremy faced Leslie, handing her the window remote and said, "I'll see you soon."

"He's turning," Fred bellowed over the wheel. "...onto M 72."

"The resort," Leslie muttered in a stricken tone.

"Yep," Jeremy said, meeting her alarmed gaze, "he's heading there all right."

Catching the green light at the intersection, Fred slowed then accelerated in the turn, following not far behind the Baddog. Leslie stumbled into Jeremy's arms, nearly dropping the remote. She straightened, catching his stare, and then pressed the 'open' button. The large glass window slowly dropped away, the roar of the highway invading the motorcoach, the wind swirling about the both of them, buffeting Leslie's long brunette hair about her shoulders. She took one of his hands and squeezed it tightly. "See you soon," she repeated back to him.

With that, Jeremy released her hand and hopped atop the queen bed, his heavy biker boots trouncing the neatly made satin slipcover. With a determined look Jeremy cautiously stuck his head through the open window, where swirling eddies danced across his face. He drew several deep breaths into his lungs just before reaching around, grabbing the ladder. Drawing on now his third wind, his body again felt energized with adrenaline as he gingerly stepped through, his right foot slowing making contact with one of the ladder rungs. He tested his footing before moving on. It was solid. Startled occupants from the string of cars following just a few lengths behind gaped in amazement, watching the drama unfolding at the back of the massive motorcoach, a few of them wondering if they were witnessing the making of a motion picture.

They were not.

Leslie held her breath and prayed as she watched Jeremy's other foot leave the edge of the window behind. She then sprinted to the front, planting herself across from Fred in the passenger seat.

"Seatbelt, my dear."

Leslie followed Fred's directive, nervously clipping the belt across herself, all the while looking through the side mirror, hoping to catch a glimpse of Jeremy.

Fred said, "You won't be able to see 'em, he's going up top."

Jeremy wasn't having second thoughts as he grabbed the top rung, easing his head up over the edge into the streaming wind, but he wished there had been another way. The airflow in his face felt like he was climbing into a jet wind tunnel. Jeremy took a moment gathering his strength, and his wits. He looked downward, nervously swallowing at the sight of the pavement whining beneath the heavy-duty wheels at a blistering sixty-five mph. He could hear the low rumble of the engine and feel its warm exhaust swirling around him. One wrong move, he thought, with his hands or feet and it would be his last.

He craned his neck, looking over the top edge.

Reaching out, one hand over the other, a grip so tight it rivaled the tightest vise-grip pliers, he pulled himself onto the roof where he immediately ran out of ladder. The hurricane-like wind screaming at his ears, parted his blond hair unnaturally. The surface of the motorcoach's roof momentarily stopped him; in front of him was an air conditioner unit. In the center was a bubbled skylight, and in front of that another air conditioner. Around them the surface looked as smooth and shiny as a freshly polished ice ring, and he hoped, not nearly as slippery.

Jeremy pressed onward, wondering if this is what it felt like to scale Mount Everest, near the summit, minus the freezing temperatures, though. Sliding along on his chest, he slowly shimmied his way forward, then toward the right side where he was able to grip the edge of the coach. Pausing, his eyes squinting in protest, he raised up slightly, spying the Baddog ahead of them a good quarter mile in the distance, and spotted the ladder along the side of it. He lowered his head, then using his right hand, clutched the smooth edge of the coach and crawled a bit farther so his legs were no longer dangling over the rear edge. He used his other hand, grabbing the air conditioner and pushed himself forward, cocking his head to the side trying to save his ears from the onslaught.

From the myriad of cars speeding along behind them, several stunned drivers and their passengers watched uncomprehendingly at the spectacle. Several had already grabbed their cell phones and called 911.

Jeremy took a rest, and a breath, then released the air conditioner, reaching out with his hand in a fist and banged three times on the roof.

Leslie flinched, looking upward. "There he is…he must be ready."

The sound of someone knocking on the outside of the coach as they sped down the highway was startling, to say the least.

Adjusting his grip on the wheel, Fred exchanged a look with Leslie and said, "All right...here we go. Hold on and pray, little lady."

Traffic along the four-lane highway was heavy in both directions. Fred applied pressure to the accelerator and eased over into in the left-hand passing lane where cars were clipping along considerably faster. Following a black Hummer, he carefully watched the Baddog in the distance, glancing at his speedometer needle, noting it rise to seventy-five.

"Is that them?"

"Yes," Leslie replied, her eyes glued on the massive Baddog RV.

Fred applied more pressure to the gas pedal, steadily diminishing the half mile or so gap between them.

Leslie caught sight of a road sign as they whizzed past reading it off. "Grand Traverse World Resort, fifteen miles."

With the assaulting wind roaring at his ears and clawing over his body, Jeremy's eyes zeroed in on the Baddog. He cleared his mind, concentrating on perhaps the most dangerous thing he'd ever done in his young life. And nothing was going to stop him!

"Better not make any sudden maneuvers for our Indian boy's sake," Whitehead spat to the henchman at the wheel as he slid into the passenger seat, spying the approaching motorcoach behind them through his side mirror. He grinned with evil intent after spotting someone on the roof. He then muttered softly to himself, "At least not until he gets here. Come and get me, Jeremy, I'm waiting for you."

He looked across at the henchman and said, "Whatta you gonna do?"

"If it's that important to him, let 'em come to us." Then he twisted his head and barked at the kids, "Close those blinds, NOW!"

Jeremy could feel Fred accelerating the motorcoach. The Baddog was now only four car lengths ahead. Still following the black Hummer, they were closing in fast. Jeremy readied himself. The cars out in front, the ones in back of them, and one off to the right beside their coach made him feel like he was in the middle of…no, scratch that. Right on top of, with a bird's eye view, a NASCAR race.

A new extreme sport; RV hopping! It was both amazingly scary and head rushing!

Concentrate, Jeremy willed himself!

Releasing his grip on the air conditioner, he used both hands, clutching the edge of the coach and pulled, easing his body toward it, his eyes focused ahead on the ladder along the side of the Baddog.

Jeremy knew he'd only have one shot at this. He cocked his head at an angle, trying to ward off the wind stream raging at his ears. Overtaking the Baddog, Jeremy grit his teeth and wrinkled his nose as he braced himself, his heart pumping fiercely beneath his sternum. Beginning to flank the Baddog, both massive vehicles racing side by side at breakneck speed, he could see nothing through the first window as it came sliding by below him. He looked ahead to the next one as it came into view, but like the preceding one, the blinds were closed. Jeremy eased himself closer to the edge. The massive motorcoaches rocked gently from side to side, the heat from the roadbed and their undercarriages wafting up between them carried the mild scent of summer and exhaust. He held his breath, getting ready. They were nearly neck and neck, the ladder coming closer and closer, bobbing to and fro.

He had only seconds now.

Coming alongside, directly across from her by feet, Leslie's eyes widened and her mouth gaped open at the sight of one of the henchmen she recognized in the driver's chair. He glared back at her with a knowing sneer. They were now side by side, racing along the highway at nearly eighty mph. Looking across the gap between them, he estimated it was less than five feet--much too far. He yelled out at the top of his lungs, not knowing whether they would hear him. "CLOSER--GET ME CLOSER!"

"That was Jeremy!" snapped Leslie craning her neck, looking overhead.

"I heard him," Fred replied, his hands carefully working the wheel, inching the RV closer, while his steady eyes kept glancing back and forth from the cars out in front to their frightening proximity to the Baddog.

At that instant, as the gap between the two motorcoaches closed to within two feet, Jeremy made his move. He reached out, first with one hand and then the other, and grabbed the top rung of the Baddog's ladder pulling himself over. The moment after his biker boots had slid across leaving the other coach, they dropped away and banged against the side of the Baddog with a clatter.

The kids snapped their heads around, startled and confused by the muffled thud along the side of the RV. Had something hit them?

"He made it!" Leslie shrilled, looking through her side mirror at Jeremy clinging to the side of the Baddog.

Fearing a collision Fred veered away letting his foot off the accelerator, allowing their speed to rapidly bleed away, dropping back.

The henchman and Whitehead watched it all from the driver's side mirror. Whitehead then rose from the passenger seat grinning and held out his empty hand. "Like I said, we're about to have company."

The henchman relented and withdrew Whitehead's Glock from his suit and handed it over to him. Stepping back to the rear, his eyes following the clattering sound along the opposite wall across from the frightened kids, Whitehead caught a shadow moving outside beside the window through the blinds.

Jeremy hung on with all his muscled strength. His feet were struggling to find one of the lowered rungs. After several attempts and slips, his right boot found purchase and snagged one of the rungs. He reached over and began inching himself upward. His eyes made contact with the roof as he kept pulling. Each agonizing baby step brought him closer until he finally crept over the top edge onto the roof. Met with an obstacle course, consisting of a dome housing for a satellite communications system at the very front, Jeremy was closest to a skylight in the middle and two air-conditioner units--one forward and the other aft of him. He gingerly crawled on his hands and knees a few feet, then dropped to his chest. Exhausted and spent he rolled onto his back, collapsing, gasping for air to fill his lungs as if he'd just passed the finish line of an *Ironman* competition.

Calmly stepping to the rear of the coach, Whitehead slipped between the two black motocross bikes secured to the floor and reached over his head for a wall-mounted box with three buttons. In vertical succession, they were marked;

OPEN

STOP

CLOSE

The kids watched him press one of them, especially Dylan. Familiar with the Baddog's equipment, he also knew the location of the release handle for each of the bikes. One of them was within his quick reach. Like the giant wooden drawbridge of a medieval castle, the entire rear section of the Baddog began to slowly crank downward.

Jeremy heard the heavy door to the rear begin to open and immediately rolled back onto his stomach.

Doubling as a ramp, the huge door extended downward on two thick cables. The kids watched it drop down in wide-eyed amazement, even Elmo from his strained position, gagged with his wrists bound over his head. Whitehead reached up and slapped the 'stop' button, halting the door to within a few inches of the streaking roadbed. Wind vortices swirled about, disturbing a heavy duty, canvas webbing attached to the top right edge of the opening next to him. Usually holding supplies, it was empty, whipping about wildly. Whitehead grabbed it in his hands, subduing it, and announced ceremoniously to the kids, "And I'll bet all you little urchins thought you'd never see Jeremy again."

In perfect timing, Jeremy's feet came clumsily into view as he slipped down onto the ramp, his outstretched hand snagging the canvas webbing for support the moment Whitehead released his own grip on it.

"Well, if isn't James Bond," Whitehead quipped in a British accent at Jeremy's sudden appearance as if on cue.

Jeremy, dazed at his own prowess and gasping to catch his breath, quickly regained his footing, steadying himself on the ramp with the canvas webbing. Catching the remark after his eyes darted about at the kids, realizing they were all safe, he replied deftly, "I guess that makes you Ernst Blofeld…and we know what happened to him."

"Don't count on it!" Whitehead gruffed at him.

"…All right…I'm here!" Jeremy snapped between breaths. "Now…let them--for crise sakes, what have you done to Elmo?"

Jeremy stepped off the ramp and into the rear of the coach toward the boy until Whitehead blocked him with his gun aimed at his chest.

"Ah-ah," sneered Whitehead.

"Why have you tied him up like that?" Jeremy snapped angrily.

"Just makin' sure the other kiddies don't look to 'em for any ideas and they all keep in line and do as they're told."

Jeremy was horrified as he stared with disbelief at the twelve-year-old. Poised atop a foot-high stool with his back against the cabinetry, his hands were bound together over his head where they clutched at a nylon cord wrapped around his neck and tied off above. Elmo stared back at him, his young dark features clearly showing the strain of trying to remain on the tiny stool while the coach gently rocked, his eyes welling with terror and the pain on hip as tiny tears in his flesh were beginning to separate the skin where it had been creased by Spear's sniper bullet in the helicopter. Jeremy glanced at Matthew and Travis side by side, then at Eric, holding Ian close on his lap in a bear hug, and Lynn beside him. All their eyes watched Jeremy expectantly. Dylan too, but he nodded nearly imperceptibly while his eyes flashed a sly, get-ready look, which Jeremy recognized.

Jeremy pretended to ignore the gun and growled, "Untie him--let him go!"

"I don't think you're in a position to be issuing orders," mused Whitehead with a grin.

Jeremy raised his hand in the kids' direction patting the air. "It's okay, it'll be okay. Peter," Jeremy said, slowly trying to reason with him, knowing it was useless. "Please, let them all go. You wanted me, here I am. Please don't hurt them. They've done nothing to you."

"BRING HIM UP HERE!" ordered the henchman from the driver's seat.

"You all breathe the air," sneered Whitehead, ignoring Jeremy's pleading expression. "That's enough for me."

"Then whatta you want from me?"

"Just your life, that's all."

Jeremy and Whitehead were locked in a deadly stare. For several terrifying moments the only sound filling the rear of the coach was the deep drone of the engine and the wind howling around them. Abruptly, it was pierced by the screeching tires of a Michigan State Police cruiser in a sharp U-turn after just passing them in the opposite lane. Jeremy spun around and watched, along with the others, as a blue Dodge Charger, its high-pitched siren and strobing red and blue lights blared to life. Spotting the cruiser through his side mirror, the henchman cursed, grinding his teeth. He wasn't about to be stopped or fail in his mission. It wasn't in his nature. Besides, his orders came from the top, from very powerful people who won't hesitate to kill him should he fail.

Irritated, he looked up again through the mirror over his head and repeated himself. "Mr. Whitehead, did you hear me?"

"One minute to the top of the hour everyone" Director Bert Mather said into his headset. Still seated beside his production assistant inside the cramped quarters of the mobile control van, parked outside the Governors' ballroom, he was in constant communication with both the station, located at the top of a scenic hill overlooking the blue waters of West Grand Traverse Bay, and his producer, Carl Thibodaux, in the ballroom. "Cue up the intro, stand by Robin. Okay people, look alive, 'cause here we go, on…three…two…one…"

"Now, live, this is Traverse City Today at noon, with Robin Carter…"

Television screens across northern Michigan flashed the eight-second opening theme and animated graphics opening, fading to thirty-year-old news anchor, Robin Carter. The attractive local native, with Scandinavian features, read easily from the teleprompter while closely monitoring her own communications through an earpiece concealed behind her shoulder-length blonde hair. "And good afternoon, Northern Michigan, Robin Carter here with a special edition of news at noon. Coming up, after nearly a year of speculation on his part…"

"Twenty-five seconds to commercial," Bert said into his headset, his keen eyes dancing across the bank of 8-inch color monitors on the panel before him. Number-1 was Robin's, number-2 and 3 were the Ballroom cameras, while number-4 was the NBC Network feed. "Camera one, stay on Miles at the podium. Camera two, let's go a little wider…yeah, right there. As the senator walks across the stage toward the podium, we'll keep it wide. When we switch to one, two, you'll swing around and we'll get a shot of the ballroom. Standby everyone, fifteen seconds."

Bert then turned to his assistant. "We set with the network hook-up?"

The young man in a baseball cap turned, slid aside his headset from one ear and said, "Ready."

Both sets of eyes were on Robin as she wrapped up her intro. "The news begins in one minute."

"And fade to commercial," Bert said, nodding, with a pleased grin at how smoothly things were flowing. "Stand by, boys and girls, sixty seconds."

Carl Thibodaux paced anxiously, as was his habit on live remotes, especially one involving a rare, live hook-up with the NBC Network in New York City. Standing out between the two cameras before the stage in the crowded ballroom, gnawing on his unlit cigar, he preferred to let Bert do his job with minimal interference. He listened to him over his headset, preparing to give his boy the five-second warning.

There was a brief pause, as everyone took a breath, before Bert's deep baritone voice could be heard again over everyone's headsets. "Heads up people, we're about to go nationwide…in ten seconds."

The Ford commercial ended, fading to black, then, two seconds later the screen brightened, displaying the NBC Network logo and opening graphic sequence, accompanied by John Williams' background theme along with Michael Douglas' voiceover.

"From NBC News World Headquarters in New York, this is an NBC News Special Report, here now is Brian Williams…"

Dressed in his iconic dark, navy blue suite, white shirt and matching striped purple tie, Williams looked directly into the camera as it zoomed in on him. "Good afternoon. He's been called one of the most influential and flamboyant individuals in business today, rivaling Donald Trump…"

Bert and the technician watched the network feed, listening over their headsets to the voice of their counterpart in the NBC control room. "Twenty seconds Carl," Bert relayed. "Stand by, Miles."

Engaging Miles eyes, Carl held out his right fist and began extending his fingers in timed intervals while he silently lipped, "Five…four…three…two…one…"

"Good afternoon Brian," Miles acknowledged the Network anchor.

"Miles, you appear to have a front row seat."

"That's right, Brian, I do. We're here in the Governors' ballroom at the beautiful Grand Traverse World Resort and Spa, in Traverse City, Michigan, where in just a few moments…"

Bert spoke smoothly and confidently, his eyes focusing on the video feeds from the two cameras in the ballroom. "Lookin' good, one. Two, lets swing around and get a shot of those excited supporters…okay…that's good. We'll do a slow pan across the room, one. Stand by."

Looking quite dashing in his charcoal gray pinstripe, Miles took a dramatic pause between breaths of his brief presentation, his eyes sweeping across the exuberant crowd in the ballroom, basking in the knowledge that he was on live television before the entire nation, with Brian Williams, no less. He kept his professional composure, never losing that toothy smile.

"Ladies and gentleman, it now gives me great pleasure, and personal pride, to introduce to you, today's honored guest…"

Bert's eyes moved swiftly across the monitors. "Switching to two, go. Start your pan. …Good job, nice and slow. One, line up on the senator…a little tighter…perfect, hold that. …Damn, he's already on the move, switching to one."

From the wings, off to the far side, a tall man with silver hair and pale complexion began his stroll across the stage to the podium like an A-list movie star strutting the red carpet at the Oscars.

"…A man who needs no further introductions…everyone, please join me in welcoming our keynote speaker today, a man we all know and respect…"

The crowed leaped to their feet in a wild frenzy of cheers and thunderous applause. Miles nodded the approach of the man in a Gucci tweed jacket with matching leather loafers. He appeared at ease before the emotional crowd, waving back at them with his large, bony hands.

Miles turned back to the anxious spectators, leaning slightly into the microphone, soaking it all in as he spoke. "Ladies and gentlemen, I give you, Senator Ellis Toddhunter. Or, as he is more affectionately known to all his friends and supporters, the Colonel!"

Miles stepped back from the podium, gesturing to the senator with an open hand.

Senator Ellis 'the Colonel' Toddhunter moved in up to the podium, nodding his thanks and approval to everyone. His cold, gray eyes, twinkling in the intense lights, swept over the rowdy gathering, soaking in the power and glory that fueled his evil, hungry heart.

CHAPTER FORTY-FIVE

Burj Dubai Tower
Dubai, United Arab Emirates

The Zentaurus Corporation, a multinational research and develop-
ment conglomerate, with its home base of operations located on the
147th floor of the world-famed Burj Dubai Tower, had already been
marred by death. A bad omen, some insiders believed. Some months
following the official opening of the tallest building in the world,
a young Asian worker, in an ongoing dispute with one of the construction companies, known for its many human rights violations,
jumped to his death from the very room where twelve men were currently seated around a large rectangular conference table. The board
members were a mix of Asian, Arab and Caucasian. Industrialists all,
each was immensely wealthy and powerful, having reached the pin-
nacle of success in their respective fields at an early age. One other
aspect each of these men shared within the Zentaurus Corporation,
which was nothing more than a front, was their association within its
clandestine operation of the syndicated global slave trade network.

Alerted by their own operative, an emergency meeting had
been convened. It was now 12:06 P.M. in Traverse City, Michigan,
9:06 P.M. on this side of the world in Dubai where ten men in business suits, two in long white Arab garments, sat riveted, watching the
large HD plasma screen on the opposite wall. A series of high-hat
lights encircling the outer perimeter of the sparse conference room

were dimmed, reflecting softly off the deep mahogany paneling. The only other amenity in the room was the fully stocked bar, attended by a tall, attractive Asian woman standing silently in the shadows. There was one additional individual in the darkened conference room, standing obediently beside the board's director at the head of the table, another tall, exquisitely beautiful Asian woman who went by the name of Kaku.

Disturbed by what they were watching, the normally breathtaking view from the room-wide floor-to-ceiling glass panels of the twinkling night lights of Dubai City, accompanied by the shimmering moon-lit surface of the Persian Gulf beyond, went completely unnoticed. The board members bristled in silence the moment the American newscaster leaned into the microphone and said, "Ladies and gentlemen, I give you, Senator Ellis Toddhunter. Or as he is more affectionately known to all his friends and supporters, The Colonel!"

They watched the live newscast, stunned as the head of the North American Slave Network stood before the cheering throng nodding and waving.

"Thank you, thank so much," said the Colonel, beaming from behind a façade of controlled emotion. He waited patiently for the crowd to simmer down until you could have heard a pin drop in the enormous room.

I have them in the palm of my hands, he thought to himself. "When…when my dear wife had passed many years ago, I had seriously considered abandoning my life-long career of public service. It was…a difficult time for me. But my love of duty and country would not allow it. My years in the private sector, then later on in the United States Senate have been enormously rewarding for myself, both professionally and personally. I have always strived to serve this great country to the best of my abilities. Over the years many friends and colleagues have urged me to seek higher political office. I have always followed my conscience. That is why I have come to a decision and to you today, my friends and supporters…to announce my bid, to run for the office of president of the United States of America."

The image on the plasma screen zoomed back, revealing the packed ballroom of people leaping to their feet in an ear-crushing explosion of cheers and clapping. It continued for several minutes, all during which the Colonel waved back warmly at his constituents.

The television screen abruptly went dark.

The gnarled, arthritic hand of Chairman Inzu, the board's Director, pressed another button on the remote, bringing up the high-hat perimeter lights to a comfortable level. He set the device aside, and then motioned for the barmaid to bring him another Andong soju, including anyone else who wished another. The sixty-two-year-old, silver-haired Director took a deep breath, clearing his throat and his mind before he spoke. The other members were equally concerned over the rapidly unfolding crisis half a world away, yet they relied on Inzu's wisdom, as always, to guide them. After the attractive barmaid had replaced his empty glass of the iconic Korean drink with a fresh one, along with three others, he settled back into his chair. The elderly gentleman looked up at Kaku sternly, then around the table at the others before he spoke.

"You have all been apprised of the situation. To recap, despite our purchase of the rights to the Yorkshire documentary 'Conspiracy of Silence' and the subsequent destruction of all copies, I regret to inform you all that a complete, surviving copy has been discovered. General Wu has informed me that the Colonel has it. Also, due to our own blundering we were unsuccessful in our attempts to silence Congressman Denis at his Italian compound. We are in a most precarious position, having now all witnessed the potential disaster the Colonel now brings to our doorstep. He was once a valued and trusted member of this organization. But he has now clearly violated that trust and our code of conduct."

Chairman Inzu drew a contemplative breath.

"I have been in constant communication with our operative," the old man continued, holding out a withered hand where Kaku deposited, on cue, a manila folder. "And it is my unhappy duty to inform you all that General Wu may in fact be dead…"

There was a hushed, but audible gasp around the table from the other members.

Opening the folder, he read from Kaku's notes. "Our last communication from the General was at five eighteen a.m., Eastern Daylight Time, United States. He advised Kaku that the Colonel was being most difficult and that he was, in fact, still entertaining the thought of continuing with his plans. That would now appear to be a moot point. And we've not heard from General Wu since. He does not respond to repeated attempts of his cell phone and he did not make his private jet at the Lodge's airstrip. We suspect the Colonel and Mr. Spear murdered him. Therefore, it is my recommendation that both he and Mr. Spear be immediately terminated."

Chairman Inzu then looked about the table at the muted faces of the board and asked, "Are we all in agreement?"

The board members bowed their heads in their silent reply. Chairman Inzu then nodded thoughtfully, glancing up at Kaku with a wrinkled, sinister smile.

"Mr. Whitehead, did you hear me? I said, bring him up here…and close that thing. Now!" the henchman barked again, gripping the wheel tightly in his hands while the wheels in his head turned, quickly formulating a revised plan to deal with the state trooper hot on their tail.

At that instant, his Bluetooth activated. Kaku's melodic voice greeted him, her delicate tone tinged in a soft Asian accent. "You are instructed to use any and all means to immediately terminate the Colonel and Mr. Spear. His private helicopter is currently located on the roof of the resort hotel."

"Let's go," Whitehead said, motioning with the gun for Jeremy to come forward off the edge of the ramp and inside. The police cruiser, his siren blaring in accompaniment with the rooftop strobing red and blue lights, raced directly behind the Baddog at a mere two car lengths behind. Nearby drivers, stunned at the sight of the unfolding drama right in front of them, had given way, easing back and out of the way of the flashing police cruiser. In the officer's view were two dirt bikes at the top of the ramp with what appeared to be a young, blond-headed man in full biker's garb standing beside one of them at the edge of the ramp, while in front of him, inside, just beyond the bikes, stood another young man, bald, in similar garb, aiming a weapon at him. Farther inside he could clearly make out several kids seated on a couch. The officer relayed this information over his radio to the police dispatcher, requesting additional backup.

Jeremy released his hold on the canvas webbing, raised his hands and cautiously stepped inside. Whitehead stepped aside pressing the ramp's 'close' button while Jeremy's eyes scanned the frightened faces of the kids. As the heavy door began lifting Jeremy's gaze stopped on Dylan, acknowledging him with a frown and a curt shake of his head. He hoped the boy would heed him. As long as Whitehead had a gun, anything was too dangerous to attempt. Dylan intensified his gaze at Jeremy then dropped his sight to the floor, hoping Jeremy would follow it, focusing on the nearby release handle for one of the bikes. Whitehead motioned for Jeremy to move forward. From the corner of his eye, Dylan watched as Jeremy, then Whitehead, slowly moved past him. He took a breath, then slyly reached forward and yanked the release handle. The ramp was half-way closed, the police cruiser vanishing from view when one of the bikes suddenly fell over, striking its companion, causing both of them finally to clank against the deck.

Whitehead spun around, his eyes flashing across the kids' muted faces, stopping at Dylan's. He grew intensely angry, waving Jeremy aside and out of the way with his gun and glared at Dylan, barking, "Pick those up and lock 'em back in place!"

Jeremy glanced at the frightened kids, then at Elmo, desperately hanging on.

The door continued inching to a close. Dylan watched it carefully as he rose up and moved over to the fallen bikes. The kids were watching him too. He bent over and picked up the bike closest to him by the handle bars.

The ramp was nearly closed.

Lynn looked over at Elmo struggling. She was catching on, they all were.

"Well?" Whitehead sneered, "secure it, the other one too-- now, Dylan!"

Lynn watched as Jeremy took a step toward Elmo.

Whitehead caught him move, spun around aiming the gun directly at him. "Ah ah, get back!"

Dylan suddenly with all his strength heaved the bike into the edge of the door where the wheel and handle bars clanked against the metal, becoming wedged along the side, jamming it to a stop. Whitehead spun back just as the motor struggled to keep working, then shut off. He bolted at Dylan, clutching him by his shirt with his one hand, while his other shoved the gun into Dylan's neck.

Lynn looked back up at Elmo.

Matthew tapped Travis' arm.

"WHAT'S GOING ON BACK THERE?" the henchman howled.

Eric's eyes flashed on the henchman up front the moment he yelled. He stood up, gripping Lynn's knee for support, squeezing it. She glanced up at him grabbing his wrist to stop him until he shook it free, whispering, "Eric, whatta you--"

"Hey! HEY!" Whitehead barked at Eric, swinging the gun in his direction.

With lightning speed Jeremy exploded, lunging for Whitehead's arm, shoving him hard against the cabinetry. The instant Whitehead's back struck the cupboards, his arm forced against the paneling he groaned, squeezing the trigger. The Glock exploded with a frightening pop! Eric and the other kids cried out, scrambling to the floor on their knees, covering their heads. Jeremy had Whitehead's arm gripped in both hands, slamming it repeatedly as hard as he could, grunting and shouting at the top of his lungs, "LET GO OF IT, DAMN YOU!"

"AAHHH," Elmo screamed, his bound hands over his head clumsily clutching at the top edge of the cabinetry in a desperate effort to keep from falling forward.

Jeremy gasped in pain the instant Whitehead kneed him in the groin.

Another round exploded from the chamber, the bullet shattering a glass cabinet.

"WHAT THE HELLL!" the henchman screeched, the coach veering suddenly as he tried to see what was happening.

"HELLLP--!" Elmo's cries were abruptly choked off as his sandaled feet slipped from the stool, knocking it over. His terror-stricken eyes bugged out as he craned his neck, straining on his tiptoes while struggling and gasping for air through the tightening cord around his neck.

Ian grabbed his backpack, opened it, and shoved his hand down inside, felt for it, then pulled it out and tossed it to Travis.

Travis caught the pocket knife, opening it and then bolted to Elmo's side followed by Matthew. The two boys gripped their friend, holding him, while Travis reached up, quickly severing the line. The three boys went down in a heap just as another shot rang out.

Panicked screams filled the interior of the Baddog.

The bullet roared past the henchman, shattering the passenger windshield in a hail of glass fragments.

The coach suddenly began weaving erratically in and out of both lanes as the henchman ducked, struggling to hold onto the wheel.

Jeremy went ballistic, smashing Whitehead in the face with his elbow just as hard as he could, over and over, until the Glock fell to the floor with a thud. He viciously clutched Whitehead's collar, plunging his knee into his chest, and then shoved him as hard as he could to the floor.

Whitehead wasn't finished.

Dylan went for the ramp control, slapping the 'open' button-- the door activated, slowly creeping back down, releasing the dirt bike.

The instant Jeremy kicked the Glock hard across the carpet, Whitehead lunged for it but missed. He pushed his upper body, twisting, reaching out with both hands, tripping Jeremy as he scrambled to get it first. As he went down, Whitehead leaped on top of him, pinning Jeremy, swinging as hard as he could at his head with his clinched fists. Jeremy tried blocking him, but he was rapidly losing ground with each painful blow.

Dylan leaped atop Whitehead, trying to pull him off, only to be thrown backward into the cabin as Whitehead violently reared back.

The heavy metal ramp came to a screeching stop, skidding over the pavement, while shooting out a stream of sparks trailing behind the wildly maneuvering coach. The police cruiser, now joined by a second one, trailed close behind them, with both sets of lights strobing like dance floor beacons. The officers could only watch in helpless dismay as a fight between two individuals in biker gear stumbled over one of the fallen bikes and out onto the sparking ramp.

Suddenly the other dirt bike, its handle bars ensnared by the heavy support cable, was sent tumbling off the ramp the moment Jeremy's shoulder crashed into it. The police cruisers veered abruptly, missing the bike as it smashed and spun wildly across the pavement.

Appearing out of the blue sky, Richard's Bell 222 slid overhead at about a hundred feet, revealing a frightening scene below of the massive motorcoach weaving from lane to lane, keeping two police cruisers at bay. As they eased over the back end with the open, sparking ramp, Charlee gasped over her headset, "That looks like Jeremy down there…fighting with…I think it's Whitehead!"

Whitehead landed back on top of Jeremy, slamming him against the ramp, delivering a devastating blow to his chest with his closed fist. He then roared off him, back into the cabin as Jeremy doubled over on his side in gasping pain, his one hand clutching the inside edge of the ramp. Dylan knew Whitehead was going for the Glock and he lunged for it, but wasn't quick enough. Whitehead snatched it from the carpet, glaring back at the boy with a satisfied grin. Dylan jumped back, tripping over Elmo, landing beside him, his hand resting next to his prosthetic leg. Beside him on the floor the kids huddled together, watching Whitehead with terrified expressions, too scared to move.

The erratic weaving subsided as the henchman saw Whitehead regaining control. He made a quick mental note to himself. The moment he stopped, before killing Spear and the Colonel, he was going to kill this idiot.

"The first bullet's for Jeremy," Whitehead snarled at Dylan. "The next one's for you!"

The moment Whitehead turned away, Dylan's hand stealthily moved up and gripped Elmo's prosthetic limb, tugging on it.

Jeremy, gasping, forcing air back into his lungs while still gripping the leading edge of the ramp, began to crawl back inside, straddling over the fallen bike. He reached out and grabbed the nylon webbing swinging next to him, pulling himself to his feet. Just behind him the ramp was still screaming and spewing sparks. Laboring to breathe, the warm, cyclone-like summer air whipping around him, Jeremy stood facing Whitehead, watching as his bitter enemy slowly moved toward him.

Elmo cautiously, and with great finesse, slipped his prosthetic limb from his leg. Dylan then gripped it tightly and waited.

Still grinning, Whitehead took careful aim directly at Jeremy.

Everything next seemed to happen in slow motion.

Dylan lunged at Whitehead wielding Elmo's prosthetic limb in both hands like a battle-axe, a pent-up guttural rage bellowing from deep within his lungs, striking him as hard as he could along his shoulder blades. Jeremy fell to the side just as Whitehead went tumbling to the ramp and onto the fallen bike, Elmo's prosthetic limb right along with him disappearing over the edge. As he went down, Whitehead grabbed at the nylon webbing. Quickly realizing he couldn't hold on while clutching the Glock, he let the weapon go, hearing it clank against the ramp and then out onto the hard pavement, disappearing as well. Struggling with the nylon webbing until a portion of it tore from its pinnings, Whitehead suddenly disappeared over the edge out onto the speeding pavement.

Dylan leaped at the ramp control button, then went for Jeremy, helping him. The two stumbled back inside as the door raised back upward. Once the huge door came to a close, the locking mechanism engaging with a click, a gasping but relieved, thankful smile eased across Jeremy's dirty face, matching Dylan's. He gave Dylan a quick embrace, then hastily withdrew from the arm pocket of his jacket the smartphone, shoving it into Dylan's hand, missing the boy's surprise and elation, sputtering, "Here, take this."

Jeremy dropped to his knees, embracing the kids on the floor. He quickly assured them and his brothers that he was fine and then told them all to stay put!

He staggered back to his feet and forward to the henchman at the wheel.

Jeremy stood behind him and snapped, "Hey you! You gonna stop this thing?"

The henchman said nothing as he weighed his options, his eyes checking the vicinity of the two Michigan State Trooper cars in his side mirror. Though they weren't far behind, with Whitehead out of the way, he could now resume his mission with minimal interference. His occupants were unimportant and a minor obstacle.

Jeremy recognized where they were the moment they crested a hill. Coming into view through the midday summer haze was the resort's expansive golf courses dotted with dense green vegetation, sand traps and ponds. And beyond was the emerald east arm of Grand Traverse Bay.

What he couldn't see was the Wojtecki wedding party set up on the outdoor pavilion just outside the conference center, and the Governors' Ballroom.

Melanie gazed down at the newly minted business card in her petite hand and read the stylish wording softly to herself for the third time as if it were poetry, "ForeverGreen Events, Inc., Melanie Michaels, Destination Wedding Designer, Extraordinaire."

She smiled privately to herself as she surveyed the lavishly decorated pavilion beneath the expansive canopy. Laid out before her were three hundred folding white chairs divided down the center by a wide red carpet leading up to a flowered archway, shrouded in purple hydrangeas and green baby's breath, flanked on both sides with multiple arrangements of red, pink and white roses. Toward the back on her right side was a large table sheathed in white linen with a matching wrap-around skirt. On it, placed in the center was her proudest accomplishment. As part of her business, she had personally designed and made a beautifully decorated, three-tiered wedding cake. Off to the side was a large cut-glass punch bowl with a center fountain spewing Dom Perignon. The gentle honking of a flock of mallards out on a distant pond stirred her gaze. The overall effect was stunning, she felt. It was perfect.

While her crew, a sister and two friends put the final touches on the flower arrangements, Melanie glowed. The Wojtecki wedding was the first real job of her fledgling business. And she couldn't have been more excited and proud.

The Baddog motorcoach began streaking past the first of the resort's golfing fairways on the right.

"Whatta you doing?" Jeremy blurted at the henchman again. "Answer me!"

Jeremy nervously watched as they flew through the intersection of Lautner Road.

"Please!" he pleaded wearily, "stop this thing!"

The henchman knew it was only a matter of minutes before the two pursuing state troopers would be joined by more. And to accomplish his mission, he was going to have to create as much chaos as possible. It was time to make his move. He glared up at Jeremy through the overhead mirror and finally answered him with deadly intent and a satirical grin, "Better hold on kid, we're goin' for a little riiide."

Jeremy's eyes widened in shock as they scanned the highway ahead, then over to the fairways streaking by. He immediately spun around, grabbing cushions from the couch and chair while barking directions at the kids.

"GET ON THE FLOOR, ALL OF YOU, RIGHT NOW--HERE--TAKE THESE!"

Jeremy ignored the look of alarm etched across all their faces and hustled the kids to the floor, pushing cushions at them. He grabbed a terrified Ian and shoved him into Eric's arms.

Frozen like a statue on the couch, Jeremy snatched Lynn, pulling her to the floor. The look of terror in her face said it all. "Where's he going?" she uttered breathlessly.

"I dunno--" he sputtered before leaning in, whispering, "stay down here with the kids."

She nodded quickly.

Jeremy hustled the terrified twins down beside Eric and Ian. "C'mon, boys--Elmo, c'mon, get down here--keep your heads down, stay under these cushions…"

Everyone cried out as the motorcoach suddenly veered right. Jeremy lost his balance, falling on his side against the couch. He grappled with it, struggling to his knees, looking out the window. He watched in horror as the coach bounced wildly, leaving M-seventy-two for a dirt access road running parallel to the highway that briefly appeared from a wooded grove. He next went for Dylan, clumsily falling again. The boy, clutching the edge of a cabinet, didn't scare easily but he was too frightened to move. Jeremy pulled him down, thrusting a cushion into his shaking hands. "Stay under this!"

Speeding at 50 mph the 63,300-pound, 45-foot Baddog motorcoach pitched violently from side to side as the heavy-duty wheels dug into the soft soil, throwing up clouds of earth.

The Michigan State Troopers, lights beaming and flashing, split up. One of them roared on down the highway toward Acme, while the remaining car trailed close behind, its rear tires fishtailing sporadically through the loose dirt.

The speeding coach narrowly missed a grove of maples where a thick low-hanging branch smashed across the broken, open passenger window in an explosion of green leaves and chunks of bark, whacking off the passenger side mirror. The massive vehicle flew off the dirt road and right onto one of the fairways, tearing up the manicured grass in its destructive wake like a freight train through snow.

George Miller, retired high school history teacher and avid golfer bent slightly at the waist over his ball on the teeing ground overlooking the ninth green, lining up his shot. The 63-year-old peered down at it, then out over the fairway toward his intended target marked with a small flag on a pole fluttering in the breeze. Behind him stood his silver-haired wife, Elaine, along with two additional friends.

It was a lovely afternoon for a relaxing foursome.

Gripping the driver firmly in both hands, his eyes spied the ball, then again down the fairway, taking careful aim. Miller drew a deep breath and held it. As his arms swung upward, Elaine gasped, abruptly breaking his focused concentration, sending him stumbling backward like a drunk.

"For cryin' out loud, Elaine!" he snapped the moment he recovered. "What the hell--you know better than to--"

"LOOK!" she blurted again and pointed.

The quiet calm of the fairway was abruptly shattered by a flock of birds squawking and leaping into the air. The group of four senior citizens did double takes in the direction of the intrusion, shielding their eyes against the noonday sun, straining to see what it was that was barreling down the fairway in their direction.

"Is that a…?" one of them started to mumble.

"That's no golf cart," someone else in the group concluded.

Then Elaine asked, "That can't be sanctioned by the PGA, can it?"

Jeremy reared up on his knees, holding onto anything for support and watched as the crazed henchman feverishly worked the steering wheel, maintaining control. Out front through the panoramic windshield, it was a wild scene of scattering carts and golfers in a mad panic as the rampaging motorcoach careened down the fairway toward the distant resort.

The henchman's large hands jerked the wheel to the left. A thunderous crash followed, sending the coach into a shuddered convulsion as if a bomb had gone off. Clipping an empty golf cart, large pieces of it, including clubs, catapulted through the air. The inside of the coach rocked ferociously, sending the kids sliding to and fro, wailing from underneath the cushions

"HOLD ON!" Jeremy shouted.

Word reached resort security that there was some sort of disturbance out on the south grounds. They in turn immediately alerted the Governors' Ballroom and the senator's head of security. Mr. Spear gathered as much information as he could, assessed the situation, then took the Colonel aside and quickly advised him.

Miles's curiosity was piqued as he watched the two men disappear out a side door.

Jeremy's eyes never stopped bulging. Up ahead he saw what looked like some kind of gathering with a large number of empty white chairs neatly lined up beneath a massive canopy. A wedding--he spotted the huge cake.

He grimaced wildly, instinctively ducking his head, as the Baddog rocketed between another grove of trees. The peaceful summer calm of the fairway was shattered by an explosive shearing of leaves and branches as the massive coach shot through and out onto an inclining sand trap like a cannonball. The heavy coach roared up the sandy hill and over the manicured edge where the front tires lost traction, going airborne until they smashed back down onto the putting green on the seventh hole. The rear tires spun out, digging into the thin delicate carpet of bentgrass, gouging out a long deep scar, spitting out turf and ripping out the flagstick in the center of the green. Grinning from the adrenaline rush coursing through his veins, the henchman gunned the gas pedal, accelerating the Baddog in the direction of a grove of trees, and the conference center beyond, in an effort to throw off the pursuing police cruiser.

The state trooper avoided the same narrow grove of trees, snapping the wheel hard over in the opposite direction and veering suddenly for a wider gap; yet misjudged the opening. Flying between two thick oak trees he spared the hapless police cruiser yet managed to neatly slice off both of his side mirrors. They ricocheted through the air, barely settling to the ground when another grove of trees appeared out of nowhere. Maneuvering quickly, like the stunt driver he fancied himself to be, the trooper spun the cruiser then slammed on the brakes. He expertly missed them. However, the blunt force trauma sustained from the head on impact with a solid maple, left the cruiser dead in its tracks. Shaken but unhurt, the trooper grimaced while gray smoke and sparks snapped from the front grill and beacon. The siren chirped feebly for a few seconds, then died, along with the strobing rooftop lights.

Jeremy was riveted by the sight of the event set up under the canopy--they were racing straight for it. "Oh, shit!" he muttered.

"STAY DOWN!" he bellowed over the racket and clatter just before he flew on top of Lynn and the others with his body. He protectively stretched out both arms covering who he could.

Melanie, after hearing the commotion and chatter over the radio from a nearby resort employee concerning a large vehicle running amuck on the fairways, ran back to her creation beneath the canopy. She had barely made it outside a few steps when she saw the marauding motorcoach cutting a swath across the lawn in a beeline for the pavilion. She watched helplessly as the catering staff began screaming, running for their lives--leaving behind her doomed wedding cake--like a sitting duck. Melanie froze, gaping with speechless disbelief. Then she simply keeled over backward, passing out on the soft green grass.

The thirteen-foot high canopy was a mere few inches shy of clearing the devastating Baddog. The leading edge's heavy duty support cable was an unforgiving executioner. In a thunderous tearing *WHOOOOOSH!* everything on the massive RV's roof; first the forward domed satellite housing, followed by the first air conditioner, the skylight in the center, then the top of the ladder, were all violently sheared off like blades of grass in a hail of screeching aluminum and metal. A millisecond later the remaining end air-conditioner unit caught the guillotine-like cable, snagging it and the canopy, taking it right along with it.

Like some stampeding bull charging the pavilion, the air was instantly filled with an eruption of white chairs. The rapid-fire slap against the front of the projectile coach was a frightening sensation drowning out everything. An instant later the flower-shrouded archway exploded into a million pieces, crushed by the front of the coach. Like confetti in a street parade pieces of wood, hydrangeas, baby's breath and hundreds of roses were violently launched and rained everywhere.

Dead ahead lay a large pond which the henchman steered directly for.

As Jeremy lay protectively across the kids Lynn cried out. Clinging to her tightly, one of his hands found hers, and he grasped it. She squeezed back--terrified.

The lumbering 45-foot Baddog, its front battered, the bumper severely mangled and deformed, flew into the pond, scattering panicked mallards and sending a wall of spray into the sun-drenched sky. Everyone slid forward over the carpet to the wall and to an abrupt stop.

There were several moments of jarring silence as the front tires slowly sank into the muddy bottom, until water began gurgling over the edge of the missing passenger window, sending a wave with floating debris over the disoriented kids. The Cummins heavy-duty truck engine wheezed, then suffocated and died in clouds of sizzling steam and dark smoke bellowing from the rear engine compartment.

"Hey--we're sinking!" shouted one of the kids.

Jeremy hustled, grabbing Lynn's arm and anyone else he could to their feet.

"Looks like we mowed through a floral shop," Lynn uttered, sweeping her hair aside, noticing the roses swirling about her ankles.

"Yeah," Jeremy muttered back, distracted, noticing the henchman had already disappeared, probably out the broken window. Water gushed over the front dash console, flooding the Baddog. He then turned to her and said, "Let's get everyone outta here--c'mon everyone, let's go!"

Lynn led the way, gingerly crawling over the edge and stepping down into the cool murky water. It was deep but she wasn't scared. Ian led the rest of the kids, after slipping on his backpack, accompanied by Eric at his side. One by one, the kids crawled over the edge of the window through the streaming water into the deep pond and swam, then waded ashore.

"Careful, you don't cut yourself on the edge there," Jeremy warned each of them.

Lynn helped Matthew and Travis, then turned to help Elmo. Without his prosthetic limb, he slung his arm over her shoulder and the two gingerly crawled over the dash and swam away from the smoldering RV.

Dylan came up behind Jeremy.

Jeremy asked him, "You all right?"

The boy nodded wearily and crawled on out the shattered window.

Jeremy followed him into the water and to shore, thankfully joining the others, noticing a crowd of golfers and curious onlookers gathering nearby on the lawn.

Fred had driven around the resort via the long perimeter drive and swung around to the rear of the conference center, converging on the south lawn just as Richard's Bell 222 touched down gently near the tennis courts. Leslie was the first to emerge from the RV, bursting through the door followed by the slacked-jawed RV salesman, after spotting the smoking Baddog in the pond. Leslie spun and kissed Fred on the cheek, thanking him for his help and dashed across the lawn for Jeremy and the others.

Fred was exhilarated as he watched her. He then turned to the RV and lovingly patted the aluminum skin and said, "Nice goin', darlin'!"

Jeremy turned just as Leslie ran into his arms. He kissed her, then hugged her tightly, thankful their nightmare was over. They were finally all home safe and sound.

Melanie awoke dazed, but not confused. She sat up, but was too terrified to look over her shoulder. Finally, she forced herself. Melanie cringed at the trail of destruction beneath the shredded pavilion and started to cry. The tornado-like swath cut by the motorcoach through the pavilion had left mangled white chairs strewn about the surrounding lawn, like fallen soldiers on the battlefield.

Then she suddenly gasped in thankful amazement.

Her exquisite wedding cake was unscathed--still sitting majestically on the table where it had been placed. Melanie frowned, though, the moment she witnessed one of the catering staff helping himself to the punch bowl. After filling one of the tiny glasses, he lifted it skyward in thankful repose, 'crossed himself', then snapped his head back gulping the Perignon.

Jeremy released Leslie to arms-length and stared into her eyes. Then suddenly, for the first time in days, they heard Ian cry out. Jeremy and the others, dripping wet as though they had all just emerged from a water park slide, whipped around, looking. Stunned by what they all saw, none of them could believe who held onto the small boy tightly, looking like he'd just emerged from a bloody car wreck.

CHAPTER FORTY-SIX

Whitehead made eye contact with his hated enemy while wrath-fully clutching Ian by the shoulder straps of his backpack, reveling in everyone's shocked expression at seeing him alive. His main objective was to get Jeremy's attention.

He got it.

"Knock it off!" growled Whitehead, jerking the boy subduing his efforts to get free.

Jeremy stared back at him with an incredulous slacked-jawed gaze, finally uttering, "...I don't believe it!"

"Where did he come from?" Leslie gasped in equal shock.

"Hell," Dylan whispered bitterly.

After Whitehead tumbled down the ramp of the Baddog, dropping his Glock out onto the streaking highway, then snagging the nylon webbing as he went over the edge, he was violently whipped around and dragged along the pavement at breakneck speed. His boots and heavy-duty polyester pants and jacket protected his muscled body for the most part, but not his hands. As he clung underhanded to the webbing, the skin along the top of both hands and knuckles was rapidly scraped to the bone.

He yelled out against the excruciating pain, while using every ounce of his brute strength to hold on.

Something in the roadway streaked beneath him, tearing a violent gash from his left shoulder to his wrist, nearly ripping the sleeve clean off, turning his exposed flesh red. When the ramp began rising, Whitehead went with it. The thick nylon webbing lifted him from the speeding pavement until it closed and he banged against it, dangling like a stranded mountain climber. Working his shredded and bloodied hands through the mesh webbing, entangling them, he managed to hold on.

Now, as he stood there before a gathering crowd of incredulous spectators, jacket torn and bloodied, he clutched a terrified Ian by his backpack straps with a hand that looked as if it had been dipped in red paint. In his other bloodied hand at his side, he held the Glock he'd recovered earlier from the dead henchman following the sniper attack outside the RV's at the abandoned barn. He grinned at Jeremy, then thrust the weapon overhead, squeezing the trigger in quick succession, firing off several explosive rounds sending the kids and onlookers alike screaming and scrambling for cover. Ian cried out, trying to get away, nearly choking on his noose-like collar. Whitehead again yanked him sharply, then stormed off in the direction of the conference center, dragging the boy with him.

Jeremy quickly rose up, helping Leslie to her feet, then said through clenched teeth, "Take care of the kids."

Before she could respond, he'd run off after them, favoring his good leg as he went.

Gathering the kids together Leslie spotted Richard, Dane and Charlee exiting the Bell 222 where it had landed near the tennis courts. She quickly sputtered to Elmo, "Keep everyone together and wait here--I'll be right back."

She then sprinted across the lawn in the direction of the Bell.

The moment Whitehead burst through the glass double-doors of the crowded conference center lobby with Ian clutched at his side, he instantly caught the attention of everyone. Spotting the weapon in his hand people froze nervously where they stood. There was a moment of curious, hushed silence followed by screams of panic as he again opened fired with the Glock, at the ceiling shattering several lighting fixtures in a hail of splintered glass and sparks. People clambered for cover as Whitehead strolled across the carpet, heading down a long wide hall where unaware people were caught off guard, gasping and cowering as he waved the weapon about. Spotting the two side-by-side scenic elevators in the main lobby, he pulled Ian along. The boy gasped and grunted in protest as he continued to struggle against Whitehead's grasp, but it was no use.

He couldn't get loose.

Gripping the Glock, his finger pressed the call button and a car arrived in short order. The door slid open and he shoved the boy inside, releasing him. Blocking Ian's escape until the door closed, Whitehead then stepped aside and pressed the muzzle end of the barrel of the Glock against the button marked, *Roof Top HeliDeck*.

Whitehead then looked down at the boy. "What's the matter, kid? Cat got your tongue?"

Shaking, too frightened to answer him, Ian could only stare back at Whitehead as they rode to the top in silence. Whitehead ignored him, looking away, staring out the glass enclosure at the green scenery around the resort. The pain, though, he couldn't ignore. To overcome it he instead focused on his hate for Jeremy. He breathed deeply as he briefly surveyed his own blood-soaked and torn biker jacket and pants. He never even heard the elevator stop and the door open behind him. He slapped the 'hold' button, locking the elevator and doors open.

"You, me and Jeremy have a date with destiny," Whitehead said to Ian prophetically.

Ian felt sudden guilt for the all the unkind things he'd said to him. Though he'd been bullied by Whitehead over the years, he suddenly realized it had brought out the bully in him. Still scared, he found his 'voice', absent for days, had returned and he somehow wanted to make it up to him when he said, "You don't hav'ta to do this, Peter."

Whitehead painfully knelt down before the boy, holding one of his injured hands close to his chest and said, "Yes I do--it's ahh--it's in my nature. It always has been. I have to admit you were an easy target, kid."

"But you can be the hero, and save us," Ian told him.

Whitehead laughed, and then frowned. "You think I'm Luke Skywalker or somethin'?"

"You can be--I know you can," Ian pleaded with him. "And if there's a trial, I can be a witness in your defense, I can help you. I'm gonna be a lawyer someday."

Whitehead said nothing as he looked at the boy. All he could think of was hurting Jeremy…maybe even kill him.

There was a moment when Ian thought he saw a glimmer of good in his eyes, but then it seemed to abruptly vanished the instant Whitehead shook his head and muttered, "…A lawyer, huh? …I'm sorry--"

"I'm sorry too…for the hateful things I said to you."

"You really mean that, don't you?"

"Yes."

Whitehead felt himself beginning to crack--to feel…empathy. And that angered him.

"Well, well," a gravelly voice said from behind. The henchman emerged from the sun-drenched deck into the elevator alcove and approached the pair. "And I thought you were dead."

"Let's go, Ian," Whitehead stood and said smoothly, ultimately ignoring the boy, herding him out the door and into the sunshine.

Jeremy tore into the lobby, abruptly sending everyone scrambling for cover again. Trying to determine where Whitehead had disappeared to, he could hear muffled cries and hushed panicked voices from people cowering behind pillars, furniture, anything for protection.

In the seemingly empty lobby Jeremy shouted, "He had a small boy with him…WHERE IS HE?"

Reluctantly, a man in slacks and a tan blazer with a 'Hello, my name is' name tag on his lapel finally stood up from behind a plush chair and pointed down the hall in the direction of the main lobby. "…He ahh, he took the elevator."

The moment Jeremy took off across the lobby people began streaming out through the doors of the Governors' Hall as instructed by resort security, filling the lobby, unaware of what was happening. Caroline and Robert, hand in hand, were among the crowd. Suddenly, Caroline tugged at Robert's sleeve.

"Huh?"

"Robert, look, is that--"

"It's Jeremy!"

Both were speechless as they watched their son sprint with a limp to the scenic elevators where an arriving car opened on cue. The instant he stepped inside he pressed one of the buttons. The doors closed and the car rose, disappearing through the superstructure and into the midday sunshine, gliding upward along the side of the tower toward the rooftop helipad.

"What's he doing here?" Caroline gasped. "Where are the other kids?"

"I have no idea," Robert uttered back in shocked confusion. He quickly recovered and said to her, "But I'm gonna find out. Get the parents together and wait here for me."

"All right," Caroline said briskly the instant before he took off across the crowded lobby.

Seeing his disheveled reflection Jeremy took a step toward the glass, and for a moment, closed his eyes. When he opened them, he drew in a deep, labored breath, watching the plush landscape below slowly slipping away from him.

He then peered up at the bright sky and whispered, "If you're really up there, I'm *not* gonna let anything happen to Ian. So, you can either help me, or get outta my way. 'Cause if you're plannin' on takin' one of us before this is over…then you take *me*, not Ian!"

His heart jumped when the elevator slowed and came to a stop. The door eased open.

Jeremy was greeted by an eerie stillness and wooden sawhorse a few feet in front of the door blocking his way. For whatever reason, the car had stopped on the floor below the roof. Then he noticed he'd pressed the wrong button. With all the construction, it should've been locked. Jeremy listened but heard nothing. He held his breath and peered inside.

At first, he didn't recognize the Trillium dining room, although having dined here in the past with his parents.

Jeremy cautiously stepped inside, going around the sawhorse. In the midst of remodeling construction, he noticed all the chairs and tables were stacked toward the back of the enormous room, draped in sheets. A long workbench, with a large tool chest on wheels standing beside it, was located off to one side. Paint cans and other supplies along with lights and scaffolding littered the room. Stained drop cloths lined the floor right up to the plate-glass windows overlooking the countryside and East Grand Traverse Bay beyond. It was then that shadows from above caught his eye. He glanced up to see three figures walking around the 35-foot-diameter smoked-glass skylight. It was the henchman, then Ian, followed by Whitehead. Jeremy quickly ducked out of sight. His head spun until he spotted what he was looking for. Directly behind him was a door marked, *To HeliDeck*.

Jeremy bolted through it.

It looked like a stairway to heaven the moment he paused looking up, the sunlight nearly blinding. All he could see was blue sky framed by the open doorway at the top. A stairway to heaven…or to hell, he wondered?

Jeremy slowly ascended the stairs. When he reached the top landing, he stepped into an alcove with a double set of elevator doors leading out onto the helideck. That's where he froze.

"We've been expecting you," the henchman said to him.

Head of resort security was 32-year-old, Toby Kellur. An ex-Navy SEAL, he had a physique rivaling a professional bodybuilder. He was an imposing individual to reckon with, standing at 5' 11" and weighing in at two hundred and thirty pounds. Possessing a deep, authoritative voice, Kellur automatically commanded respect. It didn't hurt either that he had matching rugged features with trimmed sandy blond hair. And this man took crap from no one.

The moment he heard of the disturbance concerning the marauding RV tearing up the grounds, he immediately raced to his office. His first call was to 911, then to his staff of ten over the radio to coordinate whatever had to be done. And with a visiting senator and hundreds of people in attendance, he was decisive in his actions.

Panting from his sprint, standing in the small security office located behind the front desk, Kellur quickly studied the row of closed circuit cameras, trying to determine the location of the driver after he'd disappeared. Using a hand-held remote, he brought up the cam aimed at the pond where the huge RV had crashed. Rewinding the disc just prior to impact, he then hit 'play' and watched as the RV careened into the pond. Moments later he watched as a large man dressed in a full black suit crawled out the shattered front window and took off running across the grounds, out of sight. He tried tracking him, switching to various exterior cams, but it was no use.

He'd vanished.

In his search, accessing the dozens of cameras throughout the resort, he took a step closer the instant something on the rooftop elevator alcove cam caught his eye. Switching to the wider helideck cam on the larger main monitor, he witnessed several people. One of them, oddly, was Senator Toddhunter and his security man. Opposite them, holding a weapon, was the black suited RV driver. His weapon was trained on two others, both individuals dressed in biker garb.

"Oh my God," Kellur muttered, suspecting an assassination attempt.

Bolting from the office, he brought the radio to his lips and immediately began directing his staff.

Just outside the Governors' Hall rear door, sprinting to the mobile control van, Miles bumped into Carl and his cameraman, Stan, gripping an EFP camera: a lightweight Electronic Field Production camera capable of transmitting signals back to the broadcast mobile van and light enough to be carried on the shoulder supported by a shoulder stock.

Carl said, "There you are."

"What's going on?" Miles spat, panting. "Where'd they go?"

"Who?--Look, security says there was some RV tooling down one of the fairways like a bat outta hell--already mowed through the pavilion."

"The Senator and Spear, they just vanished--the wedding?"

"No one was injured, just demolished the set-up--they probably went back to the green room, listen--"

"No, I just checked, it's empty

Carl took a breath, "Are we having two different conversations here?"

"The helideck," Miles snapped his finger and said quickly. "I'll bet they went up there."

"Well he's not the first politician to be whisked away in the middle of a crisis--forget about him for a moment, take Stan here--"

"Forget about 'em," Miles blurted, "Hey, Carl, somethin's weird going on with those two--"

Carl thought quickly then argued, "And you may be right, Miles, I'll have Stewie check it out--that's what gophers are for. In the meantime, you and Stan go outside and see if you can capture anything--security wants this place emptied..."

"But--"

"You got your radio?"

"Yeah."

Carl was off and running back to the control van, throwing over his shoulder, "I'll have Tommy radio you!"

Miles spun on his heels and said, "C'mon Stan."

Leslie ran back, flanked by Richard, Charlee and Dane, the fishing tube clutched tightly in his hand, to the kids milling at the edge of the pond and the half-sunk, smoldering Baddog in the background. The instant Charlee saw Dylan she burst into tears and sprinted for him.

Richard hung back for a moment.

Dylan abruptly broke down too the moment he embraced his sister tightly as though he'd never let her go again, his face buried in her neck, the both of them sobbing.

"Where's Jeremy--where did he go?" Travis gushed at Leslie in a near panic.

"Where'd Peter take Ian?" Matthew asked urgently. "Where'd they go?"

"I don't know," she said at a loss, exchanging a worried look with Dane.

"Is there a--" Dylan tried to say, clearing his throat while wiping his eyes. "...Is there a helipad here?"

"There is," Dane perked up and sputtered. He spun around looking up toward the resort tower. "Up there--on the roof."

"The Colonel never goes anywhere but by helicopter," Dylan continued, looking up at the tower too. "That's probably where Whitehead took Ian. I'll bet'cha they're all up there."

"Let's go!" barked Dane.

Charlee looked over at her father and waved him to come closer.

Richard's eyes began to well up as he approached the two, first focusing on Charlee, then his son.

Richard wiped his eyes, then reached out cupping Dylan's cheek and uttered, "Hi, Dylan."

Dylan looked at the man he never knew and felt the anger he'd held in his heart for so long suddenly melt away. He took a step and Richard wrapped his arms around the boy and held him tight. Richard could feel the boy trembling as he kept sobbing.

For a few moments, as Charlee embraced her father and brother, the three of them tuned out the surrounding chaos.

The instant Carl burst into the mobile control van and slid into the seat beside his director, Bert Mather, donning his headset, he said, "Get the network back on the line, Bertie, we may have something big unfolding here."

Avoiding the crowds that were exiting the conference center building, Dane led the way, sprinting across the lawn, around to a set of double doors on the north side of the tower. People were streaming out those doors as well. Squeezing their way through and into the main lobby, the kids crowded in behind Dane when he stopped in his tracks.

"Look at that mob of people at the elevators," Lynn shouted over the din, still shouldering Elmo. The twins moved in, relieving her, hoisting Elmo's arms about their own shoulders.

While people fearfully scrambled about the lobby an intermittent alarm had been activated, blaring from speakers embedded in the high ceiling, accompanied by flashing emergency lights above all the exit doors. A woman's authoritative voice over the resort PA system urged guests to remain calm and to seek safety by way of the nearest flashing exit.

"Where do we go now?" Eric asked.

"We can't go that way," Dane said, thinking, his eyes quickly scanning the lobby.

"There it is," Leslie said, pointing at a door to the right of the front desk.

"That's it--c'mon!" Dane snapped.

Threading themselves through the throng of panicked guests, Dane and the kids filed quickly through the door into the quiet stairwell marked with a placard that read, *Stairway-Lobby to Roof Top HeliDeck.*

With Leslie close behind him, Dane ascended to the fourth step then paused, facing the group of panting kids, motioning upward with the fishing tube like a pointer. "You all up for a twenty-six floor jaunt?"

Eric bolted past the two, shouting, his voice reverberating off the stairwell walls, "Just try and keep up with me!"

Dane, Leslie and the kids took off hot on Eric's heels, clamoring up the stairs, the twins helping Elmo, bringing up the rear.

Jeremy had no more fight left in him. Exhausted and drained, all he wanted to do was collapse and pass out. He moved slowly, shielding his eyes against the midday sun while a light breeze strafed across the helideck and, all the while, Ian, not far from his sight.

The helideck was large and spacious. In front of him and to his right was the 35-foot-diameter, smoked-glass skylight. To his left, directly behind the skylight, separated by a pair of sawhorses with yellow caution tape stretched across them, substituting a metal railing that had yet to be installed was the helipad. In the center, emblazoned with raised red lettering along the side was the Colonel's black Scorpion Longranger helicopter.

In the co-pilot seat with the door propped open was the Colonel, his attention buried in his smartphone. The senator sat in utter dismay. The unthinkable, the inconceivable was happening! His carefully crafted world of power and deception, years in the making, was abruptly crumbling around him--and all at the hands of a teenage boy brought about by that insipid Whitehead. And there was nothing he could do to stop it--except exact his revenge on the both of them. The mere thought of it quickened his heart of stone.

Jeremy stopped and stood, unaware of the 240,000-gallon water tank located on the far side of the deck, partially sunken through the roof. Its Caribbean blue coloring blended nearly perfectly with the equally blue Michigan skyline. Before him stood the henchman holding a gun, flanked by Spear and Whitehead, whose dried, blood-stained hand rested on Ian's shoulder.

Jeremy looked at Ian and asked, "You okay?"

The boy nodded nervously with wide eyes.

Jeremy focused on Spear when he said, "Let the boy go. It's me you want."

The henchman grinned privately to himself; they were all together now. His next and final task will be a breeze, he thought. His mistake though would be letting his guard down at the end.

"That's true," Spear said. "But first things first, as they say."

There wasn't time to process what happened next. In a split-second Spear withdrew his Glock from his shoulder holster underneath his jacket and, with expert killing skill, aimed his weapon across the deck at his forehead and pulled the trigger.

A guttural groan gushed from the henchman's lips before his back even hit the deck--dead.

Ian gasped and cried out trying to break free of Whitehead's grasp just as Jeremy jumped back, recoiling in shock.

"I've suspected that one for some time now," Spear noted calmly, more for the Colonel's sake than Jeremy's. "Turns out he's one of Inzu's operatives. As for our other mole in the organization, Henry, well, I'll deal with him eventually. A pity this poor gentleman, here, wasn't killed along with the others They were a most useful hit team. At any rate, they served their purpose, as did he."

"You're getting sloppy, Mr. Spear," groused the Colonel. "Do we know who employed Henry?"

"Probably DNI. They've had their eye on you for some time now, sir," Spear replied firmly, shifting the blame back to the Colonel. Even loyalty has its limits he thought to himself.

Jeremy glanced over at the dead henchman sprawled on the deck, his mouth gaped open in a doltish expression, vacant glassy eyes staring upward into space, then over at Spear who met his speechless gaze with piercing eyes and said, "Killing him seemed the prudent thing to do since his assignment was to kill the Colonel and me. Don't you agree?"

Spear's attention strayed for only a moment when he snapped at Whitehead, still grappling with Ian, "HOLD HIM!"

Jeremy saw an opening and bolted.

"HEY!" the enforcer erupted, spinning on his heels, taking aim with his Glock.

Tearing off toward the rear of the black Scorpion, Jeremy ducked underneath the tail boom out of sight. Spear went in the opposite direction and ran to the nose of the aircraft. Though he knew there was nowhere for him to go, Spear nonetheless instinctively held Jeremy in his gun sights and ordered him to stop.

After painfully leaping atop the four-foot ledge skirting the perimeter of the tower, Jeremy froze as ordered. He nearly regretted his move as the partially healed skin on his thigh tore open. The metal pole for the windsock embedded in the ledge provided the only support and Jeremy clutched to it tightly. He looked down and instantly felt a little woozy muttering, "Oh, god." He abruptly looked away, shuddering, his eyes avoiding the frightening 312-foot drop straight down.

He swallowed, trying to regain his composure.

"Turn around and come down from there, right now!" Spear ordered him.

Jeremy took a moment to catch his breath. When he turned an angry scowl was etched across his haggard and dirty face and he growled, "Isn't it lovely to see the rats scrambling."

"I said, come down here."

Jeremy then nodded at the helicopter and the Colonel inside.

"Don't you ever get tired of following his orders?"

"That's my job, as his enforcer," Spear explained, though not sure why.

Jeremy laughed. "His enforcer?"

Spear remained emotionless as he took a step toward Jeremy, holding out his other hand in a 'hand it over' gesture and said, "I'm sure you recovered the flash drive and smartphone from what was left of Shazuko's body. I'll take them now, if you and the boy wish to live."

"There really isn't any honor among thieves, is there?" Jeremy continued, knowing he was playing with fire, nodding in the direction of the dead henchman, blood pooling about his head like a crimson halo. "Movies, real life, you're all the same--sharks--you kill even your own people. Haven't you bozos figured it out yet--that isn't good for company morale!"

"I said--"

"Whattya gonna do, Spear? Shoot me?"

The enforcer calmly shook his head, turning his weapon on Ian and said, "How 'bout him?"

"I saw the *Godfather* movies too. You can call yourselves anything you like. The Outfit, the Syndicate, the Mob, an enforcer... you're all just thugs, thieves and killers--in expensive suits, that's all. You kill your own without hesitation. And all those lovely attributes you thugs are so fond of claiming to hold sooo dear, honor, duty, loyalty?--*baaaloney!*"

"ENOUGH, of the morality lesson!" Spear finally snapped. "I won't ask again."

Though Jeremy had turned over the smartphone to Dylan he retained his ace in the hole. He reached into the pocket on the arm of his jacket and withdrew the flash drive, holding it out.

"Hand it over," Spear reiterated with a no-nonsense tone in his cold voice.

"Ah-uh," Jeremy replied defiantly pointing at Ian. "You, first... *let him go!*"

"*I don't* think so."

"Oh, yeah? Then shoot me you sonofabitch!" Jeremy said savagely. "You're gonna anyway! Oh, I'll go over the side here, landing somewhere down there in a helluva bloody mess. And then you'll just hav'ta trot right back down those stairs and get it yourself. And I doubt you'll find it. But at least I'll have the satisfaction of knowing, you won't have--*THIS!* So go ahead you dumbass and shoot me, because that's the only way you're gonna get your fuckin' hands on it, unless you let. Him. GO!"

Spear calmly mulled over his options for a second and realized this gutsy kid had him by the balls. At least it only seemed that way, for the moment.

Jeremy swallowed nervously.

Spear finally waved for Whitehead to bring Ian to him.

When he did Spear took over, clutching Ian's upper arm firmly and said, "Are you really willing to gamble with his life?"

"*He* can't hurt you," Jeremy glared, "but *I* can--and at the moment nothing would give me more freakin' pleasure!"

Spear turned up a corner of his lip in a half grin. He admired Jeremy--he'd known many tough and hardened men, killed some of the best. But *this* teenage boy was one tough little badass.

Jeremy held his breath and prayed.

Spear released Ian. The boy looked up at him, then over at Jeremy.

"Ian," Jeremy directed him, "go over to the stairwell and go downstairs and wait for me."

Ian's tortured face shook as if he was cold in the warm sunshine when he said, "What about you?"

"Go on."

"Not without you--"

"IAN!--do as I say, go on, right now, GO!"

Ian remained for another moment, afraid to leave his friend.

Jeremy then relented with a smile. "It'll be all right," he said softly. "I promise."

Jeremy watched the boy reluctantly turn and walk over to the alcove, through the door and down into the stairwell, looking back over his backpack several times before disappearing.

"Satisfied?" Spear asked.

Jeremy nodded back wearily.

"You'll never see him again, you know that."

Jeremy said nothing.

"Let's go, then," Spear ordered, gesturing with his Glock toward the Scorpion.

Jeremy, while still holding onto the windsock pole, clumsily stepped down off the ledge, almost falling, catching himself. He walked over to the Scorpion's open passenger door along with Whitehead following closely behind. Blocking his way with an open hand Spear waited. Jeremy stared back into his hardened eyes as he dropped the flash drive onto his open palm.

"The smartphone, too," Spear said.

Jeremy looked directly at him and lied, grimacing at thought. "It was hard enough getting that…I couldn't get it…it was…in all that…blood…"

Spear then patted him down; from his arms, to his hip pockets on down to his legs, then to his ankles. "It's not on him, sir," he reported.

"And *my painting*?" the Colonel twisted in his seat and barked.

"You see it on me, Senator?" Jeremy quipped sarcastically. He labored to take in a breath when he added, "We left it in the RV wreckage back on the bridge."

"You what!" the Colonel snapped, incensed at the loss of his most valued prize. The Colonel bristled in his seat as he faced forward. Finally, he added stonily, "You know what to do, Mr. Spear."

Was this it? Jeremy wondered. Was he actually about to die? It seemed so inconceivable to him. There had to be a way out of this.

There was a cold, ever-so-slight evil grin on Spear's hardened face.

"You can't win," Jeremy said, his tone defiant, but his beleaguered face a reflection of near defeat.

"So you've said," the Colonel twisted back in his seat and replied casually. He then slid out and stood facing Jeremy. "I seriously doubt, you, a teenage boy, could destroy our global...*my* global empire--"

"But I sure gave you a run for your money--you'll have to admit that," Jeremy gleamed with a lopsided grin. "And now that you've been exposed, looks like the two of you will hav'ta crawl back under the rock you slithered out from."

The Colonel ignored the comparison. "You are merely a flea on an immense beast," the Colonel replied smoothly, refusing to concede to anything, let alone defeat.

Jeremy nodded at Spear's open hand and the flash drive. "And your Achilles' Heel there?"

The Colonel grinned diabolically, patting his neckline through his tailored cotton shirt and silk tie. "Interesting choice of words, young man. In this instance you may be correct. If you please, Mr. Spear."

Jeremy nervously watched as Spear took a few steps back. He then hefted the flash drive high into the air, took aim and blasted it from existence. Jeremy slumped at the sight of its destruction. Spear's sharp-shooting skill at hitting such a tiny target dead center was truly amazing. He then sheathed his Glock in the shoulder holster beneath his jacket and came up to Jeremy and repeated icily, "Like I said, I'm going to enjoy putting a bullet in your skull!"

Jeremy swallowed but there was little saliva left in his bone-dry throat. Thankfully, he reminded himself, the smartphone was safely in Dylan's possession.

"You have no idea what you stumbled into a few days ago," the Colonel declared in a final effort to terrorize Jeremy. "We are *the most* powerful *and* profitable cartel in the world today. No one can stop us. No police force, government, or elected official--most of whom are either murdered, blackmailed into submission, or outright bought and paid for. Do you know why the drug cartels envy us?"

Jeremy silently shook his head, mesmerized by the Colonel's emotionless explanation...and his cold, empty eyes.

"Because we have a *reusable* product. People...young people... can be *resold!*"

"We should go, Colonel," Spear interrupted.

The Colonel nodded with an arrogant smirk. "And you, Mr. Hodak, are as good as dead. And if need be, your family as well." The Colonel turned away, about to enter the helicopter, paused, then turned back displaying a broad grin and said with evil intent, "I believe you also have a new-born baby sister."

Jeremy's face lost all expression as he felt his chest tighten, his fists clenching at his sides. He blinked, nervously watching as the Colonel slid into his seat and closed his door, securing it.

Trying not to show any fear as he reached up, gripping the edge of the door, Jeremy pulled himself inside. Settling into the rear seat his eyes kept wily looking toward the alcove praying that the police, hotel security, the marines, someone would rescue him.

It was not to be.

With Whitehead, Glock in hand, following close behind, settling in beside him, there appeared to be no escape for Jeremy. Spear slid the door closed, then walked around and climbed into the pilot's seat, securing his own door. Motioning for the two of them to buckle in, Spear started the turbine engine. Immediately the rotor blades began slowly turning. After clipping his belt, Jeremy looked at Whitehead and was met by a pair of cold, vengeful eyes and a grin that could only be described as evil.

Across the helideck a muted set of terrified, wet eyes peered out from the stairwell, watching the helicopters' rotor blades spooling up, spinning faster and faster. Ian desperately tried to think of some way to stop them. His young mind could come up with only one idea and he knew he would have to act quickly. It was now or never!

CHAPTER FORTY-SEVEN

The moment Miles and his cameraman ran out onto the lawn where the sunken Baddog motorcoach was still smoldering in the pond, the two frantically looked about, searching for the occupant, or occupants. The grounds were nearly deserted. After instructing Stan to get some shots of it Miles anxiously continued looking around, though his gut told him it was a waste of time. He then looked up at the tower, shading his eyes. For a brief moment Miles thought he had seen someone standing on the ledge beside the windsock.

"Did you see that?"

"See what?"

Amid the chaos unfolding across the resort grounds, while people and vehicles were scrambling to exit the parking lot, a black Chevrolet Suburban SUV with dark tinted bulletproof windows slowly wound its way through the mob scene, pulling into a secluded service lot. After easing into a parking slot, the driver shut off the engine.

The four occupants then sat in silence and waited.

The Scorpion's turbine whined and the rotor blades were spinning at nearly full throttle. Preparing to lift off, Spear brought in the power bringing the helicopter light on the skids, then double-checked his instruments.

Jeremy leaned back in his seat and for the first time became truly terrified at what fate awaited him. Would he be dead in a few hours? In those fleeting moments he thought, I'm never going to see Elise grow up.

Like a jack-in-the-box, Ian's face popped up at the passenger door window. Hands pressing against the Plexiglas, his curly red hair whipping about his head from the rotor downwash, he looked at Jeremy and yelled as loud as he could, "JEREMMMYYY!"

Spear and the Colonel, under their headphones, hadn't heard him. Whitehead, though, saw the boy at the window. With the Glock in his right, blood-stained hand he reached across Jeremy with the gun, intending to frighten the boy away. In a lightning move, Jeremy snatched Whitehead's wrist with both hands, shoving the Glock away. Driven by sheer rage, Jeremy held Whitehead's wrist as tightly as he possibly could; Whitehead grimaced and reflexively squeezed the trigger.

Whacket!

The bullet tore through the back of the pilot's seat and into the muscled flesh of his back like a red-hot poker, ripping into his rib-cage and piercing his left lung popping clean through finally embedding itself into the instrument panel. His eyes bugged wide in searing comprehension, his hardened face awash in a stunned expression as he looked down at his chest and saw a pencil-size hole in the middle of his white, button-down collar shirt surrounded by a growing red stain. Breathing became instantly difficult as he fought to draw air in only to release it in a feeble groan. His limbs were becoming numb, his grip on the controls weakening.

Spear's final thoughts, as blackness began to close in on him...*how could this be happening? It can't be--I can't be shot...how did this...?*

The Colonel, still absorbed in his smartphone, making plans for his disappearing act to his seaside villa along the southwestern coast of Portugal in the tranquil town of Sagres, hadn't even noticed what just happened.

Trapped beneath their seatbelt harnesses, Whitehead tussled with Jeremy until he knocked him along the side of his head with the butt of the Glock. The two continued struggling for control of the weapon until Whitehead glanced out front through the wind-shield and saw the huge glass skylight sliding toward them. Spear had passed out and died, releasing his grip on the cyclic and col-lective controls. Jeremy too saw what was coming. As the Scorpion Longranger lurched forward, he reeled in panic against the rear seat scrunching his face and throwing up his arms, shielding his head. Whitehead barely had time to turn away.

Too late, glimpsing his enforcer slumped over the controls, the Colonel's head snapped around and his face distorted in a ter-rified grimace as the helicopter, rotor blades spinning at take-off RPM abruptly changed its angle after the cyclic control slipped from Spear's dead grasp, sending the Longranger twisting and gliding sideways as if on ice, right on through the yellow caution tape.

The glass paneled skylight and its reinforced aluminum frame were no match for the 2,407-pound Longranger as the skids went over the edge, crashing downward through the dome in a cataclys-mic implosion of glass and metal. The Longranger's carbon fiber composite rotor blades, spinning at 395 RPM, smashed into the polished concrete deck, grinding to a violent stop in an explosion of concrete fragments, dust and debris, tearing the turbine engine from its mounts and killing it, shearing the fuel line. The tail boom, catching the edge of the skylight, left the Longranger inverted at a 45-degree angle. In that instant one of the tail rotor blades shat-tered, snapping off from the gearbox assembly. Streaking across the helideck, the blade ricocheted off the deck like a smoking bullet, slic-ing through the 3 ½ inch thick, 26-gauge steel and shotcrete wall of the water tank…

The mangled blade, embedded into the side of the tank, stuck halfway out of it like a knife stuck in butter. For a scant few seconds it remained intact with a complete seal. Then, the enormous pressure surrounding the blade began spewing out jets of water like a geyser.

…The enormous pressure was continuous…

Just as Dane met up with Eric who was catching his breath, holding onto the hand railing, the stairwell began shaking beneath their feet. Everyone immediately stopped in their tracks behind Dane, looking and listening. While the thick concrete walls rattled, they all felt a deep rumbling, followed by a faint, thunderous crash filtering down from somewhere overhead.

"…Did you hear that?" Matthew groaned, his eyes, along with the others, looking up the stairwell.

"What the hell was that?" Miles uttered to Stan beside him. Stan slung the EFP camera up to his shoulder and began shooting again. Miles continued straining to see when he noticed a stream of black smoke drifting over the edge of the tower.

"Whatever that was, it was pretty damn loud," Stan remarked as he zoomed in.

"Yeah…see anything?"

"Just a lot of smoke...it sounded like ahh…"

"Like a…oh, Jesus," Miles gasped, "like the senator's helicopter!" Miles tapped Stan's shoulder and snapped, "C'mon!"

Clutching the camera by the handle and dropping it to his side, Stan and Miles took off running toward the building, and the main lobby.

Jeremy's first sensation that he became aware of in his darkened, semi-conscious state after the thunderous plunge down through the skylight, were his arms dangling free in space. Gradually eclipsing the abyssal blackness engulfing his mind, he began to stir to full consciousness, struggling to take in his new, sharply downward angled position. He squinted his eyes, drawing a breath and coughed, spewing the acrid air that filled his lungs. Realizing he was still alive, yet hanging precariously, straining against his seatbelt and shoulder harness pressing against his stomach and chest, he began forcing the foul air back into his lungs trying to orient himself to his new surroundings.

From the helideck, the only things visible through the rising smoke were the Longranger's mangled rotor blades protruding in an upward 'V' and the bent tail boom sticking out from the jagged edge of the crater-like shattered skylight. The remaining tail rotor blade dangled in the breeze like a broken arm. The crumpled and broken nose of the Longranger came to rest on the shattered wooden dance floor of the dining room. While Spear's body hung lifeless in his own harness, the Colonel slowly began to stir back to life in his. Whitehead too was slowly coming out of his own fog. Several colored lights on the instrument panel blinked wildly, while the overhead panel sparked and began emitting a burning odor. A second later gray smoke began seeping from the panel snaking along the roof up to Jeremy.

"Ohh, crap," Jeremy gushed with widening eyes, trying desperately to keep calm knowing he had to get out of there--fast!

He began pressing the release latch on his harness, but it refused to let go of him. His efforts quickly became frenzied as he started tugging, then pulling on the harness, trying to get free, then he froze.

"Oh, shit," he uttered as the faint smell of jet fuel began filling the cabin.

"JEREMY!" a voice cried from below him.

His eyes snapped to and he saw Ian through the cracked windshield poised out front of the demolished Longranger, standing in the rubble.

"IAN!" Jeremy called out to him. "IAN, I CAN'T GET LOOSE...I NEED YOUR POCKET KNIFE!"

Ian quickly shrugged off his security blanket and dropped his backpack to the floor atop the broken glass of the skylight, tearing into it, grabbing the knife and holding it out.

"Throw it up to me!"

Ian sped around to the passenger door, which had blown out of the door frame from the impact and leaned inside, tossing it up.

Jeremy missed it.

The knife clanked back down inside the cockpit, sliding into the bubbled chin window where the Colonel's feet had become trapped in the foot pedals.

Miles and Stan tore through the double doors into the Governors' Ballroom, running into Stewie.

"Where've you been?" Miles barked at him, noticing a small group of bewildered people gathered on the other side of the abandoned room. He then recognized them as the friends Carl had earlier introduced him to.

"Excuse me?--I've been trying to get upstairs, per Carl, to the helideck--seen the elevators lately? They're not exactly empty."

Miles nodded understandingly, sputtering, "Sorry." He then popped his forehead the moment he spotted the hotel security cameras in one of the ceiling corners on the ballroom. "What a fool I am!"

"What is it?" asked Stewie.

"You're our resident computer geek--those security cameras up there--can you access those from the mobile van?"

"Piece of cake," Stewie shrugged.

"Do it, fast! We'll take the stairs and see if we can get up there and find the senator."

The second the two took off running across the ballroom to the exit door, Stewie muttered to himself, "Twenty-six flights of stairs… knock yourselves out, boys."

Ian reached out and began to climb inside.

Jeremy watched him, then snapped, "Ian, no."

"Shut up!" the boy barked as his small hands worked their way, grabbing onto anything. He crawled behind the cockpit and between the two seats, ignoring Spear's lifeless body.

"Here son, help me" the Colonel pleaded feebly through coughs.

Ian ignored him, too, reaching into the chin window, grasping the knife. As he backed out, the Colonel grabbed at his bare, scrapped arm.

Ian yanked it free, crawling back up through the steep angled cabin to Jeremy, handing him the knife.

"Here," Jeremy said taking it. Pushing out the harness across his chest until it was taut, his other hand flipped the blade open and began cutting. On the fourth desperate swipe, the sharp blade sliced clean through the nylon strap.

"Jeremy," Whitehead uttered weakly, looking at him. "Please, don't leave me in here--I don't wanna die."

He said nothing as he went to work on the belt across his waist.

"Please, you can't leave me like this."

"...I can't...get at this thing," Jeremy muttered angrily, gritting his teeth, unable to reach around to his side, still hung up by a second strap across his other shoulder. Ian anxiously fidgeted, reaching out for the knife, trying to take it "Lemme try."

"Here," Whitehead uttered breathlessly. "Gimme the knife--I can reach it for you."

"Get back, Ian," Jeremy ordered.

The smoke was getting thicker, as was the smell of jet fuel.

Jeremy looked at Whitehead.

"C'mon Jeremy...I'll cut you free, then you help me. Okay?"

Jeremy hesitated, staring at Whitehead through the mounting haze.

"Hurry, Jeremy," Ian pleaded.

Jeremy held out the knife.

Whitehead took it into his right hand, grinning sardonically and gripped the handle as tightly as he could. The instant Jeremy became distracted with a watchful eye on Ian below, Whitehead reached out and swung the 3" shiny blade in an ark across Jeremy's chest and plunged it through his biker jacket and into his right shoulder.

"AAAHHHHHHHH!"

"NOOOOOO!" Ian screamed in shock, falling back against the bulkhead of the cabin.

Blood immediately began oozing from around the blade.

"FUUUCK!" wailed Jeremy, squeezing his eyes tightly and baring his teeth in withering agony.

Whitehead kept up the pressure, pressing the blade even deeper into Jeremy's shoulder.

"AAAAHHHHHFFFUCKIN'HELLLL!" Jeremy cried out, every muscle in his body tensing up as he struggled to get free, still held by the strap across his waist and other shoulder.

Jeremy felt light-headed, fumbling for Whitehead's hand with his other. His eyes began watering against the searing pain coursing through his arm and upper body from where the blade had neatly penetrated the trapezius muscle between his clavicle and scapula. He finally shoved Whitehead's exhausted hand away….and pulled out the bloody blade from his shoulder, letting it clatter down through the cabin.

Snatching the knife from where it landed, Ian shot back up to Jeremy, unaware of the Colonel inching his way through the bulkhead opening into the passenger cabin.

Ian frantically began sawing across the strap.

Robert ran into Caroline in the reception area outside the Governors' Ballroom.

"Did you find him?" she rasped.

Robert shook his head. "I couldn't, the elevators were jammed--c'mon."

He grabbed her hand and the two raced across the deserted lobby to the stairwell near the front desk. They burst through the door and stopped.

"Where are the other parents?" he asked her.

"They're back in the ballroom," she uttered between breaths.

He snatched her hand again and the two started briskly up the stairs.

Working feverishly, Ian hadn't noticed his other hand, holding onto Jeremy's jacket, becoming wet with Jeremy's blood streaming down his arm.

There was a moment when Ian glanced over into Whitehead's vacant, resolute eyes.

Then abruptly the strap across Jeremy's waist gave way. Jeremy instantly slipped out from the shoulder harness and the two boys tumbled down hard against the cockpit bulkhead into the corner. Jeremy cried out, grimacing from the indescribable pain in his right shoulder. He struggled up to his knees, holding his right arm close to his chest, fighting off the fuzziness that was seeping into his mind. He winced repeatedly, trying to hold on.

The Colonel, desperately struggling to orient his swirling head, clutched at anything to pull and right himself in the steeply down-angled cockpit. There was a look of utter shock--*this can't be happening*--across his haggard and bloodied face, his cheek sliced by a flying piece of the Plexiglas windshield. His normally styled white hair resembled a ratty bird's nest, his forehead furrowed in absolute terror. His overwrought expression suddenly gave way to sheer panic and he began frantically pawing at his chest, then neckline, desperately searching and feeling for the gold neck chain beneath his shirt.

He quickly loosened his tie and tore open the shirt, snapping buttons. ...*It wasn't—oh...there it is!*

Ian grabbed Jeremy's left good arm and began pulling him to the open passenger door. Waving the smoke from his face, inching their way, the two crawled tenuously against the angled carpeted floor of the helicopter.

"Wait, please, help me," the Colonel pleaded with them while blood streamed down the side of his neck. He had managed to shimmy part way through the tangled opening of the bulkhead, up to his waist. "Please don't leave me...please give me a hand, PLEASE!"

The smell of jet fuel permeated the cabin along with a faint sound like bacon sizzling.

Ian kept pulling Jeremy along, tightening the grip on his limp hand.

The Colonel reached out for Jeremy, catching his ankle with a bloody grasp and snapped, "Don't leave me here!"

In his groggy, lightheaded state Jeremy gently tugged back, halting Ian. At the edge of the door, Jeremy looked back at the Colonel and said, "So you think you're gonna hurt my family? I don't think so. Remember those photos in your office--on the *right* side--your murdered fraternity? Remember 'em? Time to join your own illustrious collection, Colonel!"

"I'M A SITTING UNITED STATES SENATOR!" Colonel Toddhunter angrily croaked at him.

"Oh yeah?" Jeremy sputtered. Recalling his repeated threats... and his newborn baby sister, he shook the fog from his mind, clenched his teeth tightly and grunted back, "Then, SIT ON THIS!" Kicking the Colonel as hard as he could in his bloodied face he sent Senator Toddhunter flailing back down into the cockpit, crashing hard against the shattered windshield where he lay unconscious. Jeremy's eyes suddenly widened in shocked recognition when he sighted what was attached to the gold chain around the Colonel's neck.

"AHHH!" Ian yelped the instant sparks began snapping above his head. Flames started pouring out from the overhead instrument panel, hugging the ceiling.

"C'mon!" Ian screamed pulling at him.

"Wait a minute," Jeremy mumbled feebly as though he were drunk.

"C'mon!"

Through the torturous pain in his right shoulder and the gathering smoke, Jeremy slipped away from Ian's grasp, inching himself down through the inverted wreckage with the speed of a tortoise and the angry determination of a bull in the ring, toward the comatose Colonel. Ian never let up, scrambling after him, finally snagging the waistband of Jeremy's biker pants and pulling with all his might. Still clutching his right arm to his chest, Jeremy stretched out his left arm and fingers with every ounce of his waning strength, reaching down for the gold chain around the Colonel's neck which had snaked through to the outside of his shirt.

Attached to the chain, Jeremy's eyes zeroed in on it--*the Colonel's flash drive!*

Then he spotted, beside the Colonel's bloodied head, his *smartphone!*

Jeremy had only seconds to make a choice. Though he knew Dylan had Ryan's smartphone, does he grab the Colonel's, potentially the mother lode or the flash drive?

The tips of his fingers were nearly close enough for him to touch one of them.

"Ian!" Jeremy pleaded with him. "LEMME GO!"

Like a high-pressure fireman's hose, a jet-stream of water was spraying out from around the embedded tail rotor blade in the tank across the deck, pooling and spreading out near the destroyed, smoldering skylight, the crumpled tail boom barely visible through the thickening black swirling smoke.

A final tug from Ian and the two fell out the Longranger through the damaged and missing passenger door opening to the carpet of broken glass. Helping each other to their feet, Jeremy noticed his hand was wet; the carpet was soaked. Rubbing the liquid between his fingers, and then smelling it, he gasped, "Jet fuel!"

Neither boy looked back as they staggered from the wreckage. Ian struggled to help Jeremy across the dining room, broken glass and debris crunching under their feet. Jeremy saw the door to the kitchen and steered Ian toward it.

Mounting flames crawled along the ceiling of the Longranger.

Still trying to free himself from his harness, Peter began to resign himself to a fate he'd always known he would meet. While sweat beaded down his face, coughing through the thickening smoke, Whitehead wrapped his arms about himself, then closed his eyes, and calmly waited for the end.

The Colonel, regaining consciousness, frantically began clawing at anything he could. With blood on his face, he pulled his large frame through the bulkhead opening again. Wriggling as far as he could, he waved his cut hands through the choking foul air laboring to breathe, seeing Whitehead.

"Whatta you doing? Don't just sit there, help me you fool-- don't leave me in here...listen--listen to me--I'll pay you whatever you want--anything!" The Colonel's face twisted in rage as he gasped, then screamed at the top of his lungs, "Just get me OUTTA HERE!"

Jeremy plowed through the kitchen door dropping to his knees, scooping Ian into his good arm shoving him to the floor, shielding the boy with his body and shouting through the withering pain in his shoulder, "CLOSE YOUR EYES!"

"Do you hear me?" the Colonel screamed at Whitehead. "Come back here--come back—"

An instant later the Longranger's fuel tank erupted in an ear-splitting blast.

An earth-moving thunderous shockwave exploded outward in all directions, piercing, shredding, loosening, splintering, rupturing, catapulting, everything in its path, instantly rippling through the tower, sprouting spider web cracks throughout the superstructure--including the concrete membrane floor of the water tank.

The kitchen door blew open, slamming against the wall, engulfing the boys in a wave of intense heat, while a trail of black flames boiled along the ceiling over their heads.

Death was instantaneous for Senator Ellis 'the Colonel' Toddhunter. The Longranger disintegrated in a blinding orange fireball along with its occupants, blowing out all twelve of the floor-to-ceiling, plate-glass windows along the northwestern side of the dining room, igniting a flash fire and sending glass fragments raining down on the resort lawn far below. While the entire superstructure of the glass tower vibrated from the blast, a black angry cloud rose from the cratered skylight. Flames spread quickly throughout the dining room accelerated by jet fuel, cans of paint, paint thinner and other combustible materials engulfed by the raging firestorm.

Jeremy's body felt the brunt of the intense, heavy wave, as if he was being pummeled by an invisible, crushing steamroller. Overhead, one of the florescent lighting fixtures tore from the ceiling in a hail of sparks, crashing to the floor, just missing the two boys. Jeremy reared up from behind Ian, looking over his shoulder, shielding his eyes from the intense glow, gaping at the raging inferno. The massive blaze roiled across the dining room floor, crawling up the walls, blanketing the ceiling in all directions.

His eyes darted about the kitchen searching for an exit.

He scooped up Ian, holding him to his chest with his good arm like a mother bear and the two crawled and stumbled on their hands and knees toward another door. The adrenalin pumping through his body overrode the pain in his wounded shoulder. When he reached it, he was dumfounded to find it locked. Jeremy struggled to his feet, pressing on the single door with his uninjured hand and twisted the knob. A tiny window revealed a narrow corridor leading to another door marked; *Emergency Exit, Stairwell.*

Jeremy held his arm and kicked at the door, cursing.

Pressure surrounding the protruding tail rotor stuck in the water tank spit the blade out across the helideck like a cork from a champagne bottle, releasing a fire hydrant flow of gushing water through the tiny hole. Within seconds, as a portion of the 4-inch concrete membrane floor of the tank began to crumble and give way, a huge section of the thick Caribbean blue steel-core wall directly above it began splitting apart, peeling downward like an invisible zipper opening up, unleashing 240,000 gallons of water.

It looked as if the sky was opening up.

A tsunami-like wave began flowing out, swiftly filling up the helideck. With nowhere to go, trapped by the 4-foot perimeter ledge, a gigantic whirlpool began swirling around the smashed skylight pouring downward like a drain, quickly dousing the flaming

Longranger and suffocating the surrounding inferno. Rapidly flooding the Trillium dining room, the roiling wave of advancing water began carrying everything it smashed into and pouring it out through the shattered windows. From below in the parking lot and lawn, it was a mesmerizing sight.

Jeremy and Ian had felt another tremor through the kitchen floor. The two stood back in shock at what they saw through the tiny window of the locked door. Water filled in behind the glass, and then began spewing out in sheets from around the door frame.

"What the--" sputtered Jeremy, clutching Ian's hand.

He then spun around toward the open dining room door just as a deluge poured in, sweeping the boys off their feet, sending them sliding to the back of the kitchen along with a wave of debris.

As Jeremy went down, the pain in his arm and leg was indescribable.

The river of tank water surging through the facility flowed in the direction of the quickest way down.

The crushing wave found it through the stairwell and twin elevator shafts.

A large crowd of guests and hotel staff had been gathering in a distant parking lot as instructed by security. Following the frightening explosion on the roof, the stunned spectators continued to gaze upward at the tower in a silent stupor as water and debris-- tables, chairs, construction equipment and supplies, including Ian's backpack--began showering out the broken windows along the top floor on a cascading waterfall.

Dane suddenly stopped in mid-stride, the kids crowding in behind him, breathing hard while listening.

"What was that!" he said, his eyes studying the stairwell ahead. Then focusing them on the wall where he placed his hand Dane muttered, "Feel that…the whole dang building is shaking." His eyes then drifted to the floor. "…Feels like an earthquake."

Within the windowless stairwell the explosion from above could be felt rattling down through the tower superstructure. The lights blinked for a moment, yet remained solid.

Paralyzed with fear, staring up the stairwell, Lynn moved past Leslie and the others toward Dane and began to cry hysterically, "It was an airplane, I know it was--we've been hit, the building's gonna…"

Dane snapped around, passing off the fishing tube to Travis, then gripped the girl's shoulders "--Look at me--look at me!"

Travis left his twin to prop up Elmo, taking the tube.

"We've not been attacked--the building is not collapsing!"

Lynn calmed, leaning into Dane's comforting embrace.

Leslie slowly ascended the stairs past the kids, trying to figure out in her mind what the strange sound and vibrations could mean. "Whaddya think?" she asked Dane with a hard stare before glancing up the stairwell.

Dane slowly shook his head.

"…Listen," she then whispered, her brow furrowing in confusion. "…what is that?"

"It sounds like…"

Leslie returned his steady gaze. "Like…like water!"

"Ohhh that's not good," Stan uttered from behind Miles as the two stood frozen on the stairs beside an exit door.

"…Yeah…" Miles murmured back distractedly.

"Miles…MILES!"

The tanned reporter turned to Stan, his eyes searching the stairway overhead and whispered, "Shhhh."

The cameraman then moaned, "I gotta bad feeling about this."

Miles leaned in toward the center of the stairwell shaft, gazing upward. A small opening running the entire length of the spiral stairwell afforded a narrow view. He suddenly heard distant screams and what looked like sloshing water--a lot of it, confirmed by drops on his face.

He suddenly gasped, "Holy water park!"

"Hold it, hold it!' Robert sputtered between breaths, grabbing Caroline's quivering hand, pulling her close. "You hear that?"

Trying to catch her breath, Caroline remarked in bewilderment, "…What is it?"

Robert's eyes narrowed, matching her confused expression, listening.

"Shit!" Dane spewed as he spun on his heels, shouting, "FACE THE INSIDE WALL--GRAB THE RAILING!"

Dane bolted back down the stairs, shoving the twins to the railing.

"WRAP YOUR ARMS AROUND IT--ERIC STAY WITH--"

The words had barely past his lips when he pulled Leslie, Lynn and Eric to the railing, shoving his muscled body up against them, protecting them as a crushing wave of cool water came crashing down the stairwell, washing over them. Everyone cried out as the roaring downpour completely engulfed them.

"HOLD OOONNN!" Dane shouted through the torrent.

While Travis clutched the fishing tube, his other hand's grasp on the railing was beginning to slip. Matthew, clutching Elmo's arm about his neck, supporting him, saw what was about to happen.

Pressing himself against the wall, he released his grip on the railing and inched his hand around his twin, grabbing the railing again, holding him tight.

Trying desperately to breath, Lynn lost her balance, dropping to her knees. Eric instantly leaned down, taking her hand into his.

Elmo cried out the instant he lost his own grip on the railing and Matthew's support and was abruptly carried away in the surging flow. Sliding down the steps past Dane, he felt the bodybuilder's tight grasp hauling him back in.

Elmo hopped up on his one leg, clutching at Dane's thick arm and held on.

No sooner had Miles grabbed the handle on the door and the two scrambled through it into the hallway when the heavy metal door slammed closed behind them from the crush of water.

The two men staggered backward with widening shocked eyes, watching the tiny window on the door completely fill with water.

"Where'd *all that* come from?" Miles gushed.

"A busted pipe?" Stan winced just as Miles's radio chimed.

Whisking it from a pocket, he heard Carl's voice boom. "Miles, get back to the van--on the double!"

Squeezing the talk button, he inquired, "Did Stewie tap into their security cameras?"

"You are not gonna believe what's happening upstairs on the helideck."

"What?"

"Just get the hell back here--the network's about to go with a live feed from here and I need *you!*"

"We're on our way!"

"When it rains it pours," Stan muttered.

Glancing over at the submerged tiny window, Miles retorted, "Don't say rain--c'mon."

The two men then dashed down the hallway and through another door.

"LOOK OUT!" Robert shouted. Abruptly pulling Caroline along with him by the arm they had just made it to the nearest exit door when sheets of cascading water came crashing down the stairs at them.

Caroline shrieked, covering her head against the downpour.

Robert turned away, gripped the handle on the door and pulled with all his strength but it wouldn't give. Suddenly, tumbling along with the raging water down the stairs a bulky man in a blue uniform grabbed at Caroline's leg.

She screamed and Robert spun around.

Pulling the man up, he and Robert hauled on the door. It finally opened and the three of them were swept inside, then knocked to the floor with a drenching wave, becoming disoriented. Recovering quickly, they helped each other, crawling around the corner into the elevator alcove. Robert and Caroline clung to each other, watching in stunned disbelief as if a dam had burst. The exit door was a roaring floodgate as a wall of churning water charged through it, flowing down the hall, taking a maid's cart with it. Twisting and cavorting with the current, the cart crashed into the door at the opposite end of the hall in a furious explosion of metal, bed sheets, towels and hotel supplies.

"Who are you? Are you all right?" Robert yelled to the stranger.

"Yeah, thanks. I'm head of security here," the man replied, wiping the water from his eyes and face. "...My name's Kellur."

In the span of some ninety seconds the water tank had emptied most of its 240,000 gallons, releasing a debris-carrying, tsunami-like wave after which it began to gradually ebb to a trickle.

It felt like a child's wading pool in the kitchen, as Jeremy rolled onto his back trying to keep his head above the water, shoving a large cart out of the way, gasping through smoke. It smelled like burning tar or oil. Lying beside him, Ian rose up on his hands looking at the devastation around them. Amazingly, one of the overhead florescent lights still burned brightly.

Jeremy surveyed the kitchen, in shambles, and quipped between breaths, "Well, I've…I've always wanted that disaster movie experience."

"Huh?" Ian uttered looking at him.

"Here…gimme a hand."

The fire alarm suddenly began to shrill, and then abruptly shorted out, going silent.

"You're just a little late," he barked at the darkened red emergency fixture in the corner of the kitchen.

As Ian helped Jeremy to his feet, the two boys continued surveying the destroyed kitchen.

"…Good thing we're not on a boat," Jeremy said quietly.

Ian caught his remark, asking, "Why?"

"'Cause then we'd have to make our way to the engine room, that's why."

"What for?"

A fan of the 1970's disaster movies Jeremy retorted, "I guess you had to be there…but then again, I'm not sure a high rise is any better--ohhhh…man," he then grimaced examining his wounded shoulder. "That *really* hurts!"

Teetering like a drunk toward the open door, Ian helped him through the maze of debris. Jeremy felt almost delirious as he held his right arm against his chest. At least the bleeding had stopped, he noticed. Though he still limped, the pain in his thigh was nothing compared to the *through the roof* burning sensation in his shoulder.

The two made their way out into the demolished dining room, pausing briefly, looking around at the blackened and scorched scene.

There was little left of the Scorpion Longranger that was recognizable but a nearly indescribable, smoldering shell.

Ian turned away when he thought of Peter.

Jeremy knew the kind of boy Ian was and knew what he was thinking. He quickly ushered him on toward the stairwell door. What was left of the singed curtains flanking the shattered, plate-glass windows swayed on a gentle breeze that wafted through the blackened dining room, gradually clearing the air.

Ian pushed the door open and the two entered a corridor. Leading up to the helideck, bright sunlight still filtered down through the stairway in front of them. They slowly ambled up the stairs, Jeremy teetering with every step.

The boys came out of the elevator alcove stepping into the warm sun, took a few more steps, and finally collapsed on the water-soaked deck. Ian looked up into Jeremy's eyes and began to break down, crying uncontrollably. With his good arm Jeremy pulled the boy to his chest, reached around and held him, whispering consolingly, "It's okay, Ian…It'll be all right now."

Jeremy's eyes surveyed the devastation around them…amazed that they survived it all. "…You go ahead and cry kid--you earned it. …If it didn't hurt so much I'd join you."

After a minute or so, Ian leaned back, wiped his eyes with his hand, and looked at Jeremy and winced, "…I think I peed my pants."

Jeremy took an exhaustive, painful breath and smiled at him. "Kid, that's nothin' compared to what I did in mine."

"Do you…do you think Arnold is okay?"

"I hope so Ian…I hope so."

Ian choked back tears as he laid his head on Jeremy's good shoulder.

Spent, barely able to move, Jeremy looked across the deck. Traces of black smoke still rose from the skylight, while the water tank across the helideck had a gaping, outward tear running the entire length, from top to bottom, as if it were made of tinfoil.

"JEREMY!" Travis shrieked from the stairway door dropping the fishing tube.

One by one the kids came streaming out from the stairwell, running across the soaked helideck. Travis and Matthew, overcome with emotion at seeing their brother, dropped to their knees embracing Jeremy, along with Ian, and burst into tears. Eric and Lynn took over helping Elmo as he hopped on his good leg. They too crouched down, wrapping their arms about each other and wept along with them.

Leslie sped past Dane bending down and melting into the group. Jeremy reached out taking her with his good arm.

Dane had picked up the fishing tube and wearily joined the group saying, "Now, that's what I call a group hug."

After several moments Jeremy looked up at his friend grinning, "If you're feelin' like a good cry come and join us."

Dane laughed, bending down, taking his friend's hand and squeezed it.

Jeremy winced painfully, and then smiled, "Thanks."

Dane winked at him, then replied, "Anytime, buddy."

When Dane stood up, his eyes caught something below in the distance, replacing his infectious smile with a relieved expression crossing his unshaven face. "Hey, look at this...now there's a sight for sore eyes."

"What is it?"

"Take a look."

With his brothers' assist Jeremy stood and the group stepped over to the 4-foot ledge, lining up along the edge. Far below in the distance, snaking up the drive of the resort with colored lights flashing was a train of police cars, fire trucks and ambulance vehicles.

Jeremy moaned as his legs began to crumble beneath him. Leslie and the twins caught him and quickly propped him back up.

"Jeremy!" Leslie gasped, seeing the blood on his arm, taking a closer look. "Your shoulder, what happened?"

"Oh this?" he winced painfully. "...It's just a little scratch."

"Scratch?"

Returning to the group, Dane passed the fishing tube back to Travis. He then peeled off the tee shirt he had switched with Jeremy, wrung out the excess water, folded it a couple of times and carefully slid it under Jeremy's biker jacket, gently pressing it over the wound.

Jeremy grimaced, and then slumped in relief, taking several measure breaths.

"Sorry," Dane said. "...okay?"

Jeremy nodded with tightly squeezed eyelids.

"Here we go." Dane said, stepping in and sliding Jeremy's good arm under his own shoulder. "C'mon, boy, we'd better get you downstairs."

"Okay," Jeremy agreed and smiled back at him.

Moving gingerly across the helideck, the kids followed Jeremy, Dane and Leslie back to the elevator alcove. They entered the wet stairwell where water still flowed, though now at a trickle and headed slowly down the steps.

"Targets are in motion," the leader of the Black-Ops team announced. Armed with a hand-held GPS computer displaying a complete layout of the hotel grounds, building and conference center, he touched the screen, superimposing a photograph. He held the device aloft for the others to see, pointing at the color image of two young individuals.

The girl had shoulder-length ebony hair, her brother the same, but much shorter.

"Our orders come from the president himself," the leader said pointedly. "You all know what to do."

The team of four men dressed in black, their faces shrouded in brown and green military camouflage makeup, exited the SUV and moved with a purpose across the service parking lot in the direction of the conference center and the Governors' ballroom.

CHAPTER FORTY-EIGHT

Miles was taken aback as he ran. He could hardly believe what he was witnessing. Nothing like this in his career had ever happened, not on this scale. After finding their way, along with a mass exodus of guests through a side emergency door, the two men decided the quickest route back to the mobile trailer was to cut through the lobby. It looked like a scene straight out of an Irwin Allen disaster movie. As Miles and Stan raced through the flooded lobby, their shoes sloshed through a good six inches of streaming water. Just off the front desk the closed stairwell door spewed water from around the frame like some bizarre fountain while the glass-enclosed double elevator shaft was a flowing vertical river. Although the blaring fire alarm had been squelched, the emergency exit lights above all the doors continued to strobe.

Miles and Stan abruptly paused, trading wide-eyed glances. Stan hoisted the EFP camera to his shoulder, about to get a shot, when all the lights went out.

A moment later the overhead emergency lights scattered throughout the lobby popped on.

They hurriedly pressed forward.

The instant the two men burst through a side exit door closest to the trailer, they were met by their wild-eyed producer. Carl immediately hustled them over to the trailer and inside.

"Have a look at this," Carl said, directing their eyes to the monitors.

While Bert huddled in a corner on the phone, the three men crouched around Stewie as he adjusted images, going back and forth on the four, eight-inch color monitors.

"Now this was taken shortly after twelve noon in the ballroom," Stewie began to explain. "You can see the Senator at the podium there. ...This image over here shows the Senator's black helicopter on the helideck upstairs. Then...back over here...we have the disturbance out on the grounds with the RV on steroids, taken from several different cameras..."

"Look at that," Stan uttered, then laughed softly. "He's tearin' everything to hell."

"Yeah," Miles mumbled, shaking his head. "Incredible--"

On hold with the network, Bert leaned in next to the others for a moment, mesmerized by the marauding RV.

"WHOA!" All four men winced.

"...And...whoosh," one of them gushed. "There goes the pavilion!"

Miles adding, "Scratch one wedding reception."

"...Along with a few hapless ducks," Stan added in dismay, and then asked, "so what happened to the driver?"

Stewie glanced over his shoulder and said, "I'm glad you asked, 'cause this is where it gets real interesting."

He adjusted the images on two of the monitors and continued, "As you can see on the right, after the RV careened into the pond, here, I'll switch vantage points...from this angle..."

"Look at that," Stan gushed, "Where'd that guy come from?"

Miles picked it up, "Was he riding on the back of that thing--on the outside?"

"Sure looks like it," Carl said. "Look how his jacket is torn and bloodied."

"Who is he?" Miles questioned, not really expecting an answer.

"Not sure, but keep watching," Stewie said. "I'll zoom in a bit."

The grainy, black and white image, showed a figure in a biker outfit, letting go of a rope or something he was clutching onto at the rear of the RV, and drop down into the water and wade off to shore.

"We'll change angles, and I'll speed it up a bit..."

All four men behind Stewie watched the monitors intently.

"...Okay, first we see, what can safely be assumed is the driver--a burly fellow in black coveralls I wouldn't wanna meet in a dark alley--crawling out through the shattered front windshield of the RV and disappears from view. Then...shortly thereafter we see a bunch of kids climbing out through the broken windshield...then our mystery exterior passenger comes up behind the little guy there, snatches him...fires his gun to frighten the crap outta everyone....and takes off in the direction of the hotel, draggin' the poor kid with him."

Stewie then froze the image on the monitor.

"Good God," Miles whispered.

"I now direct your attention to this monitor, displaying the helideck camera images."

"Hey--there he is," Stan said excitedly tapping the monitor where the bloody biker was standing, clutching the small boy.

"And look there," Miles said pointing at another figure in biker clothing. "...wasn't he with the kids?"

"Yep," Stewie said, tapping the frozen image on the other monitor. "There he is there, helping the last kid out of the RV."

"Who the hell is he?" muttered Carl.

"No idea," Stewie replied, shaking his head and pressing the play button, "Just keep watching though, this is where things get a little weird."

"Well, I'll be," Carl gushed, "There's our missing senator all right, climbing into the helicopter."

"Wait a minute, freeze that," Miles gasped. "Does the burly driver--is that a gun?"

After Stewie pressed the pause button on the console, Miles began pointing. "What the hell--okay, okay...there's our driver, holding a gun, we have two guys in biker outfits, one of 'em holding onto the kid..."

"And there's the Senator Toddhunter's security guy," Stewie finished. "Didn't you say he looked like a hit man, Carl?"

"That's what I said."

Stewie then pressed the play button, "Check this out."

"Shit--look at that!" Stan gaped, a dumbfounding expression crossing his face, along with the others.

"I don't believe it!" Carl said in exasperation. "I *was* right--the sonofabitch just shot and killed the driver!"

"Keep watching," Stewie said quietly. "The blond biker bolts around the helicopter, hops up onto the ledge where he clutches the windsock--and that's a long drop!"

"I thought I saw someone up there," Miles said. "Looks like he's stalling..."

"Or negotiating," Stewie guessed. "'Cause they let the kid go here."

"...And take the blond biker...hostage?" muttered Carl.

Miles leaned in closer and said, "This is incredible--and our good Colonel Toddhunter is just sitting there calmly through it all."

Carl shook his head. "Look at him, like he's readin' a book."

"Or dreaming of what might have been," Miles observed prophetically. "Wait...he's getting out here...he and Spear seem to be talking to the kid."

Stewie continued his commentary. "Now, watch 'em; he tosses something into the air and shoots it...then, with the blond kid at gunpoint they all pile into the helicopter..."

They watched in silence as the rotor spun up to full speed.

"Nothing's happening--" Stan observed.

"No, look," Carl blurted softly. "Here comes the little kid back to the helicopter."

Stewie pointed to the image. "Now something happens here, watch...look at the senator's hit man--he's in the pilot's seat...and I think...I think he just got shot--see 'em slumping over the controls?"

The three men held their breath, watching as the little boy in the grainy image ducked down below the helicopter as it began to slide sideways, the rotor downdraft from the near take-off thrust of the whirling blades whipping his curly hair and tee shirt. They leaned closer in utter disbelief. Like a carefully choreographed dance, as the Longranger went one way Ian went in the opposite direction, crawling right over one of the skids as it passed beneath his hands and feet. The boy then scrambled back to the alcove. Suddenly the three men reeled back, straightening where they stood.

"My God!" one of them gasped. "Right through the skylight!"

Stewie pressed the pause button.

"And all that water?" Stan asked.

"The hotel's water tank up there," Stewie clarified. "A big one."

"So the bird exploded," Miles reasoned, "rupturing the tank."

"Okay." Carl agreed, looking at the men beside him. "But how does all of this involve Senator Toddhunter? What was our good Colonel into that we don't know about?"

"Yeah, and did anyone up there survive?" Miles concluded.

"Amazingly, someone did," Stewie said, switching images. "This monitor is a *live feed* from the stairwell. There's a stair cam on each level--take a look."

"Well, I'll be damned," whispered Carl. "The blond kid in the biker suit, their hostage....and look at 'em, he's injured."

"I guess the senator didn't make it," quipped Stan. "'Cause I don't see *him*."

Miles said to him, "Where'd all those kids come from?"

"Look at 'em--those are the ones from the RV."

"You're right...and there's the little guy."

Carl stood back. "And they're coming down, right to us. You two can head 'em off at the conference center."

"All right, guys?" Bert broke in, setting the phone aside. "The network is ready--we're about to go live again."

"Good job, Bertie," Carl said, patting the man's shoulder, regaining his composure. "Have 'em stand by."

Carl then ushered his star reporter and cameraman out the door, issuing Miles instructions and a radio receiver earpiece.

Robert couldn't believe what Kellur had told him. As he and Caroline beat a path down the hall, squeezing past the wrecked maid's cart, then downstairs via a dry set of stairs off the main tower, the security chief had mentioned, in passing, how he came to be in the flooded hall prior to Robert's hauling him to safety. After some light probing by Robert, Kellur briefly stated something about spotting several people on the helideck with the senator, one of them an individual in biker clothing. That part of his story piqued Robert's interest but he dismissed it without further comment. Caroline started to say something when Robert squeezed her hand, interrupting her. He then abruptly bid the security chief good luck and they parted company.

"Am I wrong?" she asked him. "Or did that sound like Jeremy he was describing--who we both saw heading to the elevator--in biker clothes."

"I don't know. None of this makes any sense."

"What's happening, Robert--what is going on?"

He thought for a moment, gazing into her eyes and said, "Go back to the ballroom--don't say anything to the others. I'm gonna find our son."

Caroline nodded.

Robert, noticing the stress and strain distorting the soft features of her tanned complexioned face, touched her cheek and kissed it.

She then watched him jog down the hall and disappear through a doorway.

"Hold it, hold it," Jeremy moaned, his knees buckling again. "I gotta rest for a minute."

Supported on each side by Dane and Leslie, they gently lowered him to the wet steps. As he sat down, Jeremy was careful not to bend his tender leg. "Sorry to hold everyone up like this," Jeremy uttered between labored breaths.

Leslie sat beside him, gently lifting the lapel of his jacket to check his wound saying, "It's okay, take as long as you need. We're almost downstairs...it doesn't appear to be bleeding anymore. How does it feel?"

Jeremy looked at her as the kids piled in around him, kneeling, and said, "Like my whole freakin' shoulder's on fire."

"You gonna live?" Travis asked him, very seriously too.

"I think so," Jeremy replied glibly from behind sullen eyes, then smiled. He looked about at everyone, commenting, "Looks like we've all been to a waterpark."

"Feels like it too," Travis agreed with a smile.

"Ready?" Dane leaned down and said. "We gotta get that looked at, now--can you make it?"

Jeremy raised his head, nodded and said, "With a little help from my friends."

"Hey, listen," Eric piped up and said.

Lynn rose up beside him from where she was sitting saying, "Someone's coming."

Dane and Leslie straightened, along with the rest of the kids and faced an empty stairwell with anxious anticipation.

The instant Robert rounded the corner and saw Jeremy on the steps he froze in mid-step. Flanked by a collection of gaunt, soaked, refugee-like faces he almost didn't recognize, his mouth gaped open but his lungs drew no breath. It took an eternity of several seconds for his head to catch up to his eyes. He finally said in disbelief, "Jeremy?"

With Leslie and Dane's help, Jeremy rose to his feet and said weakly, "Dad."

"Jeremy--kids!"

The moment he stepped toward his son, Jeremy began to collapse again. Robert and the others caught him, bolstering him back on his feet.

Robert looked up about the stairwell at his twin sons and the others. "You're supposed to be--what are you--*what are you all doing here?*"

"It's ahh," Dane started to say.

"A really long story," Leslie concluded with a deep sigh and a faint smile.

Robert looked back to Jeremy just as he winced, grimacing from the pain in his leg and shoulder. "What's happened to you?"

Jeremy began to break down; his stalwart demeanor throughout their ordeal suddenly crumbled, giving way.

"--Oh, Dad," he muttered through eyes that began welling up.

Robert shook the confusion from his mind and took Jeremy in his arms and held him.

The boy sobbed quietly for a moment before catching himself and stifling his emotional outburst, clearing his throat.

"We gotta get him to a doctor, Mr. H.," Dane said.

Robert collected himself and said soberly, "Everyone's in the ballroom..."

He then released Jeremy to arms-length, looking at him saying, "One floor down, Dr. Gibbs is with us. Is everyone else all right?"

Jeremy nodded back, wiping his eyes, adding, "Elmo has a crease on his leg from a bullet--"

"A bullet?" Robert gasped, unable to control his shock.

"I'm okay," Elmo volunteered from behind Lynn and Eric. "It isn't bleeding."

"Jeremy, for God's sake! *What is going on?*"

"Jeremy saved all us, Dad," Travis said softly.

Robert was at a loss for words as he stared at them. "Elmo, where's your prosthetic leg?"

"Lost it in the fight with Whitehead."

"Whitehead," Robert echoed. "Peter Whitehead?"

Elmo nodded.

Still dismayed, Robert looked into their dirty faces, making eye contact with each of them. He reached over and immediately hugged Travis and Matthew.

"What's in the fishing tube?"

"A picture we found," Travis said innocently.

Robert then touched each of the kids, making sure they were indeed real. He bent down in front of Ian, who had remained seated on the damp steps and was gazing distantly off into space.

"...Ian...you all right?"

The boy looked up at him, nodded somberly and said, "I lost my backpack."

Robert straightened, still at a loss. He then scooped the boy into his arms.

"Can you two take Jeremy?" he asked. "Elmo?"

Dane and Leslie nodded silently, moving in to help him.

"I got 'em Dad," Matthew volunteered.

Robert cleared his throat and his thoughts and said, "C'mon... let's get you all downstairs."

Robert led the way with Ian's head resting on his shoulder through the exit door and down a long hall. With only the overhead emergency lights by which to navigate their way in the dimly lit shadows, Robert took a wrong turn. Adding to the confusion was the maze of halls and doors throughout the conference center. Believing he was leading them through one of the main entry doors, he brought them instead into the rear staging area.

In that instant Miles and Stan entered the staging area too through another rear door but at the opposite far side. Miles hadn't seen them at first, but Stan did. Spotting Robert carrying a small boy in his arms, followed by a troop of somber kids in tow, Stan tapped Miles shoulder.

"Huh?"

"Over there."

"The little kid," Miles said slowly in rapt recognition. "Feel free to start shooting."

"I'm way ahead of you," Stan replied, his camera already planted on his shoulder, his right eye trained through the viewfinder.

"And whatever you do, don't--" Miles interrupted himself when he heard Carl's voice coming through his radio earpiece.

"I know, I know," Stan muttered as he began shooting. "Don't even stop if I hav'ta pee."

Curtained off from the stage and dining area out front, now deserted, except for the parents, Robert set Ian down just as the kids suddenly realized their good fortune.

"FOOD!" one of them cried out loudly.

Spotting a long buffet table set up for the staff and volunteers the half-starved kids made a beeline for it.

Robert helped steer Jeremy to a folding chair where the boy grunted in relief as he sat down.

"I'll be right back," Robert said to Leslie and Dane before quickly disappearing through the curtain.

"Excuse me," a familiar deep voice said from behind.

The moment Dane and Leslie turned, Dane grinned, "Hey, I know you."

"My name is Miles Montgomery--"

"Yeah, the TV guy."

"That's right," grinned Miles. "You ahh, you all look like you've been through hell."

"I'd say that's a fair assessment," Leslie said with a weary grin coming up behind Dane.

"And we've made it back home, all of us," Dane finished, glancing over his shoulder at her with a wink.

Miles then asked them both, "Weren't you just up on the roof, with the Colonel--I mean, Senator Toddhunter?"

"--Oh, look," Leslie said pointing to the ceiling.

As suddenly as the power in the resort had gone out, the overhead fluorescent lights abruptly flickered back to life.

"Good job, Phil," Kellur whispered to himself.

For the last several minutes Kellur had been in his office intently focusing his eyes on the bank of security monitors mounted overhead. His attention had been divided among three different monitors. While he kept track of the arriving police and rescue vehicles out in the parking lot on one of them, his roving eyes scanned a second one which he was using to check various locations throughout the tower and conference center for anyone who might be hurt or in distress. One of those was the helideck cam, but it was no longer functioning and that gravely concerned him. The third monitor allowed him to observe the master electrical room. The instant the pudgy man in the background wearing an ill-fitting uniform rebooted the system breakers restoring power, Kellur radioed him.

"You just earned your pay for the week, Phil."

"Piece ah cake, Toby," his voice swaggered over the airwaves. "What next?"

Before he could respond, another voice broke in.

"Haverty to base, Toby, the police and EMS are here. Where do you wanna 'em to set up?"

Kellur thought for only a moment before replying into his radio, his eyes glimpsing across his monitors, including Phil in the electrical room. "Bobby, hav'em set up a command post there in the north parking lot. We may have casualties upstairs on the helideck, I'll be right out to--"

What followed was so startling it caught Kellur off guard.

Narrowing his eyes on one of the monitors, the one displaying the electrical room where Phil was, the grainy black and white image revealed a sudden intrusion; He watched as the door burst open. A man dressed in black with a camouflaged face confronted Phil, quickly incapacitating him. His large limp body dropped to the floor in an unconscious heap. Shocked, and before Kellur could make sense of what was happening, the intruder moved out of range of the security cam. Within moments the lights once again went out, prompting the emergency lights to switch on again. On a separate power system, to prevent what was happening, the entire closed circuit camera system also went dark.

"Say again?" Bob repeated. "I didn't catch that last part--you'll what?"

"Bobby, listen to me!" Kellur reported into the radio. "We've gotta situation in here. There appears to be an intruder dressed in black, possibly armed. Hold off on fire rescue, it may not be safe. Their location is the master electrical room, Phil's in there--he may be injured!"

Kellur's radio crackled. "Holy crap! Lemme find out who's runnin' the show out here--hold on!"

Radio in hand, Kellur bolted from his office.

"What the hell is going on here, Hodak!" Tom Thigpen barked at him as he rose from his chair.

Dressed in their 'Sunday best', the group of parents sat around the only large table directly below one of the emergency light clusters. Around them the darkened and empty ballroom was in complete disarray, following the abrupt and panicked departure of hundreds of people, as if from a sinking ship. A robust, barrel of a man, Tom ignored Robert's raised hand as he walked up to him. He'd have none of it.

"One minute we got lights and the next we're back in the dark. Why'd you want us in here anyway? Everyone else is outside."

"Everett!" Robert called out into the shadows approaching the group.

"Over here, Robert," the spry country doctor replied from where he sat beside Wyanet McCaulee.

"You find him?" Caroline whispered anxiously as she came up to him.

Robert flashed her a calming nod, taking her hand. "Listen up everyone--"

"If I didn't know better," Jeff Sumner began to say, "I'd say that voice I just heard sounded an awful lot like our son."

"Well you wouldn't be wrong," Robert quipped.

"What?" he half-laughed. He then took a step toward Robert. "Robert, are the kids back there?"

Robert leaned into Caroline's ear and whispered, "I have to run out to the car and get Everett's bag--"

"Someone's hurt!" she uttered alarmingly. "Is he hurt?"

"Who's hurt?" Jeff asked in mounting confusion.

"He's all right--he's just--"

"Robby, what is it?" Jeff approached him and asked. "What's going on?"

"What is it?" Dr. Gibbs asked immediately, threading between Tom and Lorrie.

As the group quickly closed ranks around Robert with Jeff leading the pack, Robert motioned with his hand over his head, his thumb pointing the way. "Yes, they're all back there."

"What the hell--!" Tom gruffed, suddenly taking the lead, dashing toward the stage, with the others quickly following.

The instant Tom swept the curtain aside there were audible cries from the group of stunned parents. Like horses at a food trough, the starving kids were lined up shoulder-to-shoulder at the long buffet table shoving into their mouths whatever they could grab. There were trays of cold-cut sandwiches, rolls, cookies, bags of assorted chips and a large plastic barrel at the end filled with iced down soft drinks. Turning with cheeks bulging like chipmunks preparing for a winter's hibernation, the savory, motley group of kids looked as if they had just walked out of the jungle. They stopped their piranha-like devouring, gulped and ran to their stunned parents.

Gently taking Caroline's wrist and Everett's shoulder, guiding them toward the stage, Robert said, "Jeremy's back there, he is hurt. I'll be right back with your bag"

As the three quickly parted, Caroline and Dr. Gibbs hurried backstage, while Robert bolted from the ballroom.

Kellur raced through the dimly lit maintenance shop about to enter a long corridor that led to the master electrical room when he abruptly stopped. It was more than likely he reasoned that whoever the intruder was, he was organized, well trained and professional. And there was a good chance he was armed, he reminded himself. Was this some sort of terrorist action against Senator Toddhunter, he wondered? He eased up to the heavy metal door and peered cautiously through the small window. The stark light from the emergency cluster at the far end near the ceiling revealed an empty hallway.

His mind raced. Drawing on his own tactical training techniques for clearing a room he knew that it required two people. Acting alone was dangerous. And now, as civilian security, it also required that he do it without first tossing in a hand grenade or blowing a hole through a wall to avoid the door. In a nearby corner he spotted a wooden-handled broom.

He picked it up and gripped it strategically like a ball player at home base preparing to swing away.

PART 6

THE FALL OF AN EMPIRE

CHAPTER FORTY-NINE

Kellur quietly pushed his way through the door and moved silently down the hall. When he reached the edge of the electrical room door, broomstick in hand, he hugged the wall with his back and stood there for several moments, listening.

The only sound he detected was his own slow, measured breaths.

He closed his eyes for only a moment and took another slow, measured breath. Kellur's training and experience was telling him that the intruder was very likely on the other side of the door and he'd have only a split second to incapacitate him. In his mind was the layout of the room, which he knew well. The door opened inward against the wall. With the broom in his left hand, he reached down with his right and lightly caressed the doorknob, then gripped it. Ever so slowly, he tested it, twisting the knob.

He then carefully released it.

He decided his best chance was to buttonhook the door. With cat-like reflexes, he turned with his back to the door, took a deep breath and gripped the knob. With adrenalin induced speed Kellur shoved his two hundred and thirty pound muscled body against the door and slammed it inward with explosive force. Face to face with the black uniformed intruder, Kellur handled the wooden broomstick with precision, striking the man with a succession of blows, beginning with an upward thrust to his groin and then downward against the back of his head, dropping him to the floor.

Kellur hesitated, waiting to see if he was really out. He then reached down, checking the side of his neck...there was still a pulse. He then cautiously stepped over to where Phil lay on the floor, now starting to come around.

"Easy, Phil, easy," Kellur urged his friend and coworker, helping him to sit up.

"What the hell happened?" he moaned.

Kellur spotted something near the unconscious intruder. He reached for it, picking up what looked like a weapon of some kind. It appeared to be a CED electroshock gun--a Taser. He examined it closely, saying, "You'll be all right. Rest easy for a minute, while I tie this bastard up!"

Kellur's radio started squawking. It was Bobby frantically calling him to find out what was happening. Before Kellur responded he stood erect over the intruder, tossed the broom aside, then with gritting teeth sneered down at the unconscious heap, and barked, "Never! Ever! *Screw*...with a Navy Seal!"

Tom Thigpen seethed with anger as he and Lorrie knelt, exchanging hugs with Ian. Tom then held him at arm's length, the both of them dismayed at his somber appearance. The boy looked as if he had been in a fight--they all did.

Tom finally stood and watched as Caroline and Dr. Gibbs attended to Jeremy where he sat. He looked worse. Despite that, Tom clenched his fist several times. When he began to approach them, Lorrie touched his arm saying, "Now don't lose your cool, Tom."

"Who, me?" he frowned at her.

"Jeremy...what happened to you?" Caroline cried softly as she knelt beside him, almost afraid to touch him with all the pain he appeared to be experiencing. Standing behind him Caroline glanced up into the anxious faces of Dane and Leslie as the two looked on. Jeremy tried to smile through clenched teeth as Dr. Gibbs, on his opposite side, carefully began to examine his shoulder, peeling back the lapel and collar of the biker jacket.

"Well, mom, it's kind of a long story, but--"

"Oh I'm sure we'd *allll* love to hear it," Tom barked, staring down at him with angry eyes.

Lorrie asked, "You all weren't supposed to be back until the weekend."

"Well," Jeremy began slowly, "we ran into a little trouble at the campground--Ahh--ow!" Jeremy abruptly exclaimed, pulling away the moment Dr. Gibbs eased back farther on the lapel of his jacket.

"Jeremy, this wound is rather deep, but--" the country doctor commented, continuing his examination.

"Tell me about it," he winced through watering eyes, "--and that really hurts!"

Caroline was speechless as she watched her son's tortured face react.

"That hurts, too," he winced excitedly, glancing down at where Dr. Gibbs was leaning beside his injured thigh for a closer look at his shoulder.

"Sorry son," he said straightening. He then examined the semi-healed gash on his upper leg asking, "What happen here?"

"I caught a bullet there--"

Caroline drew a gasping breath, as she looked closer at his shoulder; dark red, dried blood everywhere. "Oh my God…"

"OKAY! That's it!" Tom snapped, then blasted. "Tell me something', Hodak. Why is it every time my kid goes out with you, something happens to him? Huh?"

Miles whispered in Stan's ear. "Move in and stay on the kid in the biker suit. You'll have to use the light on your camera."

Stan nodded without saying a word. His camera poised on his right shoulder, Stan quietly stepped closer, making sure to get everything. Miles in the meantime dashed to the corner of the stage, found the lines controlling the curtain and pulled on the cord, parting the drapes open. Miles was always thinking ahead. With the group congregating near center stage, and if the power were to hopefully come back on, the overhead spotlights would provide more than enough illumination on all of them.

"Now wait a minute," Jeremy growled as he painfully leaned forward. Having had enough of Tom's open hostility he began to spew through taut lips and gritting teeth, "We've been on the run for our lives for the last three days--I've been shot at, knifed in the shoulder, almost killed in a helicopter up on the roof, and then nearly drowned up there as well. So don't gimme a hard time, okay? Frankly speaking I'm not in the mood for it!"

Jeremy abruptly broke off, slumping exhausted back in his chair, his eyes rolling back as he labored to take in several breaths.

"Take it easy, Jeremy," Caroline said.

"Last year he takes all our kids out on a midnight cruise during a winter storm," the portly man continued to growl back, pointing at him. "Well, I don't know how the rest of you feel, but you've got some explaining to do!"

"Knock it off, Tom!" Caroline snapped as she tried to quiet and comfort Jeremy, looking to Dr. Gibbs when he said, "Where's Robert?"

She too glanced over her shoulder, then said, "Here he comes."

Through the shadows, she noted he appeared to be with three others--hopefully a medical crew.

Miles had quietly slipped beside Stan, indicating with a brief hand signal that they were about ready to go to the live network hookup. Miles looked away as he listened through his earpiece to Carl back in the mobile trailer.

"I think you do owe us an explanation, Jeremy," Wyanet McCaulee said, her soft-spoken voice seeming to have a calming effect over the others.

"There, you see!" Tom quipped.

With Elmo at her side, seated due to his MIA prosthesis, she stepped forward saying, "Show them."

"It's nothing, mom--it wasn't Jeremy's fault, he--"

"Elmo, show them," she repeated sternly.

The boy lifted the bloodstained hem of his tank-top shirt, revealing a dark crease in the skin along the left side of his hip.

There were more audible gasps.

Tom's eyes widened, then narrowed with a frown.

"Here you go, Doc," Robert managed through panting breaths, handing him his black medical bag while his three companions hung back for a moment. "--How is he?"

"Here, give me a hand," Gibbs said to him after setting his bag aside. "Let's get his jacket off."

Robert stepped around, replacing Caroline as she moved out of his way. She noticed the three people, who had accompanied him, were, curiously, a man with two teens, a boy and a girl.

"Jeremy," Robert said gently to him, "Lean forward a bit."

Jeremy winced painfully as he did.

"Gently now," said Dr. Gibbs as the two men carefully slipped their hands beneath his jacket and slowly eased it down then off his arms. Robert took the jacket, setting it aside on the back of a nearby chair. As he did he couldn't take his eyes from the fleshy gash between his deltoid and breastbone. Dried blood seemed to be everywhere; streaming down along the length of his arm and up around his neck, staining a gold chain he was wearing. As Jeremy sat back, closing his eyes, Robert and Caroline exchanged slacked-jawed astonished looks.

Lorrie flinched, looking away.

Dr. Gibbs withdrew a pair of glasses from his breast pocket and slipped them on the bridge of his nose. After several moments he announced, "You're very lucky, young man. It's deep, but not too deep, between your clavicle and scapula. Give me your tie, Robert."

"Huh?--oh."

"We need to immobilize Jeremy's arm."

Dr. Gibbs realized he needed to give Caroline something to do and instructed her to clean and dress Jeremy's wound. She immediately dug into his bag and went to work.

Tom was just as shocked, and then said in mounting frustration, "I was just saying, Hodak, how we'd all love to hear your son's explanation of what they're doing here. Look at them--look at my son. What happened to his leg?"

"It's just a scratch, Daddy--I did it on a bike."

"There, you see," Jeremy quipped, trying to ignore him and the massive pain he was in.

"What bike? You didn't take your bike with you."

"I had to swipe one in order to get to the big RV to climb down onto the roof."

"*To climb down onto the roof?* I mean it, Hodak--WHAT THE HELL!"

"Please, Ian," Jeremy begged him half-heartedly, "don't help me."

Robert stood up, unknotting his tie, about to respond back to him with equal anger when Jeremy said softly. "Lynn was kidnapped two days ago."

"What?" Jeff gushed incredulously with a gaping expression, trading looks with Eric, then Lynn. "Kidnapped?--By whom?"

Travis, still clutching the fishing tube under his arm as he shoved another cookie into his mouth, swallowed, then walked over and squeezed in between Matthew beside Jeremy. Elmo bounded up from his chair, then hopped over and stood next to Matthew as well.

Robert handed Dr. Gibbs his tie asking, "Jeremy, *who* stabbed you?"

"Peter Whitehead."

Robert froze in a moment of dismay.

"That's who kidnapped me," Lynn said, softly avoiding Dylan's gaze the moment after she glimpsed him off to the side standing with Charlee and an older man she didn't recognize yet surmised he was their father. She had no desire to hurtfully implicate him in front of everyone.

"Peter Whitehead?" Jeff clarified just as Eric left his side, joining the other kids. As he did, he motioned with his head at Lynn for her to come over too.

"I don't understand any of this," Jeff said shaking his head. "Wasn't he in jail?"

"A work release program, as I recall," Robert offered. "Then I believe he was let off for good behavior."

"Our justice system in action," snapped Tom.

Jeremy cleared his throat and said, "Apparently he got involved with some really…really, bad people. When they took Lynn…Ian managed to follow them on top of their RV they were in."

Lorrie's mouth gaped open, her voice playing catch-up with her head, trying to envision her small son atop such a vehicle. "…A *moving* RV?" she gushed looking down at him with shocking disapproval. "Whatever were you thinking, young man?"

Jeremy snapped. "He was thinking of Lynn--that's who!"

"Don't you raise your voice to my wife young man!" Tom snapped back.

"Would you all just calm down?" Dr. Gibbs intervened, concentrating. With his stethoscope planted in his ears, he pressed the diaphragm pad to Jeremy's bare chest, listening. "I can't hear my patient's heart--now all of you, shut up!"

Then, placing the diaphragm pad at different positions along his back Jeremy took several breaths as instructed, and continued. "We were all held prisoner at some underground facility up north. Dylan helped us escape--that's Dylan over there."

Dylan sheepishly raised his head and said, "This is all my fault…I'm sorry."

"And just who the hell are you?" Tom gruffed.

The group of dazed parents were a captive audience as they looked over to where a teenage boy stood beside a young girl with long and equally black hair. Next to him was a tall man with short blond hair. Richard nodded respectfully to everyone, and then spoke up. "Ahh, my name is Richard Skyland. These are my children, Dylan and Charlee. Those same people have held them prisoner for nearly a year. After meeting Jeremy, when I saw Robert just now out in the parking lot, I saw the resemblance and we introduced ourselves."

"Just how are you involved, young man?" Jeff asked Dylan anxiously.

"So far so good," Dr. Gibbs said thoughtfully, setting aside the stethoscope. "Vitals are steady, no punctures to the lungs." Concerned that Jeremy may have lost a fair amount of blood, from both injuries, he coaxed Caroline to keep applying gentle pressure to the wound while he wrapped Jeremy's upper arm with a blood pressure cuff. Jeremy went on, glazing over Dylan's initial involvement. "Dylan helped us escape with one of their helicopters."

"Jeremy flew it too," Travis boasted proudly. "You should've seen him. But then we crashed."

Everyone looked even more startled than a moment ago, even Dr. Gibbs.

Jeremy resumed relating their ordeal. "We managed to get away, only later to get trapped in a cabin in the woods--that's where Peter found us."

"But we were able to get away on snowmobiles," Travis volunteered excitedly.

Matthew then picked up the story, beaming, "It was Jeremy's idea--you should've seen us. Right over the lake on snowmobiles…it was pretty cool, wasn't it Jeremy?"

"Yeah…it was cool all right," he agreed with a vague smile and little enthusiasm, remembering the real danger they had been in. "Until they caught up to us at the barn. They split us up from the kids, taking us in separated RV's, then headed south. As we were crossing the Mack, the RV Leslie and I were in crashed, tipping over."

"Tipping over?" Tom sputtered abruptly, lagging behind in dismay. "Underground facilities and snowmobiles in August? Now I've heard everything!"

"No, wait a minute," Caroline suddenly interjected, thinking aloud. "There *was* an accident on the bridge earlier today, *and it did involve an RV*--it was all over the news when we left this morning, remember Robert?"

"She's right, there was."

Tom's hands found their way to his hips when he said dubiously, "You actually expect us to believe *any of this*?"

After Ian slipped from Lorrie's grasp to join his friends she stepped beside her husband, placing an affectionate hand on his wrist and said softly, "Thomas, be quiet."

"Yes, *Thomas*, be quiet and let 'em talk," Jeff frowned. "What people, Jeremy?"

"The Colonel was behind it."

Tom gasped loudly with a doubting laugh. "The Colonel? Senator Toddhunter? Are you kidding?"

"Stop it!" Leslie admonished him. "He's telling you the truth!"

"Do me a favor, Jeremy," Tom spat calmly. "From here on just stay away from my kid, okay?"

"Are you seeing this?" Carl gushed over his headset with the NBC producer at Rockefeller Center in New York City.

Seated beside Bert in the mobile van, both men were riveted to the small monitor. "...All right," Carl acknowledged over his headset. "We're all set at this end"

Carl glanced at the monitor, then across at Bert, muttering, "Incredible. They've got Williams in his chair, tell Miles."

Miles and Stan's earpieces crackled with Bert's voice. "Ten seconds, boys."

"Where is the Senator now?" Robert asked.

"He's dead." was all Jeremy said.

Dr. Gibbs broke the uneasy silence when he said, "Robert, we've done all we can here. We need to get Jeremy to Munson hospital."

"Here we go," Bert announced in his deep baritone voice to everyone over his headset.

Following a commercial, the main monitor faded to black allowing the local feed to connect to the NBC network. A moment later television screens across the country flashed the animated NBC news opening sequence with an abbreviated John Williams theme and Michael Douglas' voiceover.

"From NBC News world headquarters in New York, this is a special report with Brian Williams."

"We have late word from the special political luncheon being held today at the Grand Traverse World Resort in Traverse City, Michigan, that Senator Ellis Toddhunter has been killed in an apparent accident. Now I must stress, this has not been confirmed. We're going now to the resort and Miles Montgomery for a live report. Miles, what can you tell us?"

Kellur had checked several panels, curious as to why the black-suited operative had cut the power to the conference center. Knowing that it was the senator's last known location, thinking it was somehow connected, he scanned the corresponding electrical panels. Satisfied there was no damage, he reached for the main breaker, pressing it downward and rebooted the entire electrical system.

Poised before Stan, microphone in hand, his eyes bristling against the camera lights' intense glare, Miles earpiece buzzed. Catching Williams voice over the fray Miles spoke calmly, "Brian, what we're hearing is nothing less than stunning. Following what appears to have been the crash of the senator's private helicopter prior to takeoff from the resort's helipad on the roof..."

Tom could hear Miles voice but ignored it, shaking his head and waving his hands at Jeremy, reacting with sarcasm. "So, Senator

Toddhunter kidnapped you. Next you'll be tellin' us how you were all pursued by government agents operatives!"

"We were!" Matthew announced flatly.

The darkness of the ballroom was suddenly chased away by the glowing chandeliers.

Everyone seemed more startled by Matthew's remark than by the sudden reappearance of the lights. Their faces were a reflection of utter silent dismay. Like members of sports team rallying to a teammate's side, all of the kids had come up and stood supportively behind Jeremy.

"Well, you're right, Mr. Thigpen," Jeremy relented with a flippant smirk and tone. "I made the whole thing up--all of it! Satisfied?"

An instant later, the east double doors burst inward with a loud bang, abruptly drawing everyone's eyes to the opposite side of the Governors' Ballroom. With frightening speed three men in black outfits and camouflaged faces swept across the littered floor toward them with guns drawn, pointing upward.

Stan spun around, focusing his camera on the Black Ops team as they bounded up onto the stage and split up, threading among the stunned and confused gathering.

Carl and Bert reeled in their seats.

Narrowing his eyes, Bert uttered, "What the--"

"Who the hell are they?" muttered Carl.

Television screens across the country clearly showed one of the men in black coming right at Miles, shoving him aside and knocking the microphone from his hand. It clanked to the floor, reverberating loudly across headphones and speakers everywhere.

The two men yelped, throwing off their own headphones gasping at the monitor screen.

One of the men in black then grabbed Stan's camera by the lens. There was a jarring, dizzying scuffle with the intruder as Stan tried to hold onto the camera until it was violently ripped from his grasp and thrust downward where it smashed against the carpeted floor.

Screens across the country went to snow.

Dazed, Stan looked down at his broken EFP shoulder camera, then stumbled backward as the Black Operative thrust a gun into his face. Bumping into a table, Stan froze with raised hands.

"Hooolee, Carl," Bert sputtered, staring at the static-filled screen. "Whatta we do now?"

Carl's mind raced at warp speed, his eyes darting, suddenly locking on one of the monitors. "Bertie, look! Are the mikes in the ballroom still hot?"

Bert quickly checked and said they were.

"Switch to camera two--quick!"

Jeremy's eyes grew wider as he watched the men in black position themselves, surrounding everyone on the stage.

No one moved after Robert and Dr. Gibbs protectively closed ranks about the kids and Jeremy.

"Two minutes!" one of the Black Ops announced sharply.

"What the hell is this?" Tom wondered aloud, as if it were some sort of a gag.

One of the men in black quickly approached him in a threatening manner, thrusting his weapon to the man's temple. Tom laughed nervously for a moment, and then started to speak. "If you think--"

Tom abruptly doubled over from the painful blow to his groin, dropping to the floor.

Leslie took a step toward him only to be stopped by Dane beside her clutching her hand.

"Daddy!" Ian cried, trying to run to him only to be held back by Eric's tight grip on his shoulders.

"Oh my God!" Lorrie screeched, rushing to Tom's side as he wheezed and coughed.

Robert started to move toward the intruders until Jeremy reached out with his good hand, stopping him and whispered, "Dad, no."

Everyone remained frozen.

Miles's eyes flashed on Stan's in a hopeless gesture. Stan's eyes replied, flashing to the left…toward the double-camera set up out front for the luncheon broadcast. Miles caught the gesture, noticing the small 'hot' light atop Camera #2. It was still glowing red. Miles winked his understanding, stifling an-ever-so-slight grin.

The leader of the Black Ops team bristled at the overhead lights. It meant something had gone wrong in the electrical room. He immediately instructed one of his men with a single word. That man then calmly but briskly exited the ballroom through the same door they'd all come in.

The leader in black, his weapon aimed toward the ceiling, then approached Jeremy where he was sitting. Flanked by Robert, Dr. Gibbs, and Caroline, along with all the kids, he focused his dark gray eyes down on Jeremy's when he said, "You either give us what we've come for or someone in this room is going to be seriously hurt. You have ninety seconds!"

Jeremy knew what he wanted.

Dylan did too and his heart sank.

Jeremy was angry and defiant to the last. In pain, his arm in a sling, tape and gauze covering both his thigh and shoulder wound, he struggled to stand until Robert and Dr. Gibbs helped him to his feet. He teetered for a moment, and then steadied himself.

Everyone's eyes, including Tom's from the floor, were on Jeremy and the man in black that faced him. They listened too to the astonishing exchange between them.

"I'm getting just a little tired of being threatened," Jeremy glared vehemently. "So tell me, what government agency are you from, anyway. CIA, NSA, FBI--?"

"Seventy-five seconds!" the other Black Ops announced with cold efficiency.

"Who are you people?" growled Robert.

The Black Ops leader, a weapon in one hand while his other held what looked like a cell phone, ignored Robert and instead drilled his gaze into Jeremy's. He leveled his gun with Jeremy's chest while his other held aloft the cell phone-like device. To everyone's quiet horror the gun was real. The leader then growled back, "I'm looking for a smartphone. This one in particular emits an electronic signature. And according to this, one of you has it…and I want it, right now!"

A sudden revelation flashed through Jeremy's mind. It had to be Ryan's smartphone, which Dylan had downloaded the Caradori file to, that they were after. However, since Spear had shut it down whose was it they were detecting? And did the Black Ops leader know that it had been deactivated? That left only one working smartphone in their possession!

Was it luck or Divine intervention, Jeremy wondered, hoping his reaction hadn't registered on his poker face.

"Sixty seconds!"

Jeremy dared not bluff him. "Dad, would you please hand me my jacket."

Robert turned, reaching for the jacket and handed it to his son.

Still wearing his poker face Jeremy dug into an interior pocket. A few feet away, flanked by Charlee and Richard, Dylan nervously watched the proceedings, his sweaty hand in his pocket, anxiously clutching Ryan's smartphone and wondering what Jeremy had up his sleeve.

"Police, forty-five seconds!" his companion announced sharply as he held up a similar device in the palm of his hand.

All eyes were on Jeremy as he withdrew the Colonel's smartphone which he had grabbed and held it up before the Black Ops leader. Facing him Jeremy could feel the weight of his stare, along with his own heart pounding beneath his sternum.

The Black Ops leader made no move, then suddenly swiped it from Jeremy's hand, examining it...

Dylan held his breath as he and Jeremy exchanged a grave momentary glance.

The man in black and camouflage then passed it over his shoulder to his companion's waiting hand. Then he said, "The flash drive too."

Jeremy drew a weary breath. He tried to swallow but he had little salvia left when he said, "We don't have General Wu's flash drive, Spear destroyed it. You can check all of us."

"No," the Ops leader barked with icy intent, raising his weapon up to Jeremy's temple. "I'm afraid I don't believe you!"

Robert suddenly interceded. "Now wait a--"

"Dad!"

Jeremy wasn't sure what to do next until he glimpsed camera #2 behind them, its lens pointed directly at the entire group. Although he'd been aware for the last several minutes that Miles' cameraman was recording their earlier exchange he hadn't paid much attention to it, until now. Then he caught Miles' sly look and subtle nod and knew. Emboldened, he straightened and stared right into the Black Ops leader's malevolent eyes surrounded by a camouflaged face and asked him belligerently, "You gonna shoot me?" He then tilted his head at the live camera out front with the glowing red light. "Right here...on national television?"

CHAPTER FIFTY

The leader of the Black-Ops team glared over his shoulder in the direction that Jeremy motioned. Spotting the two-camera setup out on the ballroom floor, one of them obviously 'hot', indicated by the red light and aimed in their direction, rather than react with shock or anger, the man in camouflaged face paint simply barked an order to his companion. Then, like scurrying cockroaches, both men in black withdrew from the stage and out the door they'd come in, vanishing, never to be seen again.

As everyone broke into cries of near hysterics and gasps of relief, Ian darted over to his mother, helping his father to his feet.

The air rushed from Jeremy's lungs the moment he dropped his gaze. Slumping back down into his chair, Robert grabbed his good arm, helping to break his fall. From weakened eyes, he watched the double doors ease shut, grateful it was over.

"Quick!" Miles directed Stan, rushing over to the podium and grabbing one of the live mikes. "Take over the camera and stay with me."

Stan was way ahead of him, briskly maneuvering himself behind the active pedestal camera, donning the headset. Adjusting the controls, he focused in on Miles.

In Midtown Manhattan, New York City, there were several stunned moments of dead air as the NBC staff in the massive control room of studio 3B caught their collective breaths. A broadcast coup like this, an elder technician recalled, hasn't been seen on live television since November 24, 1963 when millions across the nation watched in shocked dismay on the same network as Dallas nightclub operator Jack Ruby stepped from the crowd in the basement of Dallas Police Headquarters and shot Lee Harvey Oswald.

"Or 9/11," the young director reminded him solemnly.

"I stand corrected," the elder tech replied softly. "...Hollywood, eat your heart out."

Buried deep within the CIA building in Langley, Virginia the technician in the small operation center switched the network television broadcast to the main, 200-inch ultra-definition LCD flat screen. Pressing an intercom button, he spoke briefly, alerting Ops Division Director, Carol Langford.

"Ma'am, you'd better have a look at this."

Coming out from a small office her eyes were glued to the huge screen, along with the other four technicians. There was little that shocked this seasoned professional in the spy game, but an ops mission unfolding on national television was about the only thing that did. Her hand found its way to her gaping mouth, covering it.

Deputy Director, Vincent McNeil stood in the operation center at DNI headquarters in McLean, Virginia and stared at the large flat-panel HD screen along with his staff and watched the live NBC broadcast in dismay.

He shook his head and was heard to say in a hushed voice, "I'll be damned."

From his private den at the sprawling estate by the sea, Manndrake raised the volume with the remote, then sagged back into his chair behind his desk. The blood drained from his face as the shocking realization struck him of what was unfolding on his television screen across the room, and across the country.

The unflappable Brian Williams sat riveted in his chair beneath the glare of studio lights, along with the rest of the nation that was tuned into the mid-afternoon live broadcast of the disaster, watching as the black camouflaged intruders held the group hostage. Dividing his attention between his director in the control room relaying information through his earpiece and watching the intruders abruptly retreat, Williams immediately began attempting to reestablish contact with Miles.

Stan spoke briefly with Bert in the control trailer, then hand-signaled Miles. Just then, as he heard Williams's voice coming through his earpiece, Miles looked directly into the camera.

"Yes, yes, Brian, I can hear you now…"

"Miles, can you tell us what we all just witnessed?" Williams asked him.

"Brian, the young man's name is Jeremy Hodak, let's listen in."

Miles then began moving toward the group. As he did, Stan gingerly maneuvered the pedestal camera along on its wheels as far as he could, relying on the zoom lens to move in even closer. The microphone in Miles's hand easily picked up their voices.

Jeremy sat with closed eyes, his shoulder throbbing.

Still dumbstruck, Robert hesitated then asked, "Son, what did you mean when you asked that man if he was from the CIA, NSA, or the FBI?"

"Take your pick, Dad. They're all involved in it one way or the other. Even the UN! …Gee Mom, maybe you'd better sit down--before you fall down…you don't look so good."

Caroline nodded in agreement, pulling out the nearest chair and slumping into it. Then she asked, "Involved in…involved in what, Jeremy?"

"The global slave trade," Dylan answered matter-of-factly.

Robert thought he'd misunderstood as he muttered incredulously, "*The what?*"

Everyone suddenly jumped, again, and heads jerked around the moment another set of double doors across the ballroom flew open, rushed by four police officers and Security Officer Kellur. Stan abruptly swung the camera around. Guns drawn, aimed defensively, their eyes flashing about the room, one of them asked, "Everyone all right?"

"They went that-a-way," Robert replied loudly, pointing at the double-doors on the opposite side of the room through which the intruders had beaten a hasty exit.

The officer nodded with a probing eye, then he and the other officers quickly darted across the hall, along with Kellur in tow, and raced back out the other double-doors.

"Incredible," Bert uttered with a shake of his head, adding, "You think it's all true?"

Mesmerized, Carl nodded slowly and said, "Yep, and so will the rest of the country, especially after the investigations begin. I have a feeling a lot of people in Washington are gonna have a lot of explaining to do in the coming days. Oh, and remind me to tell Miles to pack his bag. I want him there covering it all."

Bert nodded.

"And tell Stan to *stay on that injured biker kid!*"

As the starving kids scrambled back to the buffet table to continue their grazing, Tom shuffled over, flanked by Jeff and Lorrie helping him, and joined the group of parents. He slumped down into the nearest chair just as Ian raced over wrapping his arms about his barrel chest.

"I'm all right, son," Tom said to Ian, wiping the boy's cheek. Ian leaned into his father, laying his head on his shoulder.

Tom then looked over at Jeremy and said, "I guess I owe you an apology."

Jeremy squinted his eyes through the pain and a languid smiled crossed his lips. "…Thanks."

After Miles hastily slid a table out of the way and moved some cables along the floor, clearing a path, Stan was able to maneuver the pedestal camera closer to the group. Miles said a few words to Williams and moved in on the group, focusing on Jeremy, looking for an opening.

"Jeremy, I don't understand any of this," Caroline uttered consolingly as she watched Dr. Gibbs give her son an injection in his good shoulder. Jeremy winced slightly then looked up giving the old country doctor a relieved grin. "…Oh, thanks, Doc."

"That'll help with the pain."

"It's all because of this," Dylan said, stepping forward. Dylan then reached into his pocket and pulled out Ryan's cell phone. "This is the one they were after. It belonged to a guy named Ryan Howland."

Charlee walked up to her brother and took the phone from him and held it in her hand for a moment before speaking. She traced it back in her mind, painfully remembering, then said, "They all had ones like these."

Still confused Caroline said, "Who's he?"

"A monster," she replied distantly.

Robert asked, "Anything particularly special about that phone?"

Dylan nodded. "That phone is our ace in the hole," he said.

"It contains the entire Caradori dossier," Jeremy winced painfully from the pain shooting through his arm. "...Proof of what's going on, and what happened to us."

Listening intently to the exchange, a keyboard at his fingertips, Williams' hands whizzed across the keys typing out instructions, immediately sending it to the control room. When it flashed across his producer's screen, it read simply:

Get me everything you've got on Caradori dossier!

Miles' intuition told him this was his cue. He intervened, moving closer with the microphone, Stan right behind him with the pedestal camera.

"Proof of what, Jeremy?"

Jeremy, feeling the effects of the drug, sighed deeply and closed his eyes as he relaxed in his chair and said, "...Proof of the existence of the Caradori dossier."

"The Caradori dossier? Does it involve the Colonel?"

"It did, right up to his corrupt beady little eyeballs," Jeremy replied flatly, gazing up at the reporter and explaining, "the Colonel was in charge of the North American slave network--his clandestine little side venture he kept neatly hidden from his constituents. The dossier was the original compilation of evidence collected back in the late eighties through the early nineties of everyone involved at the time--from the famous and well known to business leaders to high-level government officials, many of them in Washington. It's named for the original investigator, Gary Caradori, who was about to expose the whole thing in nineteen ninety until he was murdered. That's when the dossier vanished."

"Then it mysteriously showed up at the doorstep of Congressman Denis last year," Richard interjected. "Denis had the dossier with him when his plane went down in Lake Erie. Afterwards I was the one who spirited him and his family out to the country for their safety."

"Then he's alive?" Miles interrupted him in shocked tone.

"Oh, yes," Richard nodded, "It was the Colonel who tried to have him killed. Then, the dossier disappeared again."

"Until Dylan downloaded it to that phone just before we all escaped two days ago," Jeremy finished. "That's what the Colonel was so desperate to get back. The dossier exposes the entire slave net-work--its members and officers!"

Miles was incredulous. "We are talking about Ellis 'the Colonel' Toddhunter, senior United States Senator from Michigan, chairman of the House Ethics Committee. Correct?"

Jeremy nodded somberly from his chair, glancing up at Dylan as he took the phone back from Charlee. The two boys held a dumb-struck audience...from the tiny gathering in the ballroom to the entire nation.

"I don't believe it," Miles remarked in awe, nearly forgetting he was on live television. "Where was it you were all being held?"

"The Colonel's private compound estate in the Upper Peninsula."

"Where is the dossier now?"

Jeremy looked over and nodded for Dylan to come over. "Show 'em."

Dylan dropped his gaze. Despite the fact that he and Charlee had been threatened with their lives, he was nonetheless embarrassed for his complicity and it upset him terribly. Finally, he approached the gathering holding up Ryan's smartphone and said, "It's all here... on this phone."

"There it is," said the heavy-set man to his partner seated across from him in the unmarked dark blue sedan, the two men watching the live broadcast on a small portable device. "The kid had it all along."

"So whose phone was it he handed over?"

"Doesn't matter. That's the one we have orders to recover. The one with the dossier. Let's go."

Parked in a remote lot, the two men in dark business suits exited the sedan, and headed directly for the conference center.

Dylan hesitated for a moment, looking at Charlee. She smiled warmly at him, took his hand and said, "It's okay, tell them."

"Well…the Colonel's grand ambition was to have total control of the global slave network. The dossier gave him the power to blackmail a lot of influential people--*except* those within the organization--the other network bosses--whose identities are a highly guarded secret. And the only way he could achieve control over them was to go hi-tech and tap into each network's computer systems. Infiltration by computer was proving to be too difficult. So, the Colonel came up with an ingenious plan to donate a very special painting to each of the bosses. Because all of these particular paintings were widely known to have been stolen he was assured automatically and privately by each boss that they would hang them in their private offices, which meant, close to their computer terminals."

"Big deal," quipped Dane.

"It was a big deal, especially since each painting was bugged with a data-capture chip.

"A what?" Ian asked wrinkling his nose.

"A data-capture chip. Concealed on the back of the frame of each painting, it emits a signal which allowed the Colonel to bypass all their security measures and protocols. In other words, it told their computers to let him in, giving him carte blanche access into each of the network's computer systems around the globe. All their accounts were now at his disposal--*everything*. Financial records, personal information on all the bosses, who they are, along with the board of directors, including a complete global listing of participating countries and their investors and clients. He now had what he wanted most. Power. Global power...to blackmail and even control the political futures of involved government leaders."

"It's absolutely unbelievable," uttered Robert with an incredulous frown and a slow dazed shake of his head.

"The Colonel never intended to give up the painting that hung in his office to General Wu, the head of the Asian network," Dylan went on to explain. "He planned all along to kill the General and keep that one for himself."

"When I met with the Colonel," Jeremy said, picking up the story, flashing his eyes around the room at everyone, "that's when I first saw it, hanging over his fireplace. I needed something to threaten him with. He admired it so much I hoped he'd let us go. When I grabbed it I damaged the frame. The way it freaked him out I figured maybe it was valuable--at least it was to him. When we escaped that's when I spotted it in the elevator. I knew it might come in handy as a bargaining chip so I grabbed it and took it with us."

"Spear probably put it there to be taken downstairs to the repair shop," Dylan said.

"How is it you know so much about it?" Miles asked him, speaking into his microphone, then moving it closer to the boy. "Dylan, is it?"

"Yes. I'm pretty good with computers, that's why they kept me and my sister around. I programmed all the chips and Spear attached 'em to the back of the frame of each painting."

"Spear, the Colonel's security man?"

"No," Dylan corrected him emphatically. "The Colonel's *hitman*. Spear killed people--or at least, he used to. ...He can't...not anymore," he declared.

"**Ha! -- I was** right," blurted Carl in a moment of excitement as he sat beside Bert, who was still shaking his head. "I told you he was a hitman!"

Miles, a thorough professional, was racing to process what he was hearing while moving onto his next question. "How many of these stolen paintings are we talking about?"

Jeremy looked across the stage at the line of kids still feeding at the buffet and called to his brother. "Trav, would you bring over the fishing tube, please."

"...Sure," he replied after swallowing a mouthful.

All eyes were on Travis as he picked up and came forward carrying the beat-up, gray fishing tube.

"Go ahead," Jeremy instructed, the drug taking its full effect making him feel just a bit groggy.

Travis removed the lid, inverted the tube and gently, carefully tapped the top of it. For a moment the aged canvas refused to budge from the safe confines of the plastic tube, then, finally it slid out halfway. The ballroom was shrouded in silence as Matthew joined his twin, cautiously gripping the edge of the canvas and brought it out the rest of the way.

"Help me up, would you, Dad?" Jeremy asked. "Mom, would someone clear that table there?" Walking weakly, Jeremy was flanked by Robert and Dane helping him while Dylan anxiously hovered close behind them like a curious puppy. Caroline moved in and removed the centerpiece from a nearby table while Jeff quickly gathered up the round, white tablecloth along with its clanking contents and set it on an adjacent table. Delicately handling the five-by-four-foot canvas, the twins began to uncurl and open the fragile painting, exposing the back side first. The moment they turned it over and gingerly laid it flat, Dr. Gibbs gasped softly, immediately stepping forward and said, "My God...I don't believe it!"

Jeremy shrugged. "You recognize it Doc--is it worth anything? I know the Colonel sure made a fuss over it--that's why I grabbed it."

"You were right to do so, young man," Dr. Gibbs declared in rapt elation. Marveling at what his aged eyes beheld he was about to reach down to touch the old canvas until he abruptly stopped himself, as if such a thing of absolutely delicate beauty should ever be touched by human hands.

"Who are those guys?" Ian spoke up, breaking the silence.

"Those are the twelve disciples, Ian" Dr. Gibbs answered him, reverently clasping his hands together. "...And Christ. ...Jeremy, where did you get this again?"

"It was hanging in the Colonel's den," he replied. "Is it valuable?"

"*Valuable*? Please tell me you *didn't* damage the *canvas*."

"Nope, just the frame--when I was trying to get 'em to let us go. I later had the twins remove it from the frame and we carted it with us in the fishing tube."

The old doctor took his aged eyes from Jeremy's drawn face and focused them again on the painting laid out on the table. Forgetting himself, he was again about to reach out and touch a piece of history until the fingers of his hand recoiled, as though he was pulling them back from a roaring flame. In a mesmerized daze he whispered, "Look at them, just look at all of them..."

First the kids, then the rest of the curious group, including Miles, squeezed in to get a better look at the dark and moody oil painting. Stan drew closer as well, angling the pedestal camera for a clearer shot. No one spoke a word as their eyes swept over the image of a single-mast sailing sloop crowded to the brink with people aboard. The tiny boat, tilted wildly at a sharp angle, was awash in a foaming sea, engulfed by a ferocious storm. The moment Dr. Gibbs leaned over to examine the rudder more closely after mounting his spectacles across the bridge of his nose, he straightened, smiling broadly. His eyes began to glaze over as he drew a breath and said, "This is considered one of his greatest masterpieces. And it was his *only* seascape. This one, along with the thirteen others that were stolen, was estimated to be worth, from what I recall in the newspapers at the time...about...ahh...three hundred million dollars."

"What?" gasped Robert.

"Others--what others?" asked Jeff.

"Dr. Gibbs?"

Jeremy asked, "How do you know so much about it?"

"Years ago, while attending a medical conference--one of my last trips with Annie--we took in some museums. This one was one of her favorites. And I can't believe it's right here in front of us!"

"Dr. Gibbs?"

"*Who's* masterpiece?" Robert pressed.

"Vermeer's *The Concert* alone, is estimated to be worth over two hundred million dollars. And it's considered the most valuable, unrecovered stolen painting, ever."

"I still don't understand any of this," said Wyanet, looking as confused as the others.

"Which museum, Everett?" Caroline asked him.

"The Isabella Stewart Gardner Museum."

"In Boston, Massachusetts!" Caroline exclaimed. "Oh, my God!"

"Dr. Gibbs!"

"Yes, Ian, I'm sorry...what is it?"

"You said these guys were the twelve disciples, and Jesus?"

"That's right."

"Well, I count fourteen guys in the little boat, not thirteen."

Dr. Gibbs grinned. "Very good, Ian. Now, do you know which one is Jesus?"

The boy turned and pointed. "That looks like 'em there, next to the guy working the rudder."

"Top marks, Ian. Now, look closer at the rudder. See anything on it?"

Ian wrinkled his nose as he narrowed his eyes. "Welll...it's a little hard to see..."

"...Keep trying..."

"…It looks like…Rem…bran…Rembran…" he turned and announced proudly with a toothy grin, "Rembrandt, 1633!"

"Excellent, my boy!"

"Wait a minute, hold it!" Jeremy grinned, skeptically arching a brow. "Are you tellin' us…we've been draggin' around in that beat-up fishing tube, which has been dropped in a river, bounced around in an RV, and survived the equivalent of a water park waterfall in the stairwell, the actual, original, *stolen, Rembrandt* painting from the museum?"

"It would seem so--one of them, that is," the old doctor continued, his eyes aglow with excitement. "…And it appears to have come through it in remarkably excellent condition. That's Rembrandt there, see 'em? He's the one wearing the blue shirt and cap and clutching the shroud. It's titled, *The Storm on the Sea of Galilee.* In the wee morning hours of March 18, 1990, two men disguised as police officers broke into the Isabella Stewart Gardner Museum in Boston and stole this one, along with twelve others."

"Would you turn over the top right corner of it, please?" Dylan asked.

So enraptured and fearing any further chances of it being damaged after such an arduous journey, in just the last few days alone, and before the twins dirty hands could touch it, Dr. Gibbs gently, ever so gently, folded over the old and cracked corner exposing what looked like a tiny black patch attached to the fabric.

"That's it there," Dylan said pointing at the postage stamp-sized microchip affixed to the aged canvas.

Dr. Gibbs shook his head in disgust. "To risk damaging such a magnificent portrait…"

"I programmed it and Spear put 'em on, like he did with all the others."

"And they all have the same chip?" Miles probed.

"Uh-huh."

"How many are there?"

"Ahh," Dylan thought for a moment. "A painting went to each of the slave cartel bosses, and there were six of 'em. The ah, North America network, Western Europe, Eastern Europe, Africa, South America, and the Middle East. General Wu was in charge of the Southeast Asian network, and he got zip."

Miles hesitated, something he'd never done before in an interview, overwhelmed by the disclosure.

"With that chip you can locate all the other stolen paintings along with their new owners--the other network bosses. After I programmed each chip, Spear went in and created an encrypted security code," Dylan then smiled proudly with a sly twinkle in his eyes as he gazed at Ryan's smartphone in the palm of his hand, explaining, "but I can still get in. I knew what he was up to, so I created a backdoor. I just need the six-digit code, Then I can access *all* the chips. And that's in here, along with the dossier. Even though Spear shut the phone down I can still access the Caradori dossier. Piece ah cake!"

Dylan's elation suddenly faded and the smile ran from his dark complexioned face. His somber mood seemed to be contagious as the rest the kids fell silent too, trading dispiriting glances with him, as if all of it meant nothing to them.

There was an expectation of excitement at such a revelation, Dr. Gibbs thought, at least where the Rembrandt was concerned. Yet there was oddly none. After an awkward moment, in a congratulatory tone, he said, "Well, young man, this particular art theft is considered *the biggest* in US history...and it appears that you and Jeremy may have solved it!"

Jeremy grinned weakly.

Dr. Gibbs paused, frowning curiously at Jeremy, then said, "At the very least that should rate a hoot of some sort from all of you... at the very least."

Jeremy looked over at Travis and his sad boyish eyes and knew why. "Well," Jeremy admitted weakly to him, "We, ah, we had a casualty earlier today."

"Someone got hurt?" Robert blurted, his tone edging alarm, "who was it--what happened?"

"A friend," he replied softly, noticing Dane's sullen face. "His name was Arnold. He's a dog. And he quite probably saved all our lives this morning."

Jeremy took a deep breath and thought for a moment, his mind changing gears. He then narrowed his eyes on Miles, then on Dylan again and said, "I think we can trust Miles...whattya say?"

Dylan too thought for a moment and finally nodded his approval. He approached the news reporter and held out the smartphone, dropping it into Miles's hand. "Here. It's yours now. With all that's happened today, I dare you people to try and sweep this under the rug."

Miles looked back at the boy and replied earnestly, "Don't worry."

"And you might as well take the Rembrandt too." He added the moment he noticed Richard staring at him proudly, the way a father looks at his son. "We've been draggin' that thing around for the last couple of days--would you see that it's returned to the museum. I'll bet they'd like to have it back. Besides," he concluded with a sly grin, staring back across at Richard. "It just wouldn't look right hanging in my bedroom."

Miles grinned and laughed.

Jeremy did too until his legs buckled. Robert and Dane snapped into action, each grabbing an arm.

"Whoa, I gotcha, son--

"Oh, man, I don't feel so good--"

"C'mon Dane, gimme a hand with 'em."

Jeremy winced and pointed. "Doc...the Rembrandt, would you...?"

"Got it," Doctor Gibbs smiled. As gently as if he were handling a newborn he'd just delivered, he gently rolled the Rembrandt back up and carefully slid it into the fishing tube.

"Let's go, boys," Caroline said, herding the twins while keeping a concerned watchful eye on Jeremy as Robert and Dane gently escorted him from the Governors' Hall ballroom. As they all ambled down the hall Robert asked Jeremy, "By the way, son, where is our minivan?"

Through a tense, pained expression as he was helped, walking gingerly, he replied, "It's parked in the underground garage of a converted Minuteman nuclear missile silo."

"Oh…okay."

Following them in tow were the rest of the kids and their parents, heading out into the mobbed parking lot.

Left in their wake, Miles turned to the camera, deftly tucking the fishing tube containing the 1633 Rembrandt under his arm after having taken it from Dr. Gibbs, then held up the smartphone and said, "The bombshell to end all bombshells…and the world as we know it…is about to change. Back to you, Brian."

CHAPTER FIFTY-ONE

The north parking lot where the command post was set up was a sea of flashing colored lights from the numerous police cruisers, fire trucks and EMS vehicles. His clothes still damp, like the others, and despite his throbbing shoulder, Jeremy reveled beneath the bright, warm afternoon sun. Off to one corner, milling crowds were kept at bay by wooden barricades and police. Jeremy was whisked past them to a gurney, then past scores of other police officers, reporters, photographers, and firemen to one of several rescue squads where two paramedics immediately began checking his vitals and examining his shoulder and leg wounds.

"That's my husband and children," blurted a tall shapely woman as she jetted past an overburdened officer before he could stop her.

Richard walked through the busy throng, ignoring the activity, overwhelmed with relief as he held onto Dylan and Charlee flanking his sides, an arm draped across their shoulders. The instant he spotted Christine running toward them, her flowing ebony hair cascading about her back and shoulders, he steered right for her. He relinquished the kids on cue and she ran into his open arms where he closed them tightly about her. Christine couldn't help herself, as she kissed him passionately, and then hugged his neck.

She released him and stood back. "Oh, I've been so worried about you, about all of you," she said, looking at the two kids.

"You are a sight for tired eyes, my dear," he said, then proudly declared, "Christine, this is Charlee, and this is Dylan, my daughter and son."

Christine beamed with a broad smile, extending her hand to Charlee first, then Dylan. "I'm so very pleased to meet the both of you. We've been looking forward to this since we heard. I hope the ranch life appeals to you both. Richard and I own a spread just outside of Kalkaska, a large ranch with stables, riding trails…"

"You have horses?" Charlee asked her through a timid smile.

"Several. Have you ever ridden?"

"Not since I was a little girl when our mother…"

The moment her voice trailed off Christine took a step toward her and Dylan and said, "What about you, Dylan?"

Dylan only shrugged his shoulders, distrust written across his dirty face.

Christine's rose-hued lips parted in a gentle smile while her soft wet green eyes radiated warmth as she spoke. "The both of you are a part of our family now. And both Richard and I welcome you into our home."

Richard nodded affectionately at the two kids the moment they looked in his direction.

Dylan then drew closer to her and squinted in the sunlight, "Do we get to sleep in a real bed?"

"You'll each have your own room," Richard assured him, drawing up beside Christine, taking her hand and kissing it.

That broke the ice for young Dylan. Suddenly the brightest part on his soiled face were his teeth as a smile emerged across it. He allowed himself to relax and maybe even go so far as to believe them both. After all, Richard did rescue them too. Dylan then said, "Really…for real?"

"For real," Christine reassured him.

As Miles and Stan hastily made their way through the parking lot, Miles was dividing his attention between Carl's instructions over the radio receiver in his ear and the throng of people and flashing emergency vehicles around them. The fishing tube tucked under his arm, Miles acknowledged Carl curtly, then said to Stan, speaking briskly, handing him the smartphone, "Here, take this to Stewie--and take the Rembrandt--and for God's sake don't lose it. Then meet us back here--Carl's got another camera for you."

"Where is he?"

"Stewie's at the van. Tell 'em to drop whatever he's doing and download this thing, ASAP, immediately, without delay, posthaste!"

"You mean, right away?"

"I mean ten minutes ago!"

The two quickly separated in the crowd.

Jeremy's gurney had been adjusted allowing him to sit up while his shoulder was being treated by one of the paramedics, a short man with puffy but nimble fingers. At his side were Robert and Caroline, along with a Michigan state trooper, taking down his statement on a small pad. Intending only to get a few details from which to begin their investigation, the officer realized Jeremy was in no condition for a lengthy interview and politely and professionally excused himself, agreeing to resume his questioning with him in the morning, at home. Both Robert and Caroline thanked him as he departed with another officer.

Richard had taken this opportunity to introduced Christine to everyone. Following handshakes and pleasantries, she couldn't help noticing the kids' downtrodden expressions on all their faces. She whispered into Richard's ear, then to the kids she said, "My, my... what a sea of sad faces. In my profession as a trained veterinarian, dealing with horses every day, I think, in this instance, I know just the cure for all of you."

Her Ford Expedition parked just a few steps away, the engine running at idle with the air conditioning also running, Christine withdrew a key fob from her denim jean pocket, aimed it toward the rear door and pressed one of the tiny buttons. As the rear hatch slowly rose upward, the kids began to watch with mounting intrigue. Their expressions of curiosity gave way to gasps, then eruptions of excitement followed by shouts of "Arnold!"

Jeremy craned his neck to see, his teeth bursting through a relieved and thankful grin as he announced to his parents who were also looking, "Hey it's Arnold--that's Arnold…he's okay!"

The kids rushed to the edge of the tailgate, both shocked and surprised at what they had all believed was Arnold's death scene earlier that morning in the barn. They stood in awe at his miraculous recovery. Curled on a white sheet, lying on his side, a portion of Arnold's chest area and one shoulder were shaved and wrapped in white bandages. Above him, an IV bag of clear liquid, its plastic tube connected to his bandaged foreleg, hung on a clothes hanger hooked above the side window. Though weakened, Arnold responded with bright open eyes while his tail gently thumped the padding he was resting on.

"We were so worried about you, boy," Ian said to him, reaching out to gently stroke the side of his neck.

Dane approached Christine, holding out his hand.

"You must be the young man who rescued him," she said, taking his hand and gently pumping it. "Richard told me you took it pretty hard."

"This dog saved all of us," Dane uttered choking through the words. "We owe him our lives."

"He lost a lot of blood, but he's been given a transfusion," she said to him, releasing his hand with a final squeeze. "He's a fighter all right."

Dane turned and knelt down alongside Ian. He then rubbed the underside of Arnold's rough paw, working his hand gently along the dog's foreleg. Ian looked over at Dane and said, "He's gonna be okay, isn't he?"

Dane glanced up at Christine, catching her reassuring nod and said to the boy, "He sure is, Ian. He sure is."

Stewie sat beside Bert in the van, Ryan's smartphone in his hand, a cable running from it to the control deck in front of him when the side door to the mobile van suddenly tore open, sliding to a jarring stop. Startled, Bert and Stewie jumped and abruptly swiveled in their chairs wondering why in hell Miles or Carl would make such an alarming entry. They were momentarily stunned to see two men in dark business suits standing calmly before them, one of the men holding out an ID of some sort barely long enough for either one of them to recognize that it had an official seal with a photo before shoving it back inside his suitcoat.

"Sorry to burst in on you like this, gentlemen," said the rotund agent with no neck and a barrel chest. "But I believe *that* is evidence in the commission of a crime. So, gentlemen, I must ask that you to turn it over to the FBI."

Stewie frowned impishly and recoiled his hand holding the phone, blurting, "Take a hike--"

In a lightning reflex the stout agent's fat hand snatched the phone from Stewie's grasp, cable and all, followed by the other agent, slamming the door closed in their startled faces.

Stan hefted another EFP camera to his shoulder that Carl had brought out to him from the van while listening to his direction, positioning himself for the next shot. Waving his hands like a traffic cop and pointing a finger, Carl began directing Miles, "I don't wanna miss a thing out here…Miles, stand over there, let's do a recap, and then we'll move over there to where they're treating the kid."

Miles nodded, running his hand through his tousled dark hair, then faced Stan and his camera.

Standing off in the shadows away from the glare of flashing lights, two men in dark suits stepped forward and made their presence known. The one built like a gorilla with no neck and a barrel chest stepped toward Jeremy, flashing an I.D. before stuffing it back inside his suit coat. "Excuse me," he said, "Jeremy Hodak? I'm FBI Special Agent Rupert Cole. We need to speak with, if you don't mind--"

"Excuse me," Robert interjected forcefully. "My son is done for the day. We're taking him to the hospital, then home. This will have to wait until tomorrow."

"I'm sorry sir, afraid not," the agent replied impatiently. "This won't take long, and it is imperative that we speak to him now rather than later."

"Well, I'm sorry too, but--"

Jeremy watched from his gurney as agent Cole cut his father off, taking an intimidating step into Robert's personal space. Having had enough of authority figures in the last few days, in a last burst of fleeting strength Jeremy reared up on the gurney and snapped, "Hey ASSHOLE!"

You could have heard a pin drop across the parking lot.

At first Caroline and Robert exchanged startled glances, then Robert eased into an amused grin.

Though the added medication given to him by the paramedic was beginning to take effect, relaxing him even further, it didn't prevent Jeremy from locking eyes with agent Cole in an angry stare. "Did you *just hear* what my father *said to you*?" he sputtered through gritted teeth. "...I've had a really bad day, you know what I mean? And right now, we're going home, *all of us*--you got it? And if you wanna talk to me, I'll just bet you know where I live. *Now, get. Lost!*"

Jeremy slumped back into the gurney with an exhaustive gasp, closing his eyes. Agent Cole, waxing smugness, finally relented with a wave of his hand to his partner and the two stepped away, melting into the crowds and flashing lights. When Jeremy opened his eyes again, shading them against the intense summer sun, he looked up at the smoldering tower. He shook his head at the thick black smoke lazily snaking through the shattered windows of the burnt out restaurant while errant strands rose from the center, curling into the afternoon's, deep blue Michigan sky.

"What is it Jeremy?" Matthew asked him as he knelt beside the gurney. The other kids closed ranks and stood behind him.

"Son?" Robert said gently, "we're ready to go now whenever you are."

"Okay, Dad. Give me a minute, will you?"

"Sure," Robert said with a nod as he stood back with Caroline.

Feeling ever so relaxed, more than he had in days, Jeremy looked at each of the muted, filthy faces surrounding him and he said to them, "I can't believe we were all just up there...so ahh...how's everyone doin'?--Lynn?--I wanna thank *you* for being so brave."

Pushing aside her normally golden blonde hair, now soiled and matted in places, Lynn replied with a stout, confident expression.

Matthew reached for Jeremy's hand and took it into his, holding it, looking at him.

"Afraid you're gonna lose me?" Jeremy quipped with a tired grin. "Not on your life. Beside, who's gonna kick your little butts when you two bozos get outta line."

"You saved all of us, Jeremy," Matthew said seriously.

Jeremy shook his head, still grinning, focusing his gaze on Ian. "Nope. I think that distinction goes to this young man, and his utility backpack. Batman would have been very proud of you--*you* really saved the day, Ian--*you da man!*"

All the kids agreed, patting the boy's shoulder. Ian grinned at them sheepishly, wrinkling his nose. In response, they all wrinkled their noses back at him.

"Hey, Ian," Elmo chimed in, hanging onto Eric's shoulder. "where is your backpack? You're not wearing it anymore."

402

Ian looked up over his shoulder, staring at the smoking tower and said, "I left it up there."

Ian couldn't shake the image of Whitehead from his thoughts and what he had said to him after their elevator ride to the helideck.

"You know something, Ian?" Jeremy said drawing his attention.

The boy turned and looked at him solemnly with wet eyes.

Jeremy's expression grew thoughtful as he fought back the welling in his own eyes and said soberly, taking the boy's small hand. "If it weren't for you, climbing on top of that RV the way you did, going after Lynn, then calling us on the radio…there's a pretty good chance we'd have lost her. Up there on the tower helipad, you cut me free--pulled me outta that burning helicopter…you risked your life to come back and rescue me. For as long as I live Ian, I will never forget that. Never."

While all the parents stood close listening, holding back their own emotions, they were now just beginning to comprehend what had happened to all of them.

Jeremy looked up at Dylan and Charlee, standing with Richard, and sensed that, with what the entire group had experienced in just the last couple of days probably paled in comparison to what they had been through in the past year, let alone their entire lives. Though he hardly knew the two of them, they both had proven themselves to be willing to risk their own lives to save the others. And he was grateful to the two teens--they all were when he said to them, "I think the two of you are the most courageous of all."

Charlees' face was a reflection of awkwardness and gratitude as she looked at both Jeremy and Dane. When she turned away her eyes fell on Christine. In that moment Charlee could see in the woman's face a reflection of Richard's own love and affection for them. And for perhaps the first time in her life Charlee felt a deep sense of wellbeing. And something else too…something she and her brother were not used to. The young girl felt safe. Richard leaned in and kissed her gently on the temple. Dylan was still resisting, fighting back his intense feelings from becoming visible, but it was proving too difficult for him. He suddenly felt a strong presence from behind and when the boy turned he was met by Eric with open hand. Dylan took it and nodded, the tears just beginning to roll down his tanned cheeks.

"You're okay," said Eric.

Dylan acquiesced through a wave of emotion and nodded gratefully.

Jeremy wiped the moisture from his own cheeks with a towel left by the paramedic, then motioned for Eric to come closer. Jeremy tried to speak the moment the boy squeezed in between Lynn and Matt but his voice had become coarse. He cleared his throat and his thoughts and as Eric stood there silently, hands clasped in front of him, his head bowed, Jeremy said gently, "Look at me, Eric."

Eric raised his gaze and looked directly into Jeremy's eyes.

"You have nothing to be ashamed of--nothing. Do you understand me?"

Eric nodded, repeatedly clamping his eyes shut, fighting off the tears.

"...What you did in the barn this morning, Eric, was nothing short of selfless."

Eric began to weep uncontrollably.

"...And what we talked about yesterday...your mom and dad will understand, just as the rest of us do. I think I can speak for all of us here that...you're our friend...we love you...and we all care about what happens to you. And no one can ever call you a wimp. So you just hold your head high. You're a very brave young man, and I'm proud..." Jeremy wiped at his eyes again. "...*proud*, to call you my friend."

Eric looked at him, the words he wanted to say choking in his throat, and simply nodded. He then turned and walked back to his father, melding into his arms.

Jeremy again cleared the emotion that kept backing up in his throat and said to Elmo, balancing himself at the foot of the gurney,

"Sorry about your prosthesis--but it seems our little group has no shortage of heroes. Thank you."

Matt had returned to his side and while Elmo leaned on his shoulder for support, patting at his eyes with the hem of his soiled tank-top shirt, he replied with a grin, "Oh, that's okay--I need a new one anyway. I was starting to outgrow that ol' thing anyway."

Jeremy laughed, looking up at Leslie and Dane standing beside him. She knelt and leaned in, kissing him gently on the cheek. He reached and took her hand, saying, "What was that for?"

"For a lot of things," she said to him. "But mostly for getting us all back home."

"I couldn't have done it without you and Fred."

Jeremy looked around at his crew, noticing Travis hanging back. He then extended his open hand to Dane and said, "You're the best wingman a guy ever had. Thanks, Dane."

Dane grinned back at him, hooking his thumb around the tank top shoulder strap and said, "We gotta get you bigger shirts."

Jeremy laughed. "Tight is good on you."

"Excuse me," said a familiar booming voice emerging from the throng.

Jeremy's face brightened with a wide grin. "Hey everyone, this is Fred."

The RV salesman politely greeted everyone then held aloft a familiar looking backpack, dripping wet. "I understand this belongs to one of you. I heard the name of Ian earlier and just now walking through the parking lot spotted this among some of the debris. And written here..." Fred spun it around displaying the top edge along the zipper where a name had been inscribed with indelible black ink. "...It says, ah, Ian Thigpen."

Ian grinned at the happenstance discovery of his now lucky pack.

Closest to Fred, Elmo reached for it, taking the soaked backpack.

"Well, whaddya know," Elmo remarked with a laugh, "it made it over Niagara Falls." Balancing himself as he set the pack down on the pavement he slid open the zipper and withdrew a multicolored balled up article. He straightened, wringing out the excess water, shook it and held it aloft for all to see, announcing loudly with great fanfare, "Look everyone, Spiderman lives!"

"Hey, gimme those!" Ian barked as he lunged, swiping his now embarrassingly infamous underwear from Elmo's hand.

Everyone in the group broke out into laughter. Everyone with the exception of Travis, Jeremy noticed.

"You all right, little bro?"

Jeremy cupped his chin with his hand and said, "C'mon, what is it?"

The boy bowed his head and leaned into his brother, hugging him.

"Hey, hey," he whispered to him softly, "c'mon, didn't I say I'd get us all home? What's wrong--what is it?"

Trav finally pushed himself back, wiping his nose and eyes with the hem of his tee shirt and gazed at his brother, nodding. "I'm okay."

Matt dropped to his knees next to Trav and said, "Bet I know."

"You do not," Trav chided him with a gentle shove of his shoulder into Matt's.

Matt gently shoved him back, asking Jeremy, "Does it hurt much?"

"Only when I go camping," he smiled, then laughed, wincing painfully.

The boys laughed too for a moment.

"Soon as we get home and I'm placed under Doctor Mom's care, I'll be as good as new."

"Just in time to help us finish painting the garage?" Matt asked him.

"You bet. We'll finish it together."

"Hey, yeah," Elmo broke in, "we'll have a painting party--what 'bout it, Mr. H?"

Robert grinned. "I think we can do that. Burgers on the grill, along with your mother's killer bacon potato salad...not a bad idea, Elmo."

The kids broke into unbridled cheers.

After the paramedics finished up treating Jeremy and Elmo, and examining the other kids, Caroline bent down, easing herself beside him, taking his hand while Robert thanked the medical technicians.

"How you are you feeling?" she asked him.

"I'm tired, mom, really tired. Can we go home now? I don't wanna spend the night in the hospital, I wanna go home--sleep in my own bed, hold Elise...can we?"

"You bet," she said to him stroking his matted and tangled blond hair. Her voice became distracted when she noticed a gold chain around his neck. It had caught her eye earlier, after Robert had helped Jeremy remove his jacket, though now she noticed it more clearly as it glinted brightly in the afternoon sunlight. "The paramedics said that would probably be fine after they check you out at Munson more thoroughly--Jeremy?"

"Yeah, Mom?"

"Jeremy, that's a lovely necklace. I never noticed you wearing it before. It looks like real gold. Where did you get it?"

"I'm sure it is real--"

"WHAT?" Miles gasped into his radio, his deep voice piercing the somber mood.

"What is it?" Carl asked.

Stan kept filming.

Miles held up his hand in a *hold on* gesture. "Okay...all right... don't worry about, it wasn't your fault."

"Miles, what happened?"

"You're not gonna believe this, Carl." Miles spat in a shocked tone. "That was Stewie--he says two gorillas in business suits showed up at the van and announced they were from the FBI, then swiped the smartphone from him and took off with it. It's gone!"

Hearing the exchange Dylan bolted over to the reporter gushing, "I knew it, I knew this was gonna happen!"

Jeremy struggled to sit up, his mind fighting through the fog of the medication to make sense of what he was hearing.

Dylan then glared at Jeremy, defeat in his voice, waving his hands about excitedly. "*That phone* was our ace in the hole. With the Caradori file we could have proven what was happening. Now it's gone--all of it. And *they've* got it *back!*"

"Now hold on, Dylan," Jeremy calmly urged him.

"Jeremy...that was our *only* proof. All the codes are on that phone and the flash drive. Without either one, that's it--the bad guys win...*again!*"

"You're jumping to conclusions."

"Don't you get it?" Dylan cried, frantically smacking a clenched fist into the palm of his other hand several times. "We've lost the flash drive...no smartphone, no dossier, and without the codes on the paintings, *which are in the dossier*, we'll never find 'em--check-mate--game over!"

Jeremy slowly shook his head, his deadpan expression giving way to a spreading, lopsided grin.

Dylan frowned at him and said, "I'm glad you find this so amusing!"

"Oh, ye of little faith."

"...Whaddya mean?" the boy uttered warily. "Whaddya talkin' about?"

Jeremy reached up, patted the gold chain around his neck and sang brightly, "Ka-ching!"

Dylan watched him curiously, his angry, skeptical frown unchanged.

Attached to the gold chain, which had worked its way around to the back of his neck, Jeremy took hold of it from behind and brought it around and held it out under his chin between his thumb and index finger as if it was an Olympic gold medal.

At first Dylan couldn't believe his widening eyes. His mouth gaped open but the words were slow to arrive. "...Is that what I think it is--it can't be."

"Oh, but it is," replied Jeremy with a wide satisfied smile. "He hid it in plain sight by *wearing it!*"

"...But, how did you--?"

"Hey, Miles...c'mere."

The reporter, watching their exchange, curiously furrowed his brow. As he stepped toward Jeremy, Stan followed behind him with the camera.

"How would you like to have the *Colonel's* flash drive?--got it right here!"

Sitting up in his gurney Jeremy yanked the gold chain from his neck, breaking the clasp, and tossed it, along with the flash drive, to the reporter's open hand. Miles, catching it squarely in his palm, shook his head in excited disbelief, gripping it tightly in his fist as if the chain held a great diamond. He nodded and winked at the two boys. "Where did you get it?"

"He had it with him all the time." Jeremy's eyes then flashed up toward the smoldering tower. "At the last moment I relieved him of it."

Miles arched his brow, reaching out and grasped Jeremy's hand, pumping it. "Thank you, Jeremy!"

He then flashed Dylan a thumbs up and quickly departed with Stan and Carl hot on his heels, heading back to the station's mobile van.

Jeremy took a moment, noticing Trav's distant, sad expression had remained. He reached up, grabbing his brother's attention by patting his cheek. "So what still troubles you, little bro?"

"What about Jacob?" Trav asked him directly. "He's still missing, Jeremy. Jacob is still out there. It isn't right that all of us made it home and he didn't. ...Why were we saved and he wasn't?"

Jeremy's expression softened, becoming serious as he looked back into Trav's eyes. "You said once, 'God only wants to know what's in our hearts'. You know what I wanna know?"

Trav shook his head.

"I want to know what's in God's heart. Somewhere, someone out there knows where Jacob is, and what happened to him. ...You also said God is Omniscient. If He is, then He too knows what happened to Jacob--but refuses to reveal it to anyone."

For the first time Travis was starting to doubt.

"I'm sorry Trav, I guess I was pretty hard on you."

Travis thought for a moment then said, "I saw what you did back there."

"What was that?"

"After you landed the helicopter in the river you went back to get stuff and you did something. Then after the snowmobiles broke down you went back to get stuff and you did it again."

"What'd I do?"

Travis hesitated then finally said, "You looked up into the sky and said something."

Jeremy bowed his head for a moment in remembrance, recalling both instances, surprised that anyone had even noticed his actions.

"What did you say, Jeremy?"

"...I was thanking Him. Does that surprise you?"

Travis nodded that it did.

Jeremy took a long moment, then, looking at each of his twin brothers, said to them, "Maybe He can't...or won't do anything. I just don't know--I don't have all the answers. But I do know this, there is something *we* can do. Never forget Jacob Wetterling...always remember him."

The boys stared back into their brother's wet eyes with their own.

"I love you guys--I love you so much."

The twins melted into Jeremy's chest, saying nothing more.

Amid the flashing lights of police cruisers, fire trucks and EMS, among the frenzied activity of the uniformed people and officials that surrounded them in the busy parking lot, before they were descended upon by the swarm of reporters and photographers that had been arriving throughout the afternoon, corralled by police and security on the south lawn, before they all headed home to Wolf's Head Bay, the Hodak brothers took a few moments and held tight to each other like there was no tomorrow.

…And they never forgot.

On Sunday evening, October 22nd, 1989, eleven-year-old Jacob Wetterling of St. Joseph, Minnesota, along with his brother and a friend, while biking home from a convenience store were confronted by a masked gunman. He ordered Jacob's brother and the other boy to take off or he would shoot them.

Jacob was never seen again.

As of September 2016, the remains of Jacob were found in a field not far from his home, revealed by the man who had abducted him.

Jacob Wetterling loved sports. His dad coached his soccer team. He wanted to be a football player. He was a skilled hockey goalie. Jacob also believed in a fair and just world, a world where all children know they are special and deserve to be safe.
To remember and honor Jacob, there are a number of ways you can help or contribute. Please visit online
The Jacob Wetterling Resource Center

EPILOGUE

The terrifying three-day ordeal endured by Jeremy, his brothers and their friends at the hands of the Colonel and his enforcer, Spear, was now worldwide news making international headlines. In a tiny corner of the globe, standing in the middle of the Hodak's living room was Special Agent Rupert Cole of the FBI, conferring privately with a fellow agent. Despite his professional attire of a dark brown suit and matching leather loafers, with his thick body and no neck, the man resembled a linebacker with the NFL rather than a federal agent. And he had the temperament to match.

"Well? Where the hell are they?"

The other agent shook his head. "They've vanished."

"All of them?"

"We've canvassed the entire neighborhood, no sign of 'em."

"Take Branson and Evans and sweep it again--go door to door, room to room if you have to, but *find those kids*! This is all I need now, for something to happen to 'em, especially Hodak, who goes on the air--" he paused, checking his digital watch with a snap of his wrist, "--in forty-five minutes."

"What are you so steamed about?" asked the other agent. "You're still running the show."

"We blew the assignment. I'm gonna be stuck in that Detroit office for the rest of my life."

"You had no way of knowing the kid had the Colonel's flash drive."

"Try explaining that to the director. I've just become the agency's newest whipping boy. And to top it off I gotta protect this kid now."

"Well, it could be worst."

"Ohh, believe me, with what's happening, this is only the beginning."

Agent Cole turned his back and stepped to the large picture window looking beyond the plush green lawn outside the white with blue trim, Cape-Cod house to where the media circus that had been gathering out in the street since the story broke. He huffed a breath and growled, "After this I'll be lucky if they don't ship me off to the Siberian outpost."

The other agent then quickly replied with an innocently taunting grin, "The ahh--Mackinaw City field office?"

A dark angry expression clouded Agent Coles chubby face. "That's the one--get going!"

The loft in Elmo's barn had proven to be a port in the storm that had engulfed the Hodak boys, their friends and their parents. Following the live broadcast of the disaster from the Grand Traverse World Resort, the resulting scandal began to take on a life of its own. With the sudden demise of the Colonel and subsequent early morning raids conducted by agents of the FBI and the U.S. Department of Homeland Security at both the Colonel's Northern Michigan compound and the Monarch Foundation in Detroit, dozens of individuals had been detained or arrested including Ms. Patty and Lauren Wringwater.

Since arriving home Jeremy had been uncharacteristically somber, spending most of his free time after his lengthy interviews with FBI investigators, either alone in his room under his headphones or in the nursery with his newborn sister, Elise. He knew his parents were concerned, but that concern quickly turned to shock and dismay as they sat in listening to him and the twins relay their three-day ordeal to investigators. In fact, an entire team of agents had been dispatched to interview the other kids as well. Although Jeremy was mind-numbingly exhausted, he had his own concerns. Keenly aware that he and the rest of the kids were under tight scrutiny by the team of FBI agents that had descended on his home and family, he desperately needed a break from it all. Feeling like an invalid confined to a rest home Jeremy managed to steal away to Elmo's barn loft. But not before instructing the twins to stealthily gather the other kids and meet him there.

Jeremy felt as though he was a hundred years old. Every part of his body ached, from his head down to his toes. Every movement was painful. Gingerly climbing the ladder using his good arm, the other, his right, in a sling, he was ever so careful not to disturb any of the dozen or so stitches in his upper left thigh and right shoulder, including the large bandage covering the burn on his upper left shoulder. A constant reminder of his struggle with Whitehead in the cabin and being struck by the fireball from the exploding Roman candle. Seemingly reminiscent of his climb up the tube in the Colonel's converted nuke complex, yet not nearly as agonizing, he took a deep breath when he reached the top. He then hobbled to a corner and guardedly lowered himself to a bed of hay, releasing a deep sigh of relief.

Within in a few minutes he had fallen asleep.

When Jeremy awoke, hearing the hushed activity below as the kids arrived, nearly thirty minutes had elapsed. He awkwardly sat up as one by one they climbed the ladder and settling down on the bed of hay around him.

They were a forlorn group. Although they were assured by the news media that after tonight's major news broadcast and Jeremy's brief on-camera interview they would all leave, Jeremy was still doubtful that they would keep their word. And as far as his impending interview, he was dreading it--like a root canal.

Everyone traded tired glances. Travis was the first to break the long silence saying, "What are you gonna say tonight, Jeremy?"

"I haven't a clue. I'll just wing it, I guess."

Travis then added, "This place kinda reminds me of the other loft."

"Pleeease," Jeremy pleaded shaking his head, "don't remind me."

"Is this ever going to end?" Leslie asked no one in particular. "All those reporters."

"Hopefully right after Jeremy's interview," Matthew volunteered.

Jeremy nodded. "Let's hope they keep their word and they're all gone by morning. Otherwise Mr. Coombs threatened to use 'em for buckshot practice."

The boys and Lynn laughed.

"That's all we need," Elmo gruffed.

"Hey, you got your new leg," Trav noted.

Elmo swept back his black mane, grinning proudly, tapping the flesh-colored prosthesis below his right knee and said, "This thing's indestructible."

"Dane?"

"Yeah, Lynn?"

"How's Arnold doing?"

"Resting comfortably at home."

The chit-chat continued for a minute or so during which Jeremy observed each of the kids. Dylan, seated beside Charlee interrupted the conversation and asked, "Was there something else on your mind that you wanted to see us about?"

Jeremy nodded that there was. Realizing how what they'd been through was affecting the twins, and his own psyche, he needed to make sure the others were okay, especially Ian and Eric who sat quietly. He knew that it would take time for each of them to process what they'd been through. So, he instructed the kids, imploring all of them to come to him, Dane or Leslie, if they needed to talk. They all agreed, making a pact. They sealed it with all their hands in the center as one and vowing that no one would be left alone to deal with it.

"Well, it's almost seven," Matthew noted. "We'd better get back before Agent Cole has a coronary."

"I don't think he likes you, Jeremy," Dane commented halfheartedly.

"He sure has been givin' you the evil eye, hasn't he," Matthew observed as he stood.

"That's cool," quipped Jeremy. "'Cause I don't much like him either."

They started to leave when Eric finally spoke up. "You'll know… right?"

A few comprehending glances were exchanged.

"Know what?" Elmo asked.

Eric's eyes made the rounds looking at each of them as he spoke. "That he's alive. He made it out of the helicopter, Jeremy, before it exploded." Eric slowly shook his head. "…He isn't dead."

"Who isn't dead?" Ian asked innocently, poised beside Eric and looking up at him.

Jeremy glanced at Dane, then at Leslie, before returning a hard, steady gaze at Eric. "…Yeah," he nodded back, "…we know."

"Who?" Ian repeated.

The moment the other kids began to trade wary looks with each other, Ian looked back up into Eric's eyes, and then he knew too. That's when his small hand found its way into Eric's tight grasp and he murmured, "Peter Whitehead."

Special Agent Cole paced the floor nervously in the hallway just outside the Hodak's den, alongside the Hodak's attorney and some of the parents. Inside the remaining parents had gathered around the television, anxiously waiting. They were all watching intently as the screen faded out from a commercial and returned to the live network broadcast.

"The global slave trade exposed, this is NBC Nightly News, with Brian Williams."

"We are back, with our continuing live coverage in this special, extended edition of NBC Nightly News," Williams began. Still in his iconic navy-blue suite, white shirt and purple tie, the news anchor sat comfortably in Studio 3B at 30 Rockefeller Center, flanked on his left by four additional reporters, in a split-screen effect. "If your local NBC station has rejoined us, we continue to cover all fronts in what can only be described as perhaps *the* most shocking scandal in recent memory to rock our nation's capital--and beyond. Repercussions are being felt around the globe. And the young man responsible for these remarkable turn of events is only minutes away from a scheduled news conference in which he has prepared a statement for the media who have been camping outside his home on the adjoining street for the last two days. Joining me once again, our NBC staff has been hard at work covering this incredible story, beginning with the Washington fallout is our Political Director, Chief White House Correspondent, Chuck Todd...from Detroit, Michigan, Senior Investigative Correspondent, Lisa Myers...covering the international angle from Dubai City, is our Chief Foreign Affairs Correspondent, Andrea Mitchell...and from the Grand Traverse World Resort in Traverse City, Michigan, the site where this unfolding story began, Miles Montgomery.

"Chuck, we'll begin with you on Capitol Hill. This story has it all, doesn't it? Mystery, intrigue, corruption, and murder, ensnaring a world-wide cast of the rich, the famous, and the powerful."

The image on the screen switched to a close-up of the goateed, Chuck Todd, sporting a white shirt and tie with matching dark coat, poised on the north lawn of the White House, the iconic pillared, presidential residence behind him. "That's right, Brian. It is far reaching and has more tentacles than an octopus. The last forty-eight hours has been nothing short of stunning, beginning with the death of Senator Ellis, the Colonel, Toddhunter, including revelations that he was deeply involved in human trafficking, dating back to the Franklin Credit Union scandal of the mid 1980's. The ripple effects are spreading out far and wide, possibly implicating a president. Earlier today the White House did release a statement, saying only that the United States takes seriously all instances of human trafficking and vigorously investigates and prosecutes those individuals involved. And that's just for starters, Brian."

Agent Cole's head snapped around the instant he heard a ruckus coming from the kitchen. The moment he sped down the hall, his heavy frame pounding the wood panel flooring, he was pursued by the anxious parents and the family attorney.

When he burst through the kitchen door, spotting Jeremy he spat, "Where the hell have all of you been?"

"Bite me!" snapped Jeremy while the other kids streamed in through the back door and crowded in behind him.

Relaxing peacefully together in a window seat of the kitchen, the sudden commotion spooked Alley and Hobie cat. Spying the open backdoor the two Siamese cats sprang into action and flew through the opening just before it closed, heading for their favorite hunting grounds.

Robert squeezed ahead of the other parents closing ranks between himself and his son and asked, "You okay?"

Jeremy relented with a weak smile and replied, "Yeah…I just needed a get away from all of this for a little while."

"It's okay," Robert assured him.

"Next time you let one of us know where you're going," Agent Cole chided him.

"Back off!"

"Jeremy."

"…I'm sorry, Dad."

Robert nodded his understanding.

"You listen to me young man, I'll not--"

"That's enough, from both of you," Robert interceded, focusing his eyes on his son and speaking softly, "Calm down, okay?"

Jeremy took a breath and said, "I'm trying, Dad."

"It's getting close to curtain time," the Hodak family attorney interceded in a stern tone from behind Robert. "Let's get you ready now."

"I know you are," Robert said before acknowledging his attorney. "…You sure you're up for this?"

"Yeah, I'm ready. Let's just do it and get it over with."

"Come with me, then," their attorney instructed him.

Agent Cole sneered to himself as he watched the nineteen-year-old being escorted through the gathering of parents and down the hall. As the rest of the kids joined their parents filing out of the kitchen and heading to the den, Agent Cole could only bristle angrily once again at his death-sentence assignment.

As the remaining group streamed into the den their eyes immediately focused on the television and Chuck Todd's voice-over reporting while video of the political luncheon at the resort played. "Events then take yet another bizarre turn, following the rooftop disaster when a group of armed individuals burst into the Governors' ballroom, the site of the political luncheon, and threatened at gunpoint several adults and children, while a stunned nation watches on live television. While it's unclear as to the identity of the armed intruders, due to their black outfits, they apparently were after what we now know was a document containing information surrounding the infamous Franklin Credit Union scandal of the late 80's."

There was a brief moment as the video ended and Chuck Todd appeared live again on the lawn of the White House. "And Brian, that document is the now famous, Caradori dossier, named for the private detective and former Michigan state police officer, Gary Caradori. He had been assigned with the initial investigation into the Franklin Credit Union debacle by the Nebraska State Legislature back in 1989 following numerous allegations of fraud and misappropriation of funds--forty million dollars--to be exact. Early on in the investigation portions of the dossier had been turned over to the FBI, the agency now leading the investigation. Unfortunately, that evidence went missing. Sources close to the initial investigation have privately suggested that the agency, in fact, destroyed it, due to its incriminating evidence of countries and individuals involved in the global slave trade. Just hours before Caradori was to have delivered the entire dossier, he died tragically, along with his eight-year-old son, in a plane accident. And Brian, those same sources have suggested it was no accident. Now that the dossier's been recovered, intact, it has many in Washington, and quite literally around the world, terrified."

The televised image became a split-screen of Todd and Williams.

"Chuck, I understand the circumstances surrounding his death were eerily similar to last year's downing of Congressman Ted Denis's private jet in Lake Erie."

"That's right, Brian. In an ironic twist, Congressman Denis was said to have received a copy of the dossier, and was flying to Washington, with his own young son aboard, to deliver it to a special Senate subcommittee in the hopes of reopening the investigation into Franklin, and the death of Caradori, with the ultimate goal of convening a new Grand Jury. Tragically, like Caradori, his plane may have been sabotaged as well. However, as we've learned in recent days, the Congressman and his son were not killed in the crash, but in fact, did survive, and immediately following the water landing, he and his family went into hiding, fearing for their lives. Back to you, Brian."

"Chuck, thanks, Chuck Todd, at the White House, starting us off at the top of the hour."

As the camera tightened on Williams's boyish face, he continued conversationally, speaking in his stock in trade, easy going demeanor. "We also learned late today, in a stunning footnote to this extraordinary story, that criminal investigations are already underway in more than a dozen countries, which have already produced several arrests of high ranking individuals in the private sector. I'm referring of course to the game changer in all of this, the recovery of a stolen Rembrandt painting. The discovery has led investigators, not only to the whereabouts of several others, but to also the identity of the individuals allegedly running the various global slave cartels. And all of it due to a microchip embedded into the canvas of the recovered Rembrandt painting."

Williams paused in a professional beat, taking a breath, while the camera pulled back slightly, displaying Jeremy's high school senior photo in the upper right-hand corner of the screen. "*The Magnificent Seven* were a fictitious group of heroic gunslingers. Within the last few days, a younger group of real-life heroes has emerged. Eleven Michigan kids, in the wake of their harrowing ordeal at the hands of ruthless kidnappers, are being called the courageous eleven. The young man at the epicenter of this rapidly expanding story has been identified as nineteen-year-old Jeremy Hodak. With that part of the story, joining us from the lawn of the Hodak home in Wolf's Head Bay, Michigan, from our sister station in Traverse City, is Miles Montgomery."

Ever the professional, Miles sported summer slacks, a collar shirt with matching tie and light jacket. Waiting anxiously for his cue from Carl, standing just off camera, a light breeze kicked up his dark blond hair while the soft evening glow of the setting sun highlighted his golden tanned complexion. "Good evening Brian. On the strength of the documents in the dossier, delivered to this reporter from Jeremy Hodak, the Justice Department, in just the last two days has launched an unprecedented, full-blown investigation, ensnaring, as you stated earlier in this broadcast, some very power-ful and influential people, in this country and abroad. Mr. Hodak is essentially responsible for providing, what seasoned investigators are calling, the most chilling and credible evidence of criminal activity on a massive, worldwide scale they've ever seen. It's because of this extraordinary young man that this story has finally gone public."

The screen then transitioned, first back to Brian Williams in Studio 3B… "Before we continue with Miles's report, along with our other correspondents, we're going to quickly switch gears here."

…Then to the front lawn of the Hodak home and the throng of reporters, who all suddenly began to quiet down as two men approach the foot-high stage and podium. The screen zoomed in on a middle-aged man with thick gray hair and slight build standing at the podium beside a young man, his right arm in a sling.

"Ladies and gentleman, I'm David Crane, the Hodak family attorney. Mr. Hodak has prepared a brief statement. We ask that the members of the press refrain from asking any questions at this time, and to please respect the involved families' privacy, until which time Mr. Hodak is feeling up to a more thorough interview, which he has agreed to at a later date. …Jeremy?"

The two switched places.

Jeremy nervously swallowed, took a breath, then opened his mouth. For a moment that seemed more like an eternity to him, nothing came out.

"Ah…my name is Jeremy Hodak…." he began cautiously. Feeling somewhat rested, the blond stubble shaved from his chin and jaw line, his blond hair combed back, he stood there in jeans and a polo shirt clutching the edge of the podium with his sweaty free hand. He looked out over the battery of microphones at the largest gathering of news reporters he had ever seen. While some of them gripped hand-held recorders and video cameras, others clutched writing pads, pens poised anxiously in their hands waiting for him to speak. And they were all so quiet, too. There must have been at least a dozen photographers jockeying into position in front of him, snapping away, their flashes nearly blinding him. Out in the street was the local television station's mobile van, the colorful '7&4 NBC' logo emblazoned on the side, larger than life. Jeremy then noticed the wagon train of vans parked behind it in a line; FOX, CNN, CBS, ABC and C-SPAN. He imagined the neighbors were thrilled with the circus. On the roof of every one of them was someone standing behind a camera, aimed right at him.

He abruptly reminded himself to close his mouth.

Jeremy turned away from the massive media gathering and looked out across the yard over his shoulder, spotting Matt, Trav, along with all the other kids crowding in the two windows of the den, watching him. After the twins waved encouragingly, his head spun around to where Robert and Caroline stood outside on the veranda. Both of them nodded firmly, his mother's warm smile giving him strength as she held Elise in her arms.

Jeremy looked down briefly at his injured arm and his sweating palm next to his chest.

He cleared his throat. "…Five days ago…my brothers, and my friends--all of us--were kidnapped and held against our will at Senator Toddhunter's underground facility located in Michigan's Upper Peninsula."

Jeremy felt as though his throat was drier than the Saharan desert. "…During our brief captivity, I had an opportunity to talk with the Colonel--Senator Toddhunter. …And in no uncertain terms, he told me that because of what we had seen there, and heard, we were to be taken out of this country and sold--all of us--into the global slave network, essentially getting rid of us without actually killing us. But he made it very clear to me that if we tried to escape, he wouldn't hesitate to do just that…"

While the throng of reporters listened, hanging onto his every word, writing feverishly on pads, some of them held out microphones and small audio recorders while others clutched video cameras aimed in his direction. Jeremy was certain the drumbeat of his heart could be heard by everyone as a pall of absolute silence hung across the crowded and trampled yard.

"May I have some water, please," he turned and whispered to Crane.

The attorney handed him a bottle of water. Jeremy fumbled for a moment as he twisted the cap off, took a long swig, and then a deep breath and handed the bottle back to Crane.

"…We ah…we did manage to escape, and with proof. Proof not only of the Colonel's involvement, but also of the world-wide conspiracy to cover-up the proliferating global slave trade. The Caradori dossier reveals an organized and massive cover-up by authorities over the years, both abroad and here in this country, in an unrelenting effort to protect and shield those countries and individuals involved in human trafficking."

Jeremy paused, feeling overwhelmed and fatigued. He looked downward and began to step back from the podium.

That's when the feeding frenzy began.

"MR. HODAK--!"

"JEREMY!"

Crane quickly stepped in with a raised hand. "Thank you, folks, that'll be--"

"--WOULD YOU ANSWER A FEW--?"

"IS IT TRUE--?"

"WHEN YOU TESTIFY NEXT MONTH BEFORE CONGRESS--?"

"THE REMBRANDT, HOW DID YOU--?"

"WERE YOU THE LAST PERSON TO SEE THE SENATOR ALIVE?"

"DO YOU ALLEGE THAT THE SENATOR WAS THE HEAD OF THE NORTH AMERICAN SLAVE NETWORK--?"

At a loss for words Jeremy began to step back farther from the podium when he heard a calm, familiar voice. Searching the anxious mob, he called out, "What was that?"

The multitude of clamoring reporters settled down the moment Jeremy slipped in front of Crane and back up to the podium with a raised hand, singling out one of them with his index finger.

Miles spoke calmly, engaging Jeremy with a wink and cocky grin. "We're gonna have to stop meeting like this, Jeremy. Thank you for the dossier…and the Rembrandt. I passed both of them on."

Jeremy smiled privately and nodded back, remembering their last encounter when Miles interviewed Travis after his near-death drowning.

"Jeremy," Miles began, "The media has dubbed all of you, the courageous eleven. How do feel about that?"

"After what we've been through," Jeremy nodded, "I would agree with that assessment. My brothers and our friends, including two others, Charlee and Dylan Oconee…well…if it weren't for them, I don't think any of us would be here today. *They are all* the most courageous people I've ever known."

Miles's expression then grew serious. "A few days ago you said you wanted to know what was in God's heart. Has this experience shaken your faith?"

Suddenly the words came to him. Facing the anxious crowd of reporters, he blurted angrily, "I don't *allege* anything! The Senator *was the head* of the North American slave network…until a few days ago. And I would imagine he and his trained cobra, Mr. Spear, are now enjoying the warmer parts of hell!"

Miles grinned for a moment before he asked him, "Jeremy, what do you want to see happen as a result of your exposing the global human slave market?"

Jeremy's expression grew thoughtful as his eyes swept the faces of the horde of reporters. It made him uncomfortable the way they all stared back at him as if he was about to make a great pronouncement. It was a little unnerving. "Organized, global slavery is the single most destructive threat to our society that we've ever faced. There are more human slaves in the world today than at any other time in our history. Globalization has made it possible for every country on our planet to become involved in human trafficking. Here in our country, it's been reported in all fifty states including Washington, D.C., with women and children the number one targets of traffickers."

Jeremy's voice began to falter as he fought back the emotion building up inside, focusing his wet eyes on the intently listening crowd of reporters. They seemed to hear him, but he wondered, were any of them really listening. David Crane leaned in whispering into his ear but Jeremy cut him off, stepping around the podium and entered the crowd of reporters, looking them in the eyes. They silently engulfed him when he stopped.

As both Caroline and Robert looked on they were never prouder of their son.

"...Even infants are bought and sold on the black market, for the expressed purpose *and* profit, of the global slave market. Every year thousands of boys and girls, from here to China, are swallowed up by the child trafficking industry. If you live in China and your child is abducted, you can expect two things from the government and local law enforcement. Threats and jail time if you persist in your search to find your missing son or daughter. *Anyone* can be a victim. Even those *you* love. ...We almost were--and right here in our own, *safe*, backyard."

Jeremy paused, wiping his nose and eyes. "Stop writing and look at me."

An audible hush fell over the crowd of reporters as all of their eyes focused on Jeremy. Pens and pads were laid to rest as were small hand-held audio recorders . . . but the moment Jeremy began to speak . . . the recorders, like pesky flies chased away by the wave of his verbal hand, annoyingly returned.

"...Pick any country and you will find that prosecutions are few, even here in the United States. How many of our useless politicians, motivated by their own politically correct agendas, would have you believe that the most serious threat to our world is global warming, I just don't know. But *this* I do know. Our world is facing a more immediate danger that none of our useless politicians, including most of the world's leaders, will even acknowledge. It is currently engulfing our entire society—it threatens *all people, everywhere* around the world—and not sometime in the vague future, but, right now, today. It's called *global slavery!* And it's long past due, but the truth is finally coming out. Unless the good people and governments of this planet band together and take a bold stand saying *loud and clear*--no more--to

those governments and institutions that foster and protect human traf-
fickers--and that includes *you*, United Nations, are you listening?—
then, and only then, can the scourge that President Abraham Lincoln
attempted to abolish back in 1863...which continues to this day...be
ultimately banished from our society!"

Jeremy paused thoughtfully. "...And as for my faith...I would
ask a question."

His voice abruptly trailed off matching his distant and reflective expression. He dropped his gaze for a moment. When Jeremy
lifted his eyes and swept them across the sea of faces surrounding
him he stopped and focused on Miles standing directly before him,
and, as if they were speaking privately, said, "It's been written--in the
Bible no less--that God communicated with the people in Biblical
times. Yet today...where is He? With evil fueling and manifesting the
enormous pain and suffering all across our world, more so than at
any other time in our human history...I would ask God a question...
why are you so silent?"

The Drake Hotel

140 E. Walton Place, Chicago, Illinois

The man in the private booth sat pensively watching the wall-
mounted flat screen television across the lounge in the elegantly
appointed Executive Lounge on the tenth floor. Just as it appeared
the interview with Jeremy Hodak was wrapping, up his gaze floated
across the lounge and stared out the large picture window across
from him. Sipping his Blackhawk martini, his eyes focused on the
visual symphony of Lake Michigan's horizon melting into a fiery sky,
a painted mural of red and orange. The cobalt-hued water beneath it
sparkled brightly like a carpet of glitter as great sheets of wind swept

across the lake. Off in the hazy distance he could see sailboats moving lazily across the great expanse of open water.

Though his background and training identified this lone man as an elite government assassin, it was his ten year, deep cover assignment that he most identified with. It had touched him on an emotional level. And in the spy game that can be dangerous. To that end, his alter ego had served its purpose. Now that it was over it felt as though he'd been resurrected from the dead. To abruptly relinquish his decade-long identity left this man seated alone in the booth with ambivalent, even surreal feelings. He had grown to like his alter ego just as one grows fond of an old but comfortably fitting plaid shirt. It warms you when you put it on. Gone was his alter ego's mop of brown hair, now neatly trimmed and slicked back with gel. Absent too was his drab attire consisting mainly of jeans, button collar shirts and the occasional overalls. The tall, thinly built man now sported a gray tailored suit and suede shoes. He was actually quite handsome. Settling back comfortably into the plush fabric of the bench seat he'd nearly forgotten the simple pleasure of savoring his favorite drink while immersed in the stunning views of Big Blue from his old haunt.

Just as his thoughts wandered again to his recently acquired island home in the South China Sea his cell phone began to vibrate on the table beside his martini. He picked it up, recognized the private number, then pressed it to his ear and said, "Quite an impressive young man, isn't he, Vinny?"

"I would imagine there are a few members of Congress who do not share your praise."

He instantly recognized the raspy voice of his employer, Deputy Director Vincent McNeil. "The kid's right though. The global slave trade is on the rise, and few nations, if any, do much to stop it. Oh, sure, there have been a few prosecutions, but overall, little is done. Not a single country, including the United States, aggressively goes after these people or organizations. It's just not a priority."

"You'll get no argument from me," Vincent continued, his eyes glossing over the New York Times on his desk and musing over the headline screaming a mounting causality list of public celebrities and government officials around the world. "That kid is a material witness, they all are, and they're not taking any chances. At any rate, the FBI's already been assigned to protect them and their families until they testify." Vincent then changed the subject, "Time for you to come in."

"Just what I had in mind. I've decided to retire--"

"No retirement for you...you're too valuable an asset."

Snatching the toothpick pierced with a bleu cheese olive from his near empty martini glass, he popped it into his mouth and uttered between chews, "I'm done, Vinny."

"Perhaps something along the lines of nine to five."

"You're not listening to me. I'm done, finished--no more assignments. It's time for Henry Bartholomew to slip away into oblivion--permanently. I've already buried him."

"Okay, okay. ...By the way. What is your real name?"

Both men laughed for a moment.

"Admit it...this stuff's in your blood. So, congratulations. It was a very successful mission. I'm happy, and so is the Director. You've seen the news broadcasts. The scope of this thing, which is worldwide, is unprecedented. Even as we speak, agents from the Justice Department have already detained dozens of people here in Washington alone for questioning. The fallout from this will probably eclipse the Bay of Pigs, the Kennedy assassination and Nixon's impeachment--combined."

"Well, you know what they say, Vinny?"

"Yeah, I know, timing is everything, ah huh."

Silence hung in the booth for a moment. "Okay Vinny, lay it on me...what's my new assignment--should I decide to accept it?"

"Director of Operations at the Salt Pit."

"Bin Laden? So, that's where you've got 'em---and he's alive."

"Oh, hell yes. When SEAL Team Six raided his compound in Abbottabad, and took 'em out, they shot him all right--with a Magnum XP dart gun. Bissonnette's admission in his book that he was, ahh," McNeil paused clearing his throat, "buried at sea . . . all a ruse to dispel any lingering rumors that he's alive. That old terrorist has been a wealth of information. So, my friend. Ready to come in from the cold?--I'll even give you a new name if you'd like."

"I'll settle for my real one. I often feel like I'm forgetting who I really am." Although the DNI operative couldn't see him, McNeil smiled. "There's one thing I'm still in the dark about, although I've got a pretty good idea."

"And you'd be correct. That *was* Carol's Black-Ops team at the resort."

"I thought so. I understand she's in need of a very good lawyer."

"So are a lot of folks these days."

The DNI operative smiled and then ended the connection saying, "I'll be in touch, Vinny."

As he slid out of the booth and stood, he slipped the phone into a pocket, then strolled across the executive lounge toward the outer foyer. Passing a table where an attractive brunette was seated, he gave her a sly grin. She returned it with her own coquettish smile. Pausing at the elevator, he turned and approached the attractive brunette. Moments later the pair headed downstairs. Hand in hand, they exited the car, crossed the spacious lobby and walked out onto North Michigan Avenue. It was going to be a lovely Lake Michigan sunset, he thought to himself. Perhaps the last one he'd see for a while. Blending and disappearing was this man's specialty. And so, deciding to head down to a nearby pier where they could enjoy the dusky evening, he offered her his jacket against a cool lake breeze which she gratefully accepted and the pair promptly vanished among the strolling crowds, the man confident in the knowledge that the world in which we all live would never be the same because of the heroic actions of a young man, his twin brothers and their friends while on a camping trip into northern Michigan.

POSTSCRIPT

Human trafficking--modern-day slavery--is the trade in humans for the purpose of sexual exploitation, forced labor, and the extraction of organs. It is the fastest growing criminal industry in the world today, subjugating twenty million people world-wide. A multibillion dollar, international business, it is estimated that the global slave trade will eventually eclipse the drug industry in terms of generated revenue. Drugs cannot be resold, but people can. Its most heinous form is the selling of children, mostly males, as young as six years old, for sex. Street hustling involving children is nothing new. Today, however, there are fewer boys working as prostitutes, due, in large part, to the organized prostitution networks around the globe that provide sexual services of young boys and girls to some of the most powerful people in this country and abroad.

According to the U. S. Justice Department despite the many laws enacted against human trafficking within the past decade, due to the lack of training of law enforcement, public awareness and fear on the part of victims to seek help, or simply not knowing where to turn, prosecutions are rare. Many countries do not take these horrendous crimes seriously.

The National Human Trafficking Resource Center (NHTRC) is a national, toll-free hotline, available to answer calls and texts from anywhere in the country, 24 hours a day, 7 days a week. Call them at 1.888.373.7888 or text HELP or INFO to BeFree (233733).